Berkley Books by James Carlos Blake

THE PISTOLEER
THE FRIENDS OF PANCHO VILLA

THE PISTOLEER

A NOVEL

JAMES CARLOS BLAKE

BERKLEY BOOKS, NEW YORK

THE PISTOLEER

A Berkley Book / published by arrangement with
the author

PRINTING HISTORY
Berkley trade paperback edition / August 1995
Berkley mass market edition / August 1996

All rights reserved.
Copyright © 1995 by James Carlos Blake.
This book may not be reproduced in whole or in part,
by mimeograph or any other means, without permission.
For information address: The Berkley Publishing Group,
200 Madison Avenue, New York, New York 10016.

The Putnam Berkley World Wide Web site address is
http://www.berkley.com

ISBN: 0-425-15412-2

BERKLEY®
Berkley Books are published by The Berkley Publishing Group,
200 Madison Avenue, New York, New York 10016.
BERKLEY and the "B" design
are trademarks belonging to Berkley Publishing Corporation.

PRINTED IN THE UNITED STATES OF AMERICA

10 9 8 7 6 5 4 3 2 1

To Old Bill, for the lessons;
Allen, for the encouragement;
Nat, for the faith.

What though the field be lost?
All is not lost; th' unconquerable will,
And study of revenge, immortal hate,
And courage never to submit or yield;
And what is else not to be overcome?
　　　　—John Milton, *Paradise Lost*

Oh, I'm a good old rebel, that's what I am . . .
I won't be reconstructed, and I don't give a damn.
　　　　　　　—Innes Randolph (1837–87)

CONTENTS

THE
PISTOLEER

PROLOGUE

He was the deadliest man in Texas, on that they all agreed. Otherwise, they might well have been talking about two different men. . . .

Some said he was nothing but a hero. Hellfire, didn't he take up a gun against the bluebellies riding roughshod over Texas in the dark days after the War? He was hardly more than a boy and already fighting injustice. And when the damnable State Police was bullying innocent people all over Texas, didn't he give those Davis devils plenty of their own brute hell? Didn't he run them out of Gonzales County just about single-handed? Yes, sure, he killed men, a lot of men—men who were trying to kill him! Self-defense is the First Law of Life; everybody knows that. And it's an art—an art all men wish they knew well. He'd done nothing but live by that law and master that art. Who wouldn't do the same if he but had the courage and the skill? So some said.

Others were of different opinion. He was a rebel by nature, they said, a bad seed. No, worse—he was much worse than that. He was Evil at Heart. A killer natural-born. He was a violent soul ruled by Pride, the worst of the Deadly Sins. To attribute noble cause to his murderous deeds was to set a false halo over the devil's horns. So others said.

And they all said much more. They said he killed his first man at the age of fifteen. That at eighteen he backed down the great Wild Bill on the main street of Abilene in front of a hundred witnesses. That he'd been shot so many times he carried a pound of lead in his flesh. That he'd killed forty men, maybe more, by the time he went to prison at the age of twenty-five.

They said prison could not break his spirit, though it tortured his flesh for years. That he at last tamed down behind those walls to please his beloved wife. That he took up study of the law and won a pardon after sixteen years. That by then his darling Jane had been in her grave a year.

They said he tried hard to lead an upright life thereafter but his nature would not permit it. He was sore in spirit, they said, he was desolate. He drifted west to the meanest town in Texas. He reverted to the recklessness of his youth, to the habits of whiskey and games of chance. He took a wild-hearted mistress and again carried loaded pistols. The shadow of death followed him everywhere.

They said these things and more, those who had known him in some way or other during the forty-two years of his life: friends and enemies, kinfolk and strangers, soldiers, drifters, cowhands, lawmen and outlaws, gamblers and fancy ladies, judges and jail guards and convicts— witnesses, all of them, witnesses to the pistoleer....

PART ONE

REBEL
BOY

FROM

The El Paso Daily Herald,

20 AUGUST 1895

Last night between 11 and 12 o'clock San Antonio Street was thrown into an intense state of excitement by the sound of four pistol shots that occurred at the Acme Saloon. Soon the crowd surged against the door, and there, right inside, lay the body of John Wesley Hardin, his blood flowing over the floor and his brains oozing out of a pistol shot wound that had passed through his head. Soon the fact became known that John Selman, constable of Precinct No. 1, had fired the fatal shots that had ended the career of so noted a character as Wes Hardin, by which name he is better known to all old Texans. For several weeks past trouble has been brewing and it has been often heard on the streets that John Wesley Hardin would be the cause of some killing before he left the town.

Only a short time ago Policeman Selman arrested Mrs. McRose, the mistress of Hardin, and she was tried and convicted of carrying a pistol. This angered Hardin and when he was drinking he often made remarks that showed he was bitter in his feelings toward John Selman. Selman paid no attention to these remarks, but attended to his duties and said nothing. Lately Hardin had become louder in his abuse and had continually been under the influence of liquor and at such times he was very quarrelsome, even getting along badly with some of his friends. This quarrelsome disposition on his part resulted in his death last night and it is a sad warning to all such parties that the rights of others must be respected and that the day is past when a person having the name of being a bad man can run roughshod over the law and rights of other citizens. . . .

―――――――――――― F R O M ――――――――――――

The Life of John Wesley Hardin as Written by Himself

(SEGUIN, TEXAS: SMITH AND MOORE, 1896)

"Our parents had taught us from our infancy to be honest, truthful, and brave, and we were taught that no brave boy would ever let another call him a liar with impunity; consequently we had lots of battles with other boys at school. I was naturally active and strong and always came out best, though sometimes with a bleeding nose, scratched face, or a black eye; but true to my early training, I would try, try, try again. . . . I always tried to excel in my studies, and generally stood at the head. . . . Marbles, rolly hole, cat, bull pen, and town ball were our principal games, and I was considered by my schoolmates an expert. I knew how to knock the middle man, throw a hot ball, and ply the bat."

―――――

"I was always a very child of nature, and her ways and moods were my study. My greatest pleasure was to be out in the open fields, the forests, and the swamps . . . to get out among the big pines and oaks with my gun and the dogs and kill deer, coon, possums, or wild cats. If any of those Sumpter boys with whom I used to hunt ever see this history of my life, I ask them to say whether or not our sport in those old days was not splendid."

———

"I had seen Abraham Lincoln burned and shot in effigy so often that I looked upon him as a very demon incarnate, who was waging a relentless and cruel war on the South to rob her of her most sacred rights. So you can see that the justice of the Southern cause was taught to me in my youth, and if I never relinquished these teachings in after years, surely I was but true to my early training. The way you bend a twig, that is the way it will grow, is an old saying, and a true one. So I grew up a rebel."

— Vangie Molineaux —

Oh, that baby born in a rush of blood, him. I mid-wife a thousand bornings, me, and I never seen none bring out so much blood from their mama like him. That poor woman so white. The sweat rolling on her skin like hot wax and soak her dress with a smell like low river. Her eyes big and red and blind with the pain. I put a stick in her teeth and she bite it right in two.

Two years before, I help with her first, him they call Joseph, and she hardly make a sound. But this one! Oh, how this one bring out the blood and make her scream. She scream the worst I ever hear from anybody not on fire. The lamplight jumping in the glass with her scream-ing, the walls shaking with the shadows. Hardly no air in that room to breathe, only the smell of smoke and pain sweat, and the blood pumping black out her sex and mak-ing the sheet dark under her.

I hold her knees and I try to help her push, push. I reach in and feel of him and he turn around all wrong, him. But his heart beating strong. He *want* to come out—he want to come out before she maybe die and kill him with her. He *know*, that little baby—he know he in big trouble be-fore he see the light of his first day. But I feel his heart and I talk to him, tell him be strong little man, be strong—and I got his mama's blood up to my elbows and her screams like big bells in my ears.

His daddy the Reverend, he walking around and around

the room, him, praying and praying. When her screaming get louder he start to singing hymns, loud as her screams. Then her screaming get so loud I feel it like fingers on my face, and I don't hear him no more. When he see my hands come out her all covered with the thick dark blood, he quick leave the room and I thank God for that. The way he singing so crazy, so tall and big, him, with a black beard and dressed in black like always, he look like Mr. Bones and he put the spook in me—especially on this night, the twenty-sixth night of May, a night when no gris-gris can keep away the dark spirits.

Finally I get that baby turn around and out he come, kicking and swinging his little red fists. His crying not like a baby's crying, more like yelling—like the yelling a man make when he wild and happy with whiskey or with a woman, or when he wild and mad to kill something. This one born with his eyes open and looking all round to see where the trouble going to come from. Like he already know how this world is, him.

— Gregor Holtzman —

Preacher Hardin brought his family to Polk County in '55, I guess it was, maybe '56, around eight, nine years after we settled here ourselves. They came down from up around Red River. The Reverend's people were originally from Georgia and came to Texas just a few years after Steve Austin settled his first bunch down on the Brazos. It was all kinds of people coming out here for all kinds of reasons, including the need of some to quick put distance between themselves and the law. Even in them days well before the War, "G.T.T."—"Gone to Texas"—was a common good-bye note all around the South.

When the Preacher and his family first got to Polk it was just him and his wife Elizabeth and their two little boys, Joe and John Wesley. Then came their daughters little Elizabeth and Mattie. Their third boy, Jefferson Davis, was born around the end of the War and was a good bit younger than his older brothers.

The Reverend Hardin preached the Methodist word in all the counties hereabouts. He taught school some too, and was a lawyer besides. Mrs. Hardin was a right handsome woman—I say that with all proper respect—and a learned one. Her daddy was a doctor from Kentucky and they say her momma was as refined a lady as the South ever knew. It was no wonder the Hardin children were as smart as they were, what with the Preacher for a daddy and a momma as educated and well-bred as Elizabeth. It's all the more reason some folks never could understand why John Wesley turned out the way he did. Look at Joe, they say—that's the kind of son you expect from a man like the Preacher. Well, people who say that, they didn't really know any of the three of them—Joe, John Wesley, *or* the Preacher.

I'll tell you a story about the Preacher not many ever heard. I was helping him put up a chicken coop one time and this mean, crazy-in-the-head old bull came stomping over from the neighboring farm. It started chasing the Reverend's cow all over the pasture and trying to put a horn in her. The Reverend dropped his hammer and quick went into the house and come back out with his Mississippi rifle and from over a hundred yards off he put a ball right through that bull's eye. And I mean on the run. It ain't many men can shoot like that and even fewer who knew the Preacher could. Anyhow, that evening the bull's owner comes over to the Hardin place—I was sitting to supper with them—and he's hollering mad about his animal. The Preacher never even raised his voice back at him. He told the fella all he'd done was protect what was his. And then he told him if he didn't get that dead bull off his property by sunup, he'd butcher it himself and sell it for beef. Next morning, that bull was gone.

What I'm saying is, there was a side to the Preacher some folks never saw, but it's a side that came out strong in John Wesley.

They're a proud family, the Hardins, with lots to be proud of. They are a far bigger part of Texas history than most families can ever hope to be. Benjamin Hardin, the Preacher's daddy, sat on the Texas Congress back before we joined the Union for the first time. And you take a good look at the Texas Declaration of Independence and you'll see Augustine Hardin's signature on it. He was an uncle of the Preacher's. Hardin County, just south of us, was named for another of the Preacher's uncles, Judge Will Hardin.

All I'm saying is the Hardins I knew came from damn

fine stock and were mighty good people, all of them, and
I mean John Wesley too. Doesn't matter a hill of beans
how many men he killed, not to me, not to a lot of us
around here. We know damn well that in every case he
was either protecting himself or standing up for what was
right. We know that because we knew his family. We
knew their character, and character's the only fact that
really counts.

Barnett Jones

The first hanged man either of us ever saw wasn't one we saw *get* hanged. We come across him when we were hunting coon in the Thicket one day. We were about nine or ten years old. We'd seen *dead* men before, of course—men dead from a gunshot wound or fever or a timber falling on them or drowning or a snakebite, things like that. But this was the first one we saw dead from hanging, and that's a whole different thing.

We'd gone into that mean dark swamp a whole lot deeper that morning than we ever had before, following coon tracks along the creek bank. It was hot as blazes and the air was thick as stew. Johnny suddenly pulled up and said, "Listen!" It was a low humming, sort of like a congregation sounds when everybody's praying softly. We crawled up the creek bank and pushed through the cattails into a wide clearing and there he was, hanging by the neck from a hickory tree, his hands tied behind him and his bare white feet as high off the ground as our heads.

What we'd heard was the swarm of flies feasting on his face. His tongue was black and all swole up in his mouth and a good bit of it had been ate away by the crows. His lips too. And he didn't have any eyeballs left. He hadn't been up there long enough for the maggots to start in on him, but he was starting to turn ripe. He was some stranger with reddish curly hair. A little wood sign hung around his neck on a rawhide string. On it, somebody had writ in pencil, "CUT HIM DOWN AN WELL KILL YOU." We just stood there and stared at him for a while. "Who you reckon did it to him?" I finally said. "Don't know," Johnny said, "but I'd rather be shot a thousand times than end up like that."

We went back and told Uncle Barnett, and him and three of his hands went back into the Thicket with us and cut the body down. Uncle Barnett snatched the sign off him and threw it in the bushes. They took the dead man to the sheriff's office in Moscow and put him in a coffin and stood the open box on end in front of the office with a sign resting on his chest saying, "DO YOU KNOW THIS MAN?" But after a whole day and night nobody had claimed to know him and he was stinking pretty bad by then, so they went ahead and buried him with just a plain cross on his grave.

We grew up together, Johnny and me. His brother Joe too, though Joe was a sight different from Johnny. Johnny liked to run around with the rest of us and was popular with everybody, but Joe tended to keep to himself. Always had his nose in a book, Joe. Actually, Johnny liked books too—Lord knows why—but he dang sure didn't spend all his time with them. He much preferred *doing* things— riding, rassling, foot racing, chicken chasing, hunting, things like that. We didn't either of us ever like the indoors much until we'd growed up enough to learn the pleasures of saloons and fancy houses.

Johnny was always long and lean, more on the skinny side than not, but he was strong as rawhide and twice as tough. And *run*? That boy could run like a scalded dog. He wasn't but thirteen when he outran Moscow's fast man, Oliver Weeks, and the very next year he outran Jean LeRoque, Sumpter's fast man. Hell, he was quick in all the ways a man can move, not just on his feet. It's what made him such a good rassler and boxing man. He could outrassle boys near twice his weight just because he was so fast and hard to get a good hold of. He could slip around you and pull you off-balance and have you down and pinned before you could say General Joe. If there was anything Johnny was better at than rassling or shooting it was boxing. Back in Moscow he had taught himself to box from a book writ by some Eastern professor of pugilism. Joe told me that. Johnny had practiced everything it taught—the way to stand and hold up your dukes, the ways to move your feet, the different kinds of punches, all that. "And who you suppose he practiced on?" Joe said. "I can *still* feel some of the knots he raised on my head."

Hell, we was all of us pretty rough boys back then, and me and Johnny was right among the roughest, if I say so myself. But rough as we were, we weren't old enough to lie about our age and get into the War. We felt cursed as Job's goat for being born too late to join the ranks and go off to kill us some goddamn Yankees. All we could do back then was watch the men and the bigger boys go off to the fighting. We'd follow each departing bunch out to the main trace and wave after them till they were out of sight. Sometimes we'd see huge herds of horses and cattle being drove by on the way east to provide mounts for the cavalry and beef for the whole of the Confederacy.

The one good thing about being too young to go off to war was that now it was up to us to protect our homes and put meat on the table. We went about armed at all times. Me and Johnny and a few of the other boys shot at more than game, however. We used to make scarecrow-size figures of straw and old clothes and hang them from trees as targets. Our favorite was one we put a beard and a stovepipe hat on to make it look like Lincoln. Johnny drew a pair of eyes on it and always put his shots square between them. He was such a deadeye we always had to put a new head on the Lincoln dummy after Johnny got through taking his turn with it. He could shoot like that from the time he was ten years old.

My pa used to say there's some so good at what they do best it's like they been touched by magic. Farmers who can bring things out of the ground by hardly doing more than digging their boot toe in the earth and spitting in the hole. Men who can make music from any tight piece of string or empty tin can or open bottle, who can make a fiddle or a mouth organ or a banjo sing or laugh or howl just like it's got a heart of its own. Gamblers who can make a playing card scoot like a fish or float like a feather. Bronc busters who can gentle the meanest mustang in six jumps with just a touch of their heels on its flanks and a whisper in its ear. I knew what he meant. Johnny, he had that kind of magic with a pistol.

He used to say his daddy'd taught him to shoot, but Uncle James said that wasn't so. He said all he'd done was let Johnny practice with his old Colt Dragoon from the time he was big enough to hold it with both hands. "Nobody taught that boy to shoot," I once heard Uncle James tell my pa. "He just knew. It's a knowledge he was born with." He said it the way somebody might tell you their child was born with a harelip. I guess he had a feeling about what a talent like that would do to a boy like Johnny.

Anything you ever heard about his shooting, no matter how stretched it might of sounded, was likely true. From the ime he was a stripling he could shoot better than anybody I've yet seen, and I've seen more than a few shooters in my time. He could shoot a jumping squirrel in the head from eighty feet off. I saw him put all six balls in a knothole sixty feet away and no bigger around than the top of a saddle horn. I saw him set an empty whiskey bottle in the crotch of a tree with the open end facing his way, then take forty paces and spin around and shoot through the open end and blow out the bottom of the bottle. See how good you can even make out the open end of a bottle at forty paces. He taught himself all the usual twirling tricks too. He made himself a sorry-looking holster out of a piece of cowhide and practiced quick-drawing every day. I never heard of him losing a shooting contest in his life. For damn sure he never lost any of the kind that really count—the kind where you and the other fella ain't shooting at bottles on a fence, you're shooting at each other.

Let me tell you something. Most people who talk about

gunfighting like experts ain't usually been within ten miles of a gunfight in their whole life. But I have. I want it remembered that I was standing right there, not three feet from Johnny, the day in Trinity City when that tinhorn blasted him with a shotgun. I know how quick it happens, and how loud, and how it shocks you and don't seem real either then or later. How afterward you're not exactly sure just what it was you saw. There must of been two dozen witnesses to the Trinity shooting and afterward I heard two dozen different versions of it, including my own.

But that business in Trinity City was years later when he was on the run from the State Police. Right now I want to tell about the terrible days that followed the sad news of Bobby Lee's surrender. On the day we heard of Appomattox, Uncle James told Pa that as bad as things had been during the War, they were sure to get worse now. Pa didn't disagree. How could he? The damn Yankees were coming.

But ahead of the Yankees came our own soldiers, a small bunch of them every week or so. The few horses they had with them showed ribs through their hides like barrel staves. Hardly a man among them was whole. Every one of them had at least one bloody wound bound up on him someplace. The wagons carried men missing one or both legs, blind men, and men who just stared like they were blind. One-armed men stumbled along in the dust, men without hands, men missing an eye or some other part of their face. Twenty-year-olds looked like gray old men. But the most awful thing about it was how quiet they went by. They didn't hardly say a word. All you heard was dragging feet and coughing and groaning, the tired clopping of horse hooves, the creaking of wagons. It was a sorely pathetic sight to behold. It made you curse and want to kick the ground. For years after, it was cripples everywhere you looked.

But it wasn't till the Yankee army started showing up in our part of the country that we really got to know the hard consequences of losing the War. To make things worse, to rub salt in our open wounds, the Union generals

had put a shitload of niggers in the companies they sent
to enforce the Yankee law in Texas. Like most everybody
else in East Texas, Johnny and me had knowed a good
many colored folk and we had always got along with them
just fine. Hellfire, there wasn't a kin among us that owned
so much as a single slave. But God damn, all them bluebelly troops to back up the land-grabbing, conniving, son
of a bitch carpetbaggers and scalawags and federal bureau
agents and God know who-all was bad enough—without
having to put up with niggers carrying guns and giving
orders to white people. That was more than we could endure. All them Union woolies was from someplace else—
Alabama and Georgia, mostly—and they were a mean and
insolent lot, I'm telling you.

And still things got worse. A cousin of ours, Simp
Dixon, came down from Navarro County with a terrible
tale to tell. Simp was son of Silas, who was brother to
Johnny's momma. His story poured coal oil on the hate
we all felt for every Yankee in the world. What happened
was, a bunch of Yank soldiers had rode up to the Dixon
farm one day while Simp was way off in the woods hunting and his pa was in town getting supplies. The blues
killed *everybody*—Simp's momma and his baby brother
and both his sisters, one twelve and one fourteen. Nobody
knew why they'd done it. They mighta been drunk, but
not necessarily. Simp said his ma had a sharp tongue and
hated Yankees worse than the blackest sin, so likely she
said things that set them off. They burned down the barn
and shot their old milk cow and stole all four horses in
the corral. They blew his little brother's head off and took
his ma and sisters into the house and violated them in the
most dishonorable way before shooting them dead too.
When Simp's pa got back and found his neighbors gathered round the bodies of his family laid out in the front
room of the house, he near lost his mind with grief. They
told Simp later that his pa had cried and cried and started
to drinking, and by nightfall he was in a drunken, sorrow-
ing rage. He picked up the body of his youngest daughter,
who'd always been his favorite, and let out a howl you

could of heard clear to the Brazos. When his pa grabbed
up his rifle and pouch of ammunition and rode off hell-
for-leather toward the Yankee camp, Simp said, nobody
would of been able to stop him if they tried. Late the next
day, the county sheriff brought him back in a flatwagon,
just as dead as a man can be from eighteen Yankee bullets.

Simp had got back home by then and helped to dig all
the graves. That evening, he sold the house and property
to a neighbor for twenty dollars cash money and the promise of eighty more someday when the neighbor had it.
Then he saddled up and rode off to a place where the road
between Corsicana and the Yankee camp curved through
a thick grove of oak. He set himself up in a clump of trees
and waited with his Sharps carbine loaded and cocked.

The next day three Yanks came riding down from Corsicana, laughing and half drunk. Simp shot one soldier in
the head and then another in the spine as he tried to ride
off. The third one hightailed it around the bend before
Simp could load and cock the Sharps again. The one shot
in the spine was still alive, but he was paralyzed and crying, and he begged Simp for his life. He had a sweetheart
back home in Ohio he was fixing to marry, he said. Simp
laughed at him while he scalped the other Yankee. He said
the wounded Yank's eyes about popped out of his head
when he saw him do that. But we really should of seen
his face, Simp said, when he did the same thing to *him*.
The fella's screams, Simp said, was music to his ears. He
let the Yank have a good close look at his own bloody
hair in his hand, then blasted his brains into the dirt. "It
was about the most enjoyable fifteen minutes of my life,"
Simp said, and the way he smiled when he said it, you
didn't doubt him a bit. But now the Yankees were on the
hunt for him, and the word was out that they meant to
shoot him on sight. He had the scalps hung on his saddle
horn and he allowed me and Johnny to feel of them. The
skin part was stiff and rough and left flakes of dry blood
on your fingers.

Simp wasn't but sixteen years old at the time, about
three years older than me and Johnny. He had a smile like

a wolf and his eyes were hot and bright as fire. He was
the first wanted man we'd known, and we thought he was
nothing but a hero for what he'd done. Still, there were
times when he'd be off sitting by himself and looking like
he might cry, and you knew he was thinking about his
family and what those murdering Yankee bastards had
done to them.

Simp's wasn't the only story of its kind that came to
us. We heard tale after tale of Yankee cruelty all over
Texas. The way they carried on in Texas after the War
was pure hateful, and it's something none of us will ever
forget. They shot more than one man dead just for still
wearing a Confederate cap. They'd throw you in jail for
just staring hard at a Yankee. They stole any damn thing
they wanted—stock, wagons, goods. They burned farms
for the pure meanness of it—hell, they burned down whole
towns. A bunch of drunk nigger soldiers burned Brenham
to the ground and wasn't a one of them arrested for it, and
that's a fact. It was clear enough those Yankee sons of
bitches wouldn't be satisfied till there wasn't nothing left
of Texas but burnt dirt. It ain't a bit of wonder that for so
many years after the War Texas was full of more bad
actors than you could shake a hanging rope at. The way
a lot of young fellas saw it, if the Yankees were the ones
to make the laws, then the only proper thing to be was an
outlaw.

Johnny and me used to spend a lot of time at our Uncle
Barnett Hardin's farm, and we sometimes helped to harvest his crop of sugarcane. That's where the thing with
Mage happened. At harvest time Uncle Barnett always
hired extra hands to cut the stalks and that year Mage was
one of them. He was a huge muscular man with hard yellow eyes—and about the best cane cutter in the county.
He was said to have a temper as ugly as his face—which
was just covered with warts—and he was given to bullying
the other niggers something fierce. They said he'd killed
a man in the Big Thicket by drowning him in a bayou.
He'd been one of Judge Holshousen's slaves before the

War, and the judge will tell you he was trouble even then.
After the War, the judge wouldn't have him on the place
as a hired man.

Anyhow, one afternoon me and Johnny were working
in the same cane row as Mage and I got to wondering if
the two of us could best him in rassling. He had a reputation as a rough rassler, and I knew he could take either
of us by ourself, but I reckoned we could best him if he
fought us two at once. So I put the challenge to him. He
gave a mean laugh and tried to stare us down, but we just
hard-eyed him right back. "Sure," he finally said. "Some
rassling be just fine." The other hands got all excited and
started making bets as they followed us down to the clearing at the end of the row.

He was stronger but we were smarter, and we worked
him like a pair of dogs on a wild hog, one in front and
one in back, yelling and distracting him every which way,
then moving in fast and tripping him down, me grabbing
one of his arms and Johnny the other and pinning him for
fair. It happened so fast the other niggers couldn't help
laughing at Mage and riding him about it. He was so
steamed his eyes looked like yellow fires. He naturally
wanted to go another one, which was fine with us. And
we took him down again. But before we could pin him he
butted me in the face and broke my nose. I rolled away
from him with blood running off my chin. Him and
Johnny pulled apart and jumped to their feet. Johnny was
smoking mad and told him there wasn't any need of that,
but Mage just spat and said did we want to rassle or did
we want to cry about a bloody nose. Johnny asked me if
I could go another and I nodded yes, although my eyes
were watering so bad I couldn't hardly see. So we locked
up again—and Johnny dug his fingernails into Mage's face
and clawed open a bunch of his warts. Mage yowled and
tore free of us and wiped his hand across his face and
stared at the blood on his fingers. "You white shit son of
a bitch!" he hollered—and grabbed Johnny by the hair
and got him in a headlock and probably would of broke
his neck if me and three big field hands hadn't ganged up

on him and pulled him off. "I'll kill you!" he yelled. "I'll cut your damn head off with my cane knife! I'll *kill* you!"

Well, Johnny didn't have a reason in the world to think he didn't mean it, so he lit out for the house, me right on his heels. I knew he was going for his pistol, the big Dragoon his daddy had give him for his last birthday. He always brought it with him from home, even though his momma was always telling him not to.

We nearly bowled over Uncle Barnett as we tore into the house. "Whoa there!" he shouted and grabbed each of us by an arm. He said we looked like the devil himself was on our tail and demanded to know what was going on. So we told him. He ordered us to stay in the house—and specifically ordered Johnny not to even touch his gun—then hurried out to the cane field. I don't know if Johnny's heart was beating as hard as mine while we waited for him to get back—I just know we couldn't stop grinning at each other.

Pretty soon Uncle Barnett came back and said he'd fired Mage off the place, so our trouble with him was over and done with. He asked us to stay to supper and then spend the night. Johnny accepted his offer, but I had early chores to do back home and had to excuse myself after we ate.

Damn, I wish I'd stayed. It would of been worth a hiding from Pa to have been with Johnny the next morning when he shot down that bad-acting nigger after all.

Judge Clabe
Holshousen

I believe my sister Anne made an excellent choice in Barnett Hardin from the flock of suitors who so ardently courted her. He was an industrious and widely respected man of temperate personal habits, and his Long Tom Creek plantation consistently produced handsomely profitable harvests in cotton and sugarcane. I very much enjoyed his company, and, over time, I fell in the habit of attending Wednesday supper and Sunday dinner at his home. We were often joined at one or another of these family repasts by his nephew, young John Wesley Hardin, of whom both my sister and Barnett were quite fond.

John was a tall, lean lad whose aspect suggested speed and a ready grace. But his most striking feature was his eyes. They were bright with intelligence and wit, fully attentive and yet seemingly alert to the smallest movement in the room. Interestingly, their color wavered between blue and gray, and their hue twixt dark and light. He was well schooled and properly mannered, and he had an excellent propensity for recounting humorous anecdotes about his hunting adventures and sporting endeavors. His narratives were marked by an intense animation and much dramatic gesture, and unfailingly inspired us to appreciative laughter.

And yet, despite his charm and good humor, I must admit that I detected in him an inclination to recklessness. There was an aura of a cocked pistol about him, a readi-

ness to action without forethought. Thus, when he came
to me and told me he had shot a man, I was distraught,
of course, and saddened—but not altogether surprised.

On the morning in question, I was taking my second
cup of chickory when I heard a horse galloping up to the
front of the house, then a loud calling of my name. I went
immediately to the door and there found young John in a
highly agitated state. Before I could say a word, he
plunged into a torrential narrative so utterly confusing that
I was compelled to insist that he come into the house, sit
down and catch his breath, then proceed in more measured
fashion.

And thus he did. I learned that he had come to me
directly from a violent confrontation with a man named
Mage, a Negro who had once been among my holdings. I
remembered the troublesome rascal well enough. John told
me he'd had an altercation with Mage in the cane fields
the day before. The Negro had threatened to kill him, and
in consequence Barnett had fired Mage off his land. But
then just this morning, as John had been riding toward
home on the Sumpter Road, he came upon Mage at the
bend in the road where the creek abuts a cottonwood
grove, a point some seven miles from my home.

When Mage caught sight of John, he became enraged
and began to curse him vehemently. John told him he
wanted no further trouble with him and wished only to
pass by and continue on his way. But Mage raised his big
walking stick with both hands like a club and advanced
upon him, still cursing vilely. John tried to rein his horse
around him, but Mage lunged with the stick and struck
the horse on the hindquarters, making it rear in fright.

"When he hit Paint," John said, "I shot him."

"Good Lord, John!" I said. "Is he killed?"

"He wasn't when I left him," he said, "but he wasn't
looking any too spry, either. Far as I know, he's still laying
back there in the road."

The revelation that Mage was not dead came as some
small comfort, and I asked about the severity of his
wound.

"Well, sir," John said, "it's not just one wound, it's four." He hastily explained that Mage had not fallen on receiving the first ball in the stomach, but had only become more furious and intent on his attack. "I couldn't believe how he kept right on coming," John said. "So I shot him again—in the chest this time—and he took a step back—but be damn if he didn't come at me *again*." So he shot him twice more in the belly and Mage finally fell. "Lord Jesus," John said, "it was pure-dee amazing!" He spoke as if recounting a marvel witnessed at a tent show. "I reckon it's like they say," he said, "if you want to be sure a man goes down and stays down, you best shoot him in the head."

We hastened to the stable and I directed my foreman Paul to saddle our horses and bring his shotgun. The sun was nearly overhead when we arrived at the cottonwood bend, yet the soft breeze carried a distinct chill. Mage had dragged himself to the creek and was dipping water with his hand. As soon as he saw us he began cursing loudly. My viscera stirred at the sight of his wounds—they were raw and gaping and pulsing with blood. The instant I saw those wounds, I knew he was dying and could not be helped. It defied belief that he was still alive.

"That sonbitch shoot me down like a dog!" he said in a thick voice. "Come right up and shoot me. He murder me! He murder a unarmed man!"

John said, "You attacked me and wouldn't take warning to leave off. You gave me no choice."

"Liar!" Mage shouted hoarsely. "White trash murdering liar, you!" His fury prompted him to cough up a gout of bright blood, and my stomach twisted sickly.

John dismounted and drew his pistol and stepped closer to Mage. He aimed it squarely at his face and cocked the hammer.

"Do it," Paul urged him. "Do it, boy."

"Sure," Mage said, looking up at John with blood dripping off his chin. "Go ahead on and murder me some more."

I do not like to think that he would have pulled the

trigger on Mage in cold blood. I prefer to believe he was simply gesturing. And yet I couldn't keep from calling out sharply, "No, John!"

He looked at me without expression. "Do you want to swing on a Yankee rope for killing such a worthless creature?" I said. "Put up your pistol."

And he did. I heard Paul swear softly in disappointment, and I instructed him to go back to the farm and get a wagon and two field hands to load Mage onto it. They would then take him to the Negro settlement near Moscow and leave him to his people to tend him the best they could.

As Paul rode away, I told John I believed Mage was going to die. "The Union troops will come looking for you," I said. I advised him to go directly to his father and tell him what had happened. I gave him a twenty-dollar gold piece in case he got cut off by the Yankees and was forced to take refuge in strange towns.

For a moment he once again looked like the fifteen-year-old boy he was. Then his aspect assumed an air of resolve. He mounted up, tugged his hat low on his brow, reached down to shake my hand, and spurred off toward Trinity County.

Two days later Mage was dead, and John Wesley Hardin was a wanted man.

—— Charles Morgan ——

I was chopping stove wood early one morning when the weather had already turned chilly enough to show your breath, and I looked out across the meadow and saw a rider come out of the heavy pine. The farmhouse was on good high ground and you could see a ways over the trees along the creek that cut through the meadow. Wasn't often we had visitors, set so far off the trace as we were. What's more, this fella was acting cautious as a cat. He stepped his paint pony out of the trees and reined up to take a look all around, staring specially hard off to the east. I couldn't see a thing out that way but the sun just starting to blaze through the trees. I figured the only thing he could be considering so hard was that anybody wanting to have the advantage on him would likely come from that direction so as to catch him with the sun in his eyes. But I am a cautious man myself, and in those days the countryside was just crawling with all sorts of bad actors left mean and rootless by the War, so I eased over to the door and called low to my old woman to pass me out my shotgun. I checked the loads and set it against the chopping block where I could snatch it up right quick if the need came.

Turned out to be none other than John Wesley, the Reverend's second boy. I didn't recognize him till he got up close enough to halloo me. I'd see the elder boy, Joe, fairly often because he was the schoolteacher in Logallis Prairie and lived just a few miles the other side of the big hollow from us, but I hadn't seen John Wesley in a couple of years, and he'd growed some in that time. He looked to be getting close to six feet high now, and though he was still a rangy thing he'd put on some thickness through the shoulders and had him a good-sized pair of hands. Biggest change, though, was in his face. It wasn't no boy's face anymore. One look in his eyes and I knew he was bringing hard news.

He said he had a letter for me from his daddy, but he didn't hand it over till he'd taken his paint around back to the stable and got it out of sight, which he seemed mighty eager to do. I was raised up to believe it ain't polite to ask a man his business right out, but if a feller's putting his horse in your stable and has got a double-barreled shotgun at the ready and keeps taking looks over his shoulder, well, I reckon that gives you some right to be a little forward. So I say to him, "Is it somebody else likely to be coming this way, John Wesley?" And he says, "Could be, Mr. Morgan. I reckon you best read my daddy's letter now." And he hands it over.

It was some letter, all right, full of the bad news I'd felt coming on from the minute I got a close-up look at John Wesley's face. Turns out he'd shot some Nigra dead in Polk County and now the Yankees were after him. The Reverend said he believed it was a clear case of self-defense, just as John Wesley had told him, but he could not believe his boy would get a fair trial, not with the Union army setting the law in Texas. He had no doubt that if the Yankees didn't shoot John Wesley on sight, the trial they'd give him would be a mockery. He'd likely be hanged, or at the very least packed off to prison for a lot of years. "Not until the courts of Texas are again halls of true and impartial justice," the Reverend wrote, "will I encourage my son to stand himself before their judgment."

I knew John Wesley's trouble must of been paining Reverend Hardin a good deal. From the time John Wesley was born, the Reverend had hoped he would grow up to be a preacher like himself. I heard him say so more than once. He thought the world of his eldest boy, but it was John Wesley who he saw spreading the Gospel. It's why he named him after the Great Methodist. Now here the boy was, on the run from the law for killing a man.

What the Reverend wanted of me was to put the boy up for a time, till he could arrange for him to live with kin in Navarro County. As out of the way as my place was, he thought there wasn't much chance the soldiers would come looking for him there. He said Joe would come over every few days to keep us up on things and let us know if any Yankee soldiers had been spotted in our neck of the woods. I got my two boys, Will and Harold, who weren't but eleven and nine then, to clear out the lean-to I'd added to the back of our dog-run cabin and help John Wesley get himself settled in there. When they heard the Yankees were after him, they looked at him like he was Jeb Stuart himself.

The next day Joe Hardin showed up and said there was a line of families between Sumpter and Logallis Prairie keeping a lookout for Yankee patrols. He stayed to supper with us that night, and afterward my boy Will took down the fiddle his granddaddy had passed on to him, and Harold joined in with his mouth organ, and we had us a time. I mean, we shook the walls with our foot-stomping—we really made the lantern lights jump! My old woman was always kind of shy about dancing in front of people she didn't know too good, but pretty soon she let her hair down and couldn't stop smiling and blushing with all the swinging around we gave her. My three girls were youngsters yet, but we took turns dancing with them too, even little Sarah, who wasn't but six years old. Brenda and Lorrie—the one ten and the other eight—were laughing and bright in the face and just couldn't get enough of the dancing. Joe and John Wesley would bow to them when asking for a dance and kiss their hand afterward. Those two girls weren't much use at all for the next two days, they were so moony from all the gentlemanly attention they got that night.

After Joe told us about all those folks keeping an eye out for Yankees and being ready to warn us if any were to head our way, John Wesley took to riding out every day to look for cows. There was wild cattle around there in those days and you didn't need to be no cowboy to lasso one and tug it on home. You just had to have the time to do it and be willing to get yourself and your pony all scratched up rassling a longhorn through the rough brush on the end of a rope. I'd take the animal to town and trade it for goods. John Wesley helped us out plenty that way. And every evening after supper my children couldn't hear their fill of his stories about hunts he'd been on with his brother or his cousin Barnett. Those who have anything bad to say about him best never say it around me or my children—and I mean my girls too—if they don't want a fight on their hands.

One afternoon, Jules Halas, who had a small spread east of Logallis Prairie, came by in his buckboard with a message from Joe. A half-dozen Yankee soldiers had shown up on the other side of the hollow during the night. Two were keeping watch on Joe's house, one was watching the schoolhouse, and three were riding around asking folks questions about John W. Hardin. They had to know he wasn't at Joe's or they likely would of busted in on the place, but it sure looked like they knew he was somewhere around. Jules had seen the two bluebellies watching the schoolhouse when he went to retrieve his young ones. Joe had asked him to bring the news to John Wesley but to be careful about not being followed. "Joe says you best keep a sharp eye out," Jules told us. "He says it's some people around here not above giving the Yanks information in exchange for a piece of silver."

The morning after we got word of the soldiers closing in, John Wesley stayed in the house rather than go out to hunt cows and run the risk of being spotted. And then, sometime around midmorning, here they came. I was out in the hog pen and caught sight of them as they came in from the far end of the meadow, about a half mile off,

three of them. From the careless way they was coming—
riding all abreast and slow and easy, right out in the open
instead of staying close to the trees on either side—it was
clear they wasn't expecting to find him here. Likely they
were just nosing around, trying to find out if anybody had
seen him.

I looked over to the window where John Wesley had
been sitting and keeping watch, but he wasn't there anymore. I heard a low whinny from the stable and then his
horse hoofing off into the woods behind the house, and I
reckoned he was heading for the main trace to make his
getaway.

The meadow creek was less than a quarter mile away,
but you couldn't see it from the house because of the
heavy growth of hardwoods lining the steep banks and
blending into the pine forest to the south. It took the troopers a while to reach the creek, they were coming so slow.
There was a small break in the trees where they could
cross fairly easy, but they had to come across single file.

As the first soldier eased his horse down the bank, I
heard a shotgun blast and saw a puff of smoke from the
clump of sweet gums to their left. The lead rider went
backward like he'd been lassoed. I don't think he hit the
ground before John Wesley blew the second rider out of
the saddle too. The third Yank jerked his horse around and
gave it the spurs, heading back the way he'd come.

John Wesley came charging up out of the trees on his
horse, whipping the paint up the bank with the reins, yelling something I couldn't make out, and went straight after
the third soldier. The Yank cut over toward the east tree-
line, trying to get to cover. As he rode he turned and fired
two quick shots with his pistol—but John Wesley kept
charging hard and gaining on him fast, and before the
Yank could make the trees he closed to within ten feet of
him and shot him in the back. The soldier's arms went up
in the air and he tumbled off his horse and John Wesley
rode right over him at full gallop.

I tell you, it was something to see.

I took off running, hearing Will and Harold coming be-

hind me, hearing their momma shrieking for them to get
back to the house, sounding like she was near out of her
mind. The boys passed me by and got to the creek a good
ten yards ahead of me. I was plumb out of breath when I
got to the bank and stood beside him, looking down at the
two dead Yankees. One laid faceup, except he didn't have
a face anymore—it got blowed away along with half his
head. The other was belly-down and the hole in his back
where the charge had come out was big enough to throw
a cat through. John Wesley had hid himself in the trees
awful good to get such close shots at them—and they'd
been careless, like I said. Their blood was flowing down
the creek in lacy red swirls.

The boys were so excited they were just about dancing.
Harold kept saying, "Did you see it, Daddy? Did you *see*
it?" Then they were off and running again, splashing
through the creek and up the opposite bank and off toward
where John Wesley had reined up beside the other Yankee.

When I caught up to them, huffing hard again, John
Wesley was down off the paint and holding his hand tight
around his other arm. There was blood oozing through his
fingers and he was grinning like a crazy man. The dead
man at his feet was a Nigra. His eyes and mouth were
open wide and one of his cheeks had been crushed by a
hoof. The pistol ball had come out just under his collarbone and the thick patch of bright blood looked like a
large red flower crushed on his jacket. "I been shot," John
Wesley said. "First damn time." He said it like it was
something he'd been waiting on, like a letter. He was trying hard to stay calm, but there was no hiding his excitement. I couldn't hardly blame him, not really. I'd seen
fellers killed before, but never seen three killed so quick
by just one—and never in such a yeehaw way as John
Wesley had just done.

"I think we best get these bluebellies out of sight quick
as we can, don't you, Mr. Morgan?" John Wesley said. I
said I thought we damn sure should, and I sent Will off
to the DuBois place, which was down the creek and into
the woods a ways. Gerard DuBois and his boys were good

people and I knew they'd be glad to lend us a hand.

The Nigra's bullet hadn't taken but a small bite out of John Wesley's arm, but it was bleeding real free. I tore a strip off his shirtsleeve and used it to tie off the wound, then we got busy stripping down the Nigra. If anybody ever did find the bodies, we didn't want anything on them to identify them as soldiers.

Just as we'd got back to the creek and started in on the other two dead Yanks, Gerard DuBois and his boys showed up. They'd been in the middle of stringing trot-lines across the river, but when Will told them what happened, they hustled right on over to help us out. They about busted John Wesley's shoulders, pounding them so much in congratulations.

We toted the bare-ass bodies way on down the creek to a special place and buried them deep in the clay. There was lots of wash down at that spot and every rain from then on helped to bury them deeper. It was more than one dead man had been buried around there. We burned all their clothes to ashes. John Wesley didn't want any of the dead men's goods, so the DuBois boys rode off with the Yank horses, heading for the Thicket, where there was a fella always ready to pay top money for good horseflesh without a question of where it came from, not even if it carried the U.S. brand. Gerard DuBois took two of the Yankee carbines and I took the other. I couldn't pass up that Spencer.

The sun was down in the treetops by the time we got back to the house. When my old woman saw the Yankee rifle, she didn't say anything but she got awful tight in the face, knowing what it would mean if the wrong person ever caught a look at it. I kept it next to the bed but never did take it outside to shoot till long after the Yanks pulled out of Texas.

But even though she was too mad to say anything, she got right to work stripping the binding off John Wesley's wound and then bandaging it up proper. John Wesley could see how upset she was, and I think he was more uncomfortable about that than about the pain in his arm.

When she finished up with him, he said he reckoned he'd best go back home and let his daddy know what happened.

During supper he said he'd leave as soon as it got dark. My old woman wrapped up some corn bread for him. She started to leave the room, then quick came back to him and touched his face and said, "God bless you, boy." Then she went into the other room and didn't come out again. I never understood her and never will.

The boys offered their hands and he shook them as seriously as if they were grown men. He hugged the girls and kissed their cheeks. They started to cry, but I told them if they were going to do that they could leave the room, so they quit. We sat around till the last of the daylight faded, then went out to the stable. He saddled up, thanked me again for my hospitality, and rode off. It was a full moon out, but he cut over close to the trees and we lost sight of him in their deep shadow.

Next we heard, his daddy'd got him a schoolteacher job in Navarro County. They say he was a natural-born good teacher of reading and lettering and ciphering. For sure he'd of had a more peaceful life if he'd stayed at it rather than turn cowboy like he did.

— Hannie Willingham —

The very first time he walked into the schoolroom and said, "Good morning. My name's Wes Hardin and I'm your new teacher," I thought to myself, *Well now, Mr. Wes Hardin, I might could teach you something too*. I knew just by looking at him he hadn't ever done it, not yet.

I'd been teaching boys things they were mighty glad to learn since just before I turned thirteen—which was when my Uncle Andy introduced me to the original sin, as some call it, on a pile of hay at the back of his barn. I didn't begrudge Uncle Andy for plucking my cherry—I wanted him to do it as much as he did. All these women who say they never have liked it, I don't understand them. I loved it right from the first.

The first time Johnny and me did it back there in Pisga was on a blanket under a cottonwood by the lake with a big silver moon blazing through the branches over our heads. Like most boys on their first time with a girl he was quick as a gunshot about it. But then he was ready to go again—and again and again. Lord, there was no quit to that boy. I didn't keep count, but I bet we did it more than a half-dozen times that night. Like a lot of the tall skinny ones, he was hung like a horse. I mean, he could of cracked pecans with that big thing of his. And talk about a fast learner! That boy wanted to know *every*thing—how's this feel to you here, how's that feel to you there, how you like if it I do this, or this, or this? What if I do this here with my tongue? What if I do that there with my finger? He wanted to learn everything all at once. I know I taught him everything *I* knew at the time—and he damn near wore me out with all his learning and practicing.

He liked to talk too—I mean while we were at it. And laugh. And make me laugh. I remember how, right after one of the first few times we did it, he raised up on his hands and knees and looked at me like he was about to say something really serious, then said, ''You know what, Miss Hannie? I believe a man could learn to enjoy this sort of thing.'' He tickled me with silly jokes about bucking broncos and saddle sores and God-knows-what-all. He was fun. And he was really and truly nice. He talked so sweet and kissed so soft and stroked my hair so gentle. But best of all—the thing about him I'll always remember, the thing that made me think I was in love with him at the time—was that he kept right on treating me with respect in public. He'd call me *Miss* Hannie whenever we met in front of other people. He always tipped his hat to me. The fact is, he was a gentleman. I guess his momma wouldn't have approved of me in a million years, but I surely do approve of the way she raised him.

When he gave up teaching to join his crazy cousin Simp Dixon in the cattle trade, he went to live out at Jim Newman's cow camp and only came to Pisga now and then. Once in a while I'd see him in town, usually in the company of Simp and other rough characters like Frank Polk. Whenever he saw me, he'd say hello and smile sweetly, but that was all. He never whispered in my ear anymore to meet him out by the lake late at night. I heard that him and his friends were taking their pleasures with the painted cats in Jennie Ann's sporting house. For a while I pined for him so hard I thought my heart would fall to pieces— but I swore I'd never pine for a man again and I never have.

*   *   *

I got out of Pisga with a fella named Pierson who came to town one day with his two girls in a blazing-red covered wagon and gave me a wink while he hawked patent medicine to the crowd. Charlie Leamus, one of the boys I'd fooled with, told me Pierson was really a whoreman and would be peddling the girls in the wagon after dark, out at Jackson's Hollow, a mile or so out of town. That night I snuck out of the house and walked on out there and hid in the bushes until the last of the men who'd been standing in line had gone in the wagon and done his business and left. Then I went up to Pierson as he was tying everything down tight and had a talk with him. And when they rolled away from Pisga before sunup, I went too.

I worked my way north with them and then went on my own when Pierson cheated me once too often. I ended up in a house in Abilene, Kansas, the wildest town I ever worked. The first gunfight I ever saw was right in the middle of Texas Street—two drunk cowboys who missed each other six shots each from twenty feet apart. They busted windows and killed a horse and hit a dog, but missed each other every time—and then while one was busy reloading cap and ball, the other pulled out an extra pistol and walked up to him and shot him square in the face from about two feet away.

I saw a dozen fistfights a night. I saw two men cut each other up with knives till they both fell down from the loss of blood and died with faces white as powder. I saw a madam named Stella Raye shoot a man in the ear with a derringer for cutting a nipple off one of her girls. The girl wasn't too bright and had laughed at the hardass because he was too drunk to get it up. Funny thing is, after that she got to be one of the most popular girls in the house. Everybody wanted to fuck the girl with only one nipple. Oh, hell, the things I saw back then, the things I learned.

But the thing I'll always remember best about Abilene is the time Wild Bill came up to the rooms and right there with him was none other than Johnny, who I'd thought I'd never in my life see again. Ain't life a damn wonder!

Jim Newman

Simp Dixon had been cowboying for me off and on for a couple of years when he came into the Tall Hat Saloon one day with this young lean honker at his side and they bellied up next to me at the bar. This was in the spring of '69. He laid that damn Sharps of his on the bar and said, "Hey, Jim, this here's my cousin Wes Hardin. Wants to be a cowhand. Reckon we can make him one?"

I was running a cow camp for Luke Matthews a few miles west of Pisga in those days. Luke was a big drover out of San Antonio. Every year, toward the end of spring, he'd start driving cattle north along the Chisholm, a new herd every few weeks, bringing them up by way of our camp. It was my job to have more cows ready to add to every herd he sent by. Early in the spring, when there was still frost in the mornings, I'd already have a crew out popping the brush for wild cows and mavericks. We'd bring them back to camp, burn them with Luke's Bar-M, cut them, and herd them up in the grassland near the trail, ready to join the next big herd.

I always hired Simp on because he always asked for the job and I wasn't about to tell him no. The man was crazy. He'd killed a dozen or so Yankee soldiers by then and carried their scalps strung on his saddle horn. Made me queasy just to look at them. I touched a scalp at a tent show one time and had the night sweats for two days after.

Anytime Simp was in my camp—hell, anytime he was *near* me—I was always half expecting a battalion of blue-bellies to come charging out of nowhere with their guns blazing, shooting at us all and sorting out their mistakes later. And now here he was with his cousin Wes, who I'd heard was wanted by the Yankee army too.

We had a few drinks and talked things over. It so happened I was short a man, and Wes did seem serious to learn the trade, so I said I'd try him on. And that's how I came to know Wes Hardin, and how he came to be a cowboy.

He made a damn good one. Took to it like a frog to a pond. He could ride as good as any white man I ever saw who wasn't a bronc buster by trade—and I know about bronc busters because we'd sometimes break horses for Luke's remudas. Whenever Luke sent word that he was going to be needing extra mounts, I'd buy some wild ponies from a mustanger I knew and hire Terry Threefingers out of Hillsboro to saddle-break them. Luke paid well for those horses, and I always turned a nice profit on them. Terry was the only one I paid to break the ponies, but there were always a few wildhairs in the crew who wanted to try their hand at it too, just for the fun of it.

You have to be a lot tough and at least a little loco to try to bust a mustang, and Wes was both. The first one he tried to bust throwed him every which way—including smack into the corral rails and even all the way over them. Christ Almighty, that boy took a thumping. He got knocked cold on one try and Terry Threefingers had to souse him with a bucket of water to bring him around. The rest of the boys gathered at the corral and ribbed him plenty about how he ought to quit bronc busting and become an acrobat in the circus since he liked to spend so much time flipping through the air. Wes took all their joshing real good. Every time he get throwed, he'd get up grinning, shake his joints back into place, hitch up his pants, tug down his hat, and mount right back up again. That bronc was as mean as they come and throwed him at least a dozen times before Wes finally broke the ornery

jughead. The next morning Wes was walking stiff-legged
and rode with his face all pinched up, he was so sore—
which naturally made the boys josh him some more. They
said the cayuse musta finally got so bored with throwing
him, it decided being saddle-broke might be a more interesting life. The truth is, they admired the hell out of him
for sticking with that horse the way he had. Wes Hardin
had sand, no question about it.

I had him working roundups with Big Len Richards and
Joe O. And there was plenty to round up out there too.
For years after the War there were more longhorns wandering loose all over Texas than you could shake a branding iron at. Most of them were mavericks, but lots of them
were just strays—cows that once upon a time belonged to
ranchers who went off to fight the Yankees and either
never came back or came back long after their ranches had
gone to hell and their herds had scattered all over the countryside. It was only a matter of time before some of them
strays started getting rounded up by fellas who couldn't
stand the temptation of seeing so many of them running
around loose. Besides, it didn't take a whole lot of artwork
with a branding iron to change a brand. I ain't saying we
ever did that sort of thing at *my* camp, mind you—only
that you couldn't help but hear of it being done here and
there and yonder, every now and then, by somebody or
other.

Anyhow, Wes already knew a good bit about roping by
the time he came to work for me. He had real quick fingers, which you have to have to be any good with a lariat.
You got to be able to size the loop—make it bigger or
smaller—with just your throwing hand, while your other
hand's paying out rope and working the reins. And you
got to be able to do this while you're riding at full gallop.
You got to be able to do it as natural as you spit and
breathe. You watch a roper's hands real close sometime
when he's working and you'll see just how fast and
smooth his fingers move. Quick and sure as a banjo pick-
er's.

After his first few days at the camp, he was roping longhorns like he'd been doing it all his life. Big Len showed him how to lasso a calf with a heel catch so you could drag it behind your horse right up to the fire to get cut and branded. Joe O showed him how two riders could team up to bring down a big steer with what we call a head-and-heel catch, and inside a week he was even making over-and-under catches, which some cowhands never get the hang of even after years of trying.

Wes learned everything real good and real quick. I showed him how to cut the balls off a calf as slick as peeling a potato and how to heat an iron just right so it leaves a good clear brand but doesn't burn too deep and set the hide on fire. I taught him the proper way to saw a pair of horns, which you sometimes had to do to cows with horns so long they couldn't help but stab other cows when they got bunched up tight. I showed him how to use an ax for the job when the horns were too hard for the saw. There wasn't anything about cattle that boy didn't want to know. He even had me show him how to doctor a cow for screwworms and lumpy jaw and other such troubles. He said he figured to have his own herds someday and ought to know how to take care of them. He had a head on his shoulders.

It wasn't all work, of course. Every now and then we'd go into town to see a horse race and wet our snouts and try our luck at the card tables. If there's a man alive who don't like horse racing I never met him. To see a couple of fast horses come galloping hard between two long lines of spectators all jumping up and down and yelling their lungs out as the horses go rumbling past, kicking up clods of dirt, huffing and big-eyed and showing their teeth, the big muscles stretched in their necks and their riders hunched down low and whipping at them with the reins and shouting in their ear—well, hell, if that don't make your heart hop faster I'd say you were ready for burial. It's something about a horse race that gets my blood jumping long before the animals even get to the starting line.

Wes was the same way. He was always talking about buying himself a racer someday soon.

He'd surely be able to afford one, the way he raked in the winnings at the gaming tables. That boy was the luckiest gambler I ever saw. And I don't mean at just one particular kind of game. He won at *everything*—poker, dice, faro, chuckaluck, seven-up, you name it. If the house offered it, he played it—and he'd win at it a good deal more than he'd lose. I've always been a fair hand at poker, if I say so myself, but even after sitting in on many a hand with Wes I never did learn to read his game. In stud and draw both, he played fast and loose. I couldn't believe some of the reckless hands I saw him play. He'd see a whopping big raise to stay in a hand, and then call for *four* cards. He'd raise you twenty dollars on a pair of treys. I never knew anybody so ready to draw to an inside straight—or to fill so many.

I won't ever forget the night he filled two of them on Frank Polk. Simp had introduced them earlier that same day and they'd taken a shine to each other, partly because they were both wanted by the Yankee army, just like Simp. I liked Frank all right, and had hired him on, but he was near as crazy as Simp in a lot of ways, another fella you had to tread lightly with. He was a big-chested, black-bearded rascal who'd shot and wounded two soldiers in a fight in Dallas a few weeks earlier and was naturally claiming self-defense. But the word on Frank was that he'd also pulled a few robberies here and there in North Texas and had killed a store clerk in one of them. The word was, the clerk had been unarmed. But that was just the word, which is wrong about as often as it's not.

Anyhow, on this particular night I'm talking about, me and Frank and Wes and Terry Threefingers and Joel Knapp were in the Tall Hat playing stud and drinking straight whiskey—all except Terry, who was drinking Grizzly Milk, a mix of whiskey and milk and sugar, because his stomach had been ailing him lately. None of the pots was big enough to talk about till an hour into the game when suddenly we were looking at one of about two hundred dollars. Wes drew to a straight and got it to take the hand, and Frank cussed and beat his fist on the table. He was about half drunk by then and had been losing heavy, and he was steamed because he'd been holding kings up over tens and had thought sure the hand was his. Wes smiled at him and said, "Tough one to lose, Frank. But hell, ain't they all?"

Except that he was fairly red-eyed himself, you never would of known Wes had put down at least as much whiskey as Frank had. Wes could drink. I don't remember whiskey ever tangling his tongue or making him do the hard-wind walk.

Frank wouldn't even look at him, he was so steamed. He growled at me, "Your deal, Newman—so deal the damn things."

Half an hour later Wes did it again. He filled a straight flush to beat Frank's full house of aces over jacks and took in nearly three hundred dollars.

"Goddamnit!" Frank yells. He shoves his chair back from the table with a loud scrape and puts his hand on the butt of his gun. Looking hard at Wes, he says, "I have never seen such goddamn luck of the draw in all my whole life." His face and voice were just full of accusation.

Things got quiet downright quick. Wes kept his eyes on Frank and his right hand was out of sight under the table as he pulled in the pot with his left. "Well, Frank," he says, "I hope you keep on seeing it for as long as I'm sitting here."

When you're at the table at a time like that, you want to get away from it as quick and as far as you can, but you're afraid any move you make might set things off like a spark to powder, so you sit still as a stone and hope for the best. All around us the barflies were scooting for cover. I'd seen Wes shoot those Colts of his a few times by then and I knew he was a deadeye, but I hadn't seen him fast-draw. I'd heard he was quick as a snake. Frank was a damn good shot too, but only fair on the draw—but he had a nerve of flint and wasn't afraid of the devil himself. The thing is, whenever a pair of fellas got into it with only

three feet of space between them, they almost always both
got hit for sure and usually both got killed.

Just then I see past Wes to where Simp's coming in the
back door from taking a piss outside, his rifle in the crook
of his arm. I can see he catches wise to what's happening
at the table, and as he heads toward us he cocks the hammer on the Sharps. Wes and Frank are locked up in a
staring match and don't see him coming. When he gets
within two feet of the table, Simp gives me a wink and
fires a round into the floor.

Sweet Christ almighty! You ever *hear* a Sharps go off
indoors? There we all were, wound up tight as cheap
clocks, and *BOOM!*

Frank jumps straight up out of his chair like he's been
stung in the ass and his pistol goes twirling out of his hand
like he's doing some kind of trick and it comes down on
the table and goes off—BLAM!—and he falls back into
his chair and crashes over backward and lays there on the
floor, stock-still.

I never saw Wes move—but there he was, turned half
around in his chair with his cocked Colt in his hand and
square in Simp's chest.

For a second nobody moved—then Wes hollers: "You
stupid dumb jackleg asshole! You looking to get shot?"

"Say now, cousin," Simp says, grinning like the damn
crazy man he was. "Mite jumpy, ain't you?" He looks at
Frank laying on the floor and says, "You don't reckon
he's done killed hisself with his own gun?" And he
laughs.

That's for damn sure what *I* thought happened. But then
I notice a thin cloud of dust floating down on the table,
so I look up and see where the ball of Frank's pistol went
through the ceiling and shook the dust loose. Now everybody else is looking up there too. Then Frank lets out a
low groan and stirs some, then sits up and rubs the back
of his head and looks all around like he ain't real sure if
he's dead or alive. Simp points at him and says, "Lookit
here, boys, it's Lazarus come back from the dead."

Not a one of us could keep from laughing, not even

Frank, he was so damn glad to find out he wasn't dead. He'd just lost his balance, was all, and knocked himself silly when he landed on the back of his head. But for years afterward, those who'd been there—and a whole lot who hadn't—would tell the story of the time they saw Frank Polk beat himself to the draw and shoot himself down.

Not too long after that, Frank got drunk and careless in a Corsicana saloon and was taken prisoner by a Yank posse. Wes had been taking his pleasure at Mary LaBelle's sporting house at the time and said he didn't learn about Frank's capture till the next day. I was sorry to hear about it myself, but I won't deny it was a relief to have one less worry at my cow camp.

—— Mike Callahan ——

I served up more than a few glasses to Frank Polk in the Empress Emporium, I did. First met the rascal when he came to Corsicana on the run for shooting some soldiers—in Dallas, I think that was. And there was a rumor about him shooting some shopkeeper. But hell, there was always rumors about Frank and all fellas like him. Sure, he had a temper when he was in his cups—but don't most other fellas as well? A bit quick with his mitts sometimes—and not afraid to fill his hand, as they used to say, when that was what was called for. But mostly he liked a good laugh and a hand of cards and a sweet time with the ladies. Just a regular fella, he was.

It was Frank who introduced me to the Hardin lad. They came in the Empress one afternoon when I'm back of the bar, see. They'd just brought over a herd of steers from Pisga, so they had gold in their pockets and were looking for a bit of fun before heading back. So I set out a bottle of the good stuff and hand over the dice cup, and they while away a few hours sipping that good whiskey and rolling the dice. Some friends join them by and by, and they're all drinking and rolling and swapping whoppers loud enough for everyone in the place to get some pleasure out of all the lying.

Well now, by that evening the whole lot of them are drunk as lords and playing poker at a table at the back of the room. They're all laughing and talking at once and so drunk they keep losing track of who's dealing and whose bet it is, everything. One time I hear Jerry Ostermann yell, "Blackjack! I got blackjack!" Everybody else laughs and curses him for a damn fool. "How do you reckon we're playing *blackjack*, you asshole," Frank says, "when you got *five* fucking cards dealt to you? Answer me that." Well, Jerry thinks it over for a moment, his face all twisted in hard thought. Then he brightens and says, "Well, hell, I thought it was a sporting new way of playing the game!"

A half hour later Frank suddenly jumps up and hollers that he's by God had enough of Vernon Leaky's cheating. Now Vernon, he owns the Hotel Lee up the street and is one of the few truly honest men I ever met. How he got into a game with fellas such as these I can't say—except that he'd been drinking harder than usual, which is sufficient explanation for almost any stupidity a man might do. He turns white as his collar, he does, when Frank calls him a cheat.

"Frank," he says in his high voice. "Frank, *I'm* not cheating." Frank stands there, swaying a bit and looking hard at him, and says, "Last time I heard some sorry son-bitch say that, turned out he had three aces up his sleeve." The Hardin fella's watching all this with his chin in his hand and a big smile on his face.

"But, Frank," Vernon says, "how can you think I'm cheating? *You're* doing all the winning!" Frank looks at his own stack of money and sees it's for sure the biggest on the table, so he grins a bit sheepish, he does, and says, "Be goddamn." He sits down and says, "Hell, maybe *I'm* the one's doing all the damn cheating." Like I say, drunk as lords, the bunch of them, and it's still early yet.

All right then, by eleven o'clock the place is packed. The pianola's plunking one tune after another and the bar's two deep from end to end. The smoke in the place is thick as Dublin fog. There's already been a couple of fistfights, but nothing serious and not much broken except one fella's arm and a beer mug or two. Behind the bar I'm as busy as a one-legged man in an arse-kicking contest.

All of a sudden it seemed the pianola was a good bit

louder, and then I see most of the fellas have shut up and are staring hard at some Yank soldiers I never even saw come in—six of them, including a pair of woolies, moving slow and careful through the parting crowd, all of them armed with repeaters, heading for the rear of the room. I glanced at the back door and saw three more blues already there. Jerry and Vernon were staring big-eyed at the Yanks as they closed in on them. Frank had his head down on his pile of money and was singing loudly to the tune on the pianola—"My Darlin' Clementine." The Hardin fella was nowhere in sight.

The Yank in charge—a bloody big brute of a sergeant, he was—motioned for Jerry and Vernon to get away from the table, and they bolted like rabbits. The Yanks formed a half circle about Frank with their rifles raised and ready. Now the only sound in the room was the music and Frank's awful singing. The sergeant gave the table a hell of a kick and some of the money went clattering to the floor. But the kick got Frank's attention, all right. He looks up, his face all sodden with drink, and stares around at all the carbines pointed at him. "Well now, shit," he says, and straightens up in his chair—and every one of the Yanks draws back the hammer on his weapon. At the sound of all those cocking rifles, I thought sure the floor would be running with Frank's blood in the next instant.

But Frank wasn't so drunk he couldn't grasp how the thing stood. Any wrong move he made would be his last in the mortal world. Still, you had to hand it to Frank for brass. He says: "I ain't gonna stand up and fucking *salute*, if that's what you're waiting for." Looking right up the sergeant's rifle when he says it.

They took his gun and yanked him to his feet, but they had to hold him up or he'd have fallen on his face, he was so drunk. Out in the street they roped him tight from his shoulders to his waist with his hands bound behind him. The whole while, the crowd's jeering the bloody Yanks, cursing them for whoresons and bastards and such. The sergeant knows they're all drunk and getting bolder by the minute, and he's urging his boys to move fast.

They get him up on his horse at last—but the instant they set off, he tumbles from his saddle and lets out a hell of a yell. He's shouting his shoulder's broke. One of the niggers jerks him up to his feet and Frank howls like a banshee and curses him for a black son of a nigger bitch. The nigger grabs him by the hair to tug him over to his horse and Frank spits full in his face. He gets a fist in the mouth for it, and he spits another bloody gob at the nigger in return.

"Enough of this shit!" the sergeant shouts. He clouts Frank on the head with his carbine and takes the fight out of him. But while they're tying him belly-down over his horse, he pukes on one of them. Didn't that get a big laugh from the crowd!—and even from some of the Yanks. They left town at a canter, poor Frank bouncing on his belly and letting fly another streak of puke as they went.

As for the Hardin fella, we figured he either saw the blues coming or somebody tipped him and he was able to make his getaway. Nobody was faulting him for deserting Frank, either—not with Frank so damn drunk he couldn't even walk. A situation like that, it's every man for himself.

Early next morning, however, when I go to the facility behind the place for my morning ease, who do I find sitting over the hole with his trousers bunched around his shins and his head against the wall, snoring like a frog in that outhouse thick with flies and smelling like a dog that's been dead a week? Sure it was the Hardin lad. So I gently wake the boy and tell him what happened with Frank and all. And he laughs, he does. Turns out he had come to the facility before the Yanks showed up and passed out in the middle of doing his business. Said it was the first time he'd been saved by a call from Mother Nature.

Anyhow, that's how the Hardin fella escaped capture by the Yankees in Corsicana in the summer of '69.

Frank went to prison for a time for killing that shop-keeper, but they say he was wild as ever when he got out. It must have been true. The way I heard it, he got into a poker game down in Limestone County and killed a fella at the table for cheating. It was poor Frank's bad luck the fella was mayor of the town. Frank made a run for it, but a posse chased him down and trapped him by the banks of the Navasota. He hollered out to them from the trees that he was willing to let bygones be bygones. "I'll forget about the ninety dollars the son of a bitch cheated off me if you fellas'll forget about taking me in," he told them. "Fair's fair." Those were his last words before they gunned him down. They buried him there beside the river. That's how I heard it.

── Len Richards ──

Jim Newman had us roaming the Richland bottoms in search of mavericks—me, Wes, Simp, Joe O, and Tim Calloway. You didn't get much breeze through there in summer and it was hot as blazes. We'd work our mounts through the brush and scare out all the cows we could handle. Then we'd herd them up near whatever clearing we'd made our camp on that day, and the next morning two of us would drive them back to the camp at Pisga while the rest of us hunted up some more.

Early one morning, just after Joe O and Tim had left for Pisga with another bunch of longhorns, Simp went off to the creek to get water to make more coffee. A minute later he comes running back, all excited. He flings my blanket over the fire and soaks it with the pot of water he's just dipped, snuffing the fire without raising too much smoke. But all I can think about just then is that he's ruined my blanket and I start to give him hell for it, but he hushes me up with a finger to his lips. Wes was seeing to the horses, and Simp gives a low bird whistle and waves for him to come over.

He tells us there's soldiers coming by way of the creek. They're only about a hundred yards downstream, he says, but they're coming slow and lazy and probably just doing some routine patrolling. He figures they must of been camped pretty near us last night. His eyes were just dancing, he was so excited about what was coming.

"How many?" Wes wants to know. Simp says three. I'm ready to mount up bareback and get the hell going in the other direction. I hadn't done a thing to the Yanks since killing some of them in Tennessee before they tore up my legs pretty good with grapeshot. I'd been walking like an old man ever since, but hell, I counted myself lucky to be walking at all. I didn't want to give them any more reason or chance to do me worse than they already had.

But Simp and Wes are already checking their loads and talking about how to set the ambush. They quick decide to lay for them in the heavy stand of willows at the creek bend about thirty yards downstream. As they start out, Simp takes a look back at me, so I hurry over to my saddle and slide my Henry rifle out of its sheath and head out after them.

Listen. Ever since Tennessee—at a place called Franklin, where I got wounded so bad—I never could stand the sound of close-by shooting. I'm not exaggerating when I say it froze me up to hear a gun go off anywhere near me—large or small gun, either one. Hell, it still does, I ain't ashamed to admit it, not anymore. And if the shooting went on for more than a round or two, I'd start shuddering like a cottonwood in a stiff breeze. Sometimes it was so bad I'd have to grit my teeth and hold tight to something solid to keep from hollering like a crazy man. It was something nobody around Pisga knew about me except for Jim Newman, who was a good man and who I was sure I could count on to keep it to himself. It wasn't an easy thing to hide, but I knew that if the boys found out about it I'd never hear the end of it. I would of constantly been made to suffer and look the fool for their entertainment. It's what happened to me when I got back home to Nacogdoches. It's why I left there.

But what could I do now except go with Wes and Simp? It was the thing I'd been most afraid of—that the Yanks would catch up to them while I was with them, there'd be a fight, and I'd be seen to be a coward. Simp glanced back at me again as we made our way into the trees, but I couldn't tell a thing from his face. I was feeling so damned scared I thought sure I was going to dirty my britches.

Just as we reached the creek bend, Simp and Wes suddenly stopped and took cover. I dropped on my belly behind a big rock and peeked around it real careful. My heart was pounding something awful and I couldn't hardly catch my breath.

Then there they were. Just up ahead and coming at a walk alongside the creek. It was six of them. *Damn* Simp and his three. They were coming closer and closer and I couldn't understand what him and Wes were waiting for. Part of me was praying for them to let the soldiers ride on by—and part of me was terrified that if they let the Yanks get any closer they'd sense right where we were. They'd smell us out. And all I'd do is lay there paralyzed while they killed us.

They were close enough for me to see the white scar running through the point rider's red beard when Wes suddenly jumped out from behind a tree and fired square into his surprised face and knocked him out of the saddle. The others jerked their mounts around, yelling "Ambush, ambush!" and trying to double back. Wes's Colt and Simp's Sharps fired at the same time and another Yank fell off his horse and went rolling into the creek. I couldn't move and I couldn't stop watching. My throat was as tight as if somebody was choking me with both hands.

Wes's pistol cracked again and a horse went down screaming. The rider landed on his feet like a cat and grabbed hold of a loose horse bolting by him and somehow managed to drape himself across the saddle, holding on for dear life, his legs flapping and his head bouncing up and down as the animal hightailed back the way they came. The wounded horse on the ground was screaming and kicking every which way, trying to get to its feet, but it wasn't going to make it.

All the Yanks were putting spurs to their mounts now and *boom-pow!*—Simp and Wes shot together again and blood flew off a soldier's neck and he slumped forward but stayed in the saddle as his horse hit full gallop. Wes ran out for a clearer shot and fired twice more just as Simp got off another round himself.

"Got him!" Simp hollers. "You see the blood pop up where I got that one in the leg?"

"Bullshit!" Wes hollers. "That was one of mine hit that leg!"

The wounded horse was still making a hell of a ruckus, and Wes went over to it and put it out of its misery. While he was doing that, Simp started scalping. That's when I was finally able to look away.

I'd been gripping my Henry so tight my hands hurt.

After a while I looked back and saw Simp stripping the Yanks of their guns and ammunition and going through their pockets. Their scalps hung from his belt and were dripping on his pants and boots. Wes was standing off a ways, rolling a smoke and paying him no mind. Up to now neither of them had looked my way. I sat on the rock I'd hid behind and felt lower than a dog.

Then Simp moseyed over to me, working the lever on one of the Yankee Spencer carbines. "I got to admit this bluebelly rifle is damn nice," he said. "Ain't got the punch of my Sharps, but it'll hold seven rounds, so you don't got to load and lock for every shot. And .56 caliber will make a big enough hole in a fella to let the moon shine through. What you think, Lenny? You think I ought to switch?"

The casual way he was talking, I knew he knew. I lifted my face to look him in the eyes, but there wasn't any scorn or mean humor in them—and no pity either, which some was full of for me back in Nacogdoches and which I hated even more than the scorn and the ridicule. He was looking at me like a friend.

"Jim told us, Lenny," he says softly. "He thought it best we knew. Hell, brother, any man who wore the gray and got tore up by cannonfire while he was killing Yankees can't ever be nothing but a *hero* to us, don't you know that? Me and Wes, Lenny, we're *proud* to know you." I guess my face probably got as red as his, then both of us just grinned and looked away. "Well, hell," he said, "let's catch that other Yank horse and get the hell back to Pisga."

And that was it. They neither one said another word about it, not to me. If they said anything about it to anybody else, I never knew of it, but I know damn well they didn't. You won't find two men in a thousand like them. Not in ten thousand.

By the following evening they were both of them long gone out of Pisga, and I never saw either one again. I believe Wes laid low with kin in Hillsboro for a while before he went to Towash and got in that trouble everybody heard about.

As for Simp, I heard he rode with a band of Kluxers for a time before telling them it was a waste of time to go nigger-spooking and barn-burning when there were still so damn many bluebellies in Texas to kill. The Klan was out to avenge all of Dixie, but Simp was mostly interested in getting even for his own kin. Then I heard he'd taken up with a cut-nose Cheyenne squaw that had tits like whiskey jugs and an ass like a mule. They said she would of been pretty but for that cut nose, which is what a Cheyenne brave did to a cheating wife before kicking her out to fend for herself. A jawhawker brought her into a Fort Worth saloon on the end of a rawhide leash, and for some reason—maybe her—Simp and the hawker got into a fight. They say that when Simp got the hawker down and started putting the boot to him, the squaw ran up and got in some pretty good kicks of her own, which sounds like she was ready for a change of men. The way the story goes, Simp took her to live with him in a cabin deep in a woods by the Navasota. They say him and the squaw were completely bare-ass and humping like hell on the riverbank one evening when a Yank hunting party snuck up and shot them more than a hundred times.

PART TWO

FUGITIVE

DAYS

FROM

The El Paso Daily Herald,

20 AUGUST 1895

Frank Patterson, the bartender at the Acme Saloon, testified before the coroner as follows:

"My name is Frank Patterson. I am a bartender at present at the Acme Saloon. This evening about 11 o'clock J. W. Hardin was standing with Henry Brown shaking dice and Mr. Selman walked in at the door and shot him. Mr. E. L. Shackleford was also in the saloon at the time the shooting took place. Mr. Selman said something as he came in at the door. Hardin was standing with his back to Mr. Selman. I did not see him face around before he fell or make any motion. All I saw was that Mr. Selman came in the door, said something and shot and Hardin fell. Don't think Hardin ever spoke. The first shot was in the head."

(Signed) F. F. Patterson

The Life of John Wesley Hardin as Written by Himself

"I liked fast horses and would bet on any kind of a horse race, a chicken fight, a dog fight, or anything down to throwing 'crack-a-loo' or spitting at a mark."

―――――

"I had been receiving letters from my father and mother urging me to quit my wild habits and turn to better ways."

―――――

"I was young then and loved every pretty girl I met."

―――――

"If there is any power to save man, woman, or child from harm, outside the power of the Living God, it is this thing called pluck."

―――――

"Everybody . . . tried to help me and everybody was my friend, but the infamous police were after me and there were several mischief-makers about me."

John Collins

y wife, Slider, was cousin to Wes and introduced us at a get-together over at Jim Page's place on the Brazos River, where Wes and his brother Joe were staying. They'd come down after visiting at Slider's momma's house in Hillsboro for a time and everybody was damn happy to know Wes was all right. We'd only recently heard of the Yankees' back-shooting murder of Simp Dixon and had been worried the blues might of got to Wes too.

We hit it off right away, me and Wes, but Joe was standoffish and we never did cotton to each other much. When I found out how much Wes liked gambling and horse races, I told him he'd surely enjoy Towash, a small but high-kicking town a few miles from the Page place. It had plenty of loud saloons and gambling halls, and just outside of town was the Boles Track where they raced quarter horses. On race days that little town was just booming with action. Wes said he liked the sound of it, and we agreed to go to the track together on the coming Saturday.

Joe wasn't keen on the idea at all. "Are you forgetting there are soldiers hunting for you?" he asked Wes. "Soldiers who intend to shoot you on sight?"

"To do that," Wes said with a big smile, "they got to see me before I see them." He tried to make light of Joe's nagging, but I could see it irritated him. I don't believe he was sorry when Joe headed on back home to Navarro County the next day.

During the next couple of weeks we spent plenty of time in Towash, me and Wes. Like I said, it was a wild place, and Wes took to it like a redbone to a hollow full of coon. That boy would gamble at anything. He was the best I ever saw at calling the turn at the faro table—at guessing the exact order of the last three cards in the tiger, the box the dealer deals the cards out of. Calling the turn pays four-to-one, and Wes won himself just fistfuls of money. We played mostly in The Alabama Star because it had the best table layout—and because they had a dealer there named Sad Horse Tom, whose real name was Tommy Flatt. He had the longest face you've ever seen, and every time somebody had a winning streak or called the turn on him, that face would get even longer. You can imagine what he looked like whenever Wes had one of his good nights at his table. Poor fella's face got so long and miserable-looking he looked like a horse about to cry. Wes started calling him Sad Horse Tom and pretty soon everybody called him that. One night, right after Wes had called the turn on him for the second time in an hour, Sad Horse Tom said to him, ''Kid, you must have Jesus whispering the cards in your ear.''

Wes liked that, and from then on, every time the last turn came up, he'd cup his hand to his ear and look up and say, ''All right, Lord, let me hear them.'' He'd nod his head like he was listening real careful, then say, ''All right, sir, I'll do it.'' If the turn came up the way he called it, he'd smile at the ceiling and say, ''Thanks, partner.'' But if he lost, he'd look around at everybody with a real exaggerated expression of disgust and say something like, ''Well, hell, if that's all the dependable the Good Lord Jesus is going to be, it's no wonder so many folk are turning heathen nowadays.'' He could always get a laugh from the boys at the table.

Except for Sad Horse Tom, most everybody was always glad to see Wes come in the Star. He was free and easy with his winnings, and I don't recall a single time he didn't buy the house a round after winning a big poker pot or calling the turn at faro. He was a damn good joke teller too, and just as good at laughing at the ones you told him. He smiled a lot and usually meant it when he did. He liked to sing along with the piano. He was just an easy young fella to like.

Besides gambling in the Towash saloons nearly every night, we went out to the Boles Track every Saturday. We both liked the races even more than the table games, and we both usually came out winners at the end of a day's matches. But the more Wes saw of the Towash races, the more he hankered for a racer of his own, since neither his old paint nor my ornery buckskin was near good enough to run against the racers at Boles. Well, he was the sort to do whatever he set his mind to, so I figured he'd get a racer, all right—I just never expected him to show up with the one he did.

Come Christmas morning, I hear him halooing me out in front of the house, so I go to the door and there he is, sitting on this beautiful roan stallion I ain't never seen before. I couldn't help but stand there with my mouth open and admire it—I mean, it was a *fine*-looking animal! Wes just grinned down at me for a minute before he finally says, "I guess you *could* stand there all day letting the cold air in on your wife and child, or you might scrape up whatever money you got, saddle up, and go with me over to Boles to increase your holdings."

It was a beautiful day—chilly but sunny, with no wind and not a cloud in the sky. As we rode over to Boles, Wes told me the horse belonged to his daddy, who'd got it as a present from a man in Polk County. He'd named it Copperhead in honor of its sire, a stud from Ohio. The Reverend had given everybody at the Page place a real Christmas Eve surprise when he showed up so unexpected. He'd written Wes a couple of letters since moving to Navarro County but hadn't said anything about coming out to see him. What he *had* done in each letter was ask him to please quit the gambling life he'd taken up and get on back to his family where he belonged. "Joe sure must of gave him an earful," Wes said. It was pretty obvious he was caught between a rock and a hard place—the rock being his daddy wanting him to lead a righteous life like Joe and start doing the family proud, and the hard place being his natural liking for the kind of life he was living, which pleasured him plenty but pained him too, because it disappointed his daddy.

He told me him and the Reverend had stayed up half the night, talking things over. His daddy said Yankee patrols had been scouting the countryside for him all over East Texas. His mother was eaten up with worry. The Reverend still believed Wes would be acquitted in a fair trial once the Union army ended its occupation of Texas, but there was still no telling when that might be. In another few weeks the Reverend would be the new schoolmaster in Mount Calm, a little place down at the south end of Hill County, and he wanted Wes to help him get the family moved and then stay put with them for a while. He figured Wes would be safer from Yankee patrols in a tiny out-of-the-way place like that.

Wes finally agreed to go with him, and the Reverend had been so pleased to hear it he'd said yes, of course, when Wes asked if he could borrow his horse to ride over to say Merry Christmas to me and show off the animal.

"I told Daddy I'd go with him," Wes said as we came in sight of the Boles Track, "but hiding out in some two-dog town for who knows how long ain't something I hanker to do." Then he smiled and said, "But hell, it's nothing to worry about till tomorrow, is it? Right now I'm smelling money from that track yonder. What say we get on over there and put some of it in our pockets, John?"

The race day had drawn its usual big crowd. Besides the aroma of money Wes mentioned, the chilly air was full of the smells of fresh fried chitlins and roast peanuts and cigar smoke and horse dung, with a tinge of whiskey weaving through it all. It's no place on earth as exciting as a horse track on race day.

And *that* Saturday was the most exciting one of them all, let me tell you. Wes paid fifty dollars to a little nigger rider named Jerome—about four feet high and weighing all of ninety pounds—to ride Copperhead in a third-of-a-mile race against Honey Boy, belonging to Dave McIntyre. Honey Boy was the favorite because he'd already won a dozen races and lost only one—to Andy Jack, Merle Hornpiper's horse, which everybody called the fastest in the county. Hornpiper'd agreed to run Andy Jack against the winner of our race with Honey Boy.

But goddamn, that Wes was one to run risks. He was so confident Copperhead could win that he took Jerome aside and said he'd pay him ten dollars extra if he'd make sure the race against Honey Boy was close. "You win," he told Jerome, "just don't win by more'n a half length or so. If you're the rider they say you are, you ought be able to see to that." Jerome was a strange little spook but nobody's fool. He gave Wes a gold-tooth grin and said, "This here *some* hoss, cap'n—and I's *some* rider. Make it *close* be hard work—'bout twenty more dollars hard." Wes cussed him for a bandit but handed over the extra twenty, then gave him a boost up on Copperhead. He was a flashy little dude, Jerome. Wore a yellow silk scarf around his neck when he rode, and it streamed behind him like a flame. A few years later somebody hung him with it from a stable rafter.

But by damn, he was some rider. I swear I thought we were going to lose that first race right up to the last twenty yards—and then Jerome eased Copperhead up by Honey Boy and crossed the finish first by a neck. He came trotting back to us over by the corrals and leaned down in the saddle to whisper to Wes, "That be close enough, cap'n?" Besides the two-hundred-dollar stake we won from McIntyre, we pulled in nearly three hundred in side bets.

Because we'd barely beat Honey Boy, but Andy Jack had beat him by three lengths in their race the month before, the odds were heavy on Andy Jack over Copperhead—just the way Wes planned. Hornpiper put up a stake of four hundred dollars against our two hundred, and we laid out about two hundred more in side bets at good odds. Then Jerome brought Copperhead home a half length ahead of Andy Jack and, by God, we were *rich*.

We kept slapping each other on the back and laughing like hell as fellas kept coming over to pay us off. When you win big, everything's funny. We'd both nearly choke to death every time one or the other of us said, "With a *minister's* horse!"

We figured we'd go over to Towash and enjoy some of our winnings, but first we got Copperhead tended to. Wes gave a track boy two dollars to scrub and curry the horse. He wanted to be sure his daddy never suspected his own horse had been used as "an instrument of the soul's perdition," as Wes put it, imitating the Reverend's tone and way with words and tickling me some more. We bought a bottle off a fella and shared it as the last few losers paid us and hurried off to bet on the next race.

One of the fellas who lost money on Andy Jack was Jim Bradley. A track buzzard named Bobby Cue—one of those jaspers who fancied himself a big-time gambler but wasn't and never would be—introduced him to Wes when they came over to pay off. Hell, I already knew Bradley— or rather knew *of* him. He was a big black-bearded stomper who'd as soon cut your throat as tell you the time of day. With him was a hard case named Hamp Davis, a tall honker with a mustache like a squirrel tail. It was common knowledge they were both wanted for murder back in Arkansas.

They were all smiles and good buddy with Wes, paying off their bet and telling him what a damn fine horse he had. Wes stood there palavering with them like they were old pals and passing our bottle to them. When Bradley mentions a poker game they're getting up, Wes was all ears. "It's Judge Moore's game," Bradley tells him. "He asked me and Hamp here to sit down with him, but he prefers four hands. If you're interested, I reckon he'd be proud to have you join us."

Judge Moore was a white-whiskered old gent who loved to gamble. He lived in a big two-story house on the Towash road, near a cotton gin within sight of the track. There was a stable and a grocery just this side of the gin, then the judge's house, and then a little farther down the road, a wooden shed where they were holding the game. Wes asked how come they weren't playing in the judge's house, which was bound to be more comfortable, and Bradley laughed and said the judge didn't think it looked right for a guardian of the law to have gambling going on in his own home.

So Wes goes off with Bradley and Davis while I put our horses up in the stable. It was late in the day now, and getting colder. When I finally headed over to the shed, the sun was down and a wind had picked up and was pushing the trees around.

Bradley wasn't lying when he said the only ones in the game would be him and Davis and Wes and the judge, but he hadn't mentioned the bunch of his friends gathered around in front of the grocery, drinking and carrying on. It was maybe seven or eight of them, and as I passed by on my way to the shed I glanced over and saw they were all armed.

The shed was small and had a low narrow door, so you had to bend down and squeeze your way through. They were sitting on the floor and playing on an old horse blanket. Hamp Davis introduced me to the judge, and the old man nodded and went on puffing his big cigar. What with the cigar smoke and the black fumes from the two oil lamps hanging on opposite walls, the air in the little room was hazy as swamp mist and the walls were streaked with soot. It didn't help the smell a bit that they'd all taken off their boots to be more comfortable and piled them in a corner—together with everybody's gunbelts. I gave Wes a look, but he didn't seem the least concerned that he was sitting unarmed among strangers and the biggest pile of money on the blanket was his.

Cards never were my game, but nobody objected to me sitting down between Hamp and the judge and just watching. For the next hour or so the steadiest sounds in the room were the card shuffles, the bets and raises and calls, the hawking and spitting, farting and coughing. Jim Bradley cussed under his breath every time he lost a hand, and he was cussing a lot.

After a while the pile of money in front of Wes was more than twice as big as it'd been at the start. The judge looked to be a little ahead and Davis had lost about half what he started with. But Bradley was taking an awful beating. His stake was down to a few dollars in silver. There was a bottle of Kentucky whiskey we'd all been sharing, but nobody'd been drinking seriously, just now and then sipping from it to warm ourselves against the cold. Now Bradley turned the bottle up and made it bubble with the long pull he took off it. Maybe it was a signal to Davis, maybe not—all I know is things turned ugly on the very next hand.

Wes raised the pot ten dollars and Davis and the judge folded, but Bradley said, "I'll see you," and showed Wes two pair. "Not good enough," Wes says, and turns over three nines. Bradley cusses and smacks down his cards and takes another big drink.

Wes pulls in the pot and says, "That's ten dollars more you owe me."

Bradley says what the hell is he talking about, and Wes tells him he didn't put in the ten-dollar raise he called on. Bradley says bullshit, he sure enough did, and what's Wes trying to pull here?

While they're arguing, the judge scoops up his money and yanks on his boots. He says, "That's it for me, gentlemen, we really must do it again sometime"—and he goes out the door in a flash.

For a second Bradley and Wes just glared at each other—then everybody moved at the same time. Bradley whipped out a huge Bowie and took a wild cut at Wes just as Hamp Davis grabbed for the old Walker Colt on my hip. We wrestled for it, his rotten breath full in my face, and he wrenched it out of my hand and gave me elbow in the mouth, knocking me on my ass. I heard Bradley holler, "Shoot him, *shoot* him!" and saw Wes going out the door on his hands and knees as quick as a kicked cat.

"You stupid shit!" Bradley yells at Davis. "Why didn't you shoot him?"

"Who you calling stupid, you Ozark hillbilly!" Davis yells back. "We got the bastard's money, so what's the need of killing him? You want more law on our ass?"

Then Bradley takes notice of me and I figure he's for sure going to stick that Arkansas toothpick in me just so he can have the pleasure of sticking *somebody*. But Davis waves the Walker at me and says, "You! Get the hell out of here! Tell your peckerwood partner we ever see him again we'll cut his balls off."

"Same goes for you, dogshit," Bradley says to me as I scrabble by them on all fours, headed for the door, expecting to get the Bowie in my ribs as I go by, but all he did was spit on me.

As soon as I cleared the door I straightened up and started running. The road was lit up nearly bright as day under a full moon and the air was cold enough to make my teeth ache. I ran about fifty yards before I thought to cut over into the trees alongside the road where the shadows were long and deep. Once I got into the dark, I leaned up against a tree to catch my breath and let my heart slow down some.

"John," somebody whispers right behind me, and I give such a start I bump my head on a low limb. Wes puts his hand on my arm and says, "Easy." I could barely make him out, it was so dark in among the trees.

"Christ sake, Wes," I say, "let's get the hell out of here." I don't mind saying I was scared.

"Not yet," he says. "It's my fault they got my money, but I ain't about to go home barefoot and without my gun. Lend me yours."

I told him Davis had it. "They take your money too?" he asks me, and that's the first I realize they didn't. I reckon they were too taken with him to think of robbing me.

Then we hear Bradley and Davis coming up the road and we hunched deeper into the shadows. They were laughing and passing the bottle back and forth. They went by within fifteen feet of us, their breath steaming in the bright moonlight. I saw my Walker in Davis's pants, and Bradley had Wes's gunbelt and Colt slung over his shoulder. Bradley was saying he knew a whore in Dallas who could smoke a cigar with her cunt. "I know one in New Orleans can do that too," Davis said. "Even blows smoke rings with it."

"Oh, *bullshit*," Bradley says, and Davis laughs. "You'll say any damn thing to go somebody better. That's why you got no friends, you damned peckerwood."

As soon as they were around the bend in the road, Wes says, "Looks like they left my boots. I'm gonna go back and see. Follow along behind them till they're past the judge's house, then see if you can borrow a gun from him." Before I could argue about it, he vanished into the dark.

The lights in the judge's house were all out, but once Bradley and Davis were on up the road, I knocked and knocked on the door until I heard the judge calling down the stairs and asking what in thunder's going on, and then I knocked all the harder. By the time he showed up at the door with a candle in one hand and a pistol in the other, here comes Wes trotting across the yard and clumping up onto the porch in his boots.

The judge leans out the door with his candle held up high to throw more light on us and says, "Hey, *you* boys . . ." his face full of surprise as he recognizes us. Wes steps up and snatches the gun out of his hand just as slick as you please.

"What the *hell* . . ." the judge starts to bluster, and Wes says, "Excuse my bad manners, Judge, but I got an awful bad need of this hogleg right now."

It was a big Remington .45. Wes broke it open to check the loads, then hopped off the porch and headed off up the road. Before I could follow along, the judge grabbed me by the arm and says, "Listen, son, I didn't hand it over willingly, you just remember that if we all end up in court." Then he slammed the door shut and blew out the light.

I ran to catch up to Wes as he moved along in the shadows of the trees. We eased by the darkened cotton gin and closed in on the lights of the grocery. We could hear Bradley's bunch laughing and swearing before we got close enough to make them out clearly. Three of them were out in front, talking and smoking. One of them was Bradley. The others were all inside.

Wes motioned for me to follow him deeper into the woods. We made our way around the grocery in the dark and came out of the trees at the stable. There was a dim light burning inside, but when we peeked, all we saw were the animals and the sleeping stable boy. I was surprised our horses were still there. Bradley must've figured we had come straight here, saddled up, and hauled hindquarters. "Get them ready," Wes said. "I'll be up there a ways where I can keep an eye on things."

I woke the boy up and helped him saddle the animals, then led the horses up to where Wes was standing in the shadow of a large oak, watching the grocery, about forty yards away. "Mount up," he tells me. "If this doesn't go right, get the hell out of here and take Copperhead with you. Be sure Daddy gets him back."

Holding the Remington down at his side, he starts heading toward the three men in front of the grocery. They don't notice him till he stops about halfway to them and hollers, "Bradley! You, Jim Bradley!"

I could see everything plain as day from where I sat on Rollo. Bradley looked over at him and yelled, "Who's that?"

"Me, you Arkansas slop bucket!" Wes yells. "I want the money you stole from me! I want my gun!"

Bradley steps out into the road and says, "Well, God damn, looka here. I thought I'd seen the last of this skinny bigmouthed son of a bitch."

"My money!" Wes hollers. "And my gun! *Now!*"

"Well, sure," Bradley yells back, taking a few steps toward Wes. His two buddies moved up alongside of him. "So happens I got your money here in my pocket. And right here's your gun." He pulls a revolver out of his belt.

"Come on over and get it." The other two laugh.

"You got the sand to meet me straight up?" Wes says. "Just you and me? Or you too damn yellow?" Now he's walking slow toward Bradley again.

Bradley says something to the other two and they laugh again, but they hold back as he starts heading toward Wes.

They were about thirty feet apart when Bradley jerked up the Colt and fired. The ball cracked into a low branch of the big oak I was next to, and the horses shied. I hunkered down in the saddle as Wes fired and Bradley jerked backward and dropped the gun. He grabbed at his belly and yelled, "Oh, Jesus shit!" and fell down.

Wes fired at the other two as he ran up to Bradley. One yelped and started limping fast back toward the grocery, hollering, "I'm hit, Jody, help me, I'm hit!" But old Jody didn't even look at his friend as he ran past him and around the side of the store and out of sight.

The door of the grocery banged open and Hamp Davis and the others crowded out on the narrow porch, laughing and shouting and wanting to know what the hell was going on. They were four or five, all of them drunk and bumping into each other. Wes fired and one of them screamed and fell off the porch and started crying like a child. The others jammed up in the door, fighting each other to get back inside. Wes fired again and they all went tumbling in, swearing and kicking at each other.

Wes retrieved his gun and flung Bradley's into the weeds, then went through Bradley's pockets. Bradley was curled up on his side with his hands on his belly. I could hear him whimpering and saying something to Wes but I couldn't make it out. Later, Hamp Davis and a couple of others who'd been in the grocery that night would claim they heard Bradley begging for his life, but *I* say they were lying their heads off. Wes Hardin wasn't one to shoot a defenseless man, not even one who robbed him and tried to kill him twice in the same night.

Somebody raised his head up over the windowsill and somebody else poked his around the edge of the door, and they both fired wild shots in our direction. Wes fired back

and the window shattered and somebody inside yelled,
"Son of a *bitch!*" Those drunk fools finally thought to
blow out the lamps and have darkness on their side—but
by the time they did that and all of them started shooting
at us, Wes was already back to the horses and mounting
up. We got out of there at a gallop, with bullets buzzing
by us like hornets.

   After we'd put some distance between us and Boles and
slowed the horses to a trot, he apologized for not getting
me back my old Walker. Hell, I said, never mind *that*. He
told me Bradley had been pretending to be hurt worse than
he was, and had pulled a derringer and tried to shoot him
when he got close up. That's a lot more like the truth than
what Davis and them said. Listen, I knew Wes. He had to
have a damn good reason to do like I saw and shoot Bradley one more time. Right point-blank in the head.

That fracas pretty well put an end to the Reverend Hardin's plans to have Wes living with him at home in Mount
Calm. In the next few days the whole region would be
crawling with Yankee troops and vigilante gangs hunting
for Wes Hardin. I was right there when Wes told his daddy
what happened at Towash, and the Reverend looked to age
ten years as he listened. An hour later Wes lit out for
Brenham, heading for the farm of some Hardin kin.

Agnes Cotter

Once Momma had taught me all she could, she finally said I could take care of a customer all on my own, and he was the next one to walk through the door. I later found out he wasn't but a couple of years older than me. He was devilish good-looking—and just as bold as you please with those blue eyes. Momma certainly wouldn't have let me tend to him if she'd been in front when he came in, but she was out in back, dealing with the dry goods man.

I'd never done an alteration like the one he wanted, never even heard of such a thing. I told him maybe I ought to go get Momma, but he just smiled real warm and said he knew I could do it and would be honored if I would. He took off the vest and spread it on the table, then placed his pistol on it to show me exactly what he had in mind. He explained how drawing a pistol out of a hip holster required three different movements—down and up and out. But how if he had holsters in his vest he'd only need to make two—in and out. He demonstrated the movements on me with his two pointing fingers, and I flinched each time like he was throwing snakes at me. But I couldn't help smiling back.

I had to use a couple of large patches of softened leather and do some careful cutting and lots of close stitching with the strongest thread I had. Then I had to cover over part of the outside of the vest so the heavy thread wouldn't show.

I was nearly done when Momma came back inside and saw what I was doing. She didn't say a word. She just nodded when he said, "Good day to you, ma'am," and she sat and watched me finish up.

The whole thing didn't take me even an hour. He put it on and tried it out right there. Momma and I jumped at the way those big pistols seemed to pop out into his hands. He was so pleased with it he paid me an extra dollar more than what we'd agreed on. And then, as he was leaving, he gave me a big bold wink—right there in front of Momma! I felt my face catch fire and thought sure I'd catch something even hotter from Momma for my shameless blushing. I didn't care. I'd never before felt anything like what I felt run through me when he gave me that wicked wink.

Momma didn't light into me, though. She just sat there staring at the door for a minute after he'd gone. Finally, she said, "Did you see how happy you made that boy?" She didn't ask in a way that wanted an answer. "Snatching out those things as quick as the devil can spit. Right under our own roof. He can't wait to put them to use." She looked at me all accusing, but I didn't feel like I'd done anything to be accused of.

"The world's full of handsome, well-mannered evils with pretty eyes, girl," she said to me. "You best start keeping that in mind."

The truth is, you couldn't have got that thought out of my mind with dynamite. But it didn't much matter, since I never again even came close to meeting anybody in the way of dangerous men. Two years later I married a storekeeper named Walter. He said his prayers every night before getting into bed with me, as if he was embarking on a perilous mission. I do believe his seed was as timid as he was, and that's why I never conceived. I don't even blush to say it anymore. His notion of a high time was to join in the singing at tent meetings. The biggest excitement of his life was when he sold a full wagonload of goods to a party of army engineers that passed through one day. If the smallpox hadn't taken him at the age of thirty-nine, he likely would have bored himself to death and never even known what it was he died of.

I never bothered to remarry, but for a long time I didn't stop yearning for an excitement to match what I felt in that one hour I spent making those holsters and feeling his eyes on me the whole time. I can't count the nights I laid awake and wished some man would step up to me and say or do a thing to make my heart jump the way it did when he gave me that wink. Then I got old and quit my foolish wishing.

But I never did feel guilty about those holsters, not even years later when I come to find out who he was. I felt just the opposite. If I hadn't made them, he'd of found somebody else to do it. But deep in my heart I just know nobody else could have made them as good.

— Sherrie Ann Shine —

Eddie Joe was cool and fancy. Wore ruby cuff links and a fat pearl stickpin. He was handsome as sin and twice as mean when the mood was on him, but I did so good with him I didn't really mind the meanness much. It was him taught me the Murphy game—which some called the badger—and on a good night we made more money with it than I had ever made in a month of flatbacking on my own. We worked the Murphy all over North Texas till we had it down just right, then headed for Houston, where there was plenty of railroad money just waiting for us.

But Eddie Joe was greedy was his problem. He couldn't wait till we got to Houston before working the Murphy again. He was twitchy to do it, and we no sooner checked into a hotel in Kosse, this little town in Limestone where we stopped for the night, than he went out to scout for a galoot. Shortly after dark he came back and said he'd found one. Said he was barely more than a kid and looked like a cleaned-up cowboy. Eddie Joe watched him playing cards in the barroom off the hotel lobby and win hand after hand, mostly by blind luck, but the other players all quit on him before his crazy luck cleaned them out. Eddie Joe was dead sure the kid hadn't paid him any mind and wouldn't recognize him later. He said he was still down in the barroom and drinking by himself, looking lonely and plumb ripe for the picking.

We quick went over the plan, then he went out the window and I went down to the bar. Sure enough, he was still drinking at the counter, but he wasn't by himself anymore. Some overpainted buck-toothed gal who likely had some arrangement with the bartender was trying to work up his interest. But it was me he gave the eye. I sat at a table and ordered a seltzer, and in less than a minute shooed away a drummer who smelled like he'd been drowned in rosewater and a red-faced young farmer in a suit too small for him. In between, I gave the kid at the bar The Look— just once, and real quick, but it was enough. He wasn't shy. When he came over and asked if he might sit with me, I figured the thing was on rails.

He introduced himself as Jeb Bishop and said he was on his way to Austin to help his daddy with his hardware store. He was truly handsome up-close—in a taller and leaner and slower-burning way than Eddie Joe.

"Jenny Borgnine," I said, extending a cautious hand and putting on a face of being skittish but under distress too. Sure enough, his blue eyes darkened with concern under the brim of his black hat. He was proud to make my acquaintance—but say now, miss, was something the matter? I quick dabbed at my eye with my hankie, took a deep breath, and started in with my sad tale.

I told him all about having run off from home in Houston with my fella Robert. My poppa, who couldn't abide him, had forbid me to see him anymore, so we'd run off to Kosse because Robert said he had friends here who could give him work in their farm implements industry. But here it was nearly two weeks later and he still didn't have work and we were still living in this hotel and practically penniless and he'd taken to leaving me all alone for most of every day. And then, when he'd finally return in the evenings, he'd get terribly cross with me if I so much as asked him where he'd been.

I kept averting the boy's eyes to convey the shame I was feeling in my predicament. He pulled his chair over beside mine and put his hand on my shoulder in a brotherly fashion. "It's some men could use a good lesson,"

he said sympathetically, "in the proper way to treat a fine
lady."

I told him how in the last two evenings Robert had
come back later than ever before—and with the smell of
women's perfume on his clothes! And he'd gone straight
to bed as though I wasn't even in the room. Then early
this morning he'd told me he was going out for cigars and
I hadn't seen him since.

By now my eyes were brimming with tears, and I put
the hankie to my mouth to keep check on my sobs. I was
a betrayed but plucky girl doing her level best not to make
a public spectacle of her distress. The boy patted my
shoulder gently and shook his head in disgust at Robert's
mistreatment of me. Listen, I was *good* at this.

I regained composure and pressed on with my story.
This evening the hotel room had been just too lonely to
bear, I said, and so, no matter how bad it might look for
me to be in such a place, I'd come down to sit in here,
where at least there were other people. I just didn't know
what else to do. I couldn't bear to go back upstairs to that
empty old room by myself. Oh, I just *knew* Robert was
right this minute with some other woman somewhere
and . . . oh, I was so mad! At Robert *and* at myself, for
being such a silly stupid danged fool!

Miss Jenny, the boy says, if there's anything he can do
to be of help, he'd be honored to do it. His voice all of a
sudden had honey in it—and his hand quit being so brotherly and slid down to my waist. I remember thinking
how all galoots were the same, all of them easy as pie. I
sniffled a few more times into my hankie before saying,
real soft and still a little choky, "Would you be so kind
as to . . . please just . . . escort me to my door?"

There was hankering in the look he gave me, but
something else too. A kind of devilment. I should've
known he was nobody's fool—but I was too wrapped up
in my big act at the moment to think about much of anything else. Anyhow, he gave me a big smile and stood up
and crooked his arm to receive mine. On our way up the

stairs my hip bumped the gun tied down on his leg and the both of us giggled like schoolchildren.

It wasn't supposed to get as far as it did, but that boy was no lollygagger. I started to ask him at the door if he'd mind coming in for a minute, but only got as far as "Would you like to—" and wham-bam, he had me in the room, shutting the door with one hand and working the buttons of my dress with the other. In half a minute he had us both bare as chickens on a spit. Then we were a-tumble on that big old bed and for the next few minutes neither of us said much of anything, we were that busy.

I didn't usually get so caught up in my work. And I've never been one to talk about the particulars, but I have to say this about the boy: he surely did know the female geography. Take it from me, a lot of men couldn't find their way around on a woman's body even if you gave them a map, a compass, and a full set of directions. But him!—he roamed over me like I was some ranch he'd growed up on. Had me frisking like a filly in spring pasture. *Me*—who'd been whoring for three years already. I was so taken up with what we were doing I was damn near as surprised as he was when Eddie Joe came through the door.

He was holding a bunch of flowers and stood there with his mouth open and his eyes big as coffee saucers, looking shocked as a man can be. Me and the kid froze on our knees. We must of been a picture, joined like we were at that moment in what is commonly called the dog fashion.

Then Eddie Joe yells, "Son of a *bitch!*" and flings a blast of flowers at us. He kicks the door shut and yanks out his little two-shot and says, "I'll kill you!"

I wasn't real sure he didn't mean *me*, he looked so steamed. That Eddie Joe was a hell of a good actor. He probably ought to have taken it up as a trade back east where he came from, or in one of them traveling shows. He likely would have lived longer if he had.

Anyhow, I give a screech and pull away from the kid and grab up some sheet to cover myself. The kid's still kneeling there with his hands half raised and his long handsome rascal drooping between his legs. His eyes weren't nearly full of devilment now.

"No, Robert!" I let out. "Don't do it, don't!" And start bawling to beat the band. I guess I was overdoing it a little, because Eddie Joe gave the bed a kick and told me to shut up, and by the look in his eyes I knew he meant it. So I cut it down to some steady sniffling.

"Say now, mister—" the kid starts to say, but Eddie Joe tells him to shut up too. Just then it dawned on me that I'd messed up the Murphy by actually getting down to it with the kid. The way it was supposed to work—the way we'd done it up to now—was for Eddie Joe to find us together in the room and be outraged at the galoot for trying to compromise his sweetheart's virtue. But it's pretty hard to accuse a fella of taking advantage of your sweetie's innocence if you find her totally bare-assed and going at it dog style. Eddie Joe had to make this one up as he went along.

"I knew I shouldn't have married no damn whore!" he says, glaring back and forth between me and the kid. "Once a whore, always a whore. That's what they say and they sure right about that!"

The kid started to ease off the bed and Eddie Joe jabbed the gun at him. "Where you think *you're* going, snake?"

"Please, mister," the boy says, "all I want is to get out of here. I didn't know she was married, I swear."

"You damn well know it now, snake." He honest-to-God looked ready to shoot him.

"I'm real sorry, mister," the boy says. "I truly am. Just let me out of here, please."

"Oh, *please*," Eddie Joe says, mimicking him. "Why in hell should I? I got every right to shoot you, snake—her too, if I want—and wouldn't nobody say a thing about it except it served you both right."

"Yessir, I guess that's so," the boy says. "But please, I didn't mean no harm to nobody. And listen—I got money! I do! You can have every bit of it. There's fifty dollars in my britches there." He pointed to the rack where his clothes were hung with his gunbelt. "And I got two hundred more hid in my saddle at the livery.''

A woman laughed as she passed by our door and said, ''Just *hold* your *horses*, cowboy!'' Eddie Joe locked the door as their voices faded down the hall, then he sidled over to the clothes rack and slipped the kid's gun out of the holster. ''Nice piece,'' he says.

''Just for scaring the coyotes off,'' the boy says.

''Feels made for me.'' Eddie Joe gave it a twirl.

''Sure now, you keep it,'' the kid says.

''Damn generous of you,'' Eddie Joe says, backing away from the clothes rack and motioning for the kid to get over to it. ''Dig out the fifty and then we'll go visit those saddle pockets.''

''Yes, *sir*,'' the kid says, looking mighty relieved as he quick gets off the bed and heads for his pants, paying no mind whatever to his manly parts swinging all about. Eddie Joe saw me staring and gave a mean frown.

The kid dug into his pants pocket and came up with a handful of money—notes and specie both. But as he reached it around to Eddie Joe, most of it slipped out of his hand and went scattering on the floor. ''Damn you, boy!'' Eddie Joe says. But he was practically chuckling as he bent down to retrieve the money at his feet.

Just as his fingers closed on a gold piece against his boot, a gun blast rocked the room and Eddie Joe's head snapped sideways and a bunch of it splattered on the wall behind him. He slumped to the floor just as dead as a sack of clothes.

My ears were ringing like they'd never stop. I couldn't take my eyes off the blood unrolling from his head like red velvet. I couldn't believe so much blood. Then through the ringing I heard, ''Hey!'' and looked over to see the kid getting into his clothes even faster than he got out of them. He already had on his pants and boots and gunbelt and was putting on his shirt. There was a stampede of stomping feet coming up the stairs.

With the gun in his hand he motioned for me to pick the money off the floor, and I quick got busy doing it. I didn't have a doubt in the world he'd shoot me too if he got the notion. When he swung his vest on I caught a look at the holsters on the insides of the flaps. He slipped the gun back into the vest and grinned at me. I'd had no idea. Neither had Eddie Joe, obviously. He retrieved his pistol from Eddie Joe's hand and stuck it back in his belt holster and kicked Eddie Joe's two-shot under the bed.

He was cool as well water about the whole thing. The hallway was in a clamor now and there was unholy pounding on the door. I handed over the money I'd scooped up and he stuck it in his pocket. All except for one silver dollar—which he held up for me to look at. "For your fine services, ma'am," he said, and he bounced it off my tit and laughed.

Then he unlocks the door and throws it open wide. He points to me still hunkered on the floor in the altogether and says to the jabbering men crowded in the hallway, "Lookee here, boys!" And while all those stupid sons of bitches just stand there gawking at my nakedness, he pushes through them and scoots off down the stairs and gets himself long gone before the sheriff arrives.

The sheriff didn't believe the kid's name was Jeb Bishop any more than I did, but he was plenty mad about the easy way he'd made off, and he took much of his displeasure out on me. Said he didn't much care for "city trash" grifting in his nice little town and threatened to lock me up for a good long time for prostitution and public lasciviousness. I had to French him in the jail house twice before he settled on letting me pay for Eddie Joe's coffin and the undertaker's fee, plus what he called "administrative expenses"—all of which just happened to total the exact amount of money I had on me. He didn't mention the money he'd taken off Eddie Joe's dead body and naturally I didn't either. He ran me out with a warning never to show my face in Limestone County again if I knew what was good for me.

I didn't work independent for very long after that. I got cheated too often and beat up too much. I finally went to work in a house in Galveston. I was twenty-two years old and looked damn near twice that.

A few years after the bad business in Kosse, I read about that boy in the Galveston newspaper. He was in jail in Austin, waiting trial for murder and claiming it was self-defense. In a big long interview with a reporter, he told about other times he'd had to kill somebody in self-defense, and one of those he mentioned was a fellow in Limestone County who'd tried to rob him in a hotel room at gunpoint after he'd been lured in there by a pretty female accomplice. That was how I found out Eddie Joe had been killed by none other than John Wesley Hardin.

Naturally I showed the newspaper to the other girls and bragged about how it was me and Eddie Joe who tried that badger on Hardin. And do you know that none of them believed me? Not a one. Laughed at me and called me a cheap-assed liar. Goddamn lousy whores.

——— Will Hardin ———

The six months cousin Wes spent hiding out on our farm was probably the most peaceful time of his life. Since the start of his troubles with the law, I mean. It was surely an exciting time for *us*, though—"us" meaning me and my brothers Aaron and Joey. What was mostly so exciting about it was the times we all spent sporting at Mrs. Miller's or Kate Vine's over in Brenham, the closest town. It was Wes who introduced us to the pleasures of such establishments. Every Saturday—and on any day it rained or was too wet to work the fields—we'd all four ride into Brenham and have a high time at one or the other of those two fine places.

Of course none of us—I mean me and my brothers—ever had the money to pay for such sporting. It was always Wes treating us to the girls. The first thing he'd do when we got into town was go straight to the gaming tables and win enough to pay for all four of us at Kate's or Mrs. Miller's. I thought he could of been a rich man if he'd gambled for a living instead of just doing it for sporting money, but he said doing it for a living would take most of the fun out of it.

It was in Brenham that he met Phil Coe, the fanciest-dressing, fanciest-talking gambling man I ever knew. He was a big fella with a close beard. He carried a gold-headed walking stick and fastened his necktie with a diamond pin. His pistola was pearl-handled and he wore it in a holster under his arm. They said he was awful good with that gun, but I don't know, I never did see him shoot. He sure saw how Wes could shoot, though—everybody in town did—because the first time we all went into Brenham together, Wes got into a contest with some of the local deadeyes and beat them all so bad they wouldn't none of them shoot against him again. He finished up the show by shooting the windcock on the church steeple at the end of the street. He started it spinning with the first shot and kept it spinning with the next five. The fellas watching clapped and whistled like they were at a hoochie show. Reverend Hart came stomping over, all red-faced and mad enough to spit nails, but he calmed down quick when Wes gave him a twenty-dollar donation toward his good work for the Lord.

Later on when Coe and Wes got to be friends, Wes challenged him to a friendly shooting match, but Coe backed off. I was standing at the bar with them when he told Wes, "I never discharge my firearm except when compelled by serious circumstance, and the only truly serious circumstance is the defense of one's own life." That's how he talked. But that was horseshit about never pulling his gun except to defend himself. He knew damn well he couldn't outshoot Wes, and he didn't want to get shown up in public, that's all.

He couldn't beat Wes at the gaming tables, either—not near as often as Wes beat him, anyway. But he was a genuine gambler, Phil Coe was, so he never got riled about losing. He'd just make a joke and play on and wait for the cards to start coming his way again, which they usually did once Wes dropped out of the game with his winnings and we headed for the sporting house.

It was Phil Coe who gave Wes the nickname "Little Seven-up," on account of Wes's constant good luck with that game. Pretty soon everybody in the saloons was calling him by it. One time Joey called him that in the house and Ma heard him and wanted to know what it meant. She knew plenty, but it was our good fortune she didn't know the names of *all* the games of chance. That quick-thinker

Wes told her it was a sort of ice cream soda he'd gotten so fond of that the fellers in town had started calling him by that name. Ma thought that was real fine. In fact, she liked the name so much she took up calling him by it. One night at supper Pa heard her use it, and he gave us a what-the-hell look. Ma caught it and explained to him about the nickname. "Oh, yes," Pa said, "I believe I've cut my thirst with that particular soda a time or two myself." When Ma went to the stove to fetch the stewpot, he gave us a wink behind her back. He'd been a hellion himself before he married Ma and she put the bridle on him.

One last thing about Phil Coe. I didn't much care for his airs and fancy talk and I've said so, but he did become a true friend to Wes, so that made him all right with me and my brothers. We were sincerely sorry a few years later when we heard he'd got himself killed up in Abilene by none other than Wild Bill.

I don't mean to give the idea it was all high times in town while Wes was living with us, because of course it wasn't. Mostly it was the same as before he came and after he went away again. What we mainly did was work. Pa made a deal with him that gave Wes a share of the crops he helped us bring in. When it came to axing timber, grubbing stumps, clearing rocks, plowing fields, hoeing cotton, splitting rails, putting up fences—all the kinds of work that keeps you at it from sunup to sundown on a farm—Wes matched our own sweat drop for drop. You might not have thought it to look at him when he was duded up in his black suit, but he was powerful strong. In his clothes he usually looked like a bean pole holding up a hat, but when he took his shirt off to swing an ax he looked like he was made of ropes and trace chains. There wasn't a thing on his bones but long hard muscle.

The end of Wes's good days on our farm came with the news that Ed Davis had formed up the State Police. Davis was a son of a bitch who got himself made governor back the previous December in the crookedest election ever held

in Texas. He did it with the conniving help of the carpetbaggers and the scalawags and President Useless Ass
Grant himself, who was the biggest son of a bitch of them
all—except for maybe Lincoln.

The only good thing about Davis's election was that
Useless Ass took it to mean Texas was "reconstructed,"
and he pulled all the Yankee troops out of the state. That
was the good news. The bad news was that we now had
the State Police.

There's never been a group of lawmen in Texas more
despised than those black-hearted bastards. They was
about half of them Nigra bullies, and the rest mostly the
worst sort of mean-minded white trash to be found anywhere—the sort of fellas who if they hadn't been made
State Policemen would've been on the run from them their
ownselfs. They had the authority to arrest you anywhere
in the state, the local sheriffs be damned—though lots of
sheriffs worked in cahoots with them, of course. It didn't
take long for the word to get around that you didn't ever
want to be pulled in by the State Police. Too many of their
prisoners got shot dead for "trying to escape."

Late that summer we got word they had a list of men
they most wanted to run down and that Wes's name was
on it. A few nights later we saw the proof for ourselfs and
came to know just what it really meant. We were all in
The Palace, watching Wes win us some money at stud so
we would all live it up at Kate Vine's, when in comes
Jules Forge with a state wanted list he'd pulled off a jail
wall in Austin. There were ten names on it, with Bill
Longley's at the top and Wes's right under it. It offered
five hundred dollars for Longley, dead or alive, four hundred for Wes, and lesser sums for everybody else.

You should of seen how fast the idea of four hundred
dollars changed the mood in the room as the list made its
way from table to table. Four hundred dollars was a *mountain* of money. There were fellers in there who'd turn in
their own sweet mommas for *forty* dollars, if they had the
chance.

Jules had showed the paper to Wes first, and Wes had

smiled and passed it on and kept playing like it hadn't been nothing but a revival notice. But I watched him close and could see he wasn't really as much at ease as he was making out to be. He began talking to me and Aaron a good deal more while he played his hands, joking and showing us his hole cards. We were sitting just back of him, and every time he turned our way I saw his eyes sweep the room behind us. We caught on quick and started keeping close watch on his back. Some of the hard cases kept looking his way out the sides of their eyes.

Just about then, Phil Coe came in, and I can't say how I knew, but I knew he'd heard about the reward list. He stared at Wes for a second with no expression at all, then nodded to him and took a seat at a table against the wall just inside the door.

Wes played for about another ten minutes, I guess, even though he'd already won even more than usual, and I have to say they were ten of the most nervous minutes I've ever knowed. Finally Wes pockets his winnings and says, "All right, cousins, let's go to Kate's and tickle the elephant."

I'd never heard it so quiet in The Palace as when we were walking out. The only sound was our heels on the floor. The damn door seemed a mile away. My back was twitching from all the eyes I felt on it, and I half expected Phil Coe to make a pull on Wes at any second. Four hundred dollars might be all the push he needed to risk his hand against Wes. But as we got closer to him, I saw that he was looking past us, watching our backs. Without looking at Wes as we went by, he smiled, and in a voice sounding extra loud in all that quiet, he said, "You take care now, John Wesley."

Two days later Wes sold his share of the crop to Pa and said so long to us all. He'd been somewhat famous when he came to us, but thanks to that State Police poster he was a whole lot more famous when he left. A few months later we heard the reward for his capture was up to a thousand dollars. A thousand! It wasn't all that surprising, though, since by then he'd killed a State Policeman.

— Calvin Littlefield —

Bill Longley and Wes Hardin met just once, in Evergreen in the summer of '70. At the time we're talking about, Evergreen *belonged* to Bill Longley. He was born and raised there, and at the time we're talking about, it was one of the toughest damn towns in Texas. For years after the War it was chock-full of bad actors and hard cases of every sort you could think of.

Oh, we had us a sheriff. He wore a badge and carried a key to the rusty old chicken coop we called a jail. His name was Rollo Somebody and he was real good at the job. Some army patrol would show up with a warrant for one of ours, and Rollo would tell them the fella had just left town two days ago, headed north to the Indian Nations or south to Old Mexico. Whenever some lawman came by with a wanted poster, Rollo would oblige him and tack it up next to the front door of the jail. He'd promise to keep a sharp ear open for any word of the wanted man's whereabouts. Then as soon as the law left, he'd tear the poster down and take it over to whatever saloon the wanted man was watching from. The hard case would use it for target practice and buy Rollo whiskey till it sloshed out his ears. I don't believe Rollo ever had to pay for his own whiskey from the day he became sheriff of Evergreen till the sad night a few years later when he fell down drunk in the street one night during a hard rain and drowned in the mud.

The summer Hardin came to town, Bill already had a wide reputation as a pistol fighter, but Hardin's was just starting to spread. Now I want to make something real clear about Bill: *he* was no bushwhacker. It's lots who got theirselves a reputation mainly by back-shooting and dry-gulching. I'm not saying Hardin was one of them, but there *were* stories. You won't hear any such tales about Bill except from liars and drunks. At the time I'm talking about, Bill had already killed over a dozen men, all of them straight-up. He had the smoothest, quickest pull I'd ever seen and could put six balls in a steady line down a porch post fifty feet away in less time than it takes to tell it. He was the best fanner there ever was. Took the triggers off his Dance revolvers and fanned the hammers to get off his shots.

It's no trouble to remember the summer of '70. That sonbitch E. J. Davis had just formed the State Police and we'd heard they had a wanted list with Hardin's name up near the top with Bill's. The word on Hardin was that he was hiding out with kin somewhere around Brenham. Bill tried not to show it, but it rubbed him raw to hear talk about what a deadeye Hardin was, or how fast he was said to be on the pull, or how he supposedly killed three blue-bellies at one time all by himself up in Navarro County when he wasn't but fifteen. Bill would usually just stare at whoever was doing the talking until the fool finally caught on and shut up. The way Bill saw it, Hardin hadn't yet earned the right to be put in the same class with him. We all knew that. So you can imagine the stir when Hardin showed up in town all unexpected one day.

I ought to tell you that in the summertime in Evergreen we used to do our gambling out in the street. Set in the forest like it was, the town had plenty of cool shade out-side. We'd put a table or a goods box under a tree and be all set to play. On Saturday, which was race day, there'd be every kind of game set up every few yards on both sides of the street—poker, faro, seven-up, dice, every-thing. If you wanted a little more privacy for some reason, there were plenty of corn cribs where you could put a box for a table and play in there. They raced the best quarter horses from four counties. There was cockfights and dogfights. On Saturdays the town was thick as fleas with gambling men from all over East Texas.

All right then, there we were at the bar in The Bear's Den—Bill and me and Ben Hinds, Jim Brown, Jody Pinto, and Blacknose Bob—when in comes Sam Ott all worked up and tells us John Wesley Hardin was right that minute playing poker at Weldon Quinn's table over by the livery. Bill went right on rolling a smoke without a change of expression. He don't say a word till he gets the smoke rolled and lit and takes a couple of long puffs. Then he asks Sam: "How you know it's him?"

Well, Sam says, he'd been sitting in on the game at Quinn's table when Hardin walked up and asked if there was room for one more. Didn't none of them know it was Hardin, though, till a few minutes later when Sheriff Rollo comes up, weaving drunk, and says to the new man that he liked to know the names of any strangers in his town and would he mind telling his. "John Wesley Hardin," he said, "and I do admire the lively nature of your town, Sheriff." He pulled a pint bottle of rye out of his coat pocket and asked the sheriff if he might care for a taste. Rollo gave a big lopsided grin and decided to join the game too. He was so drunk he was holding some of his cards backward. Sam stayed in for a coupla more hands just to be polite, then dropped out and hurried straight on over to the Den to let Bill know about Hardin.

When Sam's all done talking, Bill looks at him a minute, then says, "How you *know* it's him?"

It was a damn good question to repeat, for two reasons—the first being that none of us knew what Hardin looked like, and the second being that anybody could *say* he was somebody else. Bill knew that better than most, there'd been so many liars claiming to be him. The first time he heard of it, I think he was sort of proud to know his reputation was so fearsome that other men would use it to scare people and have their way with them. But after he heard of somebody else pretending to be him over in

Waco, and then somebody else up in Bryan, and in Livingston and a bunch of other towns, it started to grate on him that any son of a bitch who took a mind to it could benefit himself by saying he was Bill Longley. "Look here, Cal," he once said to me, "it's took me some doing to earn my reputation, and I don't much care for these shitheads making such free use of it instead of going out and earning one of their own." By the time he heard about some hard case who was calling himself Bill Longley over in Walker County, he'd had enough of it. He saddled up and rode on over there and tracked the fella down. Found him in a saloon just a few miles south of Huntsville, talking loud and bulldozing everybody in the place, making Bill Longley seem like some kind of bigmouthed bully. Bill kicked a spittoon across the floor at him to get his attention, then said: "You are too dogshit ugly and too coarse in your ways to even dream of being Bill Longley, you son of a bitch." The hard case tried to pull, but never cleared his holster before Bill fanned three rounds right through his wishbone. He fell face-first with so much blood pouring out of him he hit with a splash. "Take a good look at my face," Bill told everybody, "so you won't be played for such fools by the next fake who says he's me." He shot up the bar mirror for good measure, then mounted up and rode home. And still, every now and then, we'd hear of Bill Longley killing somebody in some town Bill had never been to in his life.

Anyhow, that's why Bill's question was a good one, and why Sam Ott's answer wasn't. All Sam could say was, "Well, hell, Bill, that's who he *told* us he was."

So Bill tells Ben Hinds to go over to Quinn's and check the fella out, and me and Jody Pinto and Blacknose Bob decided to go along. Ben Hinds was a good one for Bill to send. He was big as a mule and near as strong—and about the same-looking, some of us thought. He'd shot men dead and gouged out eyes and bitten off at least one man's nose that I knew of. He wasn't afraid of a thing in this world except for a gypsy-woman fortune-teller named Madam Zodiac who lived a few miles outside of town.

Ben and Jody went down one side of the street and me and Blacknose Bob went down the other, the idea being to come up on Hardin from different angles and spread our positions as much as we could. But by the time we got there, Rollo had passed out and was curled up under a wagon, and Hardin had taken his seat, which put the livery wall at his back and gave him a clear view of the street. I figure he saw us coming before we even knew which one at the table was him.

One of the players quick gave up his chair to Ben, and Ben tossed in his dollar ante and told Quinn to deal him in. Quinn didn't look glad to see him—or the rest of us, either, as we spread out around the table. Hardin was smiling, but he wasn't missing a thing, and he took notice of where each of us was standing among the spectators.

On his first hand, Ben opened with a big bet and everybody but Hardin folded. Hardin raised big and Ben raised big right back and Hardin called and took the hand with three tens. Ben wasn't holding but a pair of treys. He wasn't wasting time trying to get things to a head. But Hardin suddenly stood up and started sticking his money in his pockets. "Thank you, gents," he says. "Been a pleasure. Believe I'll go buck the tiger for a while."

"Hold on there, hightime," Ben says. "A man don't up and walk off winners without giving a feller a chance to win his money back. Sit your ass back down."

Hardin says, "Well, maybe if you'd of sat in a little sooner, you'd of cleaned me out by now. But we ain't never going to know because that ain't what happened."

Ben thumps his fist on the table and hollers, "Damn you, boy, don't smart-mouth *me!*" He shoves back his chair and stands up—and *zip-click!*—Hardin's got the Colt in his hand and cocked and pointed square at Ben's face. Talk about *quick*. Ben freezes, naturally—and Hardin pulls his left-hand gun and hops back so his back's against the livery wall and he's got me and Blacknose Bob covered too. Jody put his hands half up—but Bob looked about to pull, and Hardin said, "Try it, you ugly-nosed bastard, and I'll kill you quick." Without looking directly at me he says, "You too, snake-head." I wore a snakeskin band around my hat in those days, so there was no question who he meant. Hell, I wasn't even thinking about pulling, not after seeing the way that pistola jumped into his hand. I didn't get to be as old as I am by being rash in my youth. Bill didn't make it past age twenty-eight.

"Listen here, damnit," Hardin says, talking to the whole crowd that's gathering around, everybody curious but skittish about those Colts in his hands. "I came to make the acquaintance of Bill Longley and pay my respects. I have been told he is a true son of the Confederacy and a sworn enemy of every carpetbagging Yankee sonbitch in Texas. But I was not told the people of this town are so lowdown as to gang up on a friendly stranger."

Just then the crowd opened up and there was Bill, standing in the street and facing Hardin from twenty feet off in shirtsleeves and no hat on and his hand down loose by his tied-down Dance.

"I'm Longley," he says, "and I don't know that I much care to make the acquaintance of somebody who comes looking for me with his hands full of Colts."

Everybody, including Ben and Jody and Bob, quick got out of their line of fire—and I admit I didn't tarry in taking cover behind a wagon.

"And *I* don't much respect a man who has to have all these back-shooters to watch over him," Hardin says.

Bill gives a laugh and said, "Boys, any of you throw down on this desperado, I'll shoot you myself." Then he turns up his palms, like he's saying, "You satisfied?" Hardin gives his Colts a spin and drops them in his hip holsters, then stands there holding easy to his vest flaps in the manner of some rich cotton grower. We all knew why he had his hands up there. We'd heard about that vest.

"Something else I don't much care for," Bill says, "is a fucken spy. And I heard you're spying for McNelly."

McNelly was a captain of the State Police, and I knew damn well nobody'd told Bill any such thing about Hardin.

"*Horseshit*," Hardin says. "If you're looking for a fight, bubba, you don't need to tell no lie to get one." His fingers twitched on his vest. I mean, he was *ready*.

Later on, Bill admitted to me he'd been cussing himself for saying what he did. An accusation like that was nothing but fighting words, and Bill never was one to pick a fight for no good reason. He was just irritated by all the talk he'd heard about what a hero Hardin was for killing Yank soldiers—and a little jealous too, I figured, though I never said so—and his irritation had got the better of his mouth. Not that he was scared of Hardin, you understand; Bill Longley was never scared of any man alive. But there was no good reason to get to it with the boy and he knew it. Still, he had insulted Hardin, and Hardin couldn't let it pass, and so the moment was feeling mighty tight.

So Bill says, "Whooooee! You just itching to hunt bear with a switch, ain't you, boy? Pointing guns at everybody, talking nothing but fight. I don't call that friendly nor respectful."

"*You're* the one called *me* a police spy!" Hardin says.

"So I did," Bill says. "But I see you have too much sand to be a state bootlick, and I am enough man to admit when I am wrong. But if what *you* want is a fight . . ." And he gives a big hang-it-all shrug and stands ready.

That was the only time I ever heard Bill Longley even come close to apologizing to anybody about anything— and it was smooth as owl shit the way he was doing it without backing down. He was leaving it up to Hardin to call the play or not. For the next two or three long seconds you didn't hear a thing but the birds in the trees and horses blowing. Then Hardin says: "I am man enough to admit my mistakes too. I did come to make your acquaintance, and I shouldn't of let an ignorant jackass goad me into forgetting my own good manners." Everybody turned to give Ben Hinds a look, but he was staring up at the treetops like there was something of uncommon interest to see up there. Then Hardin and Bill were both grinning, and Bill says, "I hear you like card games," and Hardin says, "About as much as I hear you do," and we knew the thing was done with.

A whole lot of breath got let out—but people being the

way they are, I'd say more of it was in disappointment than in relief. It wasn't every day you got to see two pistol fighters of high reputations pull on each other.

Ten minutes later Bill and Hardin were drinking beer and playing poker together in a crib at the far end of the street where they could have at least a little privacy from the crowds that kept following them around. Me and Jim Brown sat in with them, and I can tell you for a fact that they took a true liking to each other.

The last hand of the night is proof of it. They'd been playing pretty even till then, but on the last go-round, after the pot fattens up, Bill raises two hundred and everybody drops out but Hardin. He studies his hand like he's expecting it to talk to him, then asks Bill how much he's got left. Bill says about another hundred or so, and Hardin raises him all of it. Bill laughs and says, "Thank *you*." Hardin says, "I hope you're as sure of going to heaven as you are that you got me beat."

"Beat *this*," Bill says, and lays out a full house of aces over tens. He laughs and starts to pull in the pot, but Hardin says, "Hold on. I got two pair."

"Two *pair!*" Bill says. "Two pair don't beat shit!"

"I reckon it does," Hardin says, "if it's two pair of jacks." And he lays them down soft as eggs, the whole jack family.

Bill stares at him a second and says, "You son of a bitch." Hardin's face tightened and he watched Bill without blinking. Then Bill grins and says, "You *smart*-ass *son* of a *bitch!*"—and leans back in his chair and laughs his head off. And Hardin busts out laughing right along with him. Two of a kind, them two.

They ate steaks at the Den that night and did some drinking and took a few turns at bucking the tiger. The place was so packed you couldn't of fell to the floor if you'd been shot dead. You had to holler your conversations and the tobacco smoke was thick as a grass fire. Everybody was still hoping they'd go at it and wanted to be there if they did. Bill leaned in close to Hardin and I heard him yell, "Look at 'em! Sorry bastards just hoping we'll give them something to talk about besides their saddle sores and dripping dicks. I tell you, amigo, sometimes I feel like a fucken circus freak!''

Hardin gave him a funny look and said, ''Hell, Bill, it ain't *that* bad.'' *He* loved the attention. He wasn't yet used to having so many strangers smile at him and holler ''How doing, Wes!'' and buy him drinks—being so friendly because they were afraid of him. It was still new to him, and exciting, and you could see him eating it up with a spoon. Bill gave him a look back and shook his head. He was about as used to it as he cared to be.

Bill invited him to join us at the races the next day, and Hardin said he'd be proud to. He met us at the track next morning, and I'll be damned for a liar if he didn't win on just about every race he bet. That sonbitch couldn't lose at *anything* he laid his money on. By the time he rode out that afternoon he must of had half of Evergreen's money in his saddlebags. Most of us weren't sorry to see him go.

And that's how it was, the only time Bill Longley and Wes Hardin ever got together. If you've heard different, you've heard bullshit.

They hung Bill eight years later, in Giddings, over in Lee County, on the eleventh of October, 1878. He'd killed a lot more fellas by then, but the one they got him for was Wilson Anderson, who had killed his cousin Cale. Bill ran Anderson down and killed him with a shotgun, then went off to Louisiana to hide out. He called himself Jim Black and took up farming. After a time he fell in love with some Cajun girl. Sheriff Milt Mast of Nacogdoches tracked him down and got the drop on him and offered to blow his head off or bring him back to Texas in chains to stand trial for murder; Bill went with choice number two. Mast never would of caught him without the help of that coonass bitch. I never did find out why Bill told her who he really was, nor ever knew the reason she betrayed him. I guess a man in love is bound to do foolish things, and to a naturally treacherous woman one reason to betray a man is as good as another.

Giddings made a regular jubilee out of Bill's hanging. They built a brand-new gallows for the occasion, and people came from everywhere, from Houston, Austin, from far off as San Antone. Four *thousand* of them, the newspapers said. They were crowded in the streets and up on the roofs. Every window with a view of the gallows had at least one head sticking out of it. Even the trees were full of spectators—men in the low branches and children in the high. There was hawkers of every kind selling to the crowd, and families with picnic baskets, and firecrackers and string bands and dancing. A real jubilee. It wasn't nothing I wanted to witness with sober eyes, so I spent the better part of that morning as a serious customer in the saloons.

According to the newspapers Bill had said he was at peace, but I doubt that. He was too damn mad about being given the death sentence to be feeling peaceful. He'd wrote a letter to Governor Hubbard from his jail cell asking why was he being hung for killing a no-good son of a bitch like Anderson when John Wesley Hardin hadn't got but twenty-five years for killing a damn *sheriff?* Not to mention that Hardin had anyway killed lots more men than he ever had. The governor never did write Bill back.

When they brung Bill out, a brass band struck up playing "We Shall Gather at the River." Some of the folk cheered and some hooted and made fun. You'd of thought he was a politician. He surely looked it, in his Sunday suit and with his hair all combed and his imperial nicely trimmed. I'd never seen him looking so spruce. I was on the porch of the Saddlehorn Saloon and waved to him when he got up on the scaffold, but I don't believe he saw me.

Some old yellow dog followed the hanging party up the steps and everybody laughed to see the sheriff and his deputy both nearly fall from the scaffold trying to run the mutt off. Finally Bill gave it a kick and sent it yipping off. "You'll hang for that, Bill!" some drunk hollered, and the crowd laughed it up some more.

The newspapers reported his last words as being, "I

deserve this fate for my wild and reckless life! So long, everybody!'' That's more bullshit. I was there. Even if they'd wanted to print what he really said, they couldn't of. What Bill said was: ''I never killed nobody in blood as cold as you're hanging me, you shit-face sons of bitches! Fuck you all!''

They put the hood over his head and dropped him through the trap and he bounced hard at the end of the rope but couldn't kick much because his legs had been strapped together so the frailer women and smaller children wouldn't be upset by a lot of thrashing. He was hanging still as a bag of oats when a pair of doctors went up the underladder and listened to his heart. They shook their heads at each other and whispered some and wouldn't let anybody else go up near him yet. Every now and then they'd listen to his chest some more, and after about twenty minutes they finally pronounced him dead.

Of course, there's some who'll tell you he *wasn't* any more dead than you are. They'll tell you he bribed the sheriff and the hangman and the two damn doctors and God knows who-all else—and that they rigged him with a special harness that only made it look like he was hanging by the neck but really wasn't. I ain't saying *I* believe them—I'm just telling what some say. They say he was buried in an oversize coffin that gave him enough air to breathe till his friends came out to the graveyard that night and dug him out, then reburied the empty box. They say he went down to Argentina and got himself a big cattle ranch and a beautiful wife with green eyes and tits like peaches and he lived a good long life. Go ask around Evergreen. There's lots of folks who'll tell you how Bill Longley outfoxed them all.

But now here's a true fact. Remember Jody Pinto? Well, me and him was Rough Riders in Cuba with Teddy. Jody got shot in the stomach on San Juan Hill and suffered from it ever after. His daughter and son-in-law took care of him all these years up in New Jersey till he died about five months ago. Last year he sent me a newspaper clipping he thought would interest me. It was from *The New York*

Times. It has a list of names of people who went down on the *Lusitania*. He sent it to me just a few weeks after the Huns sunk her. Well, sir—and this is a true fact now—one of the names on that list is W. P. Longley. Got him listed as a cattleman from South America. What you think of that? Right in the damn *New York Times*. I still got that clipping around somewhere—but hell, if you don't believe me, go look it up your own damn self.

Professor J. C. Landrum

I have taught legions of students in my long career as a bona fide professor of Law and the Liberal Arts, and the most dramatic exemplum I've yet seen of the dictum that character is fate was John Wesley Hardin.

In the autumn of 1870 his elder brother Joseph had enrolled in my school of preparatory legal studies at Round Rock and had persuaded John Wesley to do likewise. John Wesley was, however, a legally declared outlaw with a price on his head. I was fully aware of his situation, yet also in full accord with Joseph's view—and the Reverend James Hardin's—that the state was unjustly persecuting John Wesley for actions of self-defense, and not, as it charged, for deliberate criminal conduct. The fact remained, however, that, as a wanted man, John Wesley could not risk attending my lectures in person.

But he was both determined and resourceful. He made a secret camp in the woods just a few miles from Round Rock, and every evening Joseph took a different and roundabout route to it, lest he be followed by agents of the damnable State Police—or worse, by one or more members of the legions of bounty men in pursuit of the reward for John Wesley's capture. While John Wesley prepared their supper, Joseph summarized the day's lecture for him. Later, after Joseph departed for home, John Wesley would study by firelight deep into the night. No student of mine ever matriculated under more difficult conditions than did John Wesley during the apprehensive weeks that followed. I was immensely pleased when they both passed their examinations at the end of the term and earned their diplomas.

And yet . . . character is fate, sayeth Heraclitus.

John Wesley Hardin was a highly intelligent young man of good education and sound moral upbringing. It could hardly have been otherwise with a father like the Reverend James Hardin and a mother like Mary Elizabeth Dixon. And yet . . . there is something in a man's soul that has no tie whatever to the influence of bloodkin or books, yet is the very essence of his nature. I herewith embolden to suggest that, for John Wesley, that essence manifested itself as a lack of clear perception of The Good, of a sense of *worthy* endeavor. He was possessed of many superlatives of mind and spirit, and would certainly have achieved greatness—of that I am entirely convinced—had not, for whatever unfathomable reason, the darker angels of his nature held sway. That sway constituted nothing less than a tragic flaw.

Tragic, yes. As a lifelong student of the works of Euripedes, Seneca, the Glorious Bard—all the great tragedists of our heritage—I am well versed in the nature and design of tragedy, and "tragic" defined his character . . . and thereby sealed his fate. Alas.

Earl Gillette

The jail in Marshall was a big log cabin with a cell of iron bars set in the center of it like a cage. I don't recollect too many jailhouses in East Texas as serious as that one. Me and my brother Judson got shut in it for no reason at all except we was strangers in town. We'd only stopped to warm our innards with a touch or two of whiskey in a saloon, for it were a bitter cold winter's day.

Now I ain't saying we didn't end up having more than a couple and getting a little brain-stung. And I ain't saying we didn't have words with a few of the local jaspers at the bar after one of them passed an unkind remark about the way South Texans laugh. "Down South Texas you never know if you're hearing a feller laughing or a mule with a cob up its ass" is exactly how the jasper put it. Now it so happens me and Judson hail from South Texas, as they damn well heard us tell the perfessor behind the bar. It also happens to be a fact I had just got through laughing at a joke Judson'd told me about a traveling preacher and the daughter of a dumbshit East Texas sawyer.

So I ain't saying things didn't get a little out of hand when Judson said real loud that East Texas probably had the most experts in the world when it came to knowing about cobs in a mule's ass. I ain't saying there wasn't some glasses and chairs got busted, and I ain't saying one

of the local jaspers didn't get his arm broke and another
didn't lose most of his top teeth and still another didn't
lose an eye to the gouging nail on Judson's thumb. I ain't
saying none of them things didn't happen.

But I *will* say that the damage we did them hardly com-
pares to what them boys did to us. They stomped up and
down on Judson and busted his cheekbone and so many
of his ribs he couldn't hardly draw a painless breath for
the next few weeks. Some son of a bitch bit a piece out
of his right ear. They busted most the fingers on both his
hands so he couldn't even wipe his *ass* for more'n a
month. And me! You think my nose always set way over
to the side like this? Think I was born with this scar across
my lip? I was a good-looking fella till that sorry night. I
got hit so hard on the head with a damn spittoon I *still*
get spells of ringing in my skull. I got a big front tooth
knocked out, and some one of them bastards kicked me
in the balls so hard I thought sure they'd be stuck in my
throat forever. Me and Judson, we took a *tromping*.

Then along comes the sheriff and puts the arm on *us*.
Me and Judson, *we're* the ones on the bottom of the damn
pile, we're the ones getting the worst of it, and he arrests
us for being drunk and disorderly. That's how it is when
you're the stranger in town. A local fella can shoot you
for no reason whatever and *you're* like to get charged with
disturbing the peace for hollering too loud with the pain—
or with dirtying the floor by bleeding on it. Hell, they're
like to charge you with trying to steal the bullet the son
of a bitch put in your hide.

Anyhow, that's how me and Judson come to be in the
Marshall jail that night they brung in Hardin: we were in
for no reason a-tall except being the strangers in town.

The sheriff wasn't really a bad sort, as sheriffs go. He
didn't rob us of our money and horses like lots of sheriffs
I could name you. They called him Cookie because he
kept his coat pockets full of gingersnaps to munch on.
Anyhow, like I said, it was colder than a witch's tit out,
and wasn't much warmer in the jail. There was a potbelly
stove over by a desk in the corner, and the sheriff and his

deputy, a jasper called Shithead because that's exactly
what he was, sat right next to it, drinking coffee with bites
of whiskey in it. They kept the stove red-hot but it didn't
carry a lick of warmth over to the cell, where we could
see our breath. I'd begun to sober up some by that evening
and I don't mind saying I wasn't feeling any too fine.
Judson was laid out cold on one of the bunks and didn't
come to until the next morning, so he missed the whole
thing with Hardin.

There was another jasper in the cell with us, a local by
the name of Lowell. He said he'd had a bad set-to with
his wife, who was prone to go loco at the full moon. She'd
gone for him with a carving knife and he'd been obliged
to shoot her in the foot to slow her down enough to make
his escape. Sheriff Cookie was letting him spend the next
few nights in the hoosegow till his wife regained her wits
with the waning of the moon. "If I'd knew it was gonna
turn so cold," he said, "I'd of brung my buffalo coat. But
hell, a man can't plan for everything."

They brung in Hardin early that evening. The Longview
sheriff and a deputy brung him over to be held for the
State Police in a stronger jail than they had in Longview.
The sheriff had spotted him in a restaurant and got the
drop on him. The funny thing is, he thought Hardin was
somebody named Garlits, who he had a paper on for killing a jasper in Waco. He read the papers out loud to Sheriff Cookie, and I have to admit the description fit Hardin
like a tailor-made suit.

Hardin, however, was mighty put out. He insisted they
had the wrong man, that his name was Josephson and he
was a horse dealer from Shreveport. He sure looked the
part in his good quality range clothes and expensive-
looking boots. "There must be two dozen fellers within
twenty miles fit that description," he said. If I hadn't
known better, I'd of believed him, he was that convincing.

Sheriff Cookie looked inclined to believe him too, but
Hardin was the Longview sheriff's prisoner, and Cookie
told him he was sorry but he'd have to hold him for the
State Police. The Longview sheriff had already notified

the nearest State Police station that Garlits would be waiting for them in the Marshall jail, and they'd wired back that a team was on its way to take him into custody.

I knew it was Hardin because I'd seen him once before, about two months earlier, in a gambling saloon in Williamson County. Me and Judson had stopped in to cut our thirst and wondered why the place was so crowded and excited. Up at the bar I asked a one-armed jasper in a Confederate cavalry jacket what the hullabaloo was about, and he said, "It ain't nothing but John Wesley Hardin his ownself sitting there behind you, mister."

He was at a poker table not ten feet from us, pulling in a big pot, and everybody was talking to him at once and offering him drinks from their bottles. He had his hat pushed back on his head and was smiling big but not saying much. He looked damn well pleased.

"Hell, he don't look so all-fired fearsome to me," Judson said. That's how Judson was, always letting his mouth run ahead of his good sense.

"Is that so?" the old rebel says, looking at Jud like he was some kind of softbrain. "You prob'ly right. Hell, all he's done is kill more bluebellies than you got hair on your balls. *Shit!* What *you* done, hard case?" He moved off down the crowded bar like he couldn't stand the smell of us. Judson watched him for a minute, wondering if he ought take things personally, then just said, "That ole boy best get control of what's eating on him before it eats more of him than his damn arm."

I wasn't about to say nothing to Sheriff Cookie about who Hardin really was. The law had its own business to tend to and I had mine. Momma didn't raise no snitches.

Sheriff Cookie shut him in with us and told Shithead to go get our suppers. Then him and the two Longview badges went off to get something to eat. Before Shithead left to fetch our grub, Hardin gave him a double eagle to buy a bottle and some tobacco for everybody in the cell.

So there we were, me and John Wesley Hardin, staring each other in the face in that cold iron cell. He looks at me real close and I felt like he was reading my mind just as easy as big letters on a barn wall. "You think you know me?" he says. I say no, I sure don't. "You reckon I'm this fella Garlits?" he says. I say, "No, I reckon your name's Josephson, like you said." He smiles and claps me on the shoulder. He looks at me close again, then looks over at Judson, then says, "Damn, bubba, you boys look like you been in a hatchet fight and everybody had a hatchet but you two."

Just then, Lowell shifts around on the mattress he's sitting on and Hardin fixes on him like a hawk spotting a rabbit. "Hey now," he says in a low voice, "if that ain't a pistola you got under your jacket, mister, I'm a three-legged jackass."

And be damn if Lowell didn't have a fully loaded .44 hogleg in his belt under his leather jacket. Sheriff Cookie never even thought to ask him if he had a gun on him— most likely because he wasn't a real prisoner, and because when Cookie put him in the cell, there wasn't anybody else in it.

He had a plan laid out in less than a minute. When Shithead brought our suppers to us, Hardin would throw down on him with the pistol and tell him to unlock the cell. We'd tie and gag him, lock him in, and make our getaway before Sheriff Cookie and the others got back. He laid it all out quick and cool, like it was the sort of thing a man might have to deal with every day.

"Whoa, boy," Lowell said, looking rattled. "I ain't having a thing to do with any of that. Hell, I escaped *into* here to get away from my moonstruck wife."

Hardin looked at him like Lowell was the one moonstruck. Then he looks at me, "What about you, bubba?"

All I could think to do was point to Judson and say I couldn't leave my brother behind.

"Well, hell," Hardin says, "carry him."

That's how simple he made it all seem. And that's the exact moment I knew just how almighty different his kind are from the rest of everybody in the world.

"What if Shithead won't unlock the cell?" I say.

"He will if he don't want to get himself shot."

"It might be he's too dumb to know what's best for him," I say. "What if he *still* don't open it?"

"Then he'll get himself shot and we'll figure out what to do from there."

I knew he meant it, so I had to tell him the truth. "Listen," I said, "me and Judson are in for a drunken fight is all. I can't go along with killing a lawman to break jail for that. Besides, it's two sheriffs down the street, and two deputies and four damn shotguns, and a team of State Police heading this way. I know it's a risk *you* got to take, but I can't throw in, I just can't."

He didn't get hot about it like I thought he might. He only give me a sorrowful look. I don't blame him. When I told Judson about it later on, he chided me good and said he'd of throwed in with Hardin and dragged me along by the collar if I'd been the one out cold. I know that's true, and it's partly why I felt so low. Until then, I'd always thought I had a right amount of sand.

Shithead came back with our suppers and the tobacco and whiskey Hardin had given him the money for. Hardin asked for the difference he had coming, and Shithead said there wasn't no difference. "The difference is my fee for doing your fetching," he said. The difference was more than fifteen dollars. It's why he was called Shithead.

During supper, Hardin and Lowell made a quiet bargain for the gun. Lowell let him have it for twenty dollars in silver and Hardin's long overcoat, which Hardin didn't need anyway, since he was wearing a wolfskin vest and a short sack coat—and besides that, he had a heavy coat of bearskin he'd brung in all rolled up and slung around his shoulder with cord. He said he'd won the coat in a card game in Tyler just a few days before.

Lowell made Hardin give his word he wouldn't use the gun to try to break the Marshall jail, not while any of us was still in there with him. Hardin agreed. He said he'd already figured another plan anyhow. He opened up his sack coat and vest and pulled up his shirt and used the cord from the bear coat to rig the pistol up high under his arm. He worked slow and careful, so as not to arouse

Shithead's suspicions. But he didn't hardly have to worry about that son of a bitch, who wasn't interested in nothing but hugging close to the stove to keep his fat ass warm. Hardin tied the gun so it set under his arm with the muzzle pointing down and the butt facing front, then pulled his shirt down over it, laced up his wolfskin vest, and buttoned up the sack coat. When he put on his bear coat over all that, you never could of guessed he had that big gun in there. Then we passed the bottle around and warmed ourselfs with sips of whiskey.

The State Police showed up just before dawn. It was three of them, with a warrant for Harold Garlits, wanted for murdering some barber named Huffman in Waco. The leader was the oldest of the three, a lieutenant named Stokes who looked to be fifty or so. He sent Shithead running to fetch Sheriff Cookie from home. Hardin started explaining to him that they had the wrong man, his name was Josephson and so on, but Stokes told him to save it for the judge.

Sheriff Cookie came in looking displeased about being woke up so early in the day. He gave the lieutenant's warrant a quick once-over, then let Hardin out of the cell. The biggest of the policemen, a nigger breed of some sort with a bad white scar across one eye, put a pair of cuffs on him.

"Hey, bubba, not so tight!" Hardin said to him.

The breed socked him full in the mouth, knocking him back against the cell bars and nearly off his feet. It was so sudden I flinched back from the bars. Sheriff Cookie looked riled, but he kept his mouth shut. Most sheriffs did, when they dealt with the State Police.

"Now, boy," the lieutenant said to Hardin, "Sergeant Smolley here don't much care for back-sass. Me neither. Don't be giving us no more of it." He said it the way a man might say he hoped it wouldn't rain.

Hardin licked the blood off his mashed lips and said, "No, sir." He gave the breed a fearful look. Hell, I don't blame him. That was one scary son of a bitch.

The lieutenant told the third policeman to search the prisoner. He was a young jasper who didn't look too happy to be there.

"That ain't necessary," Sheriff Cookie said. "Don't you think I done that before locking him in? I got his guns right here." He went to the desk to get them. The lieutenant told the youngster to search Hardin anyway.

When the boy dug his hands under Hardin's bear coat, I thought sure he'd find the gun. Maybe he just wasn't any good at searching, or maybe there was some other reason, I don't know. All I know is, he patted Hardin from his neck to his boot tops, then told the lieutenant, "He's unarmed." Sheriff Cookie handed over Hardin's pistols. Then the breed pulled Hardin on outside and that was the last I saw of him.

—— Owen Prentice ——

When we went to Marshall to pick up Wes Hardin, we didn't know that's who he was. The warrant said he was somebody named Garlits, wanted for killing a man in a Waco barbershop, and our orders were to take him to Waco for trial. It was early morning when we got there—and so goddamn cold I thought my teeth would crack. Icicles hung from the eaves and our horses stepped careful on the icy patches in the street. The weather put Smolley and Stokes in even worse tempers than usual. When Hardin complained his cuffs was on too tight, Smolley punched him one in the mouth for back-sassing. Stokes had me pat him down for a weapon just to irritate the sheriff by showing he didn't trust him to've done the job right, so I only went through the motions of a search. It'd be a different tale I'm telling if I'd of searched him proper.

We took Hardin out and hobbled his feet under his mount—an ornery old black mule Stokes got for him through some kind of deal he made with the Longview sheriff who'd arrested him. The mule didn't have a saddle, and Hardin had to ride on a blanket, injun style. The Longview sheriff was looking on, and Hardin told him he wanted his own horse. "I rode in on a fine roan stallion," he said. "My saddle's Mexican leather. I got goods in the saddlebags, including a vest my sister made me that I'm special fond of." The Longview sheriff said for Hardin not to worry, he'd take real good care of his property for him. He said, "You be sure and come see me about your horse and goods if you don't get hung, or when you get out of prison in about thirty years." Stokes and Smolley gave a loud laugh at that. It was lots of thieves wearing badges in those days. Hardin started to argue about it, but Stokes told him he'd best remember what he told him about back-sass, and Hardin quit complaining.

When we got out on the trail, Stokes told him if he tried to escape we'd fill him so full of lead it'd take the three of us to lift his carcass back onto the mule. Stokes nodded at Smolley and said, "That breed'll skin you alive for the pure pleasure of it if I so much as give him the wink to do it."

That was the truth. Smolley was about the meanest I ever met of the bad lot of bullies and thieves to be found in the State Police. A good many of them was mean-ass Nigras. I never thought I'd see the day when a Nigra'd be wearing a badge, but there they were. That's how fast and strange the world was changing. All the fellers on the force were hard cases, naturally, and ain't no question some of them were on the run from the law their ownselfs. But most were like me—ex-soldiers down on their luck who'd joined up because it was the only choice other than being a robber and it seemed wiser to be among the sons of bitches who put people in jail than be among them who got put in jail. Just the same, I don't recall a single time I got the full sixty dollars pay I had coming to me every month. They was always deducting money from our pay for one damn thing or another, so it's no wonder so many on the force was prone to helping theirselves out with their badge. There was a good bit of "confiscation" from the men we arrested—money, horses, guns, whatever might be of personal use or could be sold off easy. I never did such confiscations myself. I could of been a robber, but I never was no bully nor no thief.

Jim Smolley was the worst of both. They said he'd been one of Sherman's bummers in the march across Georgia, and before that had rode with a band of Comancheros. He was part white, part Mex, and a big part Nigra, which he looked more than anything else. Stokes was near as much a bully as Smolley and an even bigger thief, and he often picked me to work with the two of them—I think because he figured I was so young and new to the force I wouldn't never make any trouble for him about the way he did things. I hate to admit it, but he was right. I never could bring myself to snitch on them, even though I saw them shoot more than one prisoner for no more reason than back-sassing or cussing them, then write in their report that the prisoner had tried to escape. Like I said, there was plenty other State Policemen just like them. But I want it known that not all of us used our badge for a license to steal and commit meanness. Some of us were on the force because it was steady pay for legal work at a time when such was hard to come by. No other reason why.

Anyhow, when Stokes said we'd shoot him dead if he tried to run, Hardin said yessir, yessir, he understood, and we didn't have to worry none about him being so foolish as trying to escape. He was a completely innocent man and all he wanted was the chance to prove it in court. "I ain't worried," he said, "because I trust in the Lord and in the justice of our courts. As soon as you fellas get me in front of a judge is how soon I'll be a free man again, or my name ain't Frank Josephson."

The Sabine was swollen bad and running fast under a thick haze. It was a hard crossing. Stokes threw a lariat over Hardin's mule and gave his end of the rope a few turns around his saddle horn, then nudged his horse into the river and led Hardin across. Me and Smolley went directly behind them—Smolley with his gun in his hand, ready to shoot Hardin if he somehow got loose and tried to swim away. We made it all right, but soaked as we were the cold wind really cut into us. As soon as we reached higher ground we made camp and got a big fire going to warm the chill out of our bones and dry our clothes and boots. We took turns guarding Hardin through the night. On my shift he didn't do nothing but sleep like a baby.

When we got to the Trinity it was way up over its banks and booming even harder than the Sabine had been. We followed it south a few miles to where there was a ferry. The ferryman said it was too rough to cross, but Stokes persuaded him that things would be a lot rougher if he didn't take us over. It was a wild crossing that had us hanging tight to the rail and nearly pitched Stokes's horse in the river. Smolley held a shotgun on Hardin the whole time. I don't know if Hardin was more scared of falling in the river and drowning or of Smolley accidentally pulling the trigger from all the tossing about.

It was mighty wet going for a while after that, and it stayed cold as the dickens. The bottoms were a foot under icy water, and the sloughs nothing but frosty mud. Hardin kept asking us to untie him from the mule. He was scared he'd drown for sure if the animal lost its footing and fell down in the water. Stokes told him to shut up or Smolley would pull him off the mule and drown him himself.

We were on higher land by nightfall and made camp. Stokes was in a short temper. He cuffed Hardin a good one for not moving fast enough when he ordered him to round up some firewood. There was a town called Fairfield a few miles off and Stokes said he was going there to get fodder for the animals. I happened to know there was a saloon and a couple of whores there, so I guess I knew what he was really going for.

After Stokes left, Smolley followed Hardin around while he searched out wood with his hands still cuffed. Smolley kept taking out his pistol and cocking it and pointing it at him. Kept saying what a pleasure it'd be to blow his brains out. He must of drawed that pistol and said that to him upward of a dozen times. I didn't much care for it, but I knew better than to butt into Smolley's fun, so I busied myself cleaning my pistol on a blanket.

Hardin looked about to cry from being so scared. He said, ''Please be careful with that gun, Sergeant. I ain't no badman, sir, believe me. I just want to get to a courtroom and prove it.'' Smolley'd uncock the pistol and twirl it a few times, then cock it again and aim at him and say "Pow!"—and laugh to see him cringe.

While he built a fireguard of rocks and set the wood in it, Hardin kept glancing scared over his shoulder at Smolley. He put a match to the kindling, then knelt over it with his back to us to shield it against the breeze. He struck a half-dozen matches trying to get it going. All of a sudden he started sobbing hard and rocking back and forth in that big coat. Smolley gave a big horse laugh and started over to him—to give him a good kick, prob'ly. He said, "What's the matter, boy? You want your momma?"

Hardin spun around on his knees with a big pistol in his hands and shot Smolley in the face. Smolley staggered back and his legs gave out and he fell on his ass and sat there with his arms hanging limp at his sides. He had a hole under his left eye and looked awful surprised. Hardin scooted over to him and snatched away his gun.

I never moved. I just sat there with my pistol in pieces in front of me and felt my guts go soft when Hardin aimed the pistol at me and cocked it.

"Hands on your head, boy!" I did it quick.

Smolley was watching him with his mouth open, like maybe he was trying to think of something to say. Hardin grinned down at him and put the pistol in his face. "Hit me *now*, nigger," he said. And he shot him in the eye.

He worked the key out of Smolley's pocket and undid the cuffs, then came over and put them on me and told me to get my hands back on my head. He kicked the pieces of my gun into the bushes, then searched all through Smolley's saddlebags—looking for his own guns, I reckoned—and cussed when he didn't find them. Stokes had took them with him. While he saddled Smolley's horse, I sat there with my cuffed hands on my head and didn't say a word. I kept expecting him to put a ball in me any second.

When he was mounted and ready to ride, he reined the snorting pony around me in tight prancing circles. "Listen here," he said, "I am John Wesley Hardin, and whatever reason you got for being a State Police, it ain't a good one." Well, I figured I was dead for sure—but then he said, "I'm obliged to you for not letting on about the gun, and whyever you did *that*, it's a *damn* good reason. But you're a State Police and I ain't shot you dead, so we're even." He tossed me the cuffs key and told me to take them off and fling them way into the brush. Then he said, "I ever see you again and you still wearing that badge, I'll do you like that nigger, you hear?" And he touched spurs to the horse and rode off into the dark.

I knew right off why he made me throw away the cuffs. Without them on me, there wasn't much chance Stokes would believe my story of how Hardin made his escape and killed Smolley but not me. He'd be sure to lay the blame on me for losing his prisoner—prob'ly even claim I'd helped him escape. That's the moment my career in the State Police come to an end. In another minute I was saddled up and out of there my ownself, riding hard for Louisiana.

Funny, ain't it? Wes Hardin, by damn! Thinking I'd left that pistola on him a-purpose!

— Howard Pearsall —

I and my youngest boy, Robert, who was fourteen that winter, came across them in the woods about ten miles north of Belton. All three were wearing badges. State Police. Two were as dead as the whitetail buck we were toting on a shoulder pole. One's head was half gone, and I knew a shotgun had to've done it. The other dead one was all shot up in the chest and crotch both. It was powerful cold and their blood had frosted purple. The third one was still alive, but he was bad gut-shot and I knew he wouldn't make it. I sent Robert for the sheriff in Belton while I waited with the dying one. It wasn't nothing but a death watch.

He said his name was Ben Parkerson, and it took him three hard hours to die. He begged for water so bad I took my canteen out from under my coat and let him have a small taste. I was wanting to do the charitable thing, but I should've known better. As soon as the water reached his gut he hollered like a burnt baby. When he wasn't wailing from the pain, he was talking a blue streak, the way some do when they're hurt bad and breathing their last. It was mostly a lot of rambling at first, but then he seemed to get a better grip on his hurting, and he told me what happened.

They'd gotten word Wes Hardin was in Bell County, and they'd been hunting him for two days. Then, in the middle of last night, Parkerson had been woke by a shot-

gun blast. He saw Davis, who was supposed to be on
guard, laid out on the ground with his head wide open.
Then he heard two pistol shots and felt a fire in his belly.
Next thing he knew, he was looking at Hardin standing in
the light of the campfire pointing his pistols at Lankford.
Lankford had his hands up and was begging Hardin not
to kill him. "Je-*sus!*" Hardin said. "Just smell of yourself,
you sorry sonbitch. You been looking all over hell's half
acre for me, and now you found me you shit your pants.
Ain't you ashamed?"

    "He shot him down like a damn dog," Parkerson said.
"He shot him over and over. The bushes lit up with every
shot. He just fired and fired till the hammers were snapping
on empty." He started crying again, and pretty soon he
was tossing and rolling his eyes with the pain and praying
out loud to the Lord Jesus. Most of everything he said
after that didn't make much sense until near the end, when
he settled down some again. He was crying real soft and
talking to somebody named Lucy when he died. That was
in January of the year 1871.

PART THREE

LEGENDS OF

ABILENE

FROM

The El Paso Daily Herald,

20 AUGUST 1895

Mr. E. L. Shackleford testified as follows:

"My name is E. L. Shackleford; am in the general brokerage business. When I came down the street this evening I had understood from some parties that Mr. Hardin had made some threats against Mr. Selman, who had formerly been in my employ and was a friend of mine. I came over to the Acme Saloon, where I met Mr. Selman. At the time I met Mr. Selman he was in the saloon with several others and was drinking with them. I told him I had understood there was occasion for him to have trouble, and having heard of the character of the man with whom he would have trouble, I advised him as a friend not to get under the influence of liquor. We walked out on the sidewalk and came back into the saloon, I being some distance ahead of Selman, walking toward the back of the saloon. Then I heard shots fired. I can't say who fired the shots, as I did not see it. I did not turn around, but left immediately. The room was full of powder smoke, and I could not have seen anything anyhow."

(Signed) E. L. Shackleford

The Life of John Wesley Hardin as Written by Himself

"In those days my life was constantly in danger from secret or hired assassins, and I was always on the lookout."

―――――

"We stopped next at Newton and took that town in good style. The policemen tried to hold us down, but they all resigned—I reckon. We certainly shut up that town."

―――――

"I have seen many fast towns, but I think Abilene beat them all."

―――――

"Wild Bill was a brave, handsome fellow, but somewhat overbearing. He had fine sense and was a splendid judge of human nature."

Jessica Clements
Brown

We're Clements women, me and my sisters Mary Ann and Minerva, Clements born and raised. And we'll die Clements, no matter our names changed when we married, two of us into the Browns and one into the Densons. It's a proud family we come from. None of us, man nor woman, ever took a step back from anybody—and I mean Huck too, our adopted little brother. We called him Maverick because he strayed onto the ranch one day when he wasn't but about eight years old. He'd been orphaned by the cholera and been wandering on his own for months. Daddy was so impressed with his natural grit, he took him in and raised him like one of our own. All our brothers—Manning, Jim, Joe, Gipson, and Huck—had hard bark, as people used to say about the kind of man who stood his ground and could take care of himself and his own. It's how Daddy raised them up to be. There wasn't a boy in the Sandies—which is what that whole region around Gonzales County was called—to ever talk vulgar or make bold with me or my sisters, not with brothers like ours to protect the family honor. I'm telling all this so you'll properly appreciate the admiration we had for Cousin Wesley. We Clements were a lot more used to getting admiration than giving it, but we'd heard all about Wesley before we ever made his acquaintance, and none of us ever felt nothing but proud for being kin to him.

You can imagine how pleased we all were when he

showed up at the family ranch over by Elm Creek one late winter morning and introduced himself to Daddy and Momma. The boys were all out at their cow camp south of Smiley getting things ready for a roundup, so Daddy took Wesley out there to meet them. He sent Huck to give the news to me and my husband Barton Brown. Soon as I heard, I went off in the buckboard to tell my sisters and their husbands, and then me and Mary Ann and Minerva went directly to the family ranch to help Momma prepare a big welcome supper.

By the time they came in from the camp that evening, you'd of thought they'd known each other all their lives, they were joking so free and easy with Wesley and he with them. They come clomping into the house laughing and trying to raise knuckle knots on each other's arms and boxing with open hands and knocking into the furniture, causing such a ruckus that Momma had to yell at them to quit before she took a hickory switch to all their behinds and she didn't care how big they all were. Jim and Joe jumped to attention and saluted and said, "Yessir, Miz General, sir!" Momma tried to look fierce at them but it was all she could do to keep a straight face. "John Wesley," she said, "I know *your* momma didn't raise her boys to sass and mock her like these disrespectful no-counts of mine."

When Daddy introduced him to me and my sisters, Wesley said he was honored—and he kissed each of us on the hand! You should've heard the boys whoop at that, but Wesley didn't seem to mind their joshing one bit. Well, *my* heart just fluttered like a bird on a string! Mary Ann turned red as a radish, and Minerva didn't hardly know where to look, she was so flustered. But they were as tickled as I was, I could tell. Listen, if I hadn't been already married, I'd of set my sights on him for myself, cousin and all. He was *so* good-looking! He had a good strong face with the sweetest smile. But best of all was his eyes. They were warm and bluish-gray and really *looked* at you. Most men are either too shy or too scared to meet a pretty woman in the eyes for more than a second without getting nervous, but not Wesley. He looked a girl in the eyes as easy as offering her his arm.

It was a real fine supper we had in his honor that evening. Barton and Ferd and Jim—our husbands—were there too, naturally, and had brought all the children, and the house was chock-full of laughter and loud talk, good smells and babies crying and the clatter of dishware. I thought the tables might split from the weight of all the dishes set on it. There was fried pork and possum stew and sweet corn, yams and snap beans, mashed turnips, red gravy, corn bread and molasses—just everything.

He'd learned a good deal about his Clements kin from his daddy the Reverend, and he wanted to be caught up on what Clementses had got married lately and what babies had been born and who'd passed on and been buried. He'd come to us direct from visiting his family up in Mount Calm, and he said all the Hardins was in good health and spirits. His daddy was busy as ever with his good works, teaching and preaching all over Hill and Limestone counties. His momma and sister Elizabeth and little brother Jefferson Davis were doing just fine, and his big brother Joseph had married a Mount Calm girl and was fixing to move to Comanche to open his own law office.

It wasn't till we moved the children to another part of the house and cleared off the table and left it to the men that he talked about his troubles with the law. Daddy brought out a jug and passed it around for them all to fill their cups. Matches flared and pipes and cigars got lit, and the room got misty with good-smelling smoke. While Momma and Minerva tended to the children, me and Mary Ann washed the pots and dishes in the open dog-run, trying not to make too much clatter so we could listen in on the men's talk.

Wesley told about having to shoot three State Policemen in self-defense up in Bell County just a couple of weeks earlier—and before them, a bounty man who'd tried to back-shoot him outside a saloon in Fairfield. "I didn't kill the bounty man," he said, "I just shot him where his

pleasure hangs.'' That got a good laugh at the table.
''Leastways *he* won't be siring any more sons of bitches
into this world,'' Daddy said. Me and Mary Ann grinned
at each other with our faces turned away from the men.

Then Barton asked him outright if it was true he'd shot
a Nigra man off a fence in Hillsboro just for looking mean
at him as he rode by. Barton said he'd read it in a newspaper. No Clements would of been so rude as to ask
Cousin Wesley such a thing, but all the Browns were man-
nerless that way and didn't know any better. Me and Minerva both knew we'd disappointed Momma by marrying
into that family, though she never said it. It's some hard
choices we all have to make in this life. Mary Ann had
done better, marrying the only Denson boy to be had.

Wesley didn't seem to mind being asked, however, and
he said what we Clements already knew to be so—that he
never killed anybody but in self-defense. There were such
stories told about him. That he'd snuck up and shot some
gambler in Towash in the back of the head to get back
some money he'd lost to him. That he shot just about
every Nigra man, armed or not, who'd ever so much as
looked cross-eyed at him. That he'd shot a fellow in a
hotel for *snoring* too loud, for Pete's sake! I always suspected Barton believed such terrible lies about him—
though he wasn't so stupid as to say so to me or mine—
so it was good to hear Wesley tell him the truth of it from
his own mouth. ''It ain't never wise to trust the word of
a stranger nor a newspaper,'' Wesley told him. I nodded
at Mary Ann and hoped Barton saw me do it.

Wesley said there were so many lawmen and bounty
men looking for him that he was starting to feel like a
duck on a hunting pond. ''I think I'd best light out for a
spell,'' he said, ''before somebody blows the feathers off
me in the middle of the night.'' He'd talked it over with
his daddy and they'd agreed it'd be best if he laid low in
Mexico until such time as the Democrats finally got control of the state and rid Texas of the State Police.

There was a lot of loud talk then about Mexico. Jim
Denson's daddy had been with the Texans who fought

under Zack Taylor in the Mexican War, and he'd given Jim a pretty picture of the country. "Daddy said it's nice weather, and the food's real good, and—" He gave a glance our way and lowered his voice, but the way they all laughed was enough to let us know he'd said something about Mexican girls. Mary Ann gave a tight-lipped look and shook her fist in front of her where Jim couldn't see it.

"That's how my daddy seen it, anyway," Jim said. "He said it'd be a fine place to live if it wasn't so damn many Mexicans down there."

But Daddy and the boys didn't have a good word to say about Mexico, even though none of them had ever set foot in it. All that mattered to them was what the Mexicans had done at the Alamo some thirty-five years before. "Going to live in Mexico's like going to live with some sonbitch who killed your kin," Daddy said.

Manning told Wesley he ought to forget about going to Mexico and instead join up with him and my other brothers on the cattle drive they were getting ready to make to Kansas. Columbus Carol was bringing up two thousand head from San Antone, and he wanted my brothers to round up another herd of a thousand head or so in the Sandies, then take both herds up to the railhead at Abilene. "We'd be proud to have you throw in with us," Manning told him. Everybody thought that was a fine idea and said so. Manning said that as far as the law was concerned, Wesley wouldn't have a thing to worry about on the trail. Columbus Carol had said there was some sort of agreement between the big Texas drovers and the governor. "Columbus ain't never come right out and said so," Manning said, "but it's a common suspicion that Ed Davis is getting a slice of every drover's profits in exchange for keeping the police away from their trail crews."

A marshal might come around to a trail camp every once in a big while, Manning said, but they were most of them smart enough to halloo the camp from far enough away to give any cowboy on the dodge time to make himself scarce. "We give the badge a plate of beans and a cup of coffee, same as we would anybody else," Manning said, "and then he goes his way and we go ours. He can say he's done his job, and nobody in the trail crew is the worst off for it."

Wesley said he'd think on it, and in the meantime he'd be proud to help them with the roundup. That suit everybody just fine, and Daddy sent the jug around the table again. Pretty soon they were all singing "Sweet Betsy From Pike," and adding a lot of verses of their own making that had me and Mary Ann blushing and laughing into our hands.

Momma came out of the other room and told them to hush all that loud profanity or she'd drag every one of them by the collar down to the creek and throw them in. So they took their party out to the barn and kept at it till nearly midnight, when I reckon Daddy ran out of jugs. I bet there wasn't one of them who didn't have a sore head the next day.

Me and my sisters wasted no time arranging a barn dance for the next Saturday night so Cousin Wesley could meet our neighbors. Of course, the neighbors we most wanted him to meet were the unmarried girls of age. We'd come to find out he didn't have a sweetheart waiting for him anywhere, and we believed such a sorrowful condition was in bad need of rectifying. Since it was me and my sisters that arranged for that barn dance, you could say it was us that were responsible for him meeting Jane.

Everybody will tell you that Jane Bowen was just the sweetest thing. Well, yes she was. She was pretty too, there's no denying that, and had attracted the boys from the time she started blooming at about twelve. Her hair was the absolute envy of all the girls—it was long and soft and bright light brown. And if she was as vain about it as some believed, well, you couldn't really fault her too much for feeling that way.

She was a quiet girl, but not really what you'd call shy—not when it came to saying directly what was on her mind if somebody happened to ask her. And when she did speak up, she hardly ever said anything that didn't have a point, and she most always got right to it. Directness of that sort can put people off, since most folks like to stroll around in a conversation for a bit before getting to the point—if there even is one. Jane just wasn't one for small talk, which was a big reason some saw her as stuck on herself. I'm not saying *I* thought so, I'm just saying there were some who did.

I did tend to agree with them who said she probably read more than was good for her. She read more books than anybody I ever knew. Books were hard to come by in the Sandies in those days, but her daddy, who was given to spoiling her, made it a point to bring her back a book or two from San Antone every time he went there on business. One time at school I heard this boy ask her what the book in her hand was about, and she said poetry, and the fella looked around at the rest of us with a smarty-pants grin and said, ''You mean like 'Roses are red, violets are blue'?'' Jane nodded and smiled sweetly, then turned away and said—just loud enough for some of us to hear— ''Even a jackass is smarter than you,'' like she was finishing the poem.

It's no wonder so many of the boys were skittish of her. They'd be attracted by her prettiness—she never did lack for dance partners at parties—but then her learning and direct way of talking would buffalo them so bad they'd be afraid to open their mouths for fear of sounding like ignorant fools to her, and so they'd shy away. It was that way with her and one boy after another until she met Cousin Wesley.

Wesley might of done some reckless things in his life, I won't deny that, but nobody would ever call him an ignorant fool unless they're a true one theirself. The fact is, as we quick came to find out, Wesley was an educated man—a lot more than most you'd ever meet. He'd read more than a few books himself, and he could speak just like his daddy the Reverend whenever he took the notion. I imagine that when he and Jane met at that barn dance they must of felt like two people from the same strange little country meeting in a place where nobody else could speak their true language.

I was right there when Gipson introduced them, and you should've seen the way their eyes lit up on each other in the first two minutes. I hadn't never believed in love at first sight till that moment. He kissed her hand like he'd done to ours, but even though her cheeks got rosy she kept cool as you please, like she'd had her hand kissed every day of her life. Mary Ann looked at me and rolled her eyes. She wanted Wesley to meet a sweet girl as much as Minerva and I did, but she'd never been as easily abiding of Jane Bowen's airs as we were.

"May I have the honor of this dance, Miss Jane?" Wesley said to her, and she said, "It would be my pleasure, Mr. Hardin."

So off they went on the dance floor—and they didn't sit down or separate from each other for more than a minute the whole rest of the evening. They danced like they'd been born to be partners. They square-danced and two-stepped and reeled—they danced every dance that Fiddler Thomason called. It was while they were Texas waltzing that they looked the most beautiful together—whirling round and round to the music of the fiddles and Elmer Quayle's five-string and Toby Franks's mouth harp. The barn was warm and close with all those people churning up such a dancing sweat, but him and Jane moved just as light and easy as a pair of birds, his open coat swirling and the skirt of her dress flaring full and sassy as they spun around the floor. I don't believe I was ever so jealous of somebody and so happy for them at the same time.

I happened to pass close by to where they were sitting and sipping punch during a short rest the band took to wet their whistles. He was talking earnest and she was looking at him like he hung the moon. I heard him tell her she had eyes "like the fairest stars in God's wide heaven."

I've never forgot that. "The fairest stars in God's wide heaven!" Declare, if any man ever said such a thing to me . . . well, never you mind.

The next morning Wesley told Manning he'd been

thinking it over and had decided not to go to Mexico after all but would join up on the Kansas drive with him. Nobody was a bit surprised by his sudden decision—nobody who saw the way him and Jane had wrapped their eyes around each other the night before. We had a barn dance every Saturday evening for the next few weeks till the herds were ready for the trail, and Wesley and Jane would dance all night like they were in a world of their own, spinning and spinning to the music, just swimming in each other's arms.

——— Huck Clements ———

When Manning told him that Wes wanted to join the drive to Kansas, Columbus Carol was so pleased he nearly popped his buttons. He didn't waste any time signing Wes on. He even made him boss of one of the two herds—the small one of twelve hundred head. Me and my brother Jim were in his crew. Manning was ramrodding the bigger herd, about twenty-five hundred head, and Gip and Joe were working with him.

Only me and a hand named Billy Roy Dixon were younger than Wes, who was still well shy of being eighteen. You might think there'd be some hard feeling among the older hands about working for one so young and who didn't have any experience on the trail—and who would get paid one hundred fifty dollars a month when the regular hands like us were getting thirty and found. But if you thought that, you'd be wrong. The fact is, they were proud as banty roosters to have a man of Wes's reputation for a ramrod, his young years be damned. "Wes Hardin, by God!" Big Ben Kelly said when he heard the news. "I'd like to see somebody just try and give this outfit trouble." That's how Columbus Carol felt about it. "That boy's reputation," he told Manning, "is gonna save me enough cows to cover his wages twenty times over."

Manning told him that if the reputation didn't do the job, Wes himself surely would. The day before him and Wes had got into a shooting contest in the draw behind

Daddy's house and Wes had outshot him every which way. That's saying something, because Manning was one of the best pistol hands you'd ever hope to see, and I'm talking about a time when that part of Texas had more pistoleros than a hound's got fleas. The Sandies was crawling with Taylors and Sutton Regulators, and there wasn't a man among them who wasn't handy with a gun. But good as Manning was, he wasn't no match for Wes. The whole family watched the contest, Jane Bowen too. She about broke her hands by clapping so hard every time Wes showed off with some extra-tricky shot. He'd look over and wink at her, and she'd smile and blush pretty as a sunrise.

Word got around fast to the other outfits that Wes had signed on with us, and trail bosses and cowhands from the camps scattered all around us came over to make his acquaintance. A few of them, like Fred Duderstadt, became his friends for life. What they were all hoping, of course, was that he'd keep rustler and Indian trouble off their cattle while he was keeping it off our own. Wes himself was looking to make all the friends he could. Even though Columbus and Manning had said he didn't have to fret about the State Police while he was on the trail, he figured it wouldn't hurt to have plenty of friends in front and back of him, both, as we made our way to Kansas.

He was likely thinking about Abilene too. The new marshal there was none other than James Butler Hickok—Wild Bill himself—who was sure to have papers on Wes. Columbus had told him not to worry about that either. He said he knew Bill real well and would square Wes with him as soon as we got to Abilene.

"He's a fine fella," Columbus said. "He'll give us room to let off steam, you bet. Hell, he's a good-time rascal hisself. Likes his whiskey and cards and fillies as much as the next man! You ain't got to worry none about Hickok."

Wes grinned and said he wasn't a bit worried. "Fact is," he said, "I'd like to have a look at them pearl-handled navies of his I've heard so much about."

*   *   *

The afternoon before we left for Kansas we all went to
the ranch to have dinner and say good-bye to Daddy and
Momma. Annie Tenelle, who was Gip's bride-to-be, was
there, and of course so was Jane.

After a fine dinner of roast pork and yams, I took my
dogs down to the creek to let them splash around and see
what they might flush out of the reeds. As soon as we got
there they spotted a rabbit and took off after it in the brush
and that was the last I saw of them. So I just skipped rocks
on the creek for a while before starting back to the house.
Then I spotted Wes and Jane coming my way down the
path, walking hand in hand. They hadn't seen me, and I
didn't want to intrude on their privacy, so I slipped into
the heavy bushes and stood real quiet to let them pass by
unawares. As they ambled on by, I heard him talking low
but couldn't make out what he was saying. You should of
seen her face. If there's such a thing as a look of love,
Jane Bowen sure had it then. They stopped on the path
about ten feet beyond where I was and Wes pulled her
gentle into his arms and kissed her. I can still see the way
her hair shone in the late afternoon light coming through
the trees. They stayed that way for a time, and I never
moved a muscle nor took a deep breath. She whispered
something and Wes chuckled low and tightened his hold
on her and they kissed again. I don't think I ought say any
more about it. Except she surely did have pretty hair.

We moved our two herds out in early March. Besides me
and Jim, the hands in Wes's crew were Alabama Bill Pot-
ter, Ollie Franks, Billy Roy Dunn, and Big Ben Kelly.
Nameless Smith was the cook and Jeff Longtree was the
wrangler. Except for Nameless we were a young and fairly
inexperienced bunch. Only Nameless and Ollie and Big
Ben had rode the trail before, and they seemed to get a
good deal of pleasure from telling us about cowhands
they'd seen killed by lightning and drowned in wild rivers
and trampled to stewmeat in stampedes. Such tales were

scarifying but made me proud to be a cowhand, if you know what I mean.

In '71 the whole of the Chisholm Trail was one long and mighty river of cattle steadily flowing north. There was so many outfits moving steers to Kansas that year, the herds ran one right behind the other as far as you could see in either direction, even from up on a rise. Our little herd of twelve hundred head stretched nearly a mile from lead steers to stragglers. Manning's herd, just ahead of ours, was average size and twice as long. Hell, I've seen herds belonging to Shanghai Pierce that stretched five miles! It was thousands and thousands of longhorns on the trail. You never saw nothing like it.

Nor heard nothing like it either. All them cows bawling and smacking horns, their joints cracking loud as wood. Horses snorting and blowing. Cowhands calling "Ho cattle, ho ho ho!" and cussing and hollering back and forth to each other. Wagons clattering and clanking and their tarps slapping against the frame rails. But mostly it was the sound of cows squalling and whining and rumbling the ground under you the whole day long. They raised a great thick cloud of dust a mile wide from one end of the trail to the other. Even if you wore your bandanna over your face—which you damn sure had to do when you rode drag if you didn't want to choke to death—that evening you'd still be spitting mud and digging dirt out of your nose and ears. The whole world smelled of cowshit.

But damn, the nights were nice. The dust would settle and the stars would be so many and so bright and looking so close you thought you'd burn your fingers on them if you reached too high. At night the ground felt strange, it was so still. The cows were bedded down and resting easy, ripping long farts and groaning sad and low. You'd see the other outfits' fires flickering like fallen stars all the way to the north and south ends of the world. You never got enough sleep, what with having to stand a guard shift every night—but hell, that didn't matter. It was so peaceful and quiet while you were on watch, you felt like the world was all yours. If you had a good night pony he'd do most of the work, watching and pacing along your side of the herd and cutting back any restless steer that seemed of a mind to stray off. You didn't have to do nothing but sit easy in the saddle and gaze up at the stars and sing soft to the cows. The night guard on the other side of the herd would be singing his own songs and pretty much in his own world too.

Nothing I've ever done since has let me feel so free and happy as those five, six years when I was trail driving—and that first time was the one I remember best, which is only natural, I guess, since it was all new to me. I saw buffalo for the first time and more antelope and turkey and such than I'd ever see so many of again. We didn't lose any hands or cows in the river crossings, and we didn't have even one stampede—things that happened more than once in drives I made in later years. But that first drive surely had its share of excitement, and the main reason was Wes.

We laid up just outside Fort Worth for a day. Fort Worth's always been the sort of town to encourage a fella to have a high time, and that's just what we did. When we pushed off again next day, Alabama Bill was sporting two black eyes and Ollie Franks had a big bite mark on his arm and Billy Roy was missing a front tooth. All of us was a good bit red in the eyes, but nobody'd got put in jail, and we were all feeling finely refreshed.

We were just shy of the Red River when as bad a hailstorm as ever I saw came pouring down on us. Some of the stones were big as chicken eggs and hit hard as rocks. There weren't no trees to take shelter under, so we had to use our folded-up blankets to protect our heads. Everybody was yelping like dogs from getting hit on the arms and legs. The hailstones spooked the remuda bad, and horses scattered every which way. Once the storm passed we spent a couple of hours helping Jeff Longtree round them up. It was a wonder we only lost two of them jugheads. It was an even bigger wonder that only a couple of dozen cows broke away from the herd and we got them all back with not too much trouble. If the whole herd had stampeded, we'd of been hunting cows all over North Texas for a week. The worst casualties among the hands were Alabama Bill, who got a knuckle broke, and Wes, who had a knot like a walnut raised on his cheekbone. "Son," Nameless Smith told him, "you don't never want to look *up* in a hailstorm."

It was a lucky thing we crossed the Red when we did. Three days after we went through it, the river all of a sudden flooded so bad and ran so hard the steers couldn't cross it. They said sixty thousand head piled up on the Texas side before the water eased up enough so they could push them through again.

North of the Red was the Indian Nations, and back then it was a whole different country, believe me—especially to a young fella like myself who'd never before set foot outside of Texas and had heard hundreds of hair-raising tales about wild Indians. One reason the outfits traveled so close together in them days was so they could help each other out in case of Indian trouble. The only Indians most of us had ever seen was the sort to be falling-down drunk in town alleyways, and they weren't no more interesting than a mangy dog. The ones in the Nations was supposed to be peaceable, but everybody knew there was some bucks among them still prone to mischief. There were plenty of stories of how they sometimes spooked a whole herd into stampeding just so they could steal a couple of head. Now some of the redskins were demanding a tax on any cattle passing through their territory. Ten cents a head in some places, two bits in others, it depended on which Indians was doing the dealing. Some trail bosses paid the tax and some didn't. Some who didn't pay would anyway let the Indians have a beef, just to avoid trouble.

Naturally we all told each other we weren't no more scared of a featherhead than we were of a feathered hen. Everybody did plenty of loud talking around the chuck wagon of what they'd do to any damn Indian who showed his red-devil face to them. Wes said he'd sooner eat a plate of horse apples than pay an Indian so much as a penny of tax or give him a beef. "Damn redskins want cows, let them go out and round up their own," he said. I did my share of lip-flapping—but the truth is, I was almost as scared that we'd run into Indians as I was afraid we wouldn't, if that makes any sense.

Two days later Billy Roy, who was riding swing, started hollering and waving to the rest of us just as we halted the herd to eat dinner. What he'd found a little ways off the trail was a grave mound. It didn't look too fresh but wasn't that old either. A wood cross made of wagon boards was stuck in it, and in pencil somebody'd writ on the cross piece, "here lies Bulshit bob—kilt by injuns."

Well, the talk about Indians got really hot then. All through dinner we spit and growled about murdering redskins and how the only good Indian was a dead one. "I hope to hell they try to steal from us," Alabama Bill said. "I'll send the lot of them to the happy hunting ground before they can say 'How.' " Jim said, "I'll show them *how*."

That night at supper, though, the talk was generally quieter. Billy Roy wondered out loud if Bullshit Bob had a family somewhere, maybe still waiting for him, missing him, not knowing he wasn't never coming back. Most of the boys sat up around the chuck fire later than usual that evening, staring into the flames and not saying much. I don't believe I was the only one who had trouble sleeping that night, or who felt skittish all through my guard shift.

Speaking of skittish, something else I won't forget about that drive is the damn wolves. Along the Chisholm south of the Red, the bounty shooters had about wiped them out. I don't recall seeing even one the whole way up through Texas. But soon as we got in the Nations we heard their howling all around us. You hardly ever saw one except way off at a distance, but at night their yodeling sounded like it was coming right out of the nearest shadows. It got on your nerves so bad you were sure you could see their yellow eyes watching you out of the dark. The howls didn't seem to bother the cows near as much as the horses, and Jeff Longtree had a hell of a time keeping the remuda from bolting. The worst night was when we butchered a steer for supper. We normally wouldn't kill a cow on the trail because it was way more than the outfit could eat and it would mostly go to waste. But this one steer had been ornery from the time we left the Sandies. It kept breaking from the herd, making the swing rider have to run it down time after time. It was mean-tempered besides—always roughing up the cows around it and trying to stick a horn in them. Wes finally had enough, and soon as we made night camp he shot it and had Nameless butcher it. We gorged on beef that evening and to hell with the waste. But Lord Almighty, you should of heard the wolves! They smelled that blood on the air and raised a howling to stand your hair on end. That whole long night sounded like one big crazy house under the moon. If I live to be a hundred I don't never want to hear nothing like that again.

We had our first run-in with an Indian near the South Canadian River. Or Wes did, I mean. While we were bedding down the herd he rode off over the near rise to see what he might shoot for Nameless's supper pot. A few minutes later we heard the crack of his pistol and my brother Jim said to me, "Sounds like we got fresh meat for supper." Not two minutes later we heard a second shot, and I said, "Sounds like we got plenty of it!"

Then here comes Wes riding hell-for-leather over the rise. He's got a big turkey in one hand and his Colt in the other, and he's yelling, "I got one! I got one!"

"I got an injun!" he hollers when he reins up beside us and tosses the turkey over to Alabama Bill, who near falls off his horse catching it. He was breathless and big-eyed with excitement. "Sonbitch tried to bushwhack me with an arrow but I was too fast for him and now he's deader'n that gobbler. Come see, come see!" He told Alabama Bill to tell Nameless and Jeff Longtree to grab up their rifles and keep a sharp lookout on the herd, then the rest of us went galloping off behind him to see the Indian.

I don't know what exactly I expected him to look like.

All painted up in the face, I guess, with pointy teeth
maybe, and feathers all in his hair and so forth. You
know—*fearsome*. But he was a sore disappointment. He
was laying beside a bush with a hole in his forehead and
flies flocking in his open mouth and ants already in his
eyes. There wasn't a bit of paint on him nor a feather on
his head. He wasn't any taller than me and looked a good
bit punier, like he'd been eating poorly for some while.
Wes got off his horse and rolled the Indian over with his
foot. There was a hole in back of his head big enough to
house a squirrel—and the flies quick swarmed over the
thick red mess on the ground where his head had lain.

Wes said he never saw the Indian till after he shot the
turkey and got off his horse to retrieve it. Then he felt
somebody watching him. He pulled his pistol as he spun
around and spotted the Indian crouching in the brush. "He
was just starting to draw back his arrow," Wes said. "If
I hadn't been quick, *I'd* be laying here now, with feathers
sticking out one ear and an arrowhead poking out the
other."

Billy Roy wanted to take an arrow for a souvenir, but
Wes said no, it'd be bad luck. He said we best hurry up
and bury the body. Ben said he didn't know why white
men ought bother burying a heathen redskin anyway. Because, Wes said, if other Indians found this one with a ball
in his brainpan they might get riled enough to stampede
the herd. "Besides," my brother Jim said—and I caught
the quick wink he gave Wes—"some of them might slip
into camp at night looking to take a scalp or two in revenge." The thought of being scalped in his sleep made
Ben go a little waxy in the cheeks, and he didn't argue
when Wes sent him back to the wagon for a spade and
ax. Then me and Billy Roy dug a good deep grave with
the flies buzzing all about us while Wes and the others
kept a close watch for more Indians. I was thankful it was
too dark to see good by the time we finished digging and
rolled him into the hole, but I still ain't forgot the feeling
of dropping that first spadeful of dirt down on him.

Maybe we kept the killing a secret from the Indians, I

don't know, but it sure didn't stay no secret on the trail.
All next day the news traveled up and down from one
outfit to another, and we had lots of visitors come by to
congratulate Wes. One was Red Larson, ramrod of the
herd right behind ours, which belonged to Peas Butler.
Since the start of the drive, Red and Wes had got to be
fast friends.

"I hear there's one more good Indian in the world because of you," Red said with a grin. They talked for a
while over coffee, and he told Wes he was having trouble
with the herd behind his, a big Mexican outfit that kept
crowding him. Red was already shorthanded and had lost
a few steers crossing the Red River. If he got in a fight
with the Mexes and lost even more cows, Mr. Butler might
not be of a mind to hire him on again.

"Tell you what," Wes said, "when we get to the North
Canadian I'll pull my herd over and you run yours ahead
of me." It's just what Red hoped he'd say, and when we
got to the North Canadian it's just what we did. For some
reason, though, the Mexes had got slowed down the day
before and were well off behind us, so we didn't have any
trouble with them, not right away.

What we did have trouble with was more Indians. Three
more times while we were in the Nations we were approached by redskins wanting a tax on the herd or a beef
from it. The ones in the first two bunches looked even
worse off than the one Wes had plugged near the South
Canadian. They was bony, hangdog-looking critters, most
of them with big sores on their arms and legs, and we run
them off by firing our guns in the air and spurring our
horses at them like we meant business. But the third time
was different. They showed up one morning as we were
closing in on the Kansas border, about a dozen of them,
most carrying bows and arrows, a couple with lances.
There wasn't a bony one in the bunch. Their leader was
a big honker with a white stripe across his nose and two
feathers dangling from his hair. He sat straight on his horse
and had a Bowie knife on his hip big enough to chop

saplings with. His eyes looked like fireholes.

He signified through hand-talk that he wanted to cut a steer from the herd, but Wes rode up to him and yelled, "Hell, no!" One of the other braves started nudging his pony into the herd, and Wes pulled his Colt and said, "Get your red ass out from my cows, you heathen sonbitch," and waved him out of there with the gun. Now their leader started jabbering real fast in injun lingo and made it plain with his hand-talk that he meant to have a steer or know the reason why. Wes waved his pistol like he was saying no with his finger. "Hell no, I said!"

Well, that big redskin slides off his pony, yanks out that Bowie, and walks over to a fat steer. Wes stood up in his stirrups and hollered, "You kill that cow, I'll kill *you!*" The other heathens were all talking at once and shaking their lances and such. I drew my pistol and heard the boys levering rifles and cocking pistols all around me.

And be damn if that injun didn't slip that knife under that steer, look over at Wes with a grin, and shove the blade way up into its heart. The animal was still dropping when *blam!* Wes shot the injun through the eye and sprayed his brains out the back of his head.

The shot stirred up the cows and our horses spooked and pulled this way and that—and for a long terrible second I just knew we were about to be killed by either injuns or a stampede. But the cows didn't bolt, and the rest of them redskins didn't do a thing but look all big-eyed at each other and jabber all at once. I guess none of them ever expected to see big Mr. Two Feathers get his head blowed apart like that. Next thing we knew they were hightailing away from us. It wasn't till they rode off that I realized how dry my mouth was and how hard my heart was pounding. That was as close as I ever came to being in an Indian fight, and it was close enough for me.

Wes was still plenty hacked, however. He got off his horse and dragged the injun over to the dead steer and used a piece of lariat to tie him sitting up between the horns. "Let them redskins see what happens when they try stealing from us," he said.

The news ran like wildfire all along the trail. Hands from outfits ahead of us rode all the way back to the spot just to have a look at the dead Indian. Of course everybody that come along after us seen it. Even a couple of the Mexicans from the outfit behind us came over that night. They had droopy mustaches and wore big hats, silver-studded chaps and mean-looking spurs. Their herd had been gaining ground on us all day. One of the visiting Mexes had been riding point and had seen the whole business with the Indian. "Our *jefe*, Hosea," he said, "he think you should have cut the head. Scare the *Indios* more if you cut the head." Wes thanked them for the advice, but said what he'd really appreciate was if they'd give our herd more room than they'd given Red Larson's. "Ah, the red-hair man," the Mex said. He shrugged and gave Wes a big grin. "You tell your boss I said give us room," Wes said. "Sure, I tell him," the Mex said. "Hosea, he don't like to go too slow, you know. But I tell him."

We no sooner crossed into Kansas, though, than they closed up tight behind us. Wes didn't say nothing but you could see he was chafed. One morning the Mexes moved right up on our heels. Our drag riders suddenly had Mexican cows all around them, and some of our stragglers were mixing with the Mexican animals. We had to stop both herds to cut each other's steers out of the tangle.

The Mexican boss Hosea came riding up looking like he'd just swallowed a pound of chili peppers. He was tall for a Mex and wore a flat-top hat, and the ends of his mustache hung down to his chin. He didn't talk American too good, but it was clear enough he was blaming the whole thing on us for moving so slow. "I'll move my herd as I see fit," Wes told him. The chili-belly blabbered at him in Mexican, then spat down between them and rode back to his own outfit. "Greasy sonbitch," Wes said. You could about see the smoke coming out his ears, he was so mad.

The next day Manning and Gip showed up in camp and clapped Wes on the back for what he'd done to the big redskin. Then Manning told him a drover named Doc Burnett had asked him to take over another herd about fifteen miles back down the trail. The herd's ramrod had got into a fight with some bad actor and they'd cut each other up good. Looked like they'd both live, but they were laid up in wagons and would be left off in Caldwell to heal. In the meantime Burnett needed a new trail boss for the outfit, somebody he could depend on and who had sufficient sand to ramrod that troublesome crew. He'd offered Manning six hundred dollars to take the herd the rest of the way to Abilene, and guaranteed he'd still get his full wages from Columbus. "It's too good to pass up," Manning said. He was taking Gip along to back him in case there was any more trouble with the hands. When Wes told him about his problems with the Mexes, Manning said, "You let a Mex take an inch and next thing you know he's wanting five yards. So don't give the greaser that inch, and don't take his guff if things come to a head." Then him and Gip headed off south.

Things did come to a head, just two days later, out on the Newton Prairie. By then everybody up and down the trail knew there was bad blood between Wes and the Mexican boss, and expectations of a fight were running high. I was riding swing when I suddenly heard a lot of loud hollering and cussing, in both American and Mexican, coming from the rear of the herd. I reined back some till I could see through the dust good enough to make out what was going on. The lead Mex steers had closed up around our drag again, and Alabama Bill and Big Ben Kelly were arguing with Hosea and another Mex about it.

Wes came galloping back, cussing a blue streak. "I told you keep them cows away from my herd, you greaser sonbitch!" He pulled his pistol—he'd been wearing just one on the trail—and put it square in Hosea's face. And that damn Mexican was either the bravest son of a bitch you ever saw or pure-dee crazy, because what he did was go for his own gun.

Some fellas I've told this story to say they don't believe what happened next. Hell, I don't blame them. I *saw* it and *I* couldn't believe it. Wes pulled his trigger and the gun didn't fire. We later come to find out there was too much play between the cylinder and the breech to pop the cap. But here's the hard-to-believe part: Hosea's gun wouldn't fire either. There they were on their horses, no more'n two feet apart, cocking and snapping their pistols in each other's face over and over and neither one's would shoot. If I've ever seen a more unbelievable thing in my life, I sure don't recall what it was.

Hosea let out a kind of choked-up scream and flung his gun at Wes's head and just missed—and Wes threw *his* pistol and hit Hosea on the arm—and next thing you know they're locked up and rolling around on the ground, and us and the Mexicans are in a big circle around them on our horses and cheering our lungs out. And all the while the Mexican cattle's still moving, going right around the group of us like we were a sandbar in a river.

Wes broke free of Hosea's grip and got to his feet and tried to box him. He knew the manly art real well and had put on demonstrations for us in camp, hitting with open hands and making one or another of us look like staggering drunks, he was so quick and smooth. He hit Hosea square in the nose with a jab, but the Mexican looked more stunned by the way Wes was dancing up and down in front of him with his dukes up. Wes hopped forward and jabbed him again and Hosea let out a shriek and rushed him. Wes tried to sidestep but the Mex was pretty quick himself and caught hold of his shirt and down they went in a snarling knot.

They must of fought for ten solid minutes without letting up for a second. I've seen dogfights that didn't have as much fury. They was punching and biting and clawing, kicking, butting heads, cussing and spitting, just flat *tearing* each other up. Finally the both of them were breathing like bellows and having trouble getting to their feet. Their clothes was all ripped, their faces all lumped up and smeared with blood and dirt. One of Wes's eyes looked like a purple egg with a red slit, he had bad scratches on both cheeks, and his lips were blowed up. Hosea's eyes were swole nearly shut and his nose was puffed big as a potato and he had an ear tore half off.

A couple of the Mex hands tried to help Hosea on his horse, but he shook them off. Wes waved off any help from Jim and Big Ben. It was a wonder either one was able to mount up by himself, but they did. Wes looked at Hosea and said, "This ain't . . . over," said it like that, hardly able to talk for breathing so hard. Hosea spit blood at him and said, "Kill you . . . son of . . . the whore mother."

Wes rode back to our wagon and it was a good bet Hosea had gone off to his—and there wasn't no question they were going for guns. Keep in mind, both herds were still moving. With nobody keeping them in columns, they'd started spreading out, and some steers had headed off on their own. The swing riders for both outfits had to work fast to cut the strays back and tighten the herds up again. At the same time, every rider on both sides was straining to keep up with what was going on twixt Wes and Hosea. Jim passed the word for us to stick to our positions on the herd and stay out of the fight unless we saw the rest of the Mexicans get into it. He told me to get up on point, intending to keep me as far out of harm's way as he could. Wes buckled on his two-gun holster and borrowed a pistol from Nameless to replace the one of his that didn't work, then him and Jim giddapped on back toward the Mexicans. They headed off on the east side of the herd, so I snuck back on the west. I was damned if I was going to stay out of it.

The dust was swirling thick, and I heard shots before I could see what was happening. Then I spotted Wes riding straight for a bunch of Mexicans at the rear of the herd. He had his reins in his teeth and a pistol in each hand and looked like Judgment Day on horseback. Behind him a Mexican was already spread-eagled on the ground. Jim came riding out of the dust to join him. The Mexican horses were spooked and their riders were having to shoot wild. There were five of them. Wes and Jim closed in and opened fire. I drew my gun, put the spurs to Who Me, and took off behind them, letting out a rebel yell like Uncle Ike had taught me to do.

There was a clatter of gunfire and three Mexes dropped as Wes and Jim rode through the bunch of them like a couple of Mosby's Rangers. Then they reined around and started back at the two still in the fight. One threw up his hands, but not quick enough to keep from getting shot off his horse. The other one tried to hightail it—and came riding straight at me. We headed for each other at full gallop, both of us shooting and yelling to beat all hell. Next thing I knew I was in the air, flying ass over teakettle—and then I didn't know a damn thing until I opened my eyes and found myself flat on my back, looking up at my brother Jim, who was kneeling over me with a great big grin and checking me for broken bones. He told everybody the first words out of my mouth were, "Am I kilt?"—which I don't recollect saying, but which gets a good laugh every time Jim tells the tale. The Mex had shot my pony from under me is what happened. "Wes evened the score for you, Maverick," Jim said. Jim had caught the Mex's horse for me, a fine blaze stallion I named Pancho, and he proved a fit replacement for Who Me.

The herds had been stopped and pretty quick we were joined by riders from outfits up and down the line who'd heard the shooting. Everybody was laughing and jabbering all excited about the fight. Wes himself, beat-up as he was, was grinning wide. He'd took a round through his hat brim and another through his sleeve but didn't get a scratch. He came over and shook my hand and said, "I'm obliged to you, Huck, for coming to our aid." Jim says I blushed a little and maybe I did, since I hadn't done a thing but get my horse killed and my back nearly broke. But hell, I couldn't help feeling proud just the same.

It was six dead Mexicans all told, including Hosea, who'd been the first to fall. Jim had put down two and Wes had dropped the other four. The rest of the Mexes, including the two who'd come over that time after Wes killed the Indian, had stayed out of it. They told Wes they were glad the rankling was done with. Must of been true, because for the rest of the drive they kept their cows well back of ours.

For the rest of the drive we didn't have any troubles worth mentioning. What we mostly talked about around the supper campfires—besides telling and retelling about the fight with the Mexicans—was the good times we aimed to have ourselves in Abilene. For those of us who'd never been there before, the tales told about it by Nameless and Ollie and Big Ben were so exciting we couldn't hardly keep from twitching. The things they said about the women! The closer we got to the end of the drive, the later I'd lay awake every night, agitated with thoughts of those painted cats, as some called them—soiled doves, fallen angels, they had lots of different names. Ollie said they had skin as smooth and tasty as warm milk and would pleasure me in ways I couldn't even imagine. Big Ben said they put cherry-flavored rouge on their nipples and dusted their pussies with French bath powder. They said Abilene had hundreds of such women, hundreds! And everything they said turned out to be true. Before I got to Abilene that first time, I'd never yet seen a grown woman fully naked, and trying to picture all that bare and willing female flesh made me feel sort of drunk. It's one more thing about that first drive I've never forgot—the excitement of closing in on Abilene and all its wickedness just waiting for me with a wide red smile. About the only one not itching to whoop it up in Abilene was my brother Jim, who was only thinking about getting back to Annie Tenelle as quick as he could. The rest of us talked about nothing but the high times ahead. And about Wild Bill, of course, who damn well knew Wes Hardin was coming his way.

Tom Carson

We had the Texas reward poster for weeks before he showed up. Besides Bill, who I mean by "we" is me and Tyler McBride and Mike Williams, his main deputies. Every cattle outfit arrived with more news on him than we'd got from the one before. It was that way all spring. We never had to ask about him, all we had to do was listen. We heard about the Indian and we knew all about the fight with the Mexicans on the Newton Prairie. When he was told Hardin had dropped four of the six Mexes that went down in the fight, Bill's blond mustache spread in a smile over his glass of whiskey—he was in his favorite chair at the Alamo at the time—and he said, "Four, was it? That's a smart of killing. The boy must be all they say."

Abilene had been booming for a couple of years. It had a schoolhouse, two churches, banks, and real estate offices. It had stores and shops of every kind. It had photography studios. It had hotels as fancy as you'd find anywhere east of Frisco and west of St. Louie. It even had a damn newspaper.

But more than anything else, Abilene had cows. One big herd after another got packed into the rail-yard pens at the end of town for shipment to the East. And with those cows came the wild boys from Texas. Outfit after outfit rode in from three hard months on the trail, looking to have a good time. And ready to give it to them were dozens of saloon-keepers and flocks of hard-eyed whores and more quick-fingered gamblers than you could shake a pair of dice at. Abilene got so damn loud they said you could hear it all the way over in K.C. Cowboys whooping and howling, cows mooing day and night, train whistles blasting at all hours. There was brawling in public and drunks reeling on the sidewalks and horse racing in the streets. And sometimes—in spite of the ordinance against carrying guns in town—there was shooting. Usually it was in fun and only busted up some glass. Sometimes it was in earnest and somebody got shot.

Right from the start, Abilene loved the cowboys' money—but as the town had prospered and grown, many of the good citizens began to take offense at the cowboys' kind of fun. Bad enough the cowboy money stank of whiskey and whorehouse perfume by the time it reached the good citizens' hands, but the cowboys' wild ways in the streets got to be more than they could bear. What was needed, they decided, was a hardcase lawman who could keep the wild boys under control. And so, in the summer of '70, they hired Bear River Tom Smith to be the town marshal.

Bear River Tom was a big redhead from back east where he'd been a policeman, and he was tough as they come. But Abilene was tough as they come too, and Tom hadn't been marshal but about five months when one night somebody chopped off his head with an ax. Nobody wanted the job after that, and the town got wilder than ever. It took months to find somebody to take Tom's place. But they finally hired themselves the best there was—Wild Bill. That was in April of 1871, about two months before Hardin got to town.

Bill was already a legend at the time he came to Abilene. The "Prince of the Pistoleers," the dime novelists called him. And he truly did love being a famous man. He was always ready to cooperate in promoting his heroic reputation, which mostly meant telling magazine and newspaper writers the kind of adventurous bullshit stories they wanted to pass on to their gullible readers back east. He had a natural flair for being a public figure, and he damn sure looked the part—the long yellow hair, the fancy Prince Albert or the fringed buckskin, the wide red sash holding his pearl-handled navies butt-forward. He spent most of every day and night at his special table in the Alamo, the fanciest saloon in town, with double-glass doors and a mahogany bar and shiny brass cuspidors as high as your knee. He drank steady and gambled and joked and told tall tales. Every now and then he'd tour the town and let the citizens see that Wild Bill was on the job. Tyler or myself would sometimes follow along to keep watch for back-shooters, but it wasn't necessary. Bill had a sixth sense for guns being pointed at him, even from behind. A gunshot would flame from the alleyway shadows and he'd already be spinning and ducking down and returning fire, all in one smooth motion. In his first month on the job he wounded two ambushers and scared off a half-dozen others. There were plenty of pistoleros hankering for some celebrity of their own, and killing Bill was a sure way to get it. But even when he was drunk—Wild Bill Hiccup, some called him, though never within his hearing—there wasn't a one who had the guts to take him on face-to-face. (His sixth sense finally quit working for him five years later—in the Number 10 Saloon in Deadwood, where some dirty-nose tramp named McCall shot him in the back of the head. But even in death, he looked the legend: the Deadwood doc said Bill was the prettiest corpse he ever saw.)

I ought mention that just before Hardin got to Abilene, Bill had some trouble with Ben Thompson that heated up a lot of Texan tempers. It started over a sign Ben and his partner, Fancy Phil Coe—both of them Texans with lots of friends—had recently hung over the door to their Bull's Head saloon, which happened to be directly across the street from the jail. The sign showed a huge red bull reared up on its hind legs, proudly displaying to all the passing world a monster pair of balls and a giant pecker ready for action.

The first time Bill saw it he looked sad. "A sight like that," he said, "is apt to make a lady feel cheated the next time a feller lets down his breeches for her. I don't generally mind a fanciful exaggeration, but it shouldn't be of a sort to disappoint the ladies nor diminish a man's sense of his own manhood." Just the same, he wouldn't have done anything about the sign—live and let live whenever possible, that was Bill's motto—except that Mayor T. C. Henry got a storm of complaints from henpecked storekeepers, red-faced mothers with giggling children, and preachers having purple fits. He came into the jail like a man being chased by yellow jackets. "You got to do something about that sign, Bill, that's all there is to it."

So Bill told Johnny Coombs the painter to get his equipment and come along with us to the Bull's Head. Johnny no sooner got up on the ladder and started to paint over the offending portions of the big bull when Phil Coe came out of the saloon and asked what was going on. When Bill told him, Phil shrugged and said, "I warned Ben that sign would rile the good folk." Fancy Phil Coe was easy enough to get along with and had fairly decent manners for a Texan—which is why it seems all the more pitiful that of the only two men Bill killed in Abilene he was one of them.

While him and Bill were talking and watching Johnny paint, Ben Thompson came stomping out. He wasn't nearly so agreeable a fella as Phil. He was as stocky as the bull on the sign and had a reputation as a good pistolman. They said he'd killed at least ten white men in Texas and served two years in prison for trying to kill his wife's brother for beating up on her. I believe Bill was one of the few men Ben Thompson ever truly feared in his life—and so naturally Ben hated him.

"If they don't like the sign," he told Bill, "tell them not to look at it, damn their eyes!" He was wearing a gun in defiance of Bill's ordinance. Sorry, Bill told him, but the sign was going to change whether Ben liked it or not.

There was but six feet between them and you could see Ben trying with all his might to beat his fear and pull on Bill. He got all sweaty and tight in the face but he just couldn't do it. When he finally broke off the stare, his face was splotchy with shame. Phil Coe looked embarrassed for him. Ben pretended to watch Johnny paint for a minute, then started back into the saloon with his back as stiff as a fence post.

"Don't wear that useless hogleg on the street again," Bill called after him. He normally wasn't one to rub a man's face in it, but Ben brought out the worst in him. Ben's ears got red as beets but he went on inside without looking back. You could smell the rank hate he left in the air.

A couple of days after the business with the sign, I arrived at the jail one morning just as Columbus Carol was coming out. He was puffing a cigar and calling "So long, Bill" over his shoulder. He saw me and gave one of those big winks that always made me want to shoot him in the eye. "Howdy, Deputy!" he yelled. "Arrested any bad hombres lately? Har-har-har!" I never did understand how Bill came to be good buddies with that loudmouth son of a bitch.

Carol had pastured his herds at the North Cottonwood, about thirty miles south of town, and intended to keep them there awhile. He wasn't the only drover doing that. The cattle market was glutted and the price of beef was on the floor. But he'd been to the bank and borrowed enough to pay off his men, and it was mostly them we heard across the street in the Bull's Head. Bill told us all this—and that the main reason Carol had come to see him was to square Wes Hardin. He smiled and said, "I want you boys to give that young hoss wide room, hear? If he gets wildhair, you fetch me. I'll be the one to deal with him." What about if we saw him wearing his guns, I asked, but he didn't answer. He was already going out the door and on his way to the Alamo for his morning toddy.

I couldn't help but admire Bill's smarts. He knew Carol

would brag to everybody in town about squaring Hardin with his good buddy Wild Bill. It was a reason everybody would understand for Bill not coming down on Hardin. They'd all think, *Hell, Hickok ain't shying from Wes, he's just doing Columbus a favor is all.* Just the same, there was only so much slack Bill could give. If Hardin pulled on his string too hard, Bill would have to do something about it, consequences be damned.

The following night Bill was wearing his best Prince Albert, so I knew something was up but couldn't figure what. I went out on a turn with him and he headed us over to the Applejack. We had to make our way through swarms of drunks and yahooing cowhands in the street. We kept a lookout for guns but didn't spot a one. The wild boys had seen Bill head-knock too many gun-toters not to take him serious about wearing guns on this side of the river.

The piano player in the Applejack was practically hitting the keys with his fists to be heard in all the clamor of talk and laughter and shouting and dealers' calls. When Bill ordered a drink for me as well as himself, I knew for sure something was going on and wished he'd let me in on it. He normally didn't like for us to drink on the job. "One drunk lawman out on the town's enough," he'd say, meaning himself. He clinked his glass against mine and said, "To love, Tommy boy, wherever it's keeping its pretty ass."

He tossed off the drink and the barkeep poured him another, but I only sipped at mine to be polite. No matter what Bill was up to, I wasn't about to do any real drinking in a crowd like that. It was practically all Texans, and we were getting a lot of eyeballing. Bill noticed the grip I had on my shotgun down alongside my leg and told me to put it up on the bar. "These fellers are mostly just gawkers," he said. "Don't let them think they got you twitchy."

Pretty soon George Johnson pushed in beside Bill and hollered, "Wild Bill! Got somebody here you ought to meet!" George was a friend of Bill's, an easygoing railroad agent who knew most of the Texas cowhands. He reached back and put his hand on the shoulder of a tall young fellow wearing a new black suit with a red plaid vest and a black hat with a silver concho band around it— and two big army .44s tied down on his legs. "Bill," George said, "meet Wes Hardin. Wes, this here is the one and only Wild Bill Hickok."

My hand instinctively went to my shotgun, but Bill tapped my arm, so I let it be. It was clear he'd had George set up the meeting, and it irritated hell out of me that he hadn't let me in on it beforehand. It's how he was about a lot of things, lousy with secrets.

Neither one put his hand out. They just nodded and said they were proud to make each other's acquaintance. Bill offered to buy him a whiskey, but Hardin insisted the drinks were on him and ordered a bottle. They clinked glasses and drank to each other's health. While they had a couple of drinks more, Bill told him he'd heard about the fight with the Mexicans on the Newton Prairie and was impressed by the shooting they said he'd done. "You did the republic a service, getting rid of so many troublemakers all at one time," he said.

Hardin smiled big as the moon. "Glad you feel that way," he said. "I'd been wondering how I stood with the law hereabouts." For all their pleasantries, they were both doing everything left-handed. Hardin kept his right hand hooked by a thumb in his gunbelt, and Bill had his on his hip, from where he could snatch the navy just quick as a blink.

"Got something to show you, Little Arkansas," Bill said. I don't know anybody who knows why in hell Bill called him by that name, but that's what he always called him from then on—and for some damn reason Hardin seemed pleased by it. Bill took the Texas reward poster out of his coat with his left hand and shook it open for Hardin to see. Hardin gave it a glance and his smile got tight. Bill crumpled it up and said, "It don't mean jackshit. Nor any other papers they send on you. The way I see it, Little Arkansas, I got enough to do just keeping all these wild hairs from tearing up the town—and *you* got enough troubles back home without adding to them here. Now you impress me as a bright fella who's his own man. I don't believe you're likely to be influenced by any bitter souls in town who try to use you for their own low purposes."

"Like Ben Thompson, you mean?" Hardin said with a smile. "Phil Coe's an old friend of mine. Soon as I come into town he invited me to the Bull's Head and introduced me to Ben. Friendly fella, Ben. Kept pushing free whiskey at me and telling me how us Texans got to stick together here in Bloody Kansas. He had a lot to say about you."

Bill nodded and said, "I'll wager he did."

Hardin poured another left-handed round of drinks and said, "He said you are a Texan-hating Yankee sonbitch and the world would be a better place without you. I'm using his words, you understand. No offense." Bill shook his head to say none taken. But George Johnson's eyes had gone wide at the sudden bluntness of the conversation, and he eased back into the crowd and vanished. I knew how he felt. Up on the bar my shotgun looked a mile away. "Ben also says," Hardin went on, "that you prefer killing Texans to even Mexicans and niggers."

Even if most the men crowded around us hadn't been as drunk and distracted as they were, they couldn't have overheard much of the conversation between Bill and Hardin, not in all the loudness. "Folks will believe what they want to believe," Bill said.

"That's a true fact," Hardin said. "And one of the things *I've* always believed is that a man ought to do his own fighting. I told Ben so. I said, 'Ben, if what you're saying is Wild Bill needs killing, why don't you just go on over there and do it?' "

Bill let out a belly laugh and said he bet that raised Ben's eyebrows some. "Damn sure did," Hardin said, "but he stayed friendly and didn't press me anymore on the subject." Bill said Ben wasn't one to press things except with them he knew he could bully. "In that case," Hardin said, "I guess it's two honkers in this town he won't be pressing things with." You should've seen them—grinning at each other like mules at their feed.

Bill tossed off his drink and said, "It's a pleasure, Little Arkansas, but I got rounds to make." They were both fairly bright in the eyes from all the quick whiskey they'd put down. I knew Bill was drunk because of the careful way he wiped his mustaches. "If I can do you a favor while you're in town," he said, "say the word."

"Thanks, Bill," Hardin said. "I'll remember that."

Bill leaned in closer to him and said in a voice so low I barely caught it: "You can do me a favor too, if you're of a mind to."

"What might that be, Bill?" Hardin asked.

"You might make it a point," Bill said, "not to wear them pistols the rest of the time you're in town."

Hardin's eyes went thin but he kept smiling and didn't say anything. Bill smiled back and nodded so long, and we shouldered our way out through the crowd.

Back on the street, I asked Bill if he thought Hardin would go on wearing his guns. He looked up at the night sky and heaved an enormous sigh. "Only till all them stars come falling down," he said.

Over the next couple of days Bill kept to his usual routine. He made his daybreak round of town, then settled in at the Alamo for his morning whiskey and breakfast beefsteak and a few early hands with anybody interested. Hardin kept mainly to the Bull's Head and the Applejack—whenever he wasn't at one whorehouse or another. The day after Bill had his talk with him I saw him come out of a photography studio, all groomed and spit-shined in his black suit and plaid vest. He was still wearing his pistols.

The next morning I saw him and a bunch of Texans go in the Bull's Head, and from my chair out on the jail portico I listened to them get louder as the day went by. All their whooping and yeehawing kept drawing more and more wildhairs over there to join the fun. That afternoon Ben Thompson came staggering out the front doors and looked straight up at his sign—then fell over backward and laid on the sidewalk like a dead man. Some of his friends came out and laughed at him, then grabbed him by the heels and dragged him back inside.

Finally, here came Bill back from the Alamo to make his afternoon check on the jail. He had his hat low on his eyes and walked smooth as a cat. A couple of fellas standing in the Bull's Head doorway spotted him and slipped back inside and out of sight. A second later the doors swung open again and Wes Hardin stepped out with his hat pushed back on his head and his guns showing under his open black coat. A slew of faces filled the saloon window and the doorway behind him.

I started across the street so I could cover Bill against anybody who might charge out the door or try coming around the corner of the building to flank him, but Bill waved me back toward the jail. I got back up on the sidewalk and stood there with the shotgun at port arms where all the wild boys could see it. Hardin stepped down into the street and said, "Howdy, Bill."

"Little Arkansas," Bill said, "I thought you and me had an understanding about not wearing them guns till you were ready to leave town."

"Well, Bill," Hardin said, "it so happens I'm about to go see some friends tending a herd south of town."

"That's fine then," Bill said. "Glad we understand each other." But as he turned to head for the jail, somebody at the saloon door let out a rebel yell loud enough to wake the dead—and Bill spun back around and it was like the navy had been in his hand all along, he pulled it so quick. Nobody—*nobody*, never, take my word for it—could pull a pistol faster than Bill Hickok. The boys in the saloon couldn't see Hardin's face, but I could: he looked like he'd just seen Bill turn water into wine. If he hadn't froze like he did, Bill would've shot his heart out. I wish to hell he had. The whole street was suddenly so quiet I would've thought I'd gone deaf except I heard Bill say, "Hand me the guns, Little Arkansas. Easy, and butt first."

What happened next is a fact. A hundred other witnesses saw it. Hardin eased the pistols from their holsters and held them out to Bill butt forward. But he'd kept a finger in each trigger guard, and when Bill reached for the guns with his left hand, Hardin flicked his wrists and reversed them just as quick and neat as a gambler can flip a card. Just *flip!* and they were cocked and pointed in Bill's face. It's called the road agent's spin and is one of the oldest tricks there is—for show. Lots of pistolmen could do it for show. But to try it on somebody holding a gun on you, well, it's a sure way to get your brains blowed out real quick. For Hardin to do it to *Wild Bill*, who knew more gun tricks than anybody alive, was more than unbelievable—it was flat crazy. He got away with it because Bill never in a million years expected Hardin to be *that* crazy. Bill had expected a pistoleer of Hardin's reputation to know it couldn't be done. Bill, of all people, ought have known better than to expect a pistoleer to use common sense.

Hardin looked more surprised than anybody that the spin had worked. I leveled the shotgun at him, but Bill said, "No, Tom," without even looking my way. I kept it pointed at Hardin anyway, both hammers cocked.

"Drop that navy!" Hardin hollered. He was about quivering with excitement. But Bill just shook his head real slow and said, " 'Fraid not, hoss," and kept the navy pointed at him.

I barely heard Bill because of the clamor coming from the wildhairs in the saloon—them and the crowd forming fast up the street, looking for a show but at the same time trying to keep out of the line of fire. With Bill under Hardin's guns, the Hickok haters were all of a sudden plenty loud and brave. "Kill him, Wes!" they were yelling. "Kill the son of a bitch!" But Hardin knew damn well he was in a Mexican standoff. The instant he shot Bill—whether in the head, heart, or wishbone—Bill would shoot him dead too, do it in a dying reflex. And *I'd* let him have both barrels—I reckon he knew that too.

Somebody in the street crowd hollered, "Hell, I'll shoot the Yankee fancy pants myself!" Hardin swung one of his pistols in the direction of the voice without taking his eyes off Bill and shouted, ''I'll kill any sonbitch who shoots!'' I was the only one close enough to hear him tell Bill, ''I'll be damned if I'm gonna give you the chance to shoot me in the back. I been told what you're up to.''

''Oh, hell, son,'' Bill said, ''if I wanted to kill you I'd of done it in the same breath when I pulled the pistol. You'd of died looking me square in the eyes. Ben Thompson's been pouring you lies with every drink, Little Arkansas. Listen, let's go have a drink.'' With Hardin's guns still in his face, Bill uncocked the navy and stuck it back in his sash. It was about the most foolish thing I'd ever seen him do, but he reckoned he had a fix on Hardin's true nature—and he always was a gambling man. ''I'm buying,'' Bill said.

Every jackass in the Bull's Head was bellowing for Hardin to shoot. But for all the Texas wildhair in him, Hardin was cut from cloth a lot like Bill's. He twirled the pistols and dropped them back in their holsters.

It wasn't only the wild boys who let out cusses and groans of disappointment—damn near *everybody* watching had been hoping for a bloody entertainment. It's how people are. Bill and Hardin didn't pay them any more mind than they did the crows cawing along the storefronts.

''I know a place,'' Bill said, ''might suit your fancy.''

''Whatever pleases you,'' Hardin said.

They went over to Cedar Street and through the Alamo to the plank walkway out back that led down the alley to Miss Violet's pleasure parlor. I trailed along behind. They stayed in there the rest of the afternoon.

Bill came out shortly after dusk, walking in that well-oiled way a man does when he's got just the proper amount of whiskey in him and has just been laid every which way to Sunday. I never much cared for whores myself, but that's not saying I never made use of them. A man ain't always got a lot of choice about how to scratch the itch in his pants. I was standing near the back door of the Alamo, and because he couldn't see worth a damn in bad light, Bill didn't recognize me. He pushed back the right flap of his Prince Albert as he approached—then he made out who I was and let the coat flap drop. He patted me on the shoulder as he went by in a cloud of whiskey breath and French perfume. "You fine boy, Tom," he said, and went inside to while away the night in his poker chair.

A couple of hours later, as I was making my rounds, I heard shots in the Daisy Restaurant halfway down the street. I ran over and saw a small crowd rushing out the door in a panic, the women shrieking and the men hunkering low, everybody moving fast to get out of the way of a man who came staggering out with the lower half of his face missing and blood gushing from his wound. I caught him as he fell and eased him down on the sidewalk just as Hardin stormed through the door with his Colt in his hand and fury in his eyes. He stuck the gun in my face and ordered me to toss my scattergun and pistol in the street, then backed up to the end of the sidewalk and ran off down the alley.

Inside the restaurant a man named Tom Pain was sitting in a chair and cussing a blue streak about his rotten luck while a waiter used a towel to try to stop the bleeding from the bad wound in his arm. It was the only arm Tom Pain had, having lost the other in the War, and he was nearly crying, he was so mad. By the time Bill showed up, Pain had told me the whole story.

He and Hardin had met in the parlor at Miss Violet's and took a shine to each other, so they'd come to the Daisy for some supper and to talk about common acquaintances back home in Texas. Two jayhawkers sitting at the next table started talking loud about what a pesthole Texas was and how Kansas would be a far better place if every Texan in it was run out for good. Hardin turned around in his chair and said that back in Texas it was common knowledge there were three kinds of suns in Kansas—sunshine, sunflowers, and sons of bitches—and didn't neither of them look like sunshine or flowers to him. One of the hawkers jumped up and grabbed him by the collar—and

Hardin whipped out his Colt and hit the fella across the nose with it. Pain said it sounded like breaking a kindling stick. The fella dropped to his knees with blood pouring down his chin as the other hawker pulled a belly gun and fired—but he missed Hardin and hit Pain in the arm. Hardin shot twice—the first bullet nicked the jayhawker's cheek and sprayed some feathers off the hat of a young woman behind him, and the second blew off the hawker's lower jaw.

While I was telling Bill what happened, we got word that Hardin had gone to the livery, saddled up, and rode off hell-for-leather to the south. "Just as well," Bill said. "This looks like self-defense, plain and simple, but I'm damned if I ever met anybody forced to do so much self-defending as that boy." He was one to talk.

Over the next couple of days a half-dozen drovers, including Columbus Carol and Jake Johnson, came to Bill to put in a good word for Hardin. Bill told them he considered the jayhawker shooting a case of self-defense and Hardin was still squared with him. He made it seem like he was doing them a favor, but he was just doing what was best for himself. All those Texans in town were looking up to Hardin like some kind of hero, and it would have been hell to pay if Bill had come down hard on him.

When Hardin paid his next visit to town, Bill invited him into the Applejack to palaver over a couple of drinks. He told him about a new Texas reward poster that was making the rounds: the price on Hardin's head was up to one thousand dollars. He offered Hardin a deal. He'd let him wear his guns in town, and he'd make fast work of any bounty men who might come into Abilene looking for him—but in trade Hardin had to keep his Texas friends unarmed and not do anything to make Bill look bad.

Hardin said that was fair enough and they touched glasses on it.

— Maggie St. John —

On the afternoon they had their famous standoff, I was getting my hair trimmed by Wanda May up in my room. Violet kept coming by to see how much longer we'd be, telling us the parlor was full of horny galoots waiting to be serviced and the other girls couldn't take care of them all. It was true. That summer in Abilene was the hardest-working I ever knew. The house was operating every hour of the day and night. But making all that money was hard on Violet's nerves. The richer she got, the bitchier she got. She got to where she wouldn't stand for anybody taking a break longer than to ease their bladder or eat a quick meal. "Time is money, ladies!" she'd say, clapping her hands like she was chop-chopping a bunch of coolies. She damn sure didn't chop-chop *me*. She knew I wouldn't have stood for it. I would've left there in a Kansas City minute and gone to work for Dapper Dan Foster or Louella Sweet. The both of them were always trying to get me to switch to their house. They wanted me for the same reason Violet didn't get bossy with me—I was Bill's special girl and everybody knew it.

Bill liked me special because he knew I was a fool for killers. I've never been able to explain it and I'm not about to try now. But the first time he was with me he must've smelled it under my perfume or felt it in my bones. There's something about a killer that's always set my

blood humming and made my skin jump at their touch.
And *Bill*, well, I'd go so hot under his hands I'd let steam.
Even if Violet hadn't allowed Bill the run of the house for
free, I never would've charged him a nickel. He sometimes
went to other houses, of course, men naturally craving
variety like they do, and he sometimes went to some of
the other girls in Violet's. But mostly he came to me. It
increased his pleasure to know how much I thrilled to the
touch of his killer hands. Hell, we all of us got our ways.

Violet didn't charge Bill because he was so damn good
for business. Other men wanted to take their pleasure
wherever Bill took his. They wanted to sit at the same
poker tables and drink from the same bottles and mount
the same women. I brought Bill to Violet's and a heap of
business followed Bill. It's why Violet Hayes wasn't about
to take a chance on losing me to Dapper Dan or Louella.

Anyhow, just when Wanda May finished my hair, Violet came to the door again and said she had a special
party waiting on us in the Meadow Room. It wasn't unusual for some flush galoot to buy himself two girls at
once—or even three, if his hankering was that much
bigger than his pecker and his common sense—and that's
what the Meadow Room was for. It was called that because it's about how big the bed in there was.

So me and Wanda May followed Violet down the hall
in our shimmies—and who do we find waiting in the
Meadow but Wild Bill and another fella. They were sitting
at the small table by the window with a near-empty bottle
and two full ones, and they were grinning at us like
wolves. I knew right off what they had in mind. Bill always was one for whorehouse adventure. I took a quick
look at Wanda May and saw her staring at the stranger
with her mouth open. "Here they are, boys," Violet said.
"The best in the house. Y'all have a real nice time, hear?"
And she scooted on out and shut the door.

The other one was a good bit younger than Bill, tall and
good-looking. Myself, I always preferred the sort of handsome that's got some wear on it, like Bill's. At first I
figured this one for a gambler, dressed as he was in a black

suit and long string tie. But then I looked square into those gray eyes and I knew exactly what he was. My blood suddenly sang it to me. Then it struck me *who* he was— hell, we'd only been hearing about him for days. Just then Wanda May said, "Johnny? John Wesley?"

He looked at her close for a minute, then jumped up all bright-eyed and said "Hannie Willingham! Be God *damned!*" He grabbed her up and swung her around, the two of them laughing like kids. Bill and me looked at each other. I silently said, "*Hannie Willingham?*" and we busted out laughing too.

"Hellfire," Wes said, hugging Wanda to him while she kissed him all over his neck and face, "I knew this sweet thing back when I was learning to cowboy in Navarro County." Bill smiled in that lazy way of his and poured us all a drink. "Damn world's getting smaller all the time, ain't it, Little Arkansas?" I said I didn't know Wes was from Arkansas, and him and Bill laughed like that was the best joke they'd heard all day.

Bill didn't waste any time warming things up. He never did. He caught hold of the hem of my shimmy and tugged me over beside his chair. "What you got on that evil mind, you bad ole injun fighter?" I said, running my hand through his long yellow hair. Wes and Wanda sat on the edge of the big bed, sipping their whiskey and nuzzling some, but also watching as Bill took out his pistola and rubbed the barrel up along the inside of my leg. He slid it real slow all the way up under my shimmy, and when the tip of it touched my bare cunny, I grabbed a fistful of his hair and held on tight. He grinned up at me like the devil himself and stroked me gently with that iron thing till my legs got all trembly and I was breathing through my mouth and cussing him low. He'd never done *that* to me before—and there he was, doing it front of Wes and Wanda May. He kept at it till I thought I was going to faint from the pure pleasure of it. He suddenly pressed the pistol up hard against me and cocked the gun—and I let a moan and fell on him like I'd been hit behind the knees.

He sat me on his lap and held the gun up so everybody

could see the barrel shining with my wetness. "*Mag*-gie!"
Wanda May said. She was grinning big and her eyes were
all lit up. "Whoooo!" Wes said. "Somebody's having
herself a *good* time." And do you know I believe I
blushed? Me, Maggie St. John, the belle of the Abilene
whores, blushing like a schoolgirl. I couldn't help but
laugh with them. "Well, somebody else looks to be enjoying the company too," I said, and gave a pointed look
at the front of Wes's pants. It looked like he had an ear
of corn stuck in there.

Next thing you know, we were all of us bare-assed and
in that big ole bed—and Lord, what a time! It started out
Bill on me and Wes on Wanda, the both of them humping
like broncos but fighting like hell to keep from being the
first to shoot off, and me and Wanda doing everything we
knew how with our hands and hips and whatnot to make
our man come first. All that contesting got so wild the bed
gave way and hit the floor like it was going to bring the
whole house down. Wanda claimed she'd got Wes off before I had Bill, which I knew to be a lie and which Wes
said was absolutely not a fact. While we were arguing
about it Violet swung open the door with a look on her
face like she expected to find dead bodies on the floor. A
bunch of grinning galoots were staring in over her shoulders. Bill flung a pillow at her and hollered, "Shut the
goddamn door, woman! This ain't no sideshow!" For
months afterward me and Wanda could make each other
burst out laughing just by imitating that look on Violet's
face.

We sat on the broken bed and passed the bottle around,
and I noticed Wes's heavy manhood showing signs of life
as he admired my titties—they were something to admire
in those days, if I say so myself. Wanda slid over by Bill
and took hold of his long skinny thing and said to it, "Pardon me, sir, but haven't we met someplace before?" And
that got us going again—this time me on Wes, Wanda on
Bill. It started out another contest, but we all got too involved in what we were doing to give a damn who shot
when.

We went at it all afternoon, now and then stopping to rest a little, take a drink, have a smoke. At one point, Wanda ran her finger along one of Bill's scars and asked him if he could remember where he'd got it. It was bright pink and thick as a curtain cord and ran from his left collarbone to under his right arm. "The McCanles scrimmage," Bill said. He was scars from neck to knees, and could tell you how he got every one. The long ones were from cuts and the tight puckered ones were from bullets. All Wes had was a tiny pale one on his lip where he'd been punched once and a little pinched one on his arm where a Yankee soldier had winged him. "Unless you die young, Little Arkansas," Bill said, "you'll look like this one day. Probably worse, since you got more of them looking to kill you than I do. With me they get a reputation. With you they get a reputation *and* a reward."

Bill used me to show Wes some humping positions he'd learned from a Pawnee medicine man back when he was scouting for the army. Damn if some of those ways weren't new to *me*. A couple felt pretty nice, but most were so god-awful awkward only an injun would've been fool enough to do it that way. Then me and Bill watched Wanda slide down under Wes and pleasure him with her special "tongue and titty trick." Then they watched me treat Bill to a trip around the world. Then me and Wanda teamed up on Wes while Bill recovered some of his sap— and then we doubled up on him too. All afternoon it was nothing but wet nakedness wherever you turned or put out your hand.

By the time the room was in shadows we were one whipped bunch. The room was just reeking of sex. The whiskey was all gone and the boys were complaining in that boastful way men do that their peckers were so sore they'd likely fall off. Bill gave me a few last kisses on the tits and belly while he got dressed, but Wanda started fooling around with Wes again before he could get his pants on. "Sweet Jesus, girl," he said, "have pity on a poor wore-out cowhand." But damn if all her licking and handling didn't get that big raw thing up on its feet again. So he crawled up on her and gave Bill a grin that wasn't nothing but a banty rooster challenge. Bill shook his head in a sorrowful way and said, "Hell no! I guess I'm too old anymore, Arkansas. You win." Hell, he wasn't beat, he was just getting bored. He couldn't wait to get to the card table and a fresh bottle, that's all. I knew him. After he gave me a good-bye kiss on the nose and went on out, I sat at the foot of the bed and watched Wes and Wanda hump each other sweet and slow.

I've had a thousand wild times with men—ten thousand!—but that's the one sticks in my mind the clearest, even after all these years. Wes and Wild Bill. God damn me, but I loved those fucking killers.

—— Hugh Anderson ——

A few days after Wes got himself squared with Hickok for shooting the mouth off some bad actor from Kansas, I joined him for a breakfast of oysters and eggs in the American House, him and Johnny Coran and Jim Rodgers. We were laughing and going on about the good times we'd been having ourselves in Abilene and about Johnny being so black-assed because somebody'd stole his Mexican head. He'd bought it from a fella in a Missouri guerrilla shirt who'd stopped by our cow camp for a cup of coffee. The fella claimed it came off a Mex who tried to steal his packhorse over in the Red Hills. He'd taken the head to Wichita, thinking there might be a reward out for the horse thief, but the sheriff there said no, he didn't have a paper on anybody that looked like that Mex. The Missouri fella didn't much know what to do with the head after that. He said he wouldn't of felt right to just throw it away, so he'd had it hanging on his saddle horn for nearly a week before Johnny bought it off him for ten dollars. It was still in pretty fair shape, all things considered, only just starting to go rank. It had a hole under its greasy hair in back where the .44 caliber slug had gone in, and a good portion of the forehead was missing where it had come out, but when you put a hat on it you could hardly see the damage. Johnny'd brought the head into town that night and it had naturally drawn a good deal of attention. At first Johnny wouldn't let any-

body else handle it, but after he got drunk enough to get
sociable he let the boys have some fun with it, putting a
cigar in its mouth and a whore's pink garter for a head-
band, such as that. But he was mad as a sunstruck dog
when he woke up in some whorehouse next morning and
found out somebody'd stole it. "I find the thieving son of
a bitch who took it," he said, "I'll be taking two heads
back." He'd spent all day asking after it in the saloons
and whorehouses but never did find out what happened to
it.

Anyhow, we'd just ordered up another pot of coffee
when who should show up at the table but Manning and
Gip Clements, Wes's cousins. They'd just rode in off the
trail and had been hunting for him all over town. They
looked tired, both of them dark around the eyes and carrying a layer of dust. Wes was damn happy to see them. He
introduced them all around and started to tell about how
he'd got the drop on Hickok with the old road agent's spin
when Manning interrupted to say Wild Bill was exactly
who he had on his mind. He said him and Gip had run
into some hard trouble out on the trail and were wondering
if Hickok might try to do something about it.

What happened was this. Manning and Gip had taken
over a herd for Doc Burnett after his first ramrod had got
himself too badly cut up in a fight to stay on the job. But
they had trouble right from the start from a couple of trail
hands named Dolph and Joe Shadden. Johnny said he
knew the Shadden brothers. "Never had no trouble with
them myself, but I know for a fact they can both of them
be mean as snakes." I'd heard of them too, though never
nothing good.

The trouble started when the Shaddens refused to take
their turn on night guard anymore. They thought the
youngsters making their first drive ought to do all the
nighthawking since they were low men on the totem pole.
Manning told them they could either take their turn on
night guard like everybody else or they could quit. They
said fine, they'd quit, but they wanted the full pay they'd
signed on for back in San Antonio. In a pig's ass, Manning

said. He'd pay them for working as much of the drive as
they had—they were at the Red River at the time—and
not a damned nickel more. So the Shaddens stayed on and
night hawked like everybody else, but as the drive moved
through the Nations they never let up trying to cause trouble in one way or another. They kept trying to turn the
rest of the outfit against the Clementses and stirred up a
deal of discontent. They complained about everything.
They were slow to follow orders and always cussing Manning under their breath. They tried to pick fights with the
few hands who favored the Clementses. The tension just
got worse and worse. Manning and Gip took turns sleeping
so they could watch over each other in the night.

Things came to a head one drizzly evening after they'd
crossed into Kansas. Manning rode out to help a night
guard round up a couple of steers that had wandered off
from the herd, and when he got back to camp he found
Dolph slapping and shoving on Little Eddie Moorhouse,
the youngest hand in the outfit. Gip was trying to get between them, but Joe Shadden kept grabbing him away and
telling him to mind his own goddamn business. Manning
ran up and shouldered Joe off Gip just as Dolph knocked
Little Eddie down into the cookfire. Little Eddie screamed
and rolled out of the flames, and some of the hands rushed
up and started tearing his smoking shirt off him. Joe pulled
his boot knife and swiped at Manning and nicked him on
the collarbone. Gip and Dolph pulled pistols and Gip shot
Joe in the arm just as Dolph blew a hole through Gip's
floppy rain slicker. Before Dolph could fire again, Manning shot him through the heart. And then, while Joe was
struggling to pull his pistol with his bad arm, Manning
shot him square in the brainpan.

Manning turned the herd over to one of the other hands,
and him and Gip got the hell away from there. They about
rode their horses to death getting to Abilene. They'd sent
a telegram to Doc Burnett in Fort Worth telling him what
happened. "There's some in the outfit who'll tell the truth
about it," Manning said, "but there's as many who'll lie
and say I shot them in cold blood." He figured the news

had likely reached Wichita by morning and already been telegraphed to Abilene.

"Hickok's sure to have papers on me," Manning said. "If I'd been thinking clear, I wouldn't of come here. I probably ought to head east right now and make my way back home by way of Arkansas."

Hell no, Wes said, there wasn't any need to do that. He had an understanding with Hickok. He'd see to it Manning got squared with him.

"*You* can square me with Wild Bill Hickok?" Manning said.

"Hey, cousin, me and Bill're the best of friends," Wes said with a sly smile. "But now listen, you boys give your gunbelts to Johnny here and he'll hold them for you out at his camp. I can square you with Bill, but if he sees you packing iron in town he might not bother asking questions before he pulls the law on you."

"What the hell?" Manning said. "*You're* packing."

Wes stood up and put on his hat. "Yes indeed," he said, and gave Manning a wink, "but I'm special." He truly enjoyed being the fair-haired boy with Hickok. "You all stay put till I get back."

The Clements boys ordered oysters and eggs and the biggest steaks in the house, then tore into it all like they hadn't eaten in a week. Pretty soon Wes was back, smiling bigger than before. He'd spotted Hickok in the Alamo, he said, but didn't want to disturb him at his poker, so he'd gone to see Columbus Carol in the Bull's Head and explained the situation to him. Carol promised he'd talk to Wild Bill and square Manning with him.

"See, cousin?" Wes said, punching Manning on the arm. "Everything's all took care of."

After eating, we all had a so-long drink together in the Applejack, then Johnny and Jim and me went back to our Cottonwood camp to wait for the rise in beef prices we'd been told would happen in the next few days.

Next morning, Manning showed up to get his guns from Johnny. He was packing a Colt he'd got from Wes before leaving town. He sat down for a cup of coffee and told us it had been a hell of a night in Abilene, though he hadn't seen much of it because Hickok had arrested him after all. He'd spent several hours in the hoosegow, passing the time with a medicine salesman accused of poisoning six citizens who'd drunk some of his special elixirs, and with a beat-up cowboy who'd rode his horse into a saloon and up on a faro table—which had made everybody laugh except the faro players, who pulled him off his cayuse and punched him bloody before one of Hickok's deputies showed up and hauled him off to jail. Anyhow, Wes had finally finagled Manning out of jail some way or other and then quick hustled him out of town.

We all wanted to hear more details, of course, and we tried to impose on him to stay with us till the next day, but he said he was itchy to get back to Texas. "I reckon Wes'll be along sooner or later," he said, "and he can tell you the story a lot fuller than I can." So we gave him provisions and wished him well, and off he went.

And early next morning here comes Wes on the fly— riding in his damn nightclothes, I ain't lying—and with the law hot on his tail.

── Tyler McBride ──

When the wire arrived from Wichita ordering the arrest of Manning Clements for the murder of two trail hands in South Kansas, it so happened that Clements was in town—him and his brother Gip— and had been for at least a couple of days. Bill got steamed when he read the telegram. "I guess the whole town's heard about this," he said, "knowing Bloomers." Bloomers was the telegrapher—and a flannel-mouth gossip. He was faster than the *Chronicle* when it came to spreading news.

Tom said he'd just seen Clements eating supper with Hardin at the American House, and he knew for a fact that Gip Clements was playing cards in the Applejack. Tom was one for keeping track of things. Bill let out a heavy sigh and cussed under his breath. We all knew what was eating on him: Hardin hadn't held to their bargain. If he'd come to Bill and asked to square his cousin, they likely would've worked something out so that Bill could keep from arresting Clements without looking bad. But now the whole town for damn sure knew we had a paper on Clements, and Bill had to arrest him or look like he lacked the grit. "Goddamn Texas trash," he muttered. The more he thought on it, the more it hacked him. He told Tom to keep an eye on Gip Clements in the Applejack, then took me with him over to the American House. At the front door of the place, he told me, "Either one even looks like

he's moving for a gun, give him both goddamn barrels."
I mean, he was *hacked*.

Hardin was smiling till he caught the look on Bill's face.
He glanced at me standing by with the shotgun and asked
Bill if I was on my way to a duck hunt. Bill just glared
at him and said, "It's buckshot loads, hoss." Then he asks
the other one, "Are you Manning Clements?" Clements
nodded. "I have a paper on you," Bill said. "You're under arrest."

Hardin got agitated, of course, but didn't seem too inclined to do anything about it, not with my shotgun
pointed at him from the hip. I wish he had. If he'd so
much as dropped his hand off the table I'd of blown him
in half—and if I'd done *that*, I'd be remembered a lot
different, you bet.

"Didn't Columbus see you about squaring Manning?"
he asked Bill.

"Sonbitch's been in the Alamo since yesterday morning," Bill said, "too damn drunk to lift his head off the
table. If you wanted this fella posted, why didn't you see
me yourself?"

The conversations in the dining room had dropped to
nervous whispers. A lot of big-eyed faces were turned our
way. They hadn't expected such an entertainment over
their supper beefsteak. The restaurant manager was standing by the rear door, looking scared and fairly worthless.
Hardin asked Bill if they might talk in private. Bill told
me to keep my eye on Clements, then the two of them
went into a back room. While they were gone Clements
told me he was unarmed and wouldn't try to escape, so
why didn't I sit down and take it easy, have some coffee,
try the apple pie. He wasn't a bad fella, you ask me.

When Bill and Hardin came back out, they'd made another deal. It was the best solution they could come up
with to protect Bill's reputation and Hardin's cousin, both.
Hardin sat down next to Clements so he could talk low
and explained the setup to him. Bill was going to put him
in jail, then give Hardin the key at midnight so he could
let him out—and then Clements would leave town im-

mediately. Clements didn't look real pleased with the plan, but he didn't say anything. Hardin stood up and patted his cousin on the shoulder. "Eight o'clock, then," he said to Bill, "at the Alamo," and Bill nodded. Then Hardin went off to arrange to have Clements's horse ready for him, and me and Bill and Clements headed off to jail.

But first Bill took him into the Bull's Head saloon and bought him and me a drink. He wanted the Texans to see Clements in his custody. He wanted to remind them who the cock of the walk was in Abilene. The looks we got were red as hate, and the meanness in the room was like a bitter smoke. I gulped down my drink and held the shotgun tight, the barrels low and ready. Ben Thompson kept scowling at us from his table and muttering to the men sitting with him. At the end of the bar, Phil Coe looked unhappy. The grumbling around us got louder and full of threat. Bill acted like he didn't hear a bit of it. Even Clements looked more worried than him. Bill smiled at himself in the back-bar mirror and casually sipped his whiskey with his left hand. When we left, the place was in a rage.

Bill played a few hands of solitaire at his desk while Tom and me stood at the door and listened to the yelling and cussing over in the saloon. Suddenly the Catfoot jumped out of the shadows at the end of the gallery and grinned to see how he'd caught me and Tom by surprise. The Catfoot was Bill's best pair of ears in town. He'd been an army scout in the southwest territories and a friend of Kit Carson's. He claimed he'd snuck up within arm's length of many an Indian without ever being seen. By the time he took up scouting for Bill in the alleyways of Abilene, his drinking habit had robbed some of the sureness off his feet, but he was still the best sneakabout in town. He wore moccasin boots and dark clothes and a black kerchief around his head instead of a hat, making him look injun. Since first meeting Bill he had let his graying hair grow down to his shoulders too. He flat idolized Wild Bill and would do any fool thing he asked. What he'd been doing just now was mingling with the crowd in the Bull's Head, and he'd come to report to Bill what he'd heard. It hadn't required any sneaking about. The way he'd crossed over to the jail was just to show off.

He told Bill the Bull's Head boys were boiling mad about Clements's arrest. They were saying Bill had put the arm on him only because he was a Texan. Besides, they knew Wes was squared with Bill and they figured the fix ought to include his cousin. The way they saw it, being squared didn't mean jackshit to a man if it didn't include his kin. "Phil Coe said Clements oughtn't to be arrested in Abilene anyway," the Catfoot said, "not for something he done someplace else. And Ben, he said it goes to show no Texan can take your word for anything."

"Piss on Ben Thompson and the damn dog he rode in on," Bill said. He sent the Catfoot back to the Bull's Head and told Tom to go round up two more deputies. He wanted four shotgun guards in the jail in case the Texans tried to break out Clements.

A few minutes later I saw Hardin go in the Bull's Head. The shouting and carrying on got louder for a time, then eased off some. Tom returned with Mike Williams and Steve Wheeler and everybody loaded their scatterguns with buckshot. A half hour later Hardin left the saloon, and here came the Catfoot back again.

He said there were forty Texas hard cases in the saloon ready to help spring Clements. They were arming from a wagonload of weapons a Comanchero friend of Thompson's had brung into the alley. Thompson had been all for storming the jail right now, but then Hardin showed up and got them to hold off. He told them about the deal he'd made with Bill to spring Clements, but most of the Texans didn't believe Bill would hold to it, not even Phil Coe. Hardin told Coe he'd send him the key to Clements's cell at midnight and he could let him out himself. "If Coe don't get the key by twelve," the Catfoot said, "that wild bunch is gonna come storming."

A few minutes before eight, Bill stood up and stretched. He checked the loads in both navies, then adjusted his tie and put on his hat. "When Coe comes here with the key," he told Tom, "don't fuss with him, just hand Clements over." He was being casual but it was all show. The situation had put him in a corner and was agitating him no end. Behind his easy smile he was in a fury.

So off Bill went to meet Hardin at the Alamo. Tom and me sat out on the jailhouse gallery, watching the street and listening hard, ready to run to help him at the first gunshot. The saloon lights blazed into the street. The crowd in the Bull's Head kept growing, and the music and the yahooing was louder than ever. Nothing like the possibility of mob action to put a bunch of peckerwoods in a high-time mood.

Later we heard all about how Bill and Hardin had done the town together. They made a big show of being pals and took turns buying a round for the house every place they went. Their gambling luck was pure gold. They won over a thousand dollars apiece on that spree. You ask me, such a profitable streak of luck ought to've pretty well made up for whatever agitation Bill's pride had to endure that evening. But unfortunately—especially for the Catfoot—Bill didn't see it that way.

Sometime around eleven a big hack stopped in front of the Bull's Head and about seven or eight painted cats lit off it, teasing each other and laughing loud, all of them drunk and bold as brass. They spotted me and Tom watching them and started whistling and cooing and having sport with us. I didn't really mind their attention, but Tom got hacked about it. He always was a little stiff-necked about the soiled sisterhood. I believe his people were hard-shell Baptists.

"Oh, *deputy*," one called out, "you *pinched* any bad girls tonight?" and they all snickered like fillies. Coe came out and snapped at them, and most of them quick followed him inside, but two of them hung back, giggling and whispering together and looking our way. One came weaving out into the street and said, "Hey, Deputies! Lookee here!" She pulled down the front of her dress and showed us her bare teats for about one enjoyable second—firm

creamy things, they were, with big pink tips—then yanked
the dress back up and laughed like she was being tickled.

"That tears it," Tom said. He jumped off the sidewalk
and stomped over to her and put her under arrest for public
indecency. "In*decency*?" she whooped. "In fucking *Abilene*?" Tom grabbed her by the arm and tugged her toward the jail, but she was a fighter and started kicking at
him and trying to bite his hand. Then the other one ran
up and jumped on his back, and he really had his work
cut out. I didn't have much choice but to lend him a hand.

As I pried the one off his back he let out a yelp and I
saw she had her teeth in his ear. Then she turned on me,
trying her level best to knee me in the jewel sack. I finally
got her in a bear hug, pinning her arms to her sides and
holding her too close to knee me—and getting a good bit
of enjoyment from it besides, I will admit. I guess she was
too, because she started chuckling and wiggling around in
my arms without really fighting to get free. Meantime,
Tom was gripping the other one's arms crossways over
her chest from behind so she couldn't turn around and hit
or kick at him anymore. Her teats were bulging out of her
dress, but she wasn't funning like mine, and she kept cussing and fussing and giving Tom a terrible time of it.

I heard laughter and saw we'd drawn a crowd of spectators, including Bill and Hardin. They were applauding
us like we were some kind of street show. "Real good,
boys," Bill said, "real fine police work. I think you'd best
put that desperado in irons, Tom, before she busts loose
of you and rawhides the whole town all by herself." Hardin thought that was funny, but Tom was in a sweaty rage
and feeling a good bit foolish to be struggling with that
feisty girl while Bill and Hardin and a bunch of gawkers
looked on and laughed about it.

Just then she bit him good on the hand. He gave a howl
and punched her so hard she would've fallen if he hadn't
been holding her tight. She tried to pull away but he held
her fast and smacked her twice more, beating her down to
her knees.

Bill rushed up and socked him on the jaw with as pretty

a roundhouse as I've ever seen. Knocked him loose of her
and down on his ass. For good measure he gave him a
kick in the belly that blew the breath out of him. Tom got
up on all fours and puked his supper into the street.

Bill helped the girl up, calling her Suzanne. Now I recognized her as a Tennessee girl who worked at Violet's.
She said she was all right and to just leave her be. The
girl I had hold of said to let go, so I did, and she went
and helped Suzanne to adjust her clothes and fix herself
up some. Hardin was grinning big about the whole thing.
Bill gave Tom a hand up and retrieved his hat for him.
Tom wiped at his mouth with his shirtsleeve and winced
at the pain of his jaw. Bill asked if it was broke and he
shook his head. He looked at Bill like a boy who's just
got whipped by his daddy. "Son, you don't *never* hit a
woman," Bill said. He dusted off Tom's back while Tom
felt of his damaged ear. "Leastways not unless she's trying to steal your money," he said. He looked thoughtful
for a moment. "Course now," he said, "if she was to try
making off with your *horse*, you'd be right to shoot the
bitch."

Bill and Hardin escorted the girls into the Bull's Head,
and me and Tom went back up on the gallery and sat there
for more than half an hour without saying anything. Tom
kept rubbing his jaw and fingering his ear. Then Bill and
Hardin left the Bull's Head together and headed off for
the Applejack. They were followed by a man named Arlo
Greaves, who worked for Phil Coe. Finally Tom said, "All
this business with Hardin is just chewing Bill's nerves to
bits, ain't it?" I couldn't help but laugh along with him.
The more I think about it, the more it seems to me Tom
Carson had enough grit to fill a cattle car. And he for damn
sure loved Bill Hickok more than the man deserved.

As the hour got close to midnight the hullabaloo in the
Bull's Head was loud enough to disturb the dead. A bunch
of hard cases were gathered at the saloon door and letting
us see they were armed and ready. There was no sign of
the Catfoot, who must've figured we sure didn't need him

just then to tell us what the Bull's Head boys were up to. At ten minutes of midnight some two dozen armed men had spilled out of the saloon and into the street and were rebel yelling and twirling pistols and passing bottles among themselves. "Get your hat, Manning!" one hollered. "Hey, Deputies," another yelled, waving his pistol at us, "I got my jail key right here!"

And then here came Arlo Greaves down the street. He pushed his way through the crowd and into the saloon. A minute later Phil Coe came out and spoke to the Texans and there were groans of disappointment. Coe crossed over to us and handed Tom the cell key. When Clements walked out the front door, the Texans cheered, and he waved his hat at them. Coe gave him a pistol. "It's one of Wes's," he told him. "He sent it along so you won't be traveling nekkid."

Clements went off with Arlo Greaves to wherever his horse was waiting for him. Phil Coe gave us a shit-eating grin and then strutted back to the Bull's Head with the wild boys at his heels. Him and Bill had always got along good, but not after that night. He'd made an enemy of Bill for life. (For Coe, that was only another two months, till the day he got drunk as a coot and shot at a dog in the street for fun—and then stupidly fired on Bill when he came out to arrest him. Bill put two bullets in Coe's gut and it took Fancy Phil two hard days to die. Sad to say, Mike Williams came running around the corner with his gun in his hand just as Bill shot Coe—and in the hot blur of the moment Bill whirled and shot him too. Killed his own deputy. The newspaper went hard on him for it. It claimed he'd become more dangerous to the town than the wild boys he was supposed to protect it from. The townsfolk agreed, and Abilene fired Wild Bill. But all that came later.)

The day after Clements was set free, Bill seemed distracted. He lost hand after hand in the Alamo and looked to be drinking more serious than usual. That evening when I got back to the jail after making rounds, he was at his

desk, sharing a bottle with the Catfoot. They were talking
about their scouting days for the Union army. Bill said he
once knew a scout, a half-breed Apache, who'd bet the
other scouts he could slip into the commanding officer's
tent while he was asleep and cut off a lock of his beard
without being discovered. "Hell, we thought we had us
some easy money and each bet him twenty dollars," Bill
said. Him and another scout watched from the bushes as
the breed crawled off toward the major's tent—and they
were still watching twenty minutes later when the breed
tapped them on the shoulder. "He was grinning to beat
hell and holding a crop of the major's red beard," Bill
said. "The next day you could see the spot on the CO's
face where the crop was taken. Damn breed was the best
sneakup I ever knew."

The Catfoot looked offended. "It's some of us could of
shaved the man without waking him," he said. "It's nothing to take a lock of hair off a sleeping man." Besides,
he said, all that could of happened to the sneakup if he'd
been caught was to get locked up overnight and then
kicked off the army payroll. "No sneakup job's worth
bragging about unless it could get you killed," he said.
"Like all them injuns I snuck up on. Now *those* sneakups
took nerve." Bill smiled and said that was mighty bold
talk. The Catfoot said he was ready to back it up anytime.
"Just you name the bet," he said, tossing off a drink.

Bill affected to think about it, stroking his mustaches
while he poured the Catfoot another. Then he dug four
fifty-dollar gold pieces out of his pocket and slapped them
on the desktop. "I'll put these against that fine new Mexican saddle of yours," he said, "that you can't take a crop
off Hardin's head tonight."

Tom Carson told me later he was fairly sure Bill was
just funning with the Catfoot, trying to get him to admit
he wasn't the sneakup he used to be, but I don't know. If
that was so, why didn't he stop the Catfoot from going
through with it when he saw he was really going to try?
Tom's answer was that Bill must of thought Hardin would
treat it as a joke if he caught Catfoot in the act. Yeah,

sure. Shows how damn blind Tom could make himself when it came to Bill's mean side, that's what I think.

Anyhow, later that night, there we were, me and Tom and the Catfoot, standing in the shadows across the street from the American House, watching Hardin and his cousin Gip Clements going in after a night on the town. There was a moon out and the Catfoot's eyes were shining with excitement as much as from all the whiskey he'd put down. His breath could've killed bugs. He was carrying a straight razor he'd honed for an hour. "I guess old Longhair will sure enough have to admit who's the best sneakup in the world after tonight, hey?" He gave us a grin and vanished into the shadows.

We passed the time watching the hotel and listening to the music from the saloons and parlor houses on the next block, the lowing of the cattle at the rail yard, the shouts and yahoos in the distance, the now-and-then sound of breaking glass followed by high female laughter. The damn town did know how to have a good time.

And then *bam-bam-bam!*—gunshots from the American House. There were three more as we raced across the street and charged into the lobby. "Upstairs!" the desk clerk yelled, peeking around from behind the counter.

The hallway reeked of gunsmoke. The Catfoot was curled up on the floor in a mess of blood, wide-eyed dead. He was hugging something tight against his chest, which turned out to be Hardin's pants—the cousin's too. Damn fool must of thought it'd be funny to take them back to Bill along with the lock of hair that he had gripped in one hand. There was no sign of the razor.

The Catfoot's blood trailed back to a shut door a few feet down the hall. For a moment I couldn't hear a thing but my own hard breathing—and then I heard a soft scuffling coming from inside the room. Tom heard it too, and signaled to me to cover him, then ran up beside the door with his pistol cocked. Behind us the stairs were suddenly full of stomping boots and loud voices. "Give it up, Hardin!" Tom hollered at the door.

Then Bill and Mike were in the hallway, both carrying

shotguns. They had to have been damn close by to get up
there as quick as they did. Bill hardly glanced at the Catfoot. He cocked the shotgun and nodded at Tom and Tom
gave the door a hell of a kick, busting it open wide. Bill
thrust the shotgun in the doorway and fired both barrels.
Christ! In that little hallway the blasts were loud as dynamite.

I followed Tom and Bill through the door, ready to
shoot anything that moved, but the room was empty. I
couldn't hear anything for the ringing in my ears. Bill
rushed to the window to take a look out on the portico
and down in the alley. I peeked over his shoulder and saw
Steve looking up at us, waving his arms and yelling
something. I saw Bill's lips say "Shit!" He shoved me
aside and hustled out of the room with the rest of us on
his tail.

There was a crowd of drunks and curious citizens already gathered on the street. Bill pulled Steve back into
the alley to question him out of their hearing. Steve looked
ready to cry—and Bill looked ready to hit him. Steve said
Hardin and Clements had dropped down off the portico
and got the jump on him. Hardin held a razor to his throat
while Clements relieved him of his shotgun and pistol.
They'd grabbed the nearest two horses off the front hitch-
ing post and rode off together to the end of town. Then
one kept going on the south road and the other broke off
to the east. He didn't know which was Hardin. Except for
their hats and boots, they'd both been in their underclothes.

That shut us all up a moment. We were all thinking the
same thing. Mike was the first to chuckle about it. Then
Tom gave a little snort like he was fighting to hold it back,
and I felt myself grinning hard. I mean, I could just see
it—Hardin the mankiller hightailing it out of Abilene in
his underwear. Then all three of us busted out laughing,
and then Steve couldn't help but join in. Bill tried not to.
He looked up at the stars and stroked his mustaches like
he was trying to think of something else, but he couldn't
pull it off, and in another minute all five of us were laugh-

ing like loonies. We just stood there in the alley, laughing and laughing, with a crowd of citizens gawking at us from the street. "They looked like plucked chickens!" Steve said—and we all doubled up again. It was a good minute before we got ourselves under control and dried our eyes.

Bill cleared his throat and then said in a loud professional voice, so all the citizens could hear, "*This* one ain't no self-defense, not when the dead man's got no gun nor any other weapon on him." I thought of the razor and gave him a look, but he stared me down quick. "You deputies," he said, still in that loud politician's voice, "you get the chance, you shoot him on sight."

He sent Mike and Steve to hunt for the fugitive who took the east trail, and told me and Tom to search for the one who went south. If we hadn't picked up a trail by midmorning we were to turn back for home. We saddled up and rode out hard, thinking we might gain some ground on our quarry if he thought he was safely distant and had slowed down.

Just after sunup me and Tom came across one of Jake Johnson's cattle camps. The ramrod was a fella named Coran, who said they hadn't seen any sign of Wes Hardin or Gip Clements, but invited us to have some biscuit and molasses and a cup of coffee. We were much obliged—and mighty hungry after riding all night. I was just started on my second biscuit when a voice directly behind us said, "Hands up, sonbitches, or I'll turn you into dogmeat." He'd got some clothes from somebody, and it was Steve's shotgun he was holding on us.

The bastard made us take off all our clothes. I mean every single damn stitch, right down to our bare feet. He had the saddles taken off our horses and thrown in the river, together with our guns and boots. Then he told us to mount up bareback—but he had to tell us twice because we couldn't hardly hear him for all the laughing them cowhands were doing at the sight of our white buck-nekkid asses and our peters and balls all a-dangle in the bright sunshine. Hardin told us not to bother trying to circle around to another outfit to ask for clothes. He'd already sent the word out for none of the outfits to help us. "Only thing any Texas outfit'll give you skinned rabbits is a bullet in the ass," he said. We rode off with their laughter ringing in our red ears.

As soon as we went over a distant rise and out of their sight, I reined up and told Tom I wasn't going back to Abilene. We'd never be able to live down the shame, I told him. He said it was shameful all right, but there wasn't anything to do but face the music. No, sir, I said, not me. The music we'd face would be humiliating laughter, and we'd hear it every time we stepped out in the public streets for the rest of our days in Abilene. Tom was hangdog as ever I'd seen, but he said there wasn't no choice, not for him, he had to go back. I called him a fool for it, but he just shrugged and rode off.

I angled off to the west before turning south, and rode for most of the day without seeing another living soul until I came on a team of buffalo wagons just before sunset. I smelled them before I caught sight of them. The wagons were heaped high with the stiff flat-cured hides they'd taken on the high plains. Naturally the skinners all had a good laugh at the sight of me. I was bright red with sunburn, and was already peeling where the blistered skin had bust open. Even my peter was burned. It was pure pain to put on the shirt and pants and moccasins they spared me, especially since the clothes were so stiff with dried blood and gore. I near choked on the stink of them, but I counted myself lucky to have something to wear, and I thanked the skinners kindly. Their generosity extended to a bundle of buffalo jerky, a canteen of water, and a rank old blanket to use for a saddle. Then they went their way and I went mine.

Later on I heard tell that Tom Carson had met his humiliation like a man. And after they'd had their laughs and their fill of jokes at his expense, the town showed Tom even more respect than ever before, and I mean Wild Bill too. Damn.

PART FOUR

BLOOD-
LETTINGS

FROM

The El Paso Daily Herald,

20 AUGUST 1895

Mr. R. B. Stevens, the proprietor of the Acme Saloon, said:

"I was on the street and someone told me there was likely to be trouble at my saloon between Wes Hardin and John Selman, Sr. I came down to the saloon and walked in. Selman was sitting outside the door. Hardin was standing just inside the door at the bar, shaking dice with Henry Brown. I walked on back into the reading room and sat down where I could see the bar. Soon Selman and Shackleford came in and took a drink. Then I understood Shackleford to say to Selman: 'Come out, now; you are drinking, and I don't want you to have any trouble.' They went out together. I then supposed Selman had gone away and there would be no trouble. I leaned back against a post and was talking to Shorty Anderson, and could not see the front door, and do not know who came in. When Selman and Shackleford came in they took a drink at the inside of the bar. Hardin and Brown were standing at the end of the bar next the door. I did not see Selman when the shooting took place. When I went into the barroom Hardin was lying on the floor near the door and was dead. I walked to the door and looked out. Selman was standing in front with several others, Capt. Carr among them. When Capt. Carr came into the saloon I asked him to take charge of Hardin's body and keep the crowd out. He said he could not move the body until the crowd viewed it. I saw Carr take two pistols off Hardin's body. One was a white-handled pistol and the other a black-handled one. They were both .41 caliber Colts. The bullet that passed through Hardin's head struck a mirror frame and glanced off and fell in front of the bar at the lower end. In the floor where Hardin fell are three bullet holes in triangular shape about a span across. They range straight through the floor.''

────────────── FROM ──────────────

The Life of John Wesley Hardin as Written by Himself

"When I married Jane Bowen, we were expecting the police to come anytime...."

─────

"Mob law had become supreme in Texas, as the hangings of my relatives and friends amply proved."

─────

"Right there over my brother's grave I swore to avenge my brother's death and could I but tell you what I have done in that way without laying myself liable, you would think I have kept my pledge well. While I write this, I say from the deepest depths of my heart that my desire for revenge is not satisfied, and if I live another year ... be the consequences what they may, I propose to take life."

─────

"I took an oath ... never to surrender at the muzzle of a gun. I have never done so, either, although I have been forced through main strength to give up several times."

─────

"It was war to the knife with me."

Henry Porter

If Wes really wanted to try and avoid trouble when he got back from Kansas that summer, the Sandies was probably the last place he ought to have come to. Then again, this was where his Clements kin all lived—and of course there was Jane Bowen, who he was in love with and wanted to marry.

It was awful hard and bloody times. Ed Davis's bullying police were getting thick as flies everywhere you looked. Davis called Gonzales and DeWitt counties the worst places in Texas for feuding and killings and outlaw carrying on, and I guess that was true enough. The Sutton-Taylor Feud was getting meaner all the time, and vigilantes and night riders roamed the countryside. It was common knowledge, however, that a lot of Sutton's night riders were white-trash bastards who wore the State Police uniform by day.

Wes lived at Manning Clements's place out at Elm Creek and spent his days helping his cousins on their ranch. In the evenings he courted Jane. Things stayed quiet for about a month after him and the Clementses got back from Kansas. Then one day two State Policemen, a pair of big Nigra honkers, came into Smiley looking for him. Some lowlife had likely tipped them to him being in town. They asked after him from house to house and store to store, scaring the womenfolk and children like they always enjoyed doing. They finally come in my barbershop, where

Wes was taking a shave. They had their hands on their guns and took a careful look at everybody in the shop. Wes had a faceful of lather, and the Nigras looked at him extra hard. "You gents ought to be careful with them pistolas," Wes said to them real pleasantlike. "You don't want to shoot somebody by accident." The Nigra sergeant was a fellow named Green Parramore, and we all knew him for the bullying bastard he was. He said they'd been told John Wesley Hardin was in town and they were looking for him. Wes wiped a towel across his face with his left hand, keeping his right under the barber sheet, and asked Parramore if he'd know Hardin on sight. The Nigra said no, but he figured somebody with a use for a share of the reward would point him out if he was around. "I believe you right," Wes said. "Hell, *I'll* point him out to you for a share of the reward." The two Nigras quick looked around all wary. "He *here*?" Parramore asked. "*Right* there," Wes tells him with a big smile.

Parramore's eyes went big as snowballs and he started to pull his pistol, but Wes fired from under the sheet and hit him over the eye and sent the back of his head splattering through the window. The other one was already running out the door as Wes fired at him and tore a chunk off his uniform jacket. Wes ran out after him with the sheet still around his neck and lather clinging to his chin, but that nigger was scooting like a scalded dog. If Wes had stopped running and took aim he'd of dropped him sure, but he kept firing on the run and so missed him every time. Folks were whooping and diving for cover every which way. The Nigra ran into an alley and hopped over a fence and disappeared into the woods north of town. He was mighty damn lucky, that one.

Well now, you can bet the town buzzed for days with the story of that shooting. Then came the rumor that a posse of a dozen hard-case vigilantes was on its way over from San Antonio to arrest Wes or kill him, whichever it took for them to get the reward. We didn't see nothing of Wes nor the Clements boys for the next two days and most of us figured they'd all rode off to hide somewhere. But didn't no vigilante bunch come around, either.

Next Saturday morning, who shows up in my shop but Manning Clements—smiling from ear to ear with a story to tell. A couple of days earlier, he'd got word the San Antone posse was only a few miles from Elm Creek and coming fast. He went straight to Wes and advised him to head for the hill country and hide out for a time.

But Wes wouldn't have any of that. He told Manning the day he'd run from a fight was the day he'd start wearing a dress and take up knitting. He wouldn't even let Manning and his brothers join with him. It was his fight, he said, and he'd be the one to fight it. He armed himself with four revolvers and rode off to meet the posse. Manning tried to do like Wes wanted and stay out of it, but after about ten minutes he said the hell with it and rounded up Jim and Gip and they headed out after him to help out.

They were just about to Salty Creek when they heard shooting. They spurred their horses up over the near rise and saw eight or nine riders hightailing it north with Wes riding hard after them, firing with two pistols at once. Two vigilantes were already stretched on the ground, and then a third went tumbling off his mount. Wes chased the others right on over the next rise and out of sight. "It was some cheerful sight," Manning said, "all them brave possemen running scared from one Sandies bad-ass."

The Clements boys started out after him, but before they reached the next rise, here came Wes loping on back, grinning big and waving at them. The last of the three men he'd shot was trying to get to his knees, and as Wes trotted by him, he shot him in the head and hollered, "One to grow on!"

One of the fellas listening to Manning's story, a drummer passing through, muttered something about how it didn't seem too awful "sporting" of Wes to shoot that third fella in the head thataway. Manning jumped out of the barber chair and grabbed him by the collar in both fists. "That son of a bitch and all the rest of them rode all the way down here to kill Wes!" he shouted in the fella's face, which turned about white as a sheet. "All of them against just one of him! So what the hell you mean *sporting*, you stupid shitbucket?" A bunch of us managed to calm Manning down just enough to let loose of the fella, and I mean that stranger cleared out *quick*.

The tale of Wes's fight against the San Antonio posse spread through the Sandies like fire in dry grass. It made all the newspapers. Some editorials called him a hero for standing up to the damned State Police and the cowardly vigilantes who supported them—but others referred to him as a bloody desperado who ought to be shot down like a dog or strung up from the highest oak in Texas.

We then got word that a mob of about fifty Nigra police and some of their white-trash amigos were threatening to come to Smiley and burn the town down for being a friend to Wes Hardin. When Wes heard about it, he went to the telegraph office and sent a wire to State Police headquarters saying, "Come on down. Won't one of you be going back." When they still hadn't showed themselves a week later, we knew they weren't ever coming. Fact is, we never did see too much of the State Police in Gonzales after Wes sent them that telegram.

Wes then left the Sandies for a time. Some said he'd gone up to Hill County to visit with his daddy and momma, and some said he'd gone to San Antone to start a horse business. I don't know. The Clementses must of known, of course, but they never said, and I don't blame them. You never knew who might be whispering into the ears of the State Police. He didn't show up around here again till shortly after Christmas, when Gip Clements got married to Annie Tenelle. Matter of fact, it was at Gip and Annie's wedding dance that Wes and Jane announced their engagement.

Julia Harper

The wedding bells rang for them in Riddleville on a cool sunny day in March. They moved into a small house out on Fred Duderstadt's ranch. Wes talked about rounding up a herd and making another drive to Kansas along with my Lucas and the Clements brothers, but then they heard the Kansas beef market was still too low to make a drive worthwhile. So the Clementses decided to work a small herd of steers over to the coast for shipment to Mobile, and Wes decided he would try the horse business for a while. My Lucas and his brother John threw in with him. They'd heard it was a good market for horses just across the river in Sabine Parish.

While Lucas and John got to work building a corral on the Duderstadt place, Wes rode down to the King ranch and made a deal for horseflesh. It was expected he'd be gone about twelve days or so, but he'd only been gone barely more than a week when Lucas went out to the corral one morning and found Wes's horse Old Bob in there, white-caked all over and too played out to even lift its head. Wes had bought that fine horse from my brother-in-law John, and now it was ruined for fair.

When Wes showed up later in the day and Lucas asked him what had happened to Old Bob, he grinned a little shamefaced and said he'd made a straight-through ride from just south of the Nueces to Gonzales County. That's over a hundred miles, and Wes said he'd rode it in a little over six hours. It's no wonder the poor animal was foundered. I never could abide mistreatment of a horse, and I asked Lucas whatever had possessed Wesley Hardin to do such a thing to Old Bob. He said Wes told him he'd all of a sudden got so lonely for his bride he couldn't stand it and just wanted to get home to her as quick as he could. When he told me this, Lucas shrugged and studied his right hand like he always did when he wasn't sure if a thing made sense or not.

But of course it did. There's lots of things somebody might do they wouldn't normally except they're neck-deep in love. Wes had rode that horse near to death for the love of Jane. I pitied the poor horse, but it made all the sense in the world.

You could see how awful much he loved her just by how he beamed on her all evening at the party Manning Clements threw for them at his house toward the end of May. We were celebrating Jane's announcement that they were expecting their first child late next winter.

They soon had the herd all ready, and Lucas and John agreed to drive it to Hemphill, and because Daddy Harper was sheriff of Sabine County, Wes thought it was as safe a town as any for them to meet up in and take care of business. He went on ahead of the herd to visit for a spell with some of his kinfolk in Livingston. As I recall, he bought himself a racer in Polk County and took that horse with him to Hemphill. Lucas said that animal won Wes just barrels of money.

After Lucas and John showed up with the herd and the horses got sold, the two of them decided to stay in Hemphill and visit with their daddy awhile. But Wes wanted to get back to Jane and said so long. The thing is, he didn't head back directly. He started back by way of his old stomping grounds in Trinity County so he could call on more kinfolk he hadn't seen for a time. It turned out to be a real bad idea, though, because it was in Trinity he got himself shotgunned.

John Gates

I wish I'd used my head sooner and not cleaned up the blood before I realized how good it would of been for business to leave it be. I should of let it dry and marked off the spot with some paint or a rope. Even so, my trade about doubled for the next few months with gawkers come to see where it happened. At least I was smart enough to pick the buckshot out of the doorjamb before they did. I sold each shot for as much as two dollars apiece, and when I ran out I just broke open some shells in the back room and sold that as the real thing. Damn fools never knew the difference.

He came in with his cousin Barnett Jones and a few other friends of theirs. Barnett lived over near Livingston and had been in my saloon many a time. I knew him real well. I was right proud when he introduced me to Wes. I had a nice ten-pin alley in the back room, and the two of them went back there to roll a few games. I had Freddie spell me at the front bar so I could go back there and watch.

After winning about four, five games in a row, Barnett said he wouldn't play him anymore. "I'm just stealing it from you, the way you play," he told Wes. "I'll play for fun, but no more betting. Daddy'd skin me alive if he found out I'd took such advantage of kin." But Wes insisted they keep playing for money. "A man's supposed to give a fella a chance to win his money back, god-

damnit.'' And so on. You know how it is with a fella
who's losing bad.

Right about then, this fella who'd been watching them
play says he wouldn't mind wagering on a few rolls. His
name was Phil Sublett. He was an overdressed dandy with
a thin mustache and a high opinion of himself, a tinhorn,
always on the lookout for a sure thing. He must of reckoned he had one just then against Wes.

''Fine with me!'' Wes says. ''Don't much matter to me
who I win it back from. What's your bet, mister?'' Sublett
says how does three dollars a ball sound? Wes says how
does five? The gambler smiles real big and says, ''It's a
bet.'' So they each put up fifty dollars to cover all ten
balls and hand the stake to me.

Well, sir, Wes wins the first two rolls and everybody in
the place is laughing and cheering at what we all figure
ain't nothing more than simple luck, considering the way
he was playing just a minute earlier. Then he wins the
next two balls and Sublett does some hot cussing and
looks at Wes out the sides of his eyes and Wes laughs and
says something about the luck of the Irish. When he wins
the fifth roll, we all just look at each other. Barnett gives
me a wink and I finally catch on how bad they've horn-
swoggled Sublett.

When Wes won the sixth roll, even Sublett knew he'd
been taken in and was pretty hot about it. He said he
wanted to lower the bet to two dollars a ball. Nothing
doing, Wes said; they made the bet for five and that was
what it'd stay. Sublett said either the bet got lowered or
he was quitting. Wes says, ''You quit and you forfeit the
whole bet.''

Well, Sublett was a tinhorn gambler but he didn't lack
for guts, just brains, and he grabbed for his pocket gun.
Wes caught his gunhand by the wrist and slapped him
three or four quick times across the mouth, then twisted
the little gun away from him and pushed it up into his
nose. I thought Sublett had breathed his last. But Barnett
grabbed Wes's arm and said, ''Hold on, cousin—it ain't
worth it!'' Sublett's eyes looked like boiled eggs and his

face was splotched red around his mouth where Wes had slapped him. Wes let go of him and said, "You best give up gambling, hoss, if you gonna take losing as hard as all that."

He hands me Sublett's derringer and I stick it under my apron. "Let's get on with it," he says, and then rolls again. Sublett loses that roll worst of all, naturally, as shook up as he was. "Oh, hell," Wes says, "now it's like playing against some softbrain. This ain't no contest." He takes the stake money from me and counts out his own fifty plus thirty-five of Sublett's and hands him the fifteen left over. "Here, bubba," he tells him, "game's over. Come on, I'll buy you a drink. Hell, I'll buy *everybody* a drink!"

We all go out to the front room and Wes stands the house a round. Then I notice Sublett's left the scene. He'd likely slipped out the side-alley door while everybody was cheering Wes and thanking him for his generosity. I reckoned he felt too damn shamed to stay and drink with us.

Ten minutes later Wes went over to the front doors to have a look outside—which was the worst thing he could of done at that moment. Somebody in the back of the room yelled, "Watch it, Wes!" And there was Sublett, standing just inside the side-alley door, aiming a shotgun. Wes started to turn and pull his pistol, but there was only thirty feet between them and Sublett had the drop on him and couldn't miss, not with Wes squared in the doorway like he was, just a perfect target.

The charge hit him just above the hip and knocked him clean out of the room. Everybody dropped to the floor and Sublett fired the second barrel at the empty doorway and took out a good chunk of doorjamb. Then he lowered the shotgun and stood there for a minute, looking like he couldn't believe he'd done it.

Sublett was just starting to smile when Wes lurched back in through the door, clutching at his mangled side, his face all twisted up in pain. He yelled, "You sonbitch!" and got off a wild shot just as Sublett dropped the scattergun and ran out.

The blood was rolling off his wound and drenching his pant leg, but he staggered back outside as Sublett came out from the alley and ran down the street. Wes stumbled out into the street after him and got off a couple of shots, and Tim Jackson swore he saw Sublett catch one in the shoulder, but I don't know. Sublett disappeared around the corner and that's the last any of us ever saw of him. He had to of had a horse all saddled and waiting to get away as fast as he did.

Wes managed to gimp about ten feet down the street before he dropped, and we all went running up to him. He was gasping and wide-eyed. "I reckon I'm killed," he said.

Barnett kept trying to soothe him as me and a bunch of the boys hoisted him up, one on each leg and one under each arm, and started toting him fast over to Doc Carrington's office. It was a hell of a wound and left a bright red trail all the way to the doc's. I thought sure he'd be empty as a tore-open water bag by the time we got him there.

On the way over, he told Barnett to take his money belt off him, that it had about two thousand dollars in gold, and that his saddlebags were holding another two or three hundred in silver. He told him to get the money to his wife and to tell her he tried to avoid this trouble but had no choice in the matter.

He was breathing rough when we got him into Doc Carrington's, but his eyes were still burning with life. We put him on the table in the office and the doc sent one of the fellas to go get Doc Lester from his office in the livery, where he tended to animals and people both. Then he ran the rest of us on outside. Barnett was the last to come out. He had the money belt with him. It was dripping blood and had seven buckshot wedged in it.

– Dr. T. C. Carrington –

If his assailant had aimed at his head instead of his middle, they would have carried him directly to the undertaker rather than to me. Or if the shooter had been standing five to ten feet closer to him so that the load had not spread quite so much before impact. Or if he hadn't been wearing a well-packed money belt which shielded him from some of the shot. But if, if, if—*if* is meaningless. It is the premise of a parlor game. What *might* have happened to him is what *did* happen to him. And thus he was not killed.

He was, however, at the lip of the abyss, as it were, when they brought him to me. The buckshot charge had torn away a sizable portion of tissue from his side and had severed several large veins. My immediate obligation was to contain the bleeding. But I was also quite concerned with two distinct entry wounds positioned rather more toward the navel. I turned him on his side but perceived no exit perforations, so it was clear the two shot were still in him. I was inclined to believe the wound was mortal, for his blood loss was quite severe. Yet his eyes showed clear focus and his breathing, though rapid, was even and strong. He was neither lung-shot nor wounded in the stomach, and his spirit seemed robust. I have seen many men die for lack of endurance against the shock of their wounds, but had Mr. Hardin expired on my table, it would not have been for want of grit.

By the time Dr. Lester arrived, I had extracted eight
scattered and relatively shallow-perforation buckshot and
had determined that the two wounds closer to the navel
had lacerated the kidney and were most likely positioned
near the lower juncture of posterior ribs and spine. It
would be difficult to extract them, but not to do so at once
would entail the greater jeopardy. Dr. Lester concurred.
Up to this point, Mr. Hardin had endured my probings and
extractions with impressive fortitude, holding tightly to the
edges of the table and giving little evidence of his pain
except for an occasional grimace and grunt. He rejected
the opiate I offered him to dull the even greater pain he
would feel when I went after the buckshot at his spine.
"If death's going to get me," he said, "I want to give it
a clear look in the eye when it does."

We labored over him for more than an hour, and though
he cursed loudly at times in reaction to my deep and sin-
uous explorations with the forceps, his tolerance of the
pain was extraordinary. He bore the cauterizing iron with
hardly more than a quivering flexion of sinew at each ap-
plication. A man of less constitution would not likely have
survived the procedure.

When at last I had removed the two buckshot, we
stitched the gaping wound as best we could and carefully
bandaged it. Lester and I looked as though we'd been in
attendance at a hog slaughter. We were blood to the elbows and our aprons were heavily stained. Mr. Hardin was
deathly pale from the loss of blood, and his sweat exuded
severe pain's prodigious reek. Yet he did not lose consciousness at any point in the procedure. He even smiled
when we told him the ordeal was over. "Damn shame,"
he said in a whisper, "it was so much fun." Grit.

I informed him quite frankly that the chance for his
survival was no better than sixty percent. The immediate
dangers, as I made clear to him, were fever and infec-
tion—and, of course, a recurrence of profuse hermorrhag-
ing if he did not keep passively to his bed while
recuperating. He thanked me warmly for his services, assured me that his kinsman would see to my recompense,

and said he would obey my instructions to the letter.

His friends made arrangements for him at a hotel across the street. Despite my protests, his kinsman, a lively fellow named Barnett, pressed a pair of twenty-dollar gold pieces on me, an exceptionally generous payment. As they were easing him onto a litter to carry him to his quarters, I heard Barnett whisper to him that they had cut the telegraph wires and posted lookouts at either end of town.

I have on many occasions been asked how it feels to have saved the life of a man who had already killed so many, and who, because of my surgical skill, survived to kill so many more. My answer has never varied. I am proud to have done it. I applied all my skill to save a man in extremis and I succeeded. As one sworn to the Oath of Hippocrates, I could have done no less than try. And I utterly reject any responsibility whatsoever for his subsequent depredations. He was the captain of his soul, I of mine—and I shall discuss it no further.

—— Billy Teagarden ——

Wes and I had been schoolmates in Sumpter. Daddy had doctored his family from the time they came to East Texas from Dallas. Then Wes went off and became the notorious John Wesley Hardin, and I didn't lay eyes on him again for nearly five years, not until the night Barnett Jones and some others brought him to our house in a wagon, burning with fever and bleeding to death.

Barnett called out for Daddy, saying he had somebody bad hurt who needed tending. We recognized his voice, so I let down the hammers on the shotgun I'd grabbed up when we first heard the horses, and I followed Daddy out the door. The moonlight cut white and sharp through the dark trees and across the hats of the mounted men. Daddy held the lantern over the man laying in the wagon and we saw it was Wes. He was unconscious and breathing rough. Daddy felt of his pulse and checked his eyes, then held the lantern close to his sopping wound. He smelled half dead already.

He'd been shot in Trinity six days before, Barnett told us. For two days Doc Carrington had thought he would die, but then his fever broke and he started taking food and looked like he'd recover. "But some son of a bitch yapped to the police," Barnett said, "and we had to quick get him out of Trinity. Wes said to bring him here."

They'd been a day and a night on the old Trinity trace,

moving slow and careful, and it was God's own wonder they didn't meet up with any police patrols. But it's a rough old trace they'd come on, and all that bouncing around in the wagon hadn't done Wes a bit of good. Barnett said he'd been passing out off and on.

Daddy had him carried around to the lean-to in back of the house. I held the lantern up close for him while he worked at cleaning the wound and patching it where the stitches had come undone. The sweat was just steaming off Wes, his fever was so high. He was pretty much out of his head and mumbling nonsense.

While Daddy did all he could for him, Momma poured coffee for the fellas who'd brought him and passed around some warmed-over pone. They gobbled it up quick and left, all except Barnett. He was still at the table when Daddy got done with Wes. He told us he'd set up in the south woods, at a spot where he could watch both the main road and the old trace for any sign of somebody coming.

As sudden as all that, Wes was our responsibility. Momma's face was hard as stone about it, but she didn't speak her objections. Still, every time she looked over toward the lean-to, it was clear how much she hated Wes Hardin for putting her family in such danger with the law.

Daddy and me sat up with him all that night. Just before Barnett had gone off to the woods to watch the roads, Daddy'd had a whispered talk with him, then gone to the shed and got a pick and spade and placed them up against the lean-to door. If Wes had died in the night, he would have been in the ground before sunrise, and nobody but us would have known whatever became of him.

I was brought out of a doze just before dawn by Wes saying, "I could sure do with a drink of water, Billy-boy, if you don't mind." Billy-boy was what he always used to call me in our school days. Daddy was sleeping with his chin in his chest in a chair by the door. I dipped some water and held Wes's head so he could sip at it. I could feel his fever was down. He smacked his lips like he was tasting the most delicious thing in the world, then said, "So, Billy-boy, what's new?"

* * *

He was with us about ten days all told. After a week, Barnett figured Wes was safe enough with us and decided to get on back home. He had his own family to tend to, and they were sure to be worried about him. He'd cleaned and loaded Wes's pistols and put them on a chair by the bed. They shook hands and looked serious for a moment, then both laughed—which made Wes wince with pain. Barnett said, "You let me know soon as you feel up to having some fun in Trinity again, hear?" And Wes said, "You can count on it." Then Barnett left for back home. He was as fine a kinsman as a man could ask for.

Three days later we got word from a close friend and neighbor named Charles Crosby that a State Police patrol had come into town that morning and was passing around a reward poster. "Somebody's probably already talked to them," Daddy told Wes. "They're likely to be all around us by tonight."

Wes had some friends called the Harrels who owned a small farm some thirty miles away, deep in the Angelina Forest. He figured he could hide out there till he finished healing. He'd have to ride, though, and he wasn't even up walking yet. Daddy bound his wound as tight as Wes could stand it, then helped him to his feet and into his clothes. He was bent nearly double, and it was all he could do to hobble on outside to his horse. Charles held the animal next to a stump that Daddy and I helped him to step up on, and then we shouldered him up on the saddle. It all took a good while to do, and the whole process left Wes sucking for breath and pouring sweat. Worse than that, it had opened his wound some. I could see the blood seeping through his shirt just over his gunbelt. Momma gave me a sack of food she'd fixed for us and kissed me on the cheek, and Daddy squeezed my shoulder and said to take care.

We couldn't ride hard but we rode steady. Charles rode in the lead about fifty yards, keeping a sharp eye for lawmen and bands of vigilantes. I stuck right next to Wes in case he started to fall, but he hung on tight. More than once we had to rein up and hide in the trees while small groups of riders passed us by. Wes would sip water and wet his face some. The bloodstain on his shirt kept getting bigger and his eyes were red with pain. That night we camped without a fire in a thick stand of oaks and supped on jerky. Wes was able to sleep a bit with the help of a bottle of bourbon I'd thought to bring along. In the morning the blood on his shirt was crusted, but it started flowing again as soon as he mounted up.

We arrived at the Harrel farm early next evening. It was a family of four—Dave, Louella, and their young twin sons, Jack and Mack. They were happy to see him, but were alarmed by the sight of his bloody wound. We helped get him into a bunk in the side room of their enclosed dog-run cabin. Louella sent one of the boys for a kettle of steaming water and the other for her needles and thread and a clean sheet she could shred into bandages. "Dang, woman," Wes said, "I been sewed up so many times in the last couple of weeks, I'm starting to feel like somebody's poorly made shirt." Louella told him to hush his mouth or she'd start by sewing up his lips.

The Harrels were fine people. When Charles and I left in the morning, I felt sure Wes would be safe there for a while. But he wasn't. He was never safe anywhere for long.

—— Louella Harrel ——

Dave put a shotgun and extra loads next to Wes's bed, and every morning and afternoon him and the boys went out to work the fields, same as always. I kept a big pot of beef-and-bean soup simmering and would spoon some into Wes every time he awoke. By the fourth day it was clear how quick he was getting his strength back because he was feeling better enough to start peeping at me in a mischievous manner.

I was good-looking in my younger days, take my word on it—but I'm not and never have been a loose woman. I always did love my husband, first to last. I'm not making excuses for what I'm about to tell. I don't think it needs any excusing, no matter what anybody else might think.

I was wearing a big loose shirt of Dave's, and when I bent over Wes to adjust the bedclothes and his pillows, I knew he was getting a good look right down into it. He smiled up at me and I guess I smiled back. He put his hand up behind my neck and pulled my face down and gave me as good a kiss as ever I got, so wet and full of tongue it was like a living sin in my mouth. He slipped his hand up under my shirt while he was at it and my teats got tight with excitement. Then my shirt was bunched up under my arms and his mouth was at my nipples and I went dizzy from the sweetness of it. Next thing I knew, he was hard in my hand and his hand was all the way up under my skirt and we were panting like dogs against each other's neck. He started twitching in my fist and it felt like hot wax flowing over my fingers just as a shiver slid up through me like a snake.

My tongue still gets a bit dry when I think on it.

We kissed and stroked each other real gentle, and a minute later he was back asleep. We never talked about it after that. I don't know why I did it. I guess because I married so young and always thought I was missing some secret excitement in life. I'd get these *yearnings*. That small wickedness with Wes satisfied me of them for good. Later on, whenever I'd get to feeling the least bit restless, I'd recollect that time with Wes and feel a blush and then be just fine again. As for him, well, I reckon he'd just plain been taking pleasure in being alive.

Pretty soon he was getting out of bed by himself and getting dressed with only a little help from me. After breakfast he'd take a chair outside and sit propped against the front wall and whittle and sing softly till Dave and the boys got back from working the cotton patch, then he'd join them at the pump to wash up for dinner. One day I was at the stove listening to them all laughing and joshing each other out at the pump when suddenly they fell quiet. I looked out the window just as the first shots cut loose.

Wes was headed for the house, running hunched over as two policemen came riding hard out of the sweet gum grove a hundred yards away, shooting their repeating rifles as they came. I couldn't see Dave or the boys, but I heard the horses nickering loud in the corral around back. A bullet ripped splinters off the edge of the window and whanged into a skillet of corn bread on the table and knocked it to the floor. Ten feet from the house Wes got a leg shot out from under him. He hit the ground hard but kept rolling right up to the door. I stepped out and grabbed him by the shirt collar with both hands and yanked with all my might as he scrabbled to all fours. A round passed through my hair and clanked on the stove. Wes tumbled in on top of me, then pulled me with him away from the open door.

The policemen reined up in front of the house and kept firing through the door and windows as fast as they could work the levers. Wes shouted, "Shotgun!" I was already running to get it from his bedside. I heard the slam of the rear door, and when I got back, Dave and the boys were hunkered down beside Wes. "Horse," Dave yelled at him, "in back!" He had his pistol in his hand but I knew he hadn't fired it at another living man since he'd been in the War. His face was pale and tight as a bare skull, and for the first time since the shooting started I felt scared. I shoved the gun and a handful of loads across the floor to Wes, then threw myself over the twins and held them down on the floor while bullets kept whizzing in and biting into the walls and blowing open the canned goods on the shelves and ricocheting off the stove and pans.

Wes scrabbled up next to the window, stood up with his back to the wall, and cocked both hammers. The new wound was low on his thigh and bleeding steady but not hard. It looked like the bullet had ripped clean through the muscle without hitting bone. But the wound in his side had opened again and was bleeding free all the way down to his boot.

The policemen were laughing like they were at a turkey shoot as they fired and fired into the house. A bullet ricocheted through the room and Dave yelped and grabbed his backside. Wes gave him a glance, then looked at me and winked. *Winked!*

Then—all in a heartbeat—he spun into the window and fired both barrels and jumped clear again as a bullet buzzed in and whacked the wall. A horse started screaming and the police let off shooting. One of them yelled, "*Mike*, help me! *Help me*, goddamnit!" I heard a horse galloping away.

Wes reloaded faster than I thought could be done, then leaned into the window and fired one barrel and the one policeman quit his hollering. The horse was still bellowing like blue blazes. Wes braced the shotgun against the window, aimed higher and more careful, and fired the other barrel. "Damnit!" he said.

He lowered the gun and stood staring out the window. Blood was running off his boot and spreading on the wood floor. All I could hear was the dying horse. The cabin was full of dust the bullets had knocked loose.

He turned to look at us and asked if everybody was all right. I was—the boys too—and I got off them. Dave stood up and felt of his backside, but the spent round had only stung him and not even torn his pants. "Reckon you'll live?" Wes asked him. I couldn't believe he was *grinning!* He saw my look and quit, then hobbled on outside.

Wes's shotgun blasted and the horse finally stopped its horrible screaming. It was suddenly so unbelievably quiet. We went out and saw the dead animal laying within twenty feet of the house. A few feet over from it was the policeman, his belly blowed open and part of his head gone.

It was the first shot-dead man the twins had ever seen, and they ran over to him and studied him and nudged each other and pointed to this and that. Their wide-eyed excitement twisted my heart in an awful way I'd never felt before. Dave saw my face and quick called the boys back away from the body. Wes must've read my face too. He looked at me kind of sheepish. I can't explain how I was feeling. I wanted to tell him I didn't hold him to blame for my home getting shot up and my family being put in such terrible danger. But I just couldn't.

We knew the policeman who got away would bring a lot more of them back real soon. Dave hitched a mule to the dead horse and dragged it into the bushes well back of the cabin, then did the same with the dead man. I did what I could for Wes's wounds. He said he didn't mean to bring all this trouble down on our family and he was awful sorry about it. "At least nobody got hurt except me," Wes told Dave, "if we don't count that slap you got on the ass from the ricochet." That got a smile from Dave. He said he was proud to be able to say he'd fought next to him against the damn State Police. Men are such jackasses sometimes. It hadn't crossed his mind yet how hard the State Police could be with them they saw as friends of fugitives.

By that evening the boys and I were in the wagon and bumping our way on the old trace toward my sister Millie's farm some twelve miles away. Dave told me to stay put there until he came to take us home. Him and Wes had rode off in the other direction, toward Till Watson's place, which was set even deeper in the forest than ours was.

"You'll be safe there," Dave had told Wes. "Till lives alone and he'll be proud to take you, seeing how you hate the State Police almost as much as he does."

Six days later Dave got back to Millie's and told us Wes had surrendered to Sheriff Dick Reagan of Cherokee County and was under arrest in Rusk.

Monte Mays

Hardin made his terms real plain to Sheriff Dick. First off, he wanted protection from mobs. It's the one thing he was scared of—being taken by a mob—and nobody could blame him for that. A mob is a murdering thing with no more mind to it than a hay barn afire: once it gets out of hand there's nothing to be done but watch it burn till all that's left is the smoking ashes. And he wanted a doctor of course. And to be kept someplace other than a jail until he was mended good enough to travel. And Dick's word that he wouldn't stand trial anywhere but Gonzales. And he wanted half the reward Dick Reagan would get paid for him.

I was Dick Reagan's chief deputy at the time. It was Dave Harrel who brought Hardin's offer to us in Rusk. Harrel said Hardin wouldn't make the offer to the Angelina County sheriff because, as everybody damn well knew, he was a natural-born son of a bitch who was a toady for the State Police. "That Angelina shithead would agree to the deal," Dave said, "then for sure turn him over to the State Police to get shot or be given over to a mob to get lynched."

Dick wanted to know what made Hardin think he wouldn't do the same himself. Harrel said Wes had heard from people he trusted that Dick Reagan was a smart and honest lawman with no love for the State Police. "Kind of him to think so well of me," Dick said, "but I wonder

if I ain't due more than just half the reward, considering
all he wants.''

Half the reward was a far sight more than no reward at
all, Harrel said. ''Five hundred dollars ain't nothing to
sneeze at. *And* you get the glory of being the man who
captured John Wesley Hardin. A heroic accomplishment
like that could do a man with political ambitions a lot of
good if he made proper use of it.'' Dick had to grin at the
truth of that. ''Just one thing,'' he told Harrel, ''it's a state
warrant, so I'll have to take him to Austin first when he's
strong enough. But the warrant's for a killing in Gonzales
County, so he can be sure of going there for trial.'' And
so they had a deal.

Sheriff Dick owned a hotel in Rusk, and that's where we
put him. The news of John Wesley Hardin's arrest had
carried ahead of us on the wind, the way such news always
does, and naturally damn near everybody in town turned
out to have a look at him. You'd of thought he was a one-
man sideshow, the way they gawked at him when we put
him on a litter and carried him inside and up the stairs. I
do believe some expected him to have horns, tail, and
hooves—and they seemed downright disappointed that he
didn't. I heard one sprout say, ''Shoot, he don't look so
dang different than us.''

A flock of folk followed us upstairs, bold as you please,
and right into the room where we laid him on the bed.
Gawkers were packed in the hallway. Dick had gone to
check things at the jail, and since he hadn't said not to let
nobody talk to him, I let them go ahead and do it. They
asked him how many men he'd killed and who was the
toughest man he ever met. (Which he answered, by the
way, by saying, ''I've killed only as many as necessary to
defend my own life,'' and ''I'd have to say Simp Dixon,
although Wild Bill Hickok is nobody's little sister, for
damn sure.'') One peckerwood made so bold as to ask if
he'd ever shot a woman. ''No, sir,'' Hardin said, ''I never
have. But that don't mean I ain't known a few who
wouldn't of been a whole lot better for it if *somebody* had

shot them every now and then.'' I'll admit I laughed right along with everybody else at that one.

All that attention seemed to pump vigor into him. His face took on good color and his eyes brightened up and he was talkative as a jay. He probably would of answered their questions all day long if Doc Jimson hadn't finally showed up and chased everybody out.

He laid up in Sheriff Dick's hotel for near three weeks, mending fast under Dr. Jimson's care and Mrs. Reagan's looking-after. Dick complained that his wife was feeding Hardin better than she was him, but she'd just tell him to hush, that Hardin was a bad-injured boy in need of nourishment to get his strength back. Mrs. Reagan had a reputation for being nobody's fool, so it was amazing to see the way Hardin could charm her into smiling and giggling every time she brought his meals to the room. He appreciated all her good cooking too. Took seconds at every meal and cleaned his plate every time. He looked to be putting on a couple of pounds a day. He wasn't but skin and bones when we brought him in, but he'd beefed up plenty by the time Dick and me moved him to Austin.

We turned him over to Sheriff Barnhart Zimpelman, who was surprised to see we hadn't put any more restraints on him than one set of handcuffs. ''No need to,'' Dick told him. ''He gave his word he wouldn't try to escape.''

Zimpelman assured Hardin he'd be transferred to Gonzales in just a few days, and he told Dick he could claim the reward money over at State Police headquarters. Dick gave Hardin a wink and went on over to collect it. Later that afternoon he went back to the jail and gave Hardin his half. Next morning Dick and me headed back to Cherokee County and I didn't lay eyes on Hardin again, but I naturally heard lots more about him.

He was in the river jail in Austin for about a week before a half-dozen State Policemen transferred him to the Gonzales lockup to await trial for killing a state lawman named Parramore. All the way from Austin to Cherokee County, as Dick and me made our way back home, we heard a good deal of saloon talk that Wes Hardin wouldn't make it to Gonzales alive. The betting was that the police would shoot him dead somewhere along the way and claim he tried to make a run for it.

But they didn't. Maybe because public opinion had got so bad about the State Police way of doing things and there'd been so much holler in the newspapers lately to punish State Policemen who shot prisoners in their custody. Or maybe because those lawmen figured that if they murdered him on the trail, his kin and close friends wouldn't rest until they'd evened the score with every policeman on the detail. Or maybe just because the detail was under the command of Captain Frank Williams, who was said to be one of the few honest men in the Davis police. Whatever the reason, it's a fact they delivered him alive to the Gonzales County jail.

Oh, he was a smart pup, that Hardin! Surrendering to Dick had been just plain foxy. He'd been bad wounded and had half the lawmen in Texas hunting for him. He needed doctoring and nourishment and time to heal up without fear of the law sneaking up on him. He got all that when he surrendered to Dick—*and* he got half of his own reward. *And* he got transferred to a jail he knew he'd be able to practically walk right out of. Like I say—smart.

And I'm glad he was. Let me tell you, I got to know Wes Hardin fairly well in the time we'd had him in Rusk, and *I* say he was a pretty good old boy who wasn't guilty of a thing except defending himself and refusing to be dogwhipped by a bunch of damn Yankees or Davis's crooked police.

— Reuben Jackson —

They had him shackled to his horse and chained hand and foot, and two of them held shotguns at his back as they made their way through the crowd toward the Gonzales jailhouse. The people were cheering Wes and yelling for him to don't worry, they'd have him out of that jail quick enough. They cussed that party of policemen up and down for the low bastards they were—them and all State Policemen—and that son of a bitch Governor Davis too. Wes wasn't nothing but a hero to them. I know how they felt. He'd killed the worst Nigra police bully in the county and scared the rest of the black sons of bitches so bad they'd pretty much let Gonzales alone ever since.

Captain Williams signed him over to Sheriff W. E. Jones while Pancho the blacksmith cut the irons off him in the cell. "We might just as well hand him over to all his friends outside as leave him in *this* jail," Williams said. W.E. tried to look offended by that remark. "We do our duty here, Captain," W.E. said, "with the same devotion as you state boys. I'm a loyal Davis appointee myself, I'll have you know."

Part of that was true: W.E. was a Davis appointee, all right, but he always did have a somewhat *lenient* attitude about loyalty—and sometimes he'd *lean* to one side of it and sometimes he'd lean to its other, depending on which side would get him the most votes come election time. He wasn't nothing but a natural-born politician.

*   *   *

The police detail no sooner left town than Manning Clements showed up. Him and W.E. had a quiet chat in the corner of the office, then came back to Wes's cell where I was on guard. W.E. took me aside and said he wanted me to be sure to respect the prisoner's privacy during his personal visits. He gave me a big wink and a slap on the shoulder and then went off to home to have supper. I dragged my chair well away from the cell so Wes and Manning could talk in private, and I didn't do a thing to interfere with their visit, not even when Manning passed Wes a long hacksaw blade and both of them grinned over at me.

Every few days the district State Police patrol would come by to check on the prisoners we were holding for them until they got official orders to take them someplace else. The day after Wes was brought in they stopped by. The patrol leader was a nasty little runt of a redhead sergeant named Ward Wilcox, and he tried his best to rile Wes good. "I'm gonna be right in the front row and laughing like hell when they drop you through the door," he told him. "I'm gonna slap my leg laughing at the sight of your tongue sticking way out and your face turning all black and your eyes popping out of your head. Your legs'll kick every which way and you're gonna shit your pants! I'm gonna laugh and laugh at you, you lowlife son of a bitch."

Wes leaned against the wall with his arms folded and smiled at him, but I could see the muscle working under his jaw, and his eyes were as hard-looking as the bars in front of him. He never said anything back until just as Wilcox was starting to leave, and then he said, "You best start sleeping with one eye open, you short pile of shit." I think it was the way he said it as much as what he said that scorched Wilcox's ass.

"*What?*" Wilcox said. "What did you say to me, you shit-eating son of a whore?" But Wes didn't say another word. He just leaned on the wall and smiled at him. Wilcox cussed him for a solid minute straight, with the veins bulging in his neck and face nearly purple. You could see he wasn't just mad, he was *scared*. I don't think I've ever seen another man so scared by a threat. It's a terrible thing to be that afraid, and the proof of it came two days later when the patrol returned to town and found out Wes had broken jail.

Wilcox went white as milk when W.E. gave him the news. He accused W.E. of conspiring in the prisoner's escape, but of course W.E. could defend himself just fine against any such notion. He even wrote a letter to the State Police headquarters in Austin explaining how on the late night of October 10, a number of persons unknown had tied several lassos to the window bars of the prisoner's cell and then used the force of their horses to rip the bars right out of the wall.

The bars surely did get pulled out of the wall—but it only took Manning Clements one small tug with both hands to do it because Wes had already just about sawed through them. His pals had made a real fine show of jailbreaking: hooting and howling and shooting up a storm—but only up in the air so as not to take any chance of hitting somebody by accident. They took the sawed-out section of window bars with them, but anybody looking close at the cell window the next morning might of been amazed to see just how smooth all the bars had broke off—so smooth a man with a saw couldn't have done it better. Nobody but us saw that, though, because W.E. had his brother-in-law Lyle, a mason by trade, out to the jail just after sunup to put a new set of bars in the window.

Anyhow, W.E. was in the clear about the jailbreak, but Sergeant Ward Wilcox of the State Police was never the same again. The sorry bastard was terrified John Wesley Hardin would try to even the score for the tormenting things he'd said to him. The story goes that he couldn't sleep at home, he was so worried about

Wes bushwhacking him in his bed in the dead of night. His wife and two young sons volunteered to stay awake and keep watch so he could sleep, but he didn't trust them not to doze off after he did. He started spending his nights in the police bunkhouse, but he'd have bad dreams about Wes sneaking up on him and he'd wake up screaming in the middle of the night. After a few nights of being woke up that way, the other policemen kicked him out. The lack of sleep on top of his fear made him so jumpy he started flinching and throwing up his carbine at every sudden sound. One night he was passing by an alleyway and heard a noise in the shadows and quick fired four rounds into a tethered horse before he knew what he was shooting at. The police didn't want him shooting his own men, so they fired him.

He took his family to a cabin deep in the woods and fired warning shots at anybody who rode too near to it. He would holler for them to tell Hardin he was ready for him, by God. One day his wife showed up at her daddy's house with one of the young ones in tow, all hysterical and half out of her mind with grief. She told a terrible tale of Wilcox waking up in the middle of the night and going crazy with fright when he saw a shadow crossing the room. Thinking it was Hardin come to kill him, he grabbed up his gun and fired. It was his older boy Robert, walking in his sleep as he had recently begun to do, and Wilcox blew his brains all over the cabin wall. He ran out into the black woods, firing his pistol and screaming, ''Come out and fight like a man, you son of a bitch! I'm right here! I'm right here!'' While he was ranting in the forest, his wife and the younger boy slipped off and made their way to the trace and walked all night and day to get to town. Mrs. Wilcox's daddy came into town and told the story to the sheriff, and then W.E. and me went out to the cabin to arrest Wilcox.

We found him hung from the center beam of the ceiling. His face was all black and his tongue stuck out and his eyes bugged from his head. He'd shit his pants and the stink was awful. There was a note pinned to his shirt saying, "try geting me now harden."

The story goes that a few months later when he was told Ward Wilcox of the State Police had gone crazy and hung himself for fear of being killed by him, Wes said, "Ward who?"

John Gay

Even my grandpa, who'd lived in the Sandies all his life, wasn't rightly sure how the Sutton-Taylor Feud began. There'd been bad blood between the clans for as long as anybody could remember. But whyever the bloodletting got started, it's a fact it got worse than ever when Creek Taylor killed Fred Sutton. Creek was head of the Taylors at the time, the old granddaddy, and one day he caught Fred trying to steal a young hog from a Taylor pen. Fred put up a good fight and cut Creek across the ribs with his Bowie before Creek shot him in the knee and took the vinegar out of him. Then Creek tied him up, slashed his belly open with the Bowie, and threw him in the hog pen. The pigs rooted in Fred's guts while he screamed to high heaven and Old Creek laughed to see him getting gobbled up alive.

Old Creek was like that. He taught all his sons and grandsons to honor the family code: "Whosoever sheds Taylor blood shall by Taylor hand shed his."

When the War came, everybody went off to fight the Yankees—but the Taylors brought the War back to DeWitt County with them. Appomattox didn't mean jack-shit to them. They refused to knuckle under to Yankee military law and kept on killing bluebellies every chance they got. Pitkin Taylor was now the head of a family of hard cases that included his sons Jim and Billy and his nephews Buck and Scrap. They were joined by friends and

kin from all over the Sandies who were still as much
Johnny Reb as ever. One Yankee patrol after another was
sent into the Sandies to bust them up, but the Taylors
bested them every time. They knew every rock and tree
in the region and ran the Yanks in circles. They made fools
or dead men of them all.

The Yank generals in charge of Texas got in a hellish
fury with the Taylors, so they authorized a band of fifty
hired guns called the Regulators to bring the whole Taylor
bunch to heel. The Regulators didn't have any trouble recruiting Bill Sutton, who knew the Sandies as well as the
Taylors did. Sutton hated Yankees, of course, but he hated
Taylors more. He signed on so many friends that the Regulators came to be known as the Sutton Party, even though
Sutton wasn't their leader. That was Jack Helm.

When the Yankee troopers finally left Texas, the Sutton-
Taylor war was going on worse than ever—but Governor
Davis had formed the State Police, and Jack Helm became
a captain in it. He quickly got to be the most hated State
Policeman of them all, which is saying something. He re-
cruited a lot of other policemen into the Sutton Party, and
the band grew to nearly two hundred strong. Besides Sutton, Helm's lieutenants were Jim Cox and Joe Tomlinson.

The best way to describe Jack Helm is to tell about the
Kelly brothers, Will and Henry. They were a pair of lik-
able wildhairs who'd both married daughters of Pitkin
Taylor. There wasn't any question about whose side they
were on in the feud, but neither one had ever killed a
Sutton man, I know that for a fact. Anyhow, one day Jack
Helm showed up at their homes with a troop of State Police and arrested them for having shot out the lights of a
traveling show where they'd been drunk a couple of nights
before. It seemed an awful small matter to call for the State
Police. Everybody figured it was just one more of Jack
Helm's ways to irritate the Taylors. So Will and Henry let
themselves be cuffed and taken away to the courthouse in
Cuero, where they figured they'd pay a fine and then be
let go. But they never made it to Cuero. Once Helm got

them way out in the open prairie, he shot them both in cold blood.

The Kellys' mother and Henry Kelly's wife had followed the troop at a distance in a wagon and witnessed the murders with their own eyes. They filed charges at the State Police headquarters in Austin. It wasn't the first time Jack Helm was accused of shooting prisoners, but it was the first time he was brought to trial for it. In court he said the Kelly women were lying. He swore he'd shot the Kelly boys because they'd tried to escape. Ten State Policemen backed up his story and he was acquitted in less than an hour. But the State Police had had enough of his maverick ways and bad publicity, and they fired him off the force.

Pitkin Taylor was at the trial. When Helm was acquitted, Pitkin had to be restrained from attacking him. He cussed Helm and swore he'd kill him for making widows of his two daughters. "There's no place you can hide I won't find you, whoreson bastard!" Pitkin shouted. Helm just stared at him with those cold eyes and spit at Pitkin's feet.

Next thing we knew, he was sheriff of DeWitt County—which didn't mean a damn to Pitkin. "I don't care what badge he's wearing or how many guns he's got under him," he said. "One of these days when he's least expecting it, there I'll be with my double-barrel in his face—and boom!"

One of these days wasn't soon enough. A week later Pitkin's wife woke him in the middle of the night, complaining that their milk cow had got loose and was tromping out in the high brush back of the house. She could hear its bell clanking. Pitkin grumbled and pulled on his boots and went out to put the animal back in its pen. It was a cloudy night and hard to see. Cussing loud enough for his wife to hear him from the door, he followed the sound of the bell toward the edge of the woods. Suddenly the brush was blasting bright with gunfire and Pitkin was spinning and jerking every which way and then fell. Pitkin's wife didn't hear herself screaming till the shooting finally stopped. The ambushers yahooed and flung the cow bell against the front of the house. "Death to all Taylors!" they hollered, and whooped off into the woods. Mrs. Taylor didn't get a look at any of them, but there wasn't any question they were Sutton men.

Even though they'd put sixteen rounds in Pitkin, they didn't kill him, not right away. He was tough as a longhorn bull and refused to give up the ghost for nearly two months. He lay in bed all that time, seeping blood and pus from just about every pore, and slowly turned into a gasping yellow skeleton. He finally whispered to his wife one night, "To hell with it," and died.

If anybody'd had doubts about who his killers were, they didn't after the funeral. He was buried in the Taylors' big family graveyard overlooking the Guadalupe River. The preacher was in the middle of the eulogy when a bunch of riders showed up on the opposite bank. It was Bill Sutton and his boys. They cussed us and laughed and said the worms that fed on Pitkin were like to die of poisoning. "You there, Miz Taylor!" Bill Sutton called over. "If you'd like a fair replacement for Pit, I got a mean-tempered, high-smelling old hog I'd be willing to sell you cheap!" The veins in Jim Taylor's forehead looked about to pop. His brother Billy grabbed him before he could pull his gun. "This ain't the time or place, Jim," he said. "We got Ma here. We got women and young ones." Sutton and his riders yeehawed awhile longer, fired in the air a few times, then rode off laughing. The Widow Taylor looked about to go insane. "I swear to you, Ma," Jim said, "I swear to you I'll water Daddy's grave with Bill Sutton's blood."

A few days later Jim was drinking with friends in a Cuero saloon when somebody told him Sutton was playing billiards in Foster's down the street. Sutton hardly ever showed his face in town anymore, so the opportunity was too good for Jim to pass up. But he'd been drinking, like I said, and he was a natural-born hothead, and so his excitement got the better of him. Instead of sneaking up quiet and getting the edge on Sutton, Jim and his friends charged into Foster's cussing a blue streak and shooting wild. One of Sutton's men was killed and one wounded badly. One of Jim's friends got shot in the balls. Sutton got his left thumb blown off but escaped through the back door.

All the Sandies was now one big battleground. Every man went armed and ready, walked careful and spoke low—even strangers passing through. Newspapers all over Texas condemned the violence in Gonzales and DeWitt and cautioned citizens to stay away from the region until such time as law and order was restored to it.

That is how things stood at the time I met Wes Hardin. Like everybody else in the Sandies, I knew he'd been living on the Duderstadt property—him and his pretty wife Jane—ever since he broke jail on Gonzales. And like everybody else, I couldn't help wondering which side of the Taylor-Sutton war he leaned toward. Jim Taylor was especially interested in finding out. "With him on our side, him and the Clementses," Jim said, "Sutton's two hundred men wouldn't look like near so many." I'd met Manning Clements at a cattle auction the year before and had taken a drink with him in Gonzales a time or two since then—so Jim sent me out to his ranch on Elm Creek to sound him out about siding with the Taylor Party.

Manning was polite as a man can be about saying no. He said he sympathized with the Taylors and had much admired them for the proud way they'd stood up to bluebelly law and against the State Police. "And everything I've heard about Bill Sutton," he said, "has made me want to spit. And Jack Helm, well, that sorry son of a bitch best give me wide passage." Just the same, he was sorry but he didn't want to get involved in the feud: "The plain and simple of it is, it ain't my fight. I've got my own family to look out for and my cattle business to tend. As long as neither party harms me or mine, I got no cause to side with one or the other." I said I supposed his cousin Wes felt the same way. He said he couldn't speak for Wes, but he and Jane were coming to visit that night, and if I'd stay to supper I could ask him myself.

Wes seemed as glad to make my acquaintance as I was to make his. They'd brought their newborn baby daughter with them. They'd named her Mary Elizabeth but called her Molly, and Wes showed her off as proud as any new poppa. Then he and Manning and I sat in the parlor with whiskey and cigars, and Manning didn't beat around the bush in telling him there was something I wanted to know. So I went ahead and asked. Wes studied my face real close for a minute, then gave me pretty much the same reasons Manning had for staying out of it. "You just met those two darlings of mine," he said. "What sort of husband and daddy would I be if I made one a widow and the other an orphan by fighting somebody I got nothing against personally?"

I asked if he knew Jack Helm had papers on him for the shooting of Green Parramore. "I don't know Jack Helm from jackshit," he said, and gave a quick glance toward the door. He went on in a softer voice. "I do know his reputation as a natural-born sonbitch, but just the same, he ain't bothered me, and that's all that counts. The most I ask of any man is that he leave me be, and Jack Helm has done that. Far as I'm concerned, me and him ain't got a quarrel."

Well, I figured that was that, and during supper the talk turned to other things. Wes told me he was back in the cattle business. Unlike Manning, though, he had no desire to make any more drives to Kansas. He'd been rounding up cows in the Sandies and driving small herds twenty-five miles to the railhead at Cuero every week. The train delivered the steers to the port at Indianola, and from there they were shipped to New Orleans.

"Matter of fact," he said, "I've got to go to Cuero tomorrow to arrange for the next shipment to Indianola." When I mentioned I was headed for Cuero too, to pick up a new saddle I'd had sent from San Antone, Wes suggested we make the trip together, and I said fine. Manning insisted I spend the night at his place, and we then made a real fine party out of the evening.

We left just after sunup on a pretty day. The air was cool but full of birdsong and the smell of fresh-plowed earth.

We rode slowly along the new road running across the prairie between Elm Creek and Cuero, talking about racehorses, mainly. We were about eight miles from Cuero, and Wes was in the middle of telling me a wild and probably made-up tale of a time he'd won a big race in the wild town of Towash with his preacher-daddy's horse, when he suddenly said, "You recognize that man?" and just barely nodded toward the Mustang Mot, more than a hundred yards off.

The mot was a grove of hardwoods standing by itself out there on the prairie. It got its name because of the herds of wild ponies that used to rest in its shade in the old days. I had to look hard before I finally spotted who he meant—a mounted man, watching us from the deep shade of the trees. "I see him," I said, "but I don't place him from here." The rider walked his horse out of the shade and onto the road. As we closed in on each other I saw who it was. "Jack Helm," I said, and felt like a fool for whispering, since he was still a good forty yards away.

Helm was carrying a Winchester with the butt braced high on his leg and wore a pistol on each hip. Wes pushed his coat flaps back over his guns. "Watch the trees in the mot," he said. "Could be he's got backups in there." We closed up to within a few feet of each other and reined up.

"Morning," Helm said. "You boys from hereabouts?"

Wes asked who wanted to know, and Helm's face went tight. "*I* do, boy. Jack Helm, sheriff of DeWitt County. Who might you be?"

"No might about it," Wes said. "Name's John Wesley Hardin."

Helm smiled, but his eyes didn't get a bit warmer. Hell, I figured he'd known all the time it was Wes. He held the Winchester with his finger on the trigger. If he let the barrel fall forward it would be pointed square at Wes's chest from four feet off.

But Wes was all set too—his right hand high on his leg and close to his gunbutt, ready to pull. What I was ready to do was hit the ground and scoot for cover.

"Do you have papers on me?" Wes said.

"I do," Helm said. "But I don't intend to serve them."

Wes laughed. "I guess you don't—not while I'm looking you in the eye."

"Don't try bullyragging me, son," Helm said. "I have no rope out for you. You're square in DeWitt County while I'm sheriff."

"Is that a fact? And why are you so kindly disposed toward me?"

"The warrant's for killing a nigger," Helm said. "That counts less than shooting a dog. Besides, you are not sided with the Taylor Party—or so I've been told. I hold no ill toward anyone with enough good sense to hate Taylors."

"I don't hate Taylors," Wes said. "But I belong to no party except my own kin and family."

"Well, hell, that's good enough," Helm said, smiling tight. He eased the Winchester down across the pommel and said, "If you're heading into town, let's ride in together. I'd like to talk to you."

He did most of the talking. He told Wes the Taylors had brought their troubles on themselves. They were puredee troublemakers, he said, and the Sandies would be a far better place without a Taylor left in it.

"Now you and me, Wesley," Helm said, talking like he and Wes were old pals, "we're smart men—and smart men can always come to an agreement that's best for the both of them. You have your troubles with the law and I have my troubles with the Taylors. I think we could help each other out, smart men like us."

"All I want is to be left alone," Wes said. "Same goes for my friends. You can be sure we'll take no side in the feud so long as both sides let us be."

"Well now," Helm said, "I can appreciate that. Mr. Sutton will appreciate it too. But just to be sure *every*body appreciates everybody else real good, what say we all meet at Jim Cox's a week from today? While we're at it, you might be interested to hear a suggestion I got for getting you clear with the State Police. I know you wouldn't mind *that*. You know where Jim's place is?"

He didn't but I did, and he told Helm all right, he'd be there.

Cuero had come in sight by now, and Helm said, "Next week then—Jim Cox's at noon." He said he had to serve papers on some jackleg a few miles south of town, and off he went.

Wes watched him ride away and said, "Every thought in that man's mind is as crooked as a sidewinder. You can see it in his eyes." Just the same, he thought it might be interesting to hear what they had to say about getting him clear with the State Police. He would've met with the devil himself for a chance to do that.

We took care of our separate business at the train station, then went into a saloon to wet our whistles before heading back home. Just as we finished our drinks, a big man with bloodshot eyes, wearing a suit and bowler hat which were both too small for him, stepped up to Wes and said, "My name is J. B. Morgan, Mr. Hardin. Deputy J. B. Morgan. I'd be right proud to buy you a drink."

"Thanks anyway, pardner," Wes said. "We're just leaving."

"Ah, hell," Morgan said. "You got time for one drink. Barkeep! Set up my friend Hardin here with a drink!" Wes gave me a look of exasperation and stepped away from the bar.

"Hey, Hardin!" Morgan said, snatching hold of Wes's sleeve. "I just bought you a drink!"

Wes shook off his hand. "Suck it down yourself, rumpot." He was in no mood to humor some pushy drunk. But as he started for the door, Morgan grabbed him by the shoulder, saying, "You goddamn puffed-up—"

Wes drove an elbow hard into Morgan's belly—just *whooshing* the air out of him—then shoved him against the bar. "Damn you!" he said. "I don't need more troubles with the law over some shitheel like you, but you want to prove something, then do it!" He stood ready for whatever Morgan might try—but the deputy stood fast and red-eyed, holding his belly with both hands, still gasping for breath. "You *ever* see me coming," Wes said, "you best quick turn around and go the other way, you understand?" The deputy gave a jerky nod. "Good," Wes said. "Understanding's what the world needs more of."

But what the world's got way plenty of is stupidity. We'd just got outside and stepped down off the sidewalk when the saloon door bangs open behind us and Morgan hollers, "You son of a—!"

Wes whirled and fanned two shots and hit him over the right eye and in the front teeth. Morgan did a spastic little two-step and squeezed off a round into the sidewalk and pitched face-first into the street.

Wes gave him a kick to make sure he was dead, then holstered his Colt and let out a long breath. He looked around at the crowd of big-eyed spectators and said, "You are all witnesses. I wanted no row but he gave me no choice. Tell the sheriff how it was."

We mounted up and rode on out. The crowd closing around the dead man was dark-eyed and silent. The only sound as we left town was from our horses' hooves.

Thomas Ford
Tenelle

I n the spring of 1873 Wes met with Jack Helm and Jim
Cox to clarify his neutrality in the Sutton-Taylor feud.
Because he didn't trust Helm any farther than he could
kick him, Wes took my big brother George and Manning
Clements with him to the meeting. It was wise that he did,
as Helm and Cox were accompanied by eight Sutton Party
pistoleros who glowered at George and Manning the
whole time they waited outside for the meeting to be over.
Bill Sutton was not present. Helm told Wes he'd been
taken ill and could not ride. I doubt that. More likely, he
was simply too afraid to show up. You can always count
on a treacherous man to suspect treachery in everyone else.

The only reason Wes went to meet with them was to
hear Helm's deal for clearing him of all the State Police
warrants against him. Helm had a number of powerful
friends in Austin and could have done it. What he wanted
was for Wes to side with the Regulators and help them
rid the Sandies of the Taylors and everyone in league with
them. He promised Wes that no charges would ever be
filed against him for anything he did in the service of the
Sutton Party.

Wes admitted to us later on that he'd been sorely
tempted to accept the offer. The idea of no longer being
a wanted man made his head swim. ''I can just imagine
how nice it'd be to walk down any street in Texas with
my wife at my side and my baby in my arms and not have

to worry about some lawman sticking a shotgun in my face around the next corner. Or to have supper with my family in a restaurant without thinking some stranger after the price on my head might shoot me in the back while I'm chewing on my beefsteak. Or to sleep with both eyes shut and without a pistol in my hand. I can just imagine how nice it'd feel to be free as all that.''

But then Jim Cox produced a list of names and said the Sutton Party intended to rid the Sandies of everybody on it. The Clementses were on the list. So was my brother George. Even I, not yet sixteen, was on it. Wes knew every man on the list and remarked that all of them were neutral. Jim Cox said there wasn't any such thing as neutral, not anymore. "Who ain't for us," he said, "is against us." Helm said that any friends Wes had on the list would be welcome to ride with the Regulators.

Wes told him he had friends who had taken no sides between the Sutton and Taylor Parties and would prefer to keep it that way. Jim Cox went to the door, glared out at George and Manning, and spat a streak of tobacco juice. "Like *them*?" he growled. I'd seen Jim Cox: he was a huge brute who was said to have beaten at least two men to death with his fists.

"Sorry," Wes told them, "I appreciate the offer, but I can't accept." If anyone ever suggests to you that John Wesley Hardin lacked loyalty, you tell that ignorant individual to go to hell. Keep in mind that none of us knew just how soon the Davis police would be out of business. All Wes knew was that if he said yes to Helm, his troubles with the State Police would be at an end and his life would be eased considerably. But he also knew the Clementses would never side with the Suttons, nor would my brother George, and he was not one to abandon kin or friend, not for any reason.

He told Helm we would all stay out of the feud so long as we were let alone in our part of the Sandies. Jim Cox scowled at him and snorted. Jack Helm shrugged and smiled and said, "All right, son, if that's how you want it." But he hoped Wes would give a little more consideration to how much safer life would be for him and his family if all state warrants against him were dismissed. "You're squared with me, son," he said, "but I'm only the county sheriff. I can't speak for the State Police." Wes said Helm's smile was oily enough to lubricate a train.

Two weeks later the Texas legislature overturned the Police Act—and then overrode Governor Ed Davis's veto of the repeal. No Fourth of July celebration I've ever seen can compare to the jubilation that greeted the end of the State Police. A kind of proud Texas lunacy prevailed—a wild exultation over the end of what one newspaper called "an infernal engine of oppression." Firecrackers and gunfire banged all day and night. Bonfires blazed as high as the trees. Dance bands fiddled and twanged. Whiskey rivers flowed in the packed saloons and rebel yells echoed in the streets. On that glorious day my big brother George bought me my first drink of whiskey in a saloon. Wes Hardin bought me my second.

Of course, not everyone was pleased by the Repeal Act. Some feared the demise of the Davis police would permit lawlessness to flourish more openly than ever. They had fair reason to think so. In many towns the repeal prompted mobs of scoundrels to storm the jails and release the prisoners. In even more towns the "arms laws" against wearing guns were widely ignored. One newspaper quoted a former State Police official as saying, "The repeal is cause for greatest rejoicing among Ku Klucks, murderers, and thieves." Of course that was true. But criminals had not been the only ones to suffer under the State Police: too many honest citizens had been victims of its depredations as well. It was little wonder the news of its death inspired such wide revelry.

Jack Helm must have reasoned that without the threat of the State Police hanging over him, Wes had no further call to consider joining the Sutton Party—and might even be inclined to side with the Taylors. I can think of no other reason to explain Helm's sudden hostilities against Wes and the Clementses except that he must have intended to kill or arrest them before they allied themselves with the Taylors. Whatever his motive, it was the foolish move of a suspicious man—and it drew Wes into the feud as nothing else would have. . . .

A couple of days after we got the news of the repeal, we were out popping the brush for longhorns, rounding up a herd for Manning and Huck Clements to take to Kansas. Their brothers Gip and Jim already had a herd on the trail. George and I had been supping at Wes's house and sleeping on his porch most nights rather than go all the way back home. That afternoon, when we got back to Wes's, we found Jane in tears, clutching little Molly tightly to her bosom. Fred Duderstadt was with them, brandishing a shotgun. His clothes were torn and sopping wet and his face and hands were gashed and bloody.

Jack Helm and Jim Cox and some forty Sutton men had come galloping up in the middle of the day. They surrounded the house and demanded in the name of the law that Wes Hardin come out with his hands up. Jane went out with the baby in her arms to tell them Wes wasn't at home and to protest their trespass. The black terrier Wes had recently brought home for Molly to play with kept barking at the intruders and Jack Helm shot it dead. Jim Cox dismounted and grabbed Jane roughly by the arm, then pushed her and the child ahead of him as he barged into the house with pistol in hand. He fired into closets and trunks before opening them to see if Wes had been hiding inside. Jane was nearly hysterical and the baby shrieked in terror.

Fred Duderstadt had been out working his field when the Suttons rode in, and he ran to the Hardin house to try to protect Jane and the baby. But he was unarmed—luckily, or they surely would have shot him. The Sutton men beat him down with their coiled lariats, then threw a lasso over him and horse-dragged him around the house for laughs. Then picked him up and dropped him down the well.

They smashed up most of the furniture in the house for sheer devilment. Some wanted to set the place afire, but Jack Helm stopped them, saying there was no need of that. He told Jane to inform Wes that he had a warrant for his arrest for the murder of J. B. Morgan, deputy sheriff of Cuero. Wes could either clear out of the Sandies immediately, Helm told her, or he could swing from a tree when they caught him, the choice was his.

As soon as the Suttons rode off, Jane got a rope from the barn, tied it off on the well's windlass brace, and lowered it to Fred so he could haul himself out. The Suttons had taken all the guns they'd found in the house, but they'd not discovered the shotgun Wes kept hidden under the back porch steps. Fred put fresh loads in the chambers and kept watch at the front window in case any of them returned. Jane kept trying to soothe the baby but she could not stop crying herself.

Wes held her close and gently stroked her hair. He spoke softly to her and told her everything was all right now, not to cry anymore. But his eyes looked crazed and his hands were trembling. "Listen, darling," he said in a strained voice, "I have to go out for a little while." She clutched him tighter and cried, "No! There's too many!" He tenderly rocked her in his arms. "Hey, girl," he said, "I ain't crazy. I'm not going after no army of Regulators by myself. I'm going to see Manning is all. I promise."

He asked me and Fred to stay and watch over Jane and Molly, and then he and George galloped off to Manning's ranch. They found him in a cursing rage. The Sutton men had been there too, searching for the Clements brothers and frightening the women with demands to know the names of all members of the Taylor Party. Manning wanted to take the fight straight to the Suttons right then, but Wes prevailed on him to use his head. We need more men, he told Manning, good men. So Manning said all right, let's talk to the Taylors.

Wes came home and retrieved Jane and the baby. He took them back to Manning's where they'd be in the company of the Clements women and children—and guarded day and night by Manning's armed cowhands. In the meantime, Huck Clements was on his way to Jim Taylor with a message: Wes wanted to meet with him that night at the Mustang Mot.

It was a perfect place to meet. The trees gave us cover as well as concealing shadow, and the wide tract of surrounding prairie, especially under the bright quarter moon, would make easy targets of anybody who tried to ride up on us. I remember our ride out there as clearly as if it happened last night. The air was rich with the smells of the bottomland along the creek. Nighthawks were swooping into the high grass. A soft breeze carried one lonely cloud across the moon. When we got to the mot—Wes and Manning and Huck, George and I—the Taylors were already there. Jim, his little brother Billy, and his cousin Scrap.

The Taylors were good people. They were possessed of quick, familiar wit and fierce Confederate spirit. They asked no quarter in a fight and never gave it. Jim had been leader of the Taylor clan since his daddy Pitkin's murder. George and Manning had agreed that Wes should do the talking for our side.

"I wanted to stay out of this fight," Wes told the Taylors. "But those sonbitches laid hand to my wife. They frightened my child. They tore up my house and bulldozed my friend. I didn't tread on them, but they surely did on me, and I aim to see they pay for it—Cox, Helm, Bill Sutton, the lot of them. But they got an army on their side, so we need one too. It's nothing but good sense for us to side with you against those sorry bastards."

Jim Taylor said they were damn proud to have us with them, and he swore the Taylor Party would henceforth protect all Hardin, Clements, Tenelle, and Duderstadt families and properties against intrusions by Sutton forces. The only condition Jim imposed was that he be the one to kill Bill Sutton and Jack Helm. "I made my ma a promise about Old Bill I intend to keep," he said. "And I owe Jack Helm for killing my sisters' husbands." Wes said all right, but he claimed the same privilege for himself with regard to Jim Cox. "He was the one dared to touch my wife and made my daughter cry in fear." Jim Taylor nodded somberly and said, "He ought be yours, all right." They shook hands and the alliance was sealed.

Three weeks later a small party of us ambushed Jim Cox and eight of his pistoleros one night on the river road near the county line. They were returning from a dance at a Sutton ranch just north of Cuero, and since we'd been lying low for three weeks, their guard was down. We set ourselves in the trees on the high ground flanking both sides of the road where it curved toward the Guadalupe Bridge. Bill Watkins and I were the two youngest, and Wes said our job was to shoot all the horses. "It's up to you boys," he said, "to make sure not one of them Suttons leaves here on anything but a pair of wings."

We had a clear full moon to shoot by, and we were armed with repeaters. We waited till they all came into view around the wide bend in the road and got to within forty feet of us. Jim Cox was in the lead and Wes's first shot took off the top of his head. In the next instant our volley cut through them like a scythe of fire. I'd been excited and eager for the shooting to start, but the sudden screaming of so many dying men and animals drew a rush of hot vomit up to my throat. It surprised hell out of me, but I swallowed it down and kept shooting like everyone else. Our crossfire allowed for no escape. They fired wildly into the trees and ran into each other. They tried to worm themselves into the ground and out of the firestorm. They tried to hide behind blades of grass. I kept shooting at the horses, even after they'd all gone down. I wanted to stop their hellish screaming. I'd had no idea.

When none of the Sutton men was returning fire anymore, we finally eased off. It seemed like we'd been shooting for hours but it was probably no more than a minute. One of the horses was still kicking and bellowing and I had to shoot it twice more before it stopped. Manning and Jim took careful aim and put another round in each of the fallen Suttons just in case anybody was playing possum. Then we came out from behind our cover and went down to them. The air was full of the itchy scent of powder and the sharp metal smell of fresh blood.

There were nine dead horses and we counted eight dead men—and then we found the last one, halfway between the road and the river, crawling for the water. He was wounded badly, and he begged us not to kill him. Manning said, "Sorry, bubba, way too late for that." And dispatched him.

Not long afterward we got a report that Jack Helm was secretly on his way to Wilson County, just west of us, to try to recruit some old State Police pals of his into the Regulators. Wes and Jim figured he'd have some men with him but probably not many, as he wouldn't expect a Taylor ambush in territory so friendly to Suttons. They decided to see if they could hunt him down. George and I went with them. Manning and Huck stayed back to keep rounding up a herd and to ramrod the guards watching over our homes. According to our spies, a couple of Helm's old State Police pals lived in Floresville, so that's where we headed.

Shortly after we crossed into Wilson County, Wes's horse threw a shoe, so we detoured about a mile over to a town called Albuquerque, where there was a blacksmith's. It was a little two-dog town with one street and about eight buildings. The only people on the street were a knot of men sitting on their heels in the shade of an oak by the blacksmith shop, and a handful of boys about to drop a mean-looking black tomcat into a burlap sack already holding another cat. "I got five dollars says that black comes up winners," Wes said to Jim. A redhead boy was clutching the cat by its scruff and back paws, and it hissed at us as we went by. "What's the other one like?" Jim asked the boys. "One-eyed calico," a boy said. "Won the most sack fights of any of them." Jim grinned at Wes and said, "You got a bet."

George and I reined up and dismounted to watch the

sack fight while Wes took his horse into the blacksmith shop a little farther down the street. ''Y'all tell me how it turns out,'' Jim said to us, and went to join the men in the shade of the oak.

Two boys held the sack up between them and a third dropped the black inside—then they quickly tied it off and hung it on a low tree limb. You've never heard shrieking till you've heard a sack fight between two big toms. George and I were so caught up in watching that howling sack tossing and twitching on the tree limb that neither of us paid any attention to the horsemen who rode into town behind us.

A minute later a shotgun blasted and we spun around and saw Wes standing in the doorway of the blacksmith shop with both barrels of the scattergun smoking. Jack Helm was sitting in the middle of the street with the whole front of his shirt bright red with blood and a coil of shiny blue intestine bulging out of his torn belly. His pistol lay a few feet from him. The three men who'd ridden in with him were reining in their spooked horses, and Jim Taylor was covering them with a pair of pistols, yelling something I couldn't make out through the caterwauling still going on alongside me. The Sutton men dismounted and put their hands up high. Wes grabbed up their horses' reins and swung up into a saddle.

Just then, Jack Helm got up on his feet and went at Jim Taylor with a skinning knife.

I couldn't believe my eyes. He was trying to hold his guts in with his free hand as he staggered toward Jim, but they were slipping through his grip and hanging wetly against his thighs. His face was pale as pig fat. Jim shot him in the chest twice and Helm dropped to his knees and his guts rushed out into the dust. He threw the knife at Jim as awkwardly as a girl. Jim shot him again and Helm fell forward on his intestines. Then Jim went and stood over him and shot him three times in the head. I'd never before seen a man so thoroughly killed.

Helm had spotted Jim as soon as he and his men rode in—and he got the drop on him before Jim even looked over and recognized him. He'd dismounted and started walking toward him with his pistol aimed right in his face, cussing him as he came. He never knew Jim wasn't alone until Wes stepped out of the shadows of the blacksmith shop and blew his belly wide open. To this day, every time I hear a cat screech I see Jack Helm lying dead with his guts in the dirt.

We galloped out of there trailing the Sutton horses on a rope, and a few hours later we sold them to a dealer in Smiley. That night we spent every nickel from the horse sale on whiskey in a Gonzales saloon. "Drinks are on the Sutton Party!" Wes announced with a loud laugh. The news had spread fast, and men kept coming to our table all evening to congratulate us for killing Jack Helm. I heard that for months afterward Wes received letters of gratitude from people who'd hated Helm. Many of the letters were from women Jack Helm had made widows.

And still the feud went on—until finally Wes and Jim met with Joe Tomlinson and his lieutenants and everybody at last agreed to the terms of a peace treaty. They had it drawn up in a law office in Clinton, the seat of DeWitt County, and everybody signed it, including Bill Sutton, who had it brought to his guarded home by a lawyer who witnessed his signature. He knew better than to show himself to Jim Taylor, who had signed the treaty with the stipulation that it did not apply to him and Bill Sutton. The treaty group agreed that henceforth the feud was a matter strictly between the two of them.

And so, with the State Police a thing of the past, and with the feud settled by treaty, life in the Sandies turned fairly peaceful for the first time in a long time. Sutton rarely showed himself anymore, conducting most of his cattle business from the safety of his home. Jim Taylor was eager as ever to kill him, but he'd pledged his word to keep the fight between the two of them and he meant it.

We turned our attention back to the cattle business and helped Manning finish rounding up a herd for Kansas, and

then we helped Wes put a herd together for movement to
the Cuero rail yard. All in all, it was a sweet and peaceful
summer, and the peace carried over into the fall. When
we weren't working, we were racing horses and gambling
and dancing down the barn roofs. Jim Taylor kept his ear
cocked for news of Sutton, but Old Bill wasn't relaxing
his guard in the slightest, and the stalemate between them
stretched out for month after month.

Shortly after the New Year, Wes took his wife and baby
to visit Comanche, where his daddy and momma had gone
to live near his brother Joe, who'd been practicing law
there for a few years. I recall how truly excited Wes was
about that family reunion. When he bid me and George
good-bye, he looked as happy as I'd ever seen him.

A few weeks later George and I received notification of
our father's death in Houston. He'd been a college-
educated man, a district manager for the railroad, and his
will provided George and me with two thousand dollars
each. And just that simply, my life changed forever. By
the time Wes got back from visiting his family in Comanche, I was on my way to enroll in college in Houston.
Eventually, I became an attorney-at-law and today I have
a thriving practice in Galveston. George had planned to
use his inheritance to buy a small ranch, but he never did.
Just a few months after I left the Sandies, he was murdered
by Sutton Regulators.

Holden Quill

Comanche was a small community less than twenty years old on the edge of the West Texas frontier. The town square was built around a stone courthouse and shaded with live oaks. The nearest rail tracks were a hundred miles away. The roads were difficult. Except for an occasional cattle crew passing by, the place had few visitors.

I'd spent the previous six years reporting and editing for a San Antonio newspaper, but a whiskey habit as relentless as a bulldog finally got me fired. I was also in pressing financial circumstances at the time—*and* under the dark shadow of an ugly legal suit for breach of matrimonial promise to a young lady who'd proved to be neither as young as she'd led me to believe nor as much of a lady as I had presumed. Thus, when the editorship of the *Chief*, Comanche's weekly newspaper, was offered to me by its devil-may-care publisher one besotted evening in a Castroville cantina, I accepted the position on the spot and accompanied him to Comanche the following morning without even a rearward glance at San Antone. And that is how I came to be there when John Wesley Hardin made his fateful trip to Comanche in the spring of 1874.

By that time his brother Joe had been a resident of the town for three years. His first child—Dora Dean Belle Hardin—had been born there, and his second, Joe Hardin, Jr., was soon to be. He practiced law and sold real estate, served as the town postmaster, belonged to the Masons, and was a member of the Friends of Temperance. But although he was generally popular and admired, he did not lack for a strong core of critics. It was rumored that he was in league with corrupt agents of the state land office in Austin who were getting rich from the sale of worthless titles to unclaimed Texas land grants. Further, a stockman in neighboring Brown County had recently claimed he'd been defrauded by Joe Hardin in a cattle deal. Joe simply ignored all such mean talk and carried on in his usual gregarious fashion.

The Reverend and Mrs. Hardin and all the rest of their brood now lived in Comanche, as well. So too did John Wesley's Anderson and Dixon cousins.

Wesley had first visited Comanche in January, and Sheriff John Carnes had been apprehensive about it. But when Joe introduced him to his famous brother on the gallery of Jack Wright's saloon, Sheriff John was much relieved to find that he was a personable young man who wished only to enjoy a short stay with his family before returning to his cattle business in Gonzales. For his part, Sheriff John assured him that state warrants were of no consequence in Comanche, which preferred to tend to its own legal business and let the rest of the counties tend to theirs. Wesley said that was an enlightened judicial attitude if ever he heard one and offered to buy Sheriff John a drink. I bellied up next to them at the bar and Sheriff John introduced me. Wesley gave me a sharp look. He said he'd been the victim of many a false newspaper story and had come to distrust all pen pushers. I said I didn't blame him a bit. "I don't trust a damn one of them myself," I told him, which was the truth. That got a laugh out of him and he stood me to a drink. Thus did we become acquaintances.

His wife Jane and daughter Molly came with him on that first visit. So did a cousin named Gip Clements and a rough-hewn little man named Dr. Brosius, who had recently hired on as his cattle crew foreman. Toward the end of January they all returned to the Sandies, and a few weeks later Joe went to visit him.

Before we saw either of them again, we got the news that Jim and Billy Taylor had murdered Bill Sutton in broad daylight at the Indianola docks. Billy Taylor had been arrested shortly thereafter and was locked up in the Galveston jail. Jim Taylor was said to be hiding out at John Wesley's cow camp in the Sandies. Rumor had it that both Joe and Wesley had been involved in the killing, although not directly. Supposedly, the Taylors had learned of Bill Sutton's intention to take a steamer to New Orleans, but their informant had not known the exact date of his departure, and so Wesley had prevailed upon Joe—the only one among them not known to Bill Sutton—to go to Indianola to try to get that information. Joe, the rumor had it, was successful. He sent this information to Wesley, who relayed it to the Taylors, who boarded Sutton's steamer as it was about to leave the dock and shot him two dozen times in front of a terrified crowd.

It was nothing new to hear such tales about Wesley Hardin, the notorious mankiller and ally of the Taylors. But *Joe*? The attorney-at-law and upstanding citizen? The Mason? The Friend of Temperance? The *postmaster*? Who could believe such a thing about him? The few who did were the same people who already thought him guilty of land swindles and cattle fraud. Most Comanche citizens scorned the idea that he'd had anything to do with Sutton's assassination. Joe *might* be a bit of a legal hornswoggler, they said, but he wasn't one to take part in a murder plot.

When Joe returned from the Sandies, he brought Jane and Molly back with him. Over coffee and honey biscuits in the Coop Cafe, he informed me that Wesley had already dispatched one herd north in charge of his cousin Joe Clements, and was busy rounding up another. While the crew finished with the branding, Wesley would come to Comanche for another visit, and then, when Doc Brosius brought the herd up to Hamilton, a little town southeast of us, Wesley would join the crew for the drive to Wichita.

Jane and Molly would live at Preacher Hardin's while
Wesley was away.

And so in April Wesley showed up—accompanied by Jim
Taylor, who had a five-hundred-dollar price on his head
for killing Bill Sutton. It was unlikely anyone in Comanche would try to collect the reward. These were not men
to let down their guard. Even in the midst of drunken
frolic, they were ever vigilant for danger. Moreover, the
entire "Hardin Gang"—as Wesley and his usual entourage of Taylor, the Andersons, and the Dixons had come
to be known—would certainly retaliate on the instant if
any among them were attacked. Yet I never once saw them
bully anyone or present a deliberately menacing aspect.
To the contrary, they took special care not to antagonize
the townfolk and were generous about buying a round for
the house wherever they went. They were popular with the
town's saloon crowd, and they had a friend in Sheriff
John, and it certainly behooved them to keep it that way.
Wes bought a beautiful racehorse named Rondo from a
local breeder and kept busy overseeing the animal's training.

They hadn't been in town long, however, before we
heard dark rumors that Charles Webb, a Brown County
deputy sheriff, was calling John Carnes a coward for his
refusal to arrest Wes Hardin and Jim Taylor. He was
threatening to come to Comanche and serve state warrants
on them himself. I was present in Jack Wright's saloon
when Jim Anderson relayed the rumor to John Wesley and
Jim Taylor at the bar. They both laughed. Taylor loudly
proclaimed that if Charlie Webb came for them, the only
thing he'd succeed in arresting would be his own life.

Toward the end of May, the Hardin brothers began promoting a set of horse races to be held on the twenty-sixth,
which would also be Wesley's twenty-first birthday. Joe
drew up a racing flier, had hundreds of copies printed, and
hired a dozen men and boys to distribute them throughout
Comanche and all the neighboring counties. He also turned
a handsome profit on the advertisements placed in the fli-

ers by a goodly number of local businesses. By then, the latest rumor out of Brown County was that Charlie Webb had arrested an entire cattle crew at Turkey Creek and pistol-whipped its ramrod, who he had insisted was none other than Wesley Hardin. When he was told the tale in the Wright saloon, Wesley spat ferociously. "You really *believe* he thought that fella was me?" he said. "I tell you, for somebody I ain't never laid eyes on, that sonbitch is starting to chafe me raw."

On the day of the races the entire county turned out, as well as a good many visitors from the neighboring regions. The town square was clamorous with people and horses and dogs. The streets were crowded with wagons, and from the moment they opened their doors that morning the saloons did a floodtide business. A huge red banner announcing "Races—May 26" had been stretched across the courthouse façade for several days, and Carl Summers's string band was strumming and fiddling on a low platform in the courthouse yard. At ten o'clock all the contestants paraded their racers around the square to permit the spectators a close look at them. The betting was loud and furious and kept up as everybody headed out to the track about a mile northeast of town.

Three races had been matched, and the Hardin Gang was represented in each one. Joe's beautiful chestnut mare, Shiloh, was entered in the first race, Wesley's Rondo was in the second, and Bud Dixon's handsome buckskin Dock was running in the third. An air of festivity pervaded the Hardin entourage. Not only was it John Wesley's birthday, but the whole family was still celebrating the birth of Joe Hardin, Jr., who'd entered the world a few days earlier.

Spectators were lined six deep along the track from starting line to finish. Their exuberant yowling could probably be heard all the way over in Brown County. Shiloh and Rondo won their matches easily, but Bud Dixon's Dock was severely tried by a speedy black from Eastland County. It was a thrilling race all the way to the finish line, but Dock crossed first by a neck. The Hardin brothers won small fortunes in cash bets, and received further winnings in the form of property. Wesley had made the most and the biggest bets, and he reaped more than three thousand dollars in specie and paper money—as well as a buckboard, a new Winchester carbine, and eight saddle horses. The entire Hardin party was jubilant, and we all rode back to town whooping like Indians.

The celebration in Jack Wright's saloon was a boisterous and thoroughly sodden affair. The place was awash in whiskey. Preacher Hardin stopped in and seemed appalled by the proceedings. He took Joe aside and spoke to him in serious aspect. Joe stared down at his feet and nodded, and a moment later they left together.

Carl Summers and his band had been coaxed into the saloon with an offer of free drinks in exchange for a steady flow of music. Wesley bought round after round for the house. He was unrestrained in his celebration. At one point he drew his pistol and shot the glass eye out of a deer head mounted on the rear wall of the saloon. Jack Wright remonstrated with him about the damage to his trophy, and was placated with a shiny double eagle. Jim Taylor suggested to Wesley that he should perhaps slow down his drinking. "If there's a scrap," he said, "you don't want to be shit-brained." Wesley waved off his concern and ordered another round for the house.

Sometime later Deputy Frank Wilson shouldered his way up next to Wesley at the bar and shouted through the din that Sheriff John wanted a word with him. Wesley hollered, "Sure!" but insisted that Frank have a drink first, which he did, and then they went outside. I followed along with Jim Taylor and Bud Dixon.

The square had cleared considerably. A few wagons were still in the street, with tight-lipped women and tired-looking children waiting for the man of the family to finish up his celebrating and take them home. A small group of men—none of whom I recognized—stood in the street flanking the building. Wesley spotted them instantly and stopped short, his demeanor suddenly and remarkably alert. At the bottom of the steps, Frank finally caught sight of them too.

"Brown County?" Wesley asked. Wilson nodded grimly. "Listen, Wes," he said in a low voice, "Sheriff John thinks you ought maybe head on home—you know, before things get out of hand. You know John's your friend, Wes. He'd appreciate the favor."

Wesley cast another look at the Brown County party in the side street. They wore dark expressions, and I caught sight of guns under coat flaps. "Sure, Frank," Wesley said. "I'll just fetch a cigar and be on my way." Then Bud Dixon said, "Here's that damn Brown County deputy."

Charles Webb was strolling our way down the street as casually as if he were on his way to supper. He had both hands behind his back and his open coat revealed a pair of six-shooters on his hips. Jim Taylor whispered, "Now ain't that a sight!" Wesley fixed his gaze on him as intently as a hawk. As he came abreast of the saloon, Webb gave us an indifferent glance, then nodded a greeting to Frank Wilson as he passed him by.

"Say, you there!" Wesley called out.

Webb paused and looked up at him. "Are you talking to me?" His manner was self-possessed but without hostility. He was not young, yet looked hardy and capable, and his eyes were black and quick.

"Is your name Charles Webb?" Wesley asked.

Webb stepped nearer the gallery and scrutinized him closely. He stroked his mustaches with his left hand but still kept his right behind him. "I don't know you," he said.

"My name is John Wesley Hardin. I am told you have made threat on my life."

"Say now, men—" Frank Wilson began, but Webb cut him off, saying, "I've heard of you. But I have never made threat on your life. You've been listening to the talk of idle fools, Mr. Hardin."

"What's that behind your back?" Wesley asked. His own right hand was inside his vest. I heard my blood humming in my skull and set myself to leap out of the line of fire. Jim Taylor and Bud Dixon eased away from either side of Wesley, and the men in the side street seemed to contract toward the corner of the building.

Webb grinned and slowly brought his hand around and displayed the unlit cigar in it. I felt my breath release and heard Bud Dixon's low chuckle. Wesley lowered his hand and said, "Well, Deputy, I reckon we got no matter between us."

Charles Webb shook his head, still smiling, and said, "Never did, son."

"I was about to take a drink before heading home," Wesley said. "Can I stand you to one?"

"My pleasure," Webb said.

Wesley turned to go inside and Webb went for his gun. Someone yelled "Wes!" and I was jostled hard and fell back against the wall as Wesley lunged sideways at the same instant Webb fired. I heard a woman scream and Wes grunted and there was a simultaneous discharge of firearms and a bullet thunked into the wall inches from my head. Webb fell to one knee and his face was smeared red above one mustache and Wes and Jim and Bud all shot him again at the same time and he pitched over on his back. Then Jim Taylor and Bud Dixon ran down and stood over him and emptied their pistols into him.

Frank Wilson stood rooted with his hands up. "Not me, boys!" he pleaded. "Not *me*!" The square had cleared completely. Jim Taylor grabbed up Webb's pistols, tossed one to Bud Dixon, and they both hopped back up on the gallery. Wesley was stuffing a bandanna against the wound he'd taken in the side from Webb's first shot. Some of the men in the side street peeked around the corner of the building, guns in hand, and more men were coming fast from the other end of the street. "It's all Brown County!" Bud said.

Sheriff John was hurrying over from the jail with a shotgun in his hands, and from farther across the square came Joe and Preacher Hardin. "Best take cover, boys," Wesley said—and I ran behind him and Jim into the saloon.

The last of the customers were bolting out through the side and back doors. Jack Wright stood behind the bar, holding a pistol. Jim Taylor leveled his gun at him and said, "Our side or theirs, Jack?" Wright said he only wanted to defend himself if he had to, and Jim let him be. Alec Barrickman and Ham Anderson had taken cover behind an overturned table. They looked scared but ready to make a fight of it.

The street resounded with outraged accusations of murder and shrill exhortations to hang Wesley. "Listen to that," Wesley said, grinning ruefully at Jim Taylor. "You boys put ten pounds of lead in the bastard to my two rounds, and it's me they're calling to hang."

"It's the price of fame, bubba," Jim said, reloading his pistols. "You're welcome to it."

I crouched down behind the far end of the bar, cursing myself for running into the saloon instead of into the alley alongside the building. That's what Bud Dixon had done, and he'd gotten clear. I peeked around the counter: through the space under the swinging front doors I saw Sheriff John at the foot of the gallery steps, trying to get the crowd under control. He said he'd already telegraphed the State Rangers for assistance and they were on their way.

"It's a damn mob," Wesley said, standing alongside the front window with a ready pistol and taking fast looks outside. His side was slick with blood.

Suddenly the shouting grew more strident and there was a cursing scuffle. I glimpsed Sheriff John struggling with several men. His shotgun was wrested from him and he was roughly pulled from my line of vision. I saw Reverend Hardin trying to break through the crowd, but he too was wrestled out of sight.

A large rock crashed through the front window in a spray of glass, followed by a volley of gunfire that shattered the back-bar mirror and gouged chunks out of the mahogany bar. Jack Wright gaped at the damage and cursed with religious fervor.

"To hell with this!" Jim Taylor shouted. "It's nothing

but peckerwoods out there. If we rush them all at once, they'll run like rabbits or goddamnit we'll kill them all!'' He looked deranged enough to try it.

"No!" Wesley said. "I got family out there, you crazy galoot!'' He ran to the side door and opened it a crack to peek outside. "By damn! Look here!'' Taylor rushed over and peered out as Wesley gestured for Ham and Alec to join them.

"Well now,'' Jim said, "ain't *that* a sight!''

"Let's do it before they get wise,'' Wesley said, tugging his hat down tight. "Let's go!''

He threw the door open wide and they raced across the side street to a line of untended horses hitched at a rail. As they swung up into the saddles, somebody shouted, "Here! Over *here*, goddamnit!'' They galloped off as a barrage of gunfire cut loose behind them. Gunfire and curses.

As the front doors banged open I ducked behind the bar and hunkered down—I don't *know* why, *I* was no outlaw. "Don't shoot, you dumb shits!'' Jack Wright cried out.

Boot heels pounded the floor. A terrible apparition in a red beard suddenly loomed above the bar, glaring down at me from the far end of the twin barrels of a shotgun. The muzzle was bare inches from my face and looked like death's own portals. My fear was paralytic—I could not speak.

The barrels abruptly flew upward and discharged and blew a hole in Jack Wright's ceiling the size of a frying pan. Sheriff John had snatched up the gun an instant before the redbeard pulled the triggers.

He shoved the man away and peered over the counter at me. "Holden,'' he said, "are you all right?'' As dust and splinters and flakes of paint descended gently on my head, I felt the content of my bladder spreading warmly over my lap.

The next two weeks were the most violent in Comanche's young history—a fortnight of marauding and murder and vigilante justice, if justice it can be called. The events that

followed did not, of course, possess the orderly coherence
with which I now present them. It was a time of furious
confusion, erratic report, wild and frightening rumor. Not
until after the terrible culmination of those events was I
able to reconstruct them in proper sequence and perspec-
tive.

Within minutes of Wesley's escape, the town square was
swarming with Brown County deputies. No, not deputies—vigilantes. Vigilantes is what they were. They were
joined by a number of armed Comanche residents who
held grudges against the Hardins. The streets were in full
clamor to hunt down Charlie Webb's killers. Less than an
hour later, posses were in pursuit.

That evening a contingent of Frontier Battalion Rangers
arrived in town. They were under the command of Captain
A. E. Waller, who went by the name Bill and who swiftly
took charge of the manhunt. His orders from Austin were
to capture or kill the outlaw John Wesley Hardin and every
member of his gang who was with him when they did,
and he duly authorized all vigilante possemen to carry out
those orders.

Wesley and his friends rode directly from Comanche to
Preacher Hardin's house, about two miles northwest of
town. They were met there by Joe, the Preacher, and Sheriff John. While Jane tended Wesley's wound, the men discussed the possibilities. They all agreed Wesley had acted
in self-defense and should therefore be acquitted in a fair
trial, but Sheriff John said if the mob got to him it was
likely he'd never be allowed to stand trial at all, never
mind get a fair one. It was a blood-smelling mob they were
dealing with, he said, and he wouldn't be able to protect
any of them against it. But the Rangers were coming, and
Preacher Hardin wondered if *they* could be trusted to be
fair with Wesley. Sheriff John said maybe. But when he
got back to town and met Captain Waller, he knew there
was no chance of that, either.

As soon as Wesley's wound was bound, they fled to

Round Mountain, some eight miles west of town. They really did believe the town's fury would slacken, and that once the Brown County posse went back home they would be able to return to Comanche and justify themselves. However, when Joe and the Preacher saw the continuing hubbub in the streets, and when guards were posted at their homes, and when they learned of Captain Waller's devout intention to see Wesley dead or jailed, they began to comprehend the full gravity of the situation.

The next morning Joe and the Dixons rode out of town before sunup, trailing a brace of racehorses on lead ropes. They were followed by a Ranger posse, but the Dixons were masters of the brush country and they managed to lose the Rangers in the mesquite thickets several miles outside of town. While the posse beat the bushes in search of their trail, Joe and the Dixons made their roundabout way to Wesley and informed him of the town's deadly mood. Joe advised him to remain in hiding awhile longer. In addition to the fresh mounts, they'd brought plenty of food and ammunition, and Joe promised to return the next day with the latest news.

But as soon as they got back to Comanche, Joe and the Dixons were arrested and clapped shut in the courthouse jail. Captain Waller charged them all with giving aid to the fugitives, though they denied having done so. Captain Bill wasn't the only one angered with them. There was mean muttering all over town about "those damned Hardins and all their kin."

Then Preacher Hardin and his family—as well as Jane and young Molly—were taken to Joe's house and there kept under arrest, together with Joe's wife and children. Alec Barrickman's family was also put under heavy guard and not permitted to leave the premises or receive visitors.

Wesley must've thought his family was still at his daddy's, however, because he tried sneaking up to the house one evening. He was spotted by one of the dozen guards posted around the property and all hell broke loose. In the poor twilight visibility, the excited and confused guards

mistook each other for members of the Hardin Gang and
shot it out for several furious minutes. Wesley escaped—
and without having fired a shot, he left two dead and five
wounded possemen behind him. Captain Bill's rage was
apoplectic.

Now Doc Brosius showed up. He had arrived at Hamilton
with the herd as planned, and then, wholly oblivious to
the situation in Comanche, he had come to town to find
Wesley. When he said he was looking for his boss, Wes
Hardin, he was promptly arrested. He was interrogated for
hours, then put behind bars. In the meantime, Waller sent
a posse to Hamilton to apprehend the rest of the crew and
take possession of the herd. Three of the cowhands eluded
capture, but three others were brought back in handcuffs
and locked up with Dr. Brosius.

Then even the weather turned mean. Daily thunderstorms
flashed and blasted. Water tumbled down the gullies and
the Leon River overflowed. Creeks swamped their banks.
The bottoms flooded. The sky turned to iron and the roof-
tops clattered all night long under the relentless rain. The
world was sopping and made of mud. Posses rode in and
out of town around the clock. Sightings of the Hardin
Gang came from every corner of the county.

A posse headed by Waller himself ran up on Wesley
and Jim Taylor in the south prairie and gave them chase
in a ferocious rainstorm. "I still don't know how in the
hell they got away," a Ranger told me that night over a
bottle of bourbon in Jack Wright's. "We must of fired a
hundred rounds at them while they was gutting it up the
slippery side of a gully we'd boxed them in. We hit everything but Hardin and Taylor theirselfs. I saw Hardin's
horse hit three times and that damn animal didn't hardly
flinch. I know I hit Hardin's saddlebags, and I saw him
get a damn boot heel shot off. One shot knocked Taylor's
hat over his eyes—and the sonbitch *laughed*, I swear. You
could hear him laughing like some kind of damn *demon*
over the gunfire and the thunder. They had a hundred-yard

lead on us by the time we made the top of the gully, and in another minute they were flat out of sight. I don't know what they paid for them racers they was riding, but they damn sure got every last nickel's worth, tell you that.''

In town the mob grew restless. Its mood worsened in the sudden cessation of news of Wesley. For three days after the Rangers lost them on the south prairie, not one reliable sighting of the Hardin Gang was reported. Hunting parties continued to comb the stormy countryside, but there was no sign of Wesley anywhere. The possibility that he might have fled Comanche County for parts unknown added to the possemen's black rage. When they were not in the saddle, the vigilantes kept to the saloons, drinking resolutely and cursing the killers of that good man Charlie Webb—whose memory grew more venerable by the day. They drank and glared through the rain at the courthouse across the square and growled more and more murderously.

Shortly before midnight on the evening of June fifth, I was awakened by a clamor in the square. I stumbled to the window of my quarters directly above the *Chief*'s office and saw a mob surging at the courthouse door. The clouds had broken, and the scene was illuminated by a bright moon and a host of flaming torches. Shadows leapt and quivered on the courthouse wall.

The crowd roared as Bud and Tom Dixon were hauled outside by several men holding them fast by the arms. The brothers were spat upon and struck with clubs, and their hands were swiftly bound behind them. Another knot of men brought out a struggling Joe Hardin and shoved him into the clutches of the mob. His hands too were bound, and someone punched him full in the face. Then the three prisoners were swept into the square as if on a river current. My heart thumped in my throat. I could not spot Sheriff John or any of his deputies in the swirling crowd.

I hastily pulled on my trousers and boots and, still in my nightshirt, plunged headlong down the stairs and out into the street. I ran toward the mob, shouting I know not what. A pair of grinning men with clubs came toward me as the mob crossed the square and headed into the oak grove at the edge of town. "This is murder!" I yelled. I was clubbed on the neck and knocked to my knees. I recognized the man who hit me as a Brown County deputy. As I started to get up I was kicked in the stomach. I sagged on all fours and vomited while my assailants hurried away to rejoin the mob. Gasping, I got to my feet and staggered after them.

The mob had halted in a clearing and was swarming before a tall spreading oak—howling, laughing, having a revel, their faces devilish with murderous glee. At the fringe of the crowd I spotted a local townsman. "The law!" I shouted at him. "Where's the damn *law*?" He stared at me as if I were speaking Chinese. In the flickering light of the torches, he looked stricken and ghostly, as stunned by his helplessness as I was by mine to do anything but bear witness to the horror taking place.

The torchfires brightly lighted the underbranches of the tree. A noose sailed over a lower limb, and then another next to it. A third flew over a separate branch. The nooses danced macabrely as they were lowered to eager hands.

A great animal howl went up as Tom and Bud Dixon suddenly ascended into the mob's full view—hanging side by side and kicking their bare feet crazily. Their faces were horrifying above the crushing nooses. The mob cheered wildly, laughed, and threw stones at the dying men.

A moment later they hanged Joe from the other branch and the cheering was greater yet, the laughter louder at his distorted face and his pale feet flailing the empty air under him. There were shrill whistles and piercing rebel yells, and he too was stoned as he died. A woman screamed—whether in anguish or celebration I could not say—and a child laughed in firelit delight from his perch on the shoulders of a grinning man.

*　　*　　*

In the morning a Ranger named Dick Wade told me the
Hardin family women were wailing with such grief in
Joe Hardin's house it broke his heart to hear them.
Preacher Hardin had asked if the report of the lynching
was true, and Wade had confirmed the terrible truth. At
dawn he had been to the site of the murders and seen for
himself the three dead men dangling in the cold mist.
"The old Preacher cried like a child when I told him,"
Wade said. "The only good news I could give him was
that his friend Matt Fleming and two of his niggermen
took down the bodies after sunup and gave them a proper
burial."

Sheriff John had been out of town at the time of the lynch-
ings. He got back late the next day. When I stopped in to
see him that evening he was red-eyed with drink and de-
spair. Bill Stones had come to him on the previous morning and told him Alec Barrickman and Ham Anderson had
been hiding on his ranch out by Bucksnort Creek for the
past two days after having separated from Hardin and Taylor. Stones said he'd let them stay at his place because
they'd once helped him round up some loose calves in the
thicket and seemed like nice fellas. But when he found out
it was Captain Bill Waller looking for them, he got scared
for his own skin. If Barrickman and Anderson were found
on his place, Captain Bill might think he was part of the
Hardin Gang too. So he'd come to Sheriff John to give
them away.
    Sheriff John went out after them with a posse of eight
men, including Stones. They reached the ranch late that
night and sneaked up to within twenty yards of the lean-
to set against the rear of the house, where Ham and Alec
were sleeping. Sheriff John spread the posse in a wide half
circle around the back of the house in case Alec and Ham
tried to run for it. He had given strict orders not to shoot
unless the fugitives fired first—but before he could halloo
Ham and Alec and tell them they were under arrest,
somebody in the posse squeezed off a shot and ignited a
blazing fusillade of rifle fire that went on for a good thirty

seconds before John was finally able to make them desist. It was too late to do Ham and Alec any good. They found them lying dead on the floor, still wrapped in their blankets, shot all to bloody hell.

"None of them would say who started the shooting," John said, "but I know it was that Stones bastard. He was scared they'd kill him one day for turning them in." He took a big pull from the bottle. "Then I get back here," he said, "and find there was a hell of a necktie party while I was gone." Frank Wilson and a handful of Rangers had been on guard in the courthouse, but they all claimed the mob had taken them by surprise and forced them to give over the prisoners. They swore they didn't recognize any of the vigilantes. All the other Rangers had been out on patrol with Captain Bill. "Ain't that something," Sheriff John said, staring at me with a face as sick as sin. "Well hell, Holden," he said, and toasted me with the bottle. "Fuck 'em all!"

And now Comanche knew true fear. The lynchers had mostly been Brown County men, but the murders had taken place in Comanche, and the good citizens reasoned that Wesley would therefore take the worst of his revenge on them. Black rumors flew through town like frightened bats. They said he would kill twenty men for each of his two cousins, and thirty to get even for Joe. He would fill Comanche's streets with blood to his stirrups. He would burn the town to the ground and scatter the ashes. Women kept to their houses and prayed for deliverance from the wrath of John Wesley Hardin. Children slept under their beds and woke shrieking in the night. For weeks a dozen armed guards walked the town square every night and kept great fires burning at every street corner, the better to see his terrifying specter when he came to murder the good people in their beds.

Ross Yarrow

Fancy Frank and me were with a pair of girls at his cabin in the cedar brakes just north of Austin, and this buck-ass nekkid thing called Sandra Jean grabs up the whiskey bottle and runs out with it, laughing like a drunk redskin, which she partly was—redskin I mean; she was way more than partly drunk. Anyhow, I go out after her—twanger and balls flapping and bouncing as I chase her around back of the house—and *wham*, she runs smack into this tall rascal standing there in the shadows and falls on her ass. He throws down on me with a big Colt which I could see just fine in the moonlight, and I thought, *Shit! Bandits!* But no, the fella says "Frank Taylor?" and I say "Nosir, name's Yarrow. Frank's inside." He looks down at Sandra Jean—who's looking up at him with her little titties shining in the light of the moon and her big bush dark as sin twixt her legs—and he says with a grin, "Looks like a nice party." It's the sort of remark don't need an answer, but I said, "Yeah, I guess." You don't know what it feels like to be nekkid till you're nekkid in the out-of-doors and somebody fully dressed is holding a gun on you.

Sandra Jean got up and brushed her ass off with one hand while she held the other over her bush like some shy little schoolgirl instead of the free-and-easy waiter girl she was at Fancy Frank's saloon in Austin. The girl in the house with Frank was a waiter girl too—Lola, a redhead with nipples you could hang hats on. "If nobody *minds*," Sandra Jean says, "I will just retire to the indoors." She turns on her heel and nearly loses her balance, then gets hold of herself and walks off twitching her pretty ass.

The fella says, "Listen, Yarrow, I got Frank's cousin Jim here. He's bad sick and I'm shot." I'd never met Jim Taylor, but I'd heard all about him from Frank. Like everybody else, I'd heard about how him and his little brother Billy had gunned down Bill Sutton on the steamer Clinton in Indianola. "Might you be . . . ?" I say—and he says, "John Wesley Hardin. Go tell Frank."

Frank already had his pants on and his hand filled—and damn near shot me when I came through the door. Sandra Jean had told him there was a man with a gun behind the house and he'd thought the same thing I had, that we were being rousted by bandits. I told him who it was and we got dressed fast. Two minutes later Frank was patting the girls on their bottoms as he helped them into the buckboard while I hitched the team. The girls were still only half dressed and mad as wet hens to be getting such a fast shove out of there. Frank pressed some money on them to ease their upset. He gave Lola a kiss so long and a squeeze of her tit, then slapped the horse's rump and said, "Git!" and the wagon rolled off down the trace toward the Austin road.

We went around back and there was Wes holding two horses. Jim was on one and coughing into a balled bandanna. While Frank and Wes got him in the house, I staked their horses back in the brakes with ours. When I got back, Jim was tucked in bed, looking sick as a dog and sweating with a rank fever. Frank got him to drink some of the juice off the stew we'd supped on, then let him drift off to sleep.

He tore up an old shirt to make a bandage for Wes's wound. We came to find out he'd taken the shot in some bad business him and Jim had got into up in Comanche. His family was still back there, and he was worried about how they were making out. He figured he'd lie low for a few days to let things cool off some, then slip on back and make sure they were all right. Frank told him he was welcome to stay as long as he liked. "Thanks kindly," Wes said. He had a heavy growth of whiskers and his hair was all wild tangles and his eyes were bloodshot with pain and exhaustion. He fell asleep at the table before he finished eating his stew.

Over the next few days Jim mostly slept and got better. His fever broke and his cough eased up. Wes was doing good too. It was the first chance for his wound to start healing since they'd made their getaway from Comanche more than a week before, and after a few days it was knitting up nicely.

Then Alf and Charlie Day showed up. They were cousins to Jim Taylor and were supposed to be with Doc Brosius and the trail crew Wes had hired to move his herd. When Wes saw them coming out of the brakes, he said, "Oh, hell."

Alf and Charlie were surprised to find Wes and Jim there, but they didn't look real happy about it, and pretty soon we found out why. We sat at the table and had a drink while Alf did most of the talking. He told us Doc Brosius and three other of the crew were under arrest in Comanche, and the herd had been confiscated by the State Rangers.

He and Charlie had been on herd guard when they saw a gang of about two dozen riders coming at a gallop over a far rise—so they quick spurred their ponies into the woods and got out of sight. Pink Burns was already there, gathering wood for the cookfire. Doc Brosius had gone to Comanche the day before to find Wes and let him know the herd was at Hamilton, but he hadn't come back yet.

They watched from the trees as Scrap Taylor and the other two men in camp threw up their hands in surrender. "We knew it wasn't rustlers," Alf said, "not a gang that size." When half the riders headed back toward Comanche with the three trail hands and the other half stayed with the herd, Alf figured them for some kind of posse, but he couldn't make heads or tails of what was going on. He and Charlie and Pink circled their way around and headed into town to see if they could find Doc Brosius to tell him what happened.

What they found was a town crawling with Rangers and vigilantes. "The place looked ready for war, there was so many guns about," Alf said. They learned Doc was in jail too, and Wes's brother Joe and his Dixon cousins—all because Wes and Jim had killed some deputy from Brown County. Wes's whole family was under arrest in Joe's house. The Rangers were arresting everybody connected to Wes by blood or friendship. There were posses criss-crossing the whole region. Alf convinced Charlie and Pink it'd be safer to stay put in the crowded town for a few days than try to leave Comanche County with so many posses on the lookout for suspicious characters.

Wes cussed like blue blazes. Now Alf was licking his lips and looking everywhere except in Wes's eyes. Charlie was looking awful uncomfortable too. I knew we hadn't heard the worst, not yet. I reckon Wes knew it too. "Get it out, Alf," he said.

"Oh, Jesus, Wes," Alf said, "I hate to be the one." The way he said it, you knew it was going to be as bad as bad gets, and it was. Talking fast and without hardly pausing for breath, he told how Joe and the Dixons had been taken out of the courthouse jail by a midnight mob and lynched in the woods. "There wasn't a thing in the world we could of done to stop them, Wes," Alf said. "If we'd tried, they'd of hung us too. You got to believe that."

"He died brave, Wes," Charlie said. "It ain't nothing but the truth."

Wes's face looked about to fall apart. He got up fast and went outside. The rest of us just sat there. I picked at the wood grain of the table top with my fingernail and wished I was someplace else. Jim Taylor looked like a kicked hound. "Sweet Christ," he said. "*Joe*. He never even shot nobody."

After a while Wes came back in. His eyes were puffy and red, but you could tell he was done with it. Jim Taylor got out of bed and joined us at the table. He was some better but still weak, and he stunk to high heaven.

Jim decided he'd go to Gonzales with Alf and Charlie to lay low among friends till he was full well again, but Wes was going back to Comanche. He had to know how the rest of his family was doing and see what he could do to get them clear of town. Alf said the family all been moved back to the Reverend's house, but advised Wes against going there. "That Ranger captain got out the word that if you so much as show your face around there he'll kill your daddy. He's the sort to do it, Wes."

Wes punched the table. "Son of a *bitch*! I can't just do *nothing*!"

"You go," Jim Taylor said. "But you step real light."

I said he could use somebody to ride with him, and I'd be proud to be the one. He looked at me for long moment, then said he'd be proud to have me. And that settled that.

Three nights later we made our way into Comanche slow and careful. We went up through the heavy oak groves at the west end of town, where Alf said the lynching had took place. A hazy slice of moon showed through the treetops. It had rained a little earlier and the trees were still dripping. Our horses' hooves sucked through the mud. We dismounted and walked the animals the last fifty yards to the rear edge of the Preacher's property.

Several of the lower windows showed light, but the upper rooms were all dark. "It's likely possemen on the first floor," Wes whispered, "and the family sleeping upstairs." He nudged me and pointed—a man had stepped out of the shadows alongside the house and was coming toward the trees, a rifle laid across his shoulders and his arms draped over its ends. He stopped at the trees, about fifteen feet from us, set his rifle against a trunk, and fumbled with the front of his pants. A moment later we heard the piss pouring and a satisfied sigh.

One of our horses snorted softly and the man's head jerked up. He probably wet himself, cutting off his piss as short as he did. He tried to tuck himself in with one hand while he held the rifle out like a pistol with the other—

but he was facing the wrong way, sound being the funny thing it is in the dark. Wes eased up behind him in the heavy shadows of the trees, and just loud enough for the fella to hear, he said, "Drop it or die."

The fella dropped the rifle and froze. "Jesus, Wes," he whispered, "don't shoot. It's me—Dick."

"Dick?" Wes says. "Dick Wade?"

Turns out they knew each other. They'd had a run-in sometime earlier when Wes had sneaked up to his daddy's house and found it full of possemen ambushers. He'd had to run for it with bullets whizzing past his ears. Dashing through the trees to get back to his horse, he'd run smack into Ranger Dick Wade. Wade had thrown up his hands and begged Wes not to shoot him, saying he was his friend and was pulling for him to get clear. He seemed so sincere that Wes not only spared him, but gave him a twenty-dollar gold piece to give to Jane as soon as he could sneak it to her.

"I snuck it to her the very next day, Wes," he said. "She was so happy to know you were alive she cried. She said if I saw you again to tell you she's all right, the baby too, and she prays for you every night. I told your daddy I'd seen you and was your friend, and him and me got to be friends too. He hired me on to tend his garden—that's what him and me told Captain Waller—but he really just wanted me around here to keep a lookout and warn you off in case you came to see Jane and Molly."

Wes asked where Joe was buried, and Wade said back in the grove about a quarter mile. Wes thought about it a minute, then said, "Show me. I want to see."

We followed him through the dripping shadows until we came to the grave mounds. They were set pretty much side by side, and even though the rains had flattened them some, they still smelled heavy of fresh-turned earth. Wade pointed to the one a little apart from the other two and said it was Joe's. "Listen," Wes said, "I want to see Jane, I want to see my little girl. Tell Daddy I'm here. Find out how I can see them." Dick said he'd be back directly and slipped off into the dark. Wes knelt in the mud beside Joe's grave and took off his hat.

I went off deeper into the woods till I figured it was safe to light a cigar, then sat on a stump and smoked my cheroot and just listened to the raindrip and frogs and hoot owls. I hoped Wes was right to trust the Ranger not to bring back a bunch of his friends. When my smoke was down to a stub, I snuffed it and went back to the gravesite. Wade had already returned and was telling Wes his daddy'd been powerful happy to hear he was alive and running free. But he'd refused to wake Jane and tell her Wes was here. She'd insist on coming to see him, and all the stirring about would alert the Rangers in the house for sure. The Reverend wanted Wes to get far out of Comanche County and stay away. "He said to tell you Waller'll kill the whole family if you're seen anywhere in the county. He's serious as church, Wes. I don't blame him. Waller's the devil's own son of a bitch."

Wes paced around in a wide circle, cussing steadily under his breath. There wasn't a thing he could do, not with his whole family hostage like they were. It's nothing in the world as bad as having to hold back from attacking something you hate with all your might because you might hurt something you love with all your heart. It's a situation to make a man howl like a moonstruck hound.

Finally he says, "All right, tell Daddy I'm headed for Uncle Bob's place in Brenham. See the word gets around. Once Waller knows I'm gone, maybe he'll ease off on the family. Tell Jane I'll send somebody for her and Molly just as soon as I can." He handed Wade some gold pieces to give to Jane, then shook his hand and gripped his shoulder. "You're a good man, Dick," he said. "You either oughtn't be a Ranger or every Ranger ought be like you."

I rode with him as far as Lampasas. We spotted more than one posse brushing the country for the Hardin Gang, but managed to avoid being seen by any of them. At Lampasas we shook hands and wished each other luck, and then I swung off on the Austin road and he pushed on toward Brenham.

Harry Swain

I was marshal of Brenham when Wes showed up in the summer of '74. I was married to Jenny Parks, a second cousin of his. Will Hardin introduced us at a calf roast they were having in his honor. I already knew about the terrible happenings at Comanche, and he'd confessed to Jenny he was worried sick about Jane and Molly and the rest of his family still back there. He didn't show it, though, when he was among people. When we were introduced, he joked about me being a marshal, and I joshed him back for being the most wanted outlaw in Texas. I liked him right off. Him and me and his cousins Will and J.D. went fishing in the creek the next day and caught a mess of catfish and perch and had us a big fish fry that evening.

After we got easy with each other, he told me he wanted to get out of Texas for a time. He believed mob law was everywhere. It had so far cost the life of his brother and of other kin, and he was sure it would get him too if he stayed in Texas. Just a week or so earlier, he'd been given even more reason to feel that way when the four trail hands of his who'd been arrested in Comanche had been taken down to Gonzales County to stand trial on trumped-up charges of some kind. The Rangers turned them over to the sheriff in Clinton and then quick left town, all of them, and in the middle of the night a band of vigilantes showed up and dragged the prisoners off to the cemetery and hanged three of them—Scrap Taylor, Shorty Tuggle, and Frog White. The fourth one, Doc Brosius, somehow got away.

"Even if it's lawmen who catch me," Wes said, "they'll either hand me over to the mob or the mob'll take me from them by force."

I argued that there were some lawmen who'd never let a mob take a prisoner from them. He laughed and asked me how many mobs I'd seen in action. I had to admit I hadn't seen a serious one yet. "Well," he said, "after you see your first serious one, I'll be interested in hearing how easy you think it is for even a brave lawman to hold off Captain Lynch."

He had written to Jane in Comanche, writing in a code they had and using her daddy's name on the envelope. In her return letter she said that when Captain Waller got the news of the Clinton lynching, he had released the family from arrest and told her she was free to go home. All she needed was somebody to come get her and Molly. But she warned him not to come himself, since the county was still full of Rangers and bounty men who would shoot him on sight. J.D. left for Comanche on horseback early the next morning. He would buy a wagon there to bring them back in.

In the meantime, Jane's father, Neal Bowen, had just got back to Gonzales from Kansas, where he'd gone at Wes's request to help Joe Clements get top dollar for Wes's cattle, and he was holding a good bit of money for him. Wes wanted to go to Gonzales to collect it, and he asked me to go with him, figuring my badge would keep the Sutton Party at a distance if they got wind of his presence. I really don't think my damn badge was nearly as much protection to him as his own reputation. We heard lots of talk in town of what the Sutton Party had said they'd do to Wes Hardin or Jim Taylor if either of them showed his face in the Sandies again, but we didn't have any trouble while we were there. Jim Taylor hadn't been so lucky. The Suttons had made several attempts on his life in the weeks since he'd come back, and he'd been

wounded in a fight near the Guadalupe. Wes wanted to
see him and try to talk him into leaving the region, but he
was pretty sure Taylor wouldn't leave again, no matter
what. Besides, Taylor was hiding out with an old pal
named Russel Hoy, who Wes distrusted so much he would
not go to his house, not even to try and see Jim.

Wes was several thousand dollars richer when we got
back to Brenham, but he was also more convinced than
ever that he had to get out of Texas fast.

A few days later J.D. got back with Jane and Molly. He'd
driven day and night and gone through three teams of
horses. I mean to tell you that was one happy reunion Wes
had with his family. During the supper party my Jenny
gave for them that evening, him and Jane couldn't keep
their eyes off each other—hardly their hands, if truth be
told. I had a feeling they couldn't wait for it to be over
so they could get to their bedroom in Bob Hardin's house.
Jenny, bless her sharp-eyed soul, saw how anxious they
were to get together in private too, and she managed to
bring the party to an early ending without offending any
of the guests. You can't do better in this life than to be
married to a wise and good-hearted woman.

Wes's problem now was how to get out of Texas without
putting Jane and Molly at risk. That's where I came in. I
said I'd accompany his wife and child to New Orleans so
he could travel alone and not have to worry about danger
to them if he should run into any trouble on the way. Jenny
corrected me—she said *we'd* take Jane and Molly. "I've
always hankered to go to New Orleans," she said. "Let's
make a high time of it."

Wes left Brenham on horseback a couple of days before
the rest of us set out in a wagon with a couple of spare
horses hitched to its rear. It was a real nice trip for us. We
slept under the stars some nights, in road inns on others,
and in hotels when we were near a town. Jenny and Jane
became true fast friends. Molly wasn't yet two years old
at the time, but she was a hardy little traveler and eye-

balled everything on the road with curiosity. I knew she was going to be a smart little scamp, that one.

We met Wes at the Prince Francis Hotel in the French Quarter as planned. He'd been there for four days by the time we arrived. He'd registered as J. W. Swain and told the hotel manager that his brother Harry would soon be arriving with the wives and child. Jane and Jenny couldn't believe the splendor of the hotel. "Makes me feel like poor kin, though," Jane whispered, "dressed like this in such a place." Wes said he'd figured that's how she'd feel, and had already informed the dress shop around the corner that she and Jenny would be in for fittings that afternoon. The next day our wives were wearing beautiful dresses and ready to see the town. You never saw two prettier gals with happier eyes. They even bought a fancy little bonnet with flowers on it for Molly to wear in her stroller.

Wes was already acquainted with the city and eager to show it to the rest of us. It was warm and the air was heavy, but a sweet breeze came off the river. None of us had seen the Mississippi before. "My Lord," Jenny said, gazing on it, "the *Big* Muddy is right." Wes laughed and said, "It ain't Sandy Crick, is it?" He had to keep reminding Jane to call him John instead of Wes.

We took long walks through the Quarter, admiring the iron lacework of the balconies and the tap dancing of the Nigra boys on the street corners and the fine jumpy music coming out of every other doorway. Wes was careful not to say anything about the fancy houses we passed on nearly every street, and naturally Jane and Jenny were too well brought up to even show they'd noticed them. But every now and then when we'd pass one and the girls weren't looking our way, Wes would nod at it and give me a big wink so I couldn't keep from grinning. He has some rascal in him, all right.

The smells from all the wonderful bakeries and restaurants kept us in a constant hunger, and it seemed like we spent half our time in New Orleans just eating. We spooned up bowls of gumbo and cleaned off platters of crayfish and iced raw oysters and trays of fancy desserts. The coffee was sweet as candy and the wines so fine it was no wonder we all drank ourselves silly at the table every night. Jenny's first sip of Bourdeaux lit her eyes up like a sudden understanding, and she said, "Oh, my." She looked so soft-eyed and beautiful, I couldn't help but lean over and kiss her on the one shoulder her pretty new dress left bare. New Orleans is the kind of place that'll make a man do a thing like that. "*Harry!*" she said, all big-eyed with happy surprise. Wes clapped me on the back and said, "Damn, Harry, if you ain't a natural-born Frenchman— pardon *my* French, ladies." And Jane—who swore her lips had never touched spirits until she took her first taste of wine with us—just smiled and smiled. She raised her glass and said, "To us all," and we drank to that.

But the girls' favorite places were the ice cream salons. Wes called them *saloons* just to make Jane blush. "Oh . . . *John,*" she'd say, "*behave!*" The city was full of them, and I swear I never tasted nothing better than the praline-and-caramel ice cream I ate in a salon on Royal Street. The first spoonful of it I put in my mouth made me think my tongue had died and gone to heaven. And for all the fun he made of the places, Wes loved them too, and it wasn't unusual for him to eat two bowls to my one.

There finally came the morning we checked out of the hotel and went with Wes and Jane and Molly down to the wharf to see them off. Wes and me shook hands and Jane and Jenny hugged and kissed and cried all over each other. Then they went aboard the steamboat and waved to us from the railing while the whistle blew and blew. Then the boat pulled away from the dock and headed on down-river for the Gulf of Mexico and steamed away to Florida.

Gus Kennedy

It was their first time at sea and it showed. As soon as we reached open Gulf and the steamer started its easy pitching on the low swells, they got a little green around the gills. By the next day, however, they had their proper color again and were back at the railing like a pair of old salts, smiling at the sea and each other, telling their little girl not to be scared of the sea gulls fluttering and screeching over the deck.

Even as he talked and laughed with his family, his eyes didn't miss a thing going on around him. He was a man with no use for surprises. His coat was open, the top two buttons of his vest were undone, and the left side of it bulged with a pistol. He was just starting a mustache. I had him figured for a Texan. We had plenty of them in Florida at the time. There were cattle wars going on from the upper St. John's all the way to the southwest coast, and some of the big ranchers were importing pistoleros to protect their interests. The prisoner I'd just turned over to a Texas Ranger in New Orleans was such a man. We'd had a DeSoto County rustling warrant on him, and one evening I spotted him coming out of a Beaver Street whorehouse, so I slipped up behind him and gave him the butt of my shotgun in the head. A little later we received the Texas warrant on him for murder and I delivered him on the steamship. But this one had his family with him, so I figured he was likely more interested in staying out of trouble than looking for it.

The weather that afternoon was nice—bright sunshine and a gentle salt breeze. I was standing only a few feet from them at the railing when the woman suddenly pointed and cried out, "Oh, look—what are *those*?" A school of porpoises had surfaced and was rolling and blowing alongside the ship. I tipped my hat and told them what they were looking at. "They're warm-blooded as you and me," I told them. "See those blowholes on their heads they breathe through? Some say they're smart and can talk to each other, though I can't guess what *about*. Maybe what kind of fish make the best eating, or whether the water feels any cooler today than yesterday, or which boy porpoise has been chasing after which lady porpoise—beg pardon, ma'am."

The man laughed and the woman blushed pretty. I introduced myself and put my hand out. "John Swain," he said as we shook—"my wife Jane and daughter Molly." Jane said she didn't know how smart porpoises were, but they sure did look like the happiest things. "Just look at those great big smiles!" she said. The man said he'd smile all the time too if all he had to do was play and eat and chase after the ladies all day long. "Now, Wes, *behave!*" she said, blushing again—and then quick put her hand up to her mouth. And just like that, I knew who he was.

Jane gaped at him like she'd spilled coffee in his lap. He patted her hand and looked around to make sure we weren't being overheard, then smiled at me and said, "Mr. Kennedy, you look like you might have something on your mind."

Of course I was a little wary. I mean, John Wesley Hardin, the Texas mankiller! "Well, sir," I said, "I'd say Miz Swain might be one to get names a little confused when she gets excited."

He smiled and said, "That's a fact. Just last week she called me Winston in the excitement of a horse race in Houston. *Winston!* I about died of shame." Then his smile closed up. "What I'm wondering is what some lawman

might do if he was to mistake a peaceable citizen like
myself for a man on the dodge, a man who ain't wanted
in the lawman's own state and for sure ain't wanted on
this boat." I said before that his eyes didn't miss much,
but I was surprised he'd spotted me for a policeman. "I'm
asking you man-to-man, Mr. Kennedy—what you aim to
do now?"

"Mr. Swain," I said, "I aim to enjoy this boat ride like
I always do, and let sleeping dogs lie like I always do. I
figure a policeman's job is to protect a citizen's person
and property from them that's trying to harm the one or
steal the other. Beyond that, I got no use for a policeman
myself." It was the truth. I'd become a law officer by
chance after getting my fill of the cow-hunter's life on the
prairie. Turned out I was a good one—I was big and probably a bit less fearful than most, and I had a sharp eye for
what was going on around me. But I never used my badge
to bully nor went looking for trouble.

He studied my face close for a minute, making up his
mind, then gave me his hand with a grin. "Proud to know
you, Gus." And I said, "Proud to make *your* acquaintance
. . . *Winston*." And even Jane laughed.

I accepted their invitation to join them for supper that
evening, and we took most our meals together every day
after that for the rest of the voyage. Jane couldn't get
enough of talking about New Orleans, and John and I always accommodated her choice of topic at the table. In
the afternoons, however, when she retired to their cabin to
put the baby down for a nap, John and I went to the upper
deck railing to smoke a cigar and talk about our adventures
in the cow trade—and about horseflesh and gambling
houses and parlor palaces where we'd taken our pleasure.
We had many similar opinions and both loved games of
chance. I told him that if he ever got up to Jacksonville,
I'd take him to some poker houses where the stakes ran
rich as mother lodes.

He said Jane had kin in the Alabama boot heel, and he
thought he might go in the lumber business up there. But
first he wanted to see an old friend of his from the trail-

driving days, a fella named Bama Bill, who was running a saloon in Gainesville. He fancied the idea of running his own saloon and wanted to see if Bill could use a partner. He didn't talk about his trouble with the Texas law but to say he wasn't guilty of a thing except defending himself and his own. I said no honest man could fault him for that. By the time the steamer bumped up against the dock at Cedar Key, it felt like we'd been friends for years.

They about smothered in the humidity. "Good Lord," Jane said, "we've got heat in Texas, but *this*!" Mosquitoes whined in our ears and horseflies stabbed the backs of our necks as our hack made its slow way around all the timber wagons delivering loads to the dock for shipment. After trading profanities with every teamster impeding our progress, our driver finally got us to the train station. But not till the train pulled out and gained enough speed to bring a breeze through the windows did we get some relief from the heat and the insects. Gazing out the coach window at the passing country of pine and cypress, John smiled and said it reminded him of the East Texas piny woods, which he loved. "Me too," Jane said, only she looked sad and far from home. We said good-bye at the Gainesville station. As the train pulled out again, heading for Jacksonville, they stood on the platform and waved so long.

One night about ten months later I arrested a bullying big drunk of a seaman named Davison in a bad saloon over by the river docks, but when I pulled him out on the sidewalk a mean crowd followed us, including three of his shipmates, and the situation got tight real fast. The sailors pulled knives and backed me and my prisoner against the wall, saying I either let their friend go or they'd cut me up for fish bait. The crowd was egging them on, wanting a show. I'd cuffed Davison's hands behind him, but he was putting up a hell of a fuss and it took both hands to hold him. I knew if I was forced to pull my gun I'd have to shoot—and with that crowd, no telling what could happen.

Then one of the sailors gave a grunt and his eyes rolled up and down he went. And there John stood, grinning at me and holding a big army Colt that he'd clubbed the fella with. "Stand fast, boys," he told the other two, and they froze in place.

I grabbed Davison by the hair and rammed his head into the brick wall, putting an end to his nuisance and freeing my hands of him. John backed up beside me, still holding his gun on the other two, and said, "Evening, Gus. They said at the station you'd been sent here to settle a row, but damn if it don't look like it's trying to settle you."

"Evening yourself, John," I said. "Real good to see you. Excuse me a minute."

I took the knives off the two tars and gave each one a hard backhand across the mouth, drawing blood both times. I told them to pick up their trash and get out of my sight before I cut their noses off. They didn't waste any time hoisting up the one John coldcocked and making off down the wharf. I told the crowd the show was over and to break it up, and they started milling back into the bar, grumbling that nobody'd been killed. I took a mug of beer from one fella and poured it in Davison's face to bring him around.

"Mr. Swain," I said, "let me check this gentleman into the Crossbars Hotel and we'll go sit ourselves down with a bottle so you can tell me why it's taken you so damn long to come to our fair city."

A half hour later we were drinking rye at a back table in Feller's Club and he was telling me he'd found the saloon his old trail friend had owned in Gainesville—but Bama Bill himself had been dead for two months. He'd got into a drunken fight with the high yella woman he lived with just outside of town and she'd broke his head open with an iron skillet. She'd covered up her crime by burning down the house and claiming the fire killed Bill. But she was a good Christian woman and her conscience bothered her too much to live with, so she went to the sheriff and confessed. Two nights later, while the sheriff was at supper, a bunch of Bama Bill's friends broke her out of the jail and took her out in the swamp and a few of them had their way with her and then they drowned her.

John heard this story from Sam Burnette, who'd come to own the saloon after Bill's death. But Sam was champing at the bit to go prospecting for silver in Colorado, and he was ready to sell. In just a couple of days they'd made the deal and John had himself a saloon.

Shack Wilson, the Gainesville sheriff, became one of his regulars, not only at the bar but in the poker room John set up in the back. They started going bass fishing together. Shack introduced him to a neighbor of his named Salter who raised a kind of hunting dog called a Texas leopard, which is the best wild-hog hunting dog there is. The three of them would go into the forest every now and then and come out with enough pig for all their families to feast on for days.

One day when he was tending bar, in walks a couple of Texans he knew from his trail-driving days. They recognized him too, mustache and all. But before they could say anything, John put out his hand and said, "Name's John Swain! Always glad to see new faces in here." He took them to a table at the rear of the room and they had a quiet talk. The Texans were in town on some cattle deal and were mighty glad to see him. They said they'd been hearing all sorts of tales about him back in Texas for the last ten months—that he'd robbed banks in Waco and Dallas, that he'd killed the sheriff in Livingston last Christmas and two Texas Rangers in San Antone just last month and four possemen near Austin the month before that. Every time somebody got shot dead in Texas and there weren't any witnesses, you could bet the blame would fall on John Wesley Hardin. "I guess it's a compliment," John told them, "to be so often remembered by my fellow Texans." The two trail partners swore they wouldn't say a word back in Texas about having seen him, and Wes told them he knew he could trust them. The Texans were in town a week and spent every night in John's saloon, drinking and gambling and having a high time. Three days after they left back for Texas, John had sold the saloon and set out with his family for Jacksonville without letting anyone know where he was going. "It's not that I don't trust them old boys," he said, "I just thought it'd be wise to proceed as if I didn't."

He did real well in Jacksonville—got into cattle shipping and bought himself a butcher shop, and both businesses prospered. Their little rented house on the bank of the St. Johns was shaded by palms and cooled by the river breezes. Jane loved living in the midst of all that lush greenery. They often took the wagon out to the beach with a picnic lunch and played in the breakers. Jane was rosy with sun and the glow of pregnancy, and Molly was dark as an Indian. In August "J. H. Swain, Jr." was born, and for the next two weeks John handed a cigar to every man he met. I got into the habit of taking supper at their house two or three evenings a week. I taught John the fun of fishing in the surf, and we'd go hunting in the swamps for deer and pig. He shot a couple of good-size alligators one day and we dragged them out on ropes and had them skinned by an old Creek from the St. John backwater. John hung the skin of the sixteen-footer on the front porch of his house and had the fourteen-footer made into belts and hat bands and two fine pairs of boots, one for me and one for himself. We got to be damn fine friends and got to talking about going partners in the timber business up in the Panhandle.

Of course we did a little gambling every so often. We sat in on Bobby Chiles's poker game on Tuesday nights in the back of his saloon, and in Fred Johnson's game every Thursday. I always did all right, but John most always came out the big winner. The fellas used to cuss me half joking and half not for introducing him to our games. "Don't seem we can do much about your luck, Swain," Bobby Chiles said to him one time, "but we ought to take a damn horsewhip to Kennedy for bringing you around here in the first place."

*   *   *

One night—he'd been in Jacksonville about a year, I guess—we came out of Bobby Chiles's with a nice bourbon glow and bumped into a pair of strangers coming through the doors. They were big rascals and wore tight black suits and derby hats. One had a black handlebar and the other's face was full of orange freckles. "Pardon me, friend," I said to the Handlebar, then saw the look he gave John and I knew they'd come for him. Freckles stood aside to let us pass and John nodded thanks.

We paused under the streetlight in front of the saloon to fire up cigars, and John whispered, "Looks like they're on to me." I glanced real casual up at the saloon window behind him and saw Handlebar peeking out. "Best go your own way, Gus," he said. "It ain't your fight." Hell it ain't, I told him. In my best copper's voice I said I was an authorized agent of the law, sworn to protect the honest citizens of Jacksonville from those who would interfere with the exercise of their civil liberties. John smiled and said, "Well hell then," and we headed off toward the deserted section of town by the old port on the river.

They followed us down the lighted streets, keeping half a block back. Music twanged from the swinging doors of every saloon. We went around a corner and onto a dark street of empty warehouses facing a line of rotted piers that hadn't been used by the river steamers in years. The lots between the empty warehouses were littered with shipping debris. "Fill your hand," John whispered—but I'd drawn my revolver as soon as we'd turned the corner, and I held it cocked under my coat. "I'll take the street-side one," he said, "you the inside." The saloon music was fainter now, and I thought I heard their footsteps crunching up behind us in the broken glass. My back muscles quivered. Then one of them called out, "Mr. Swain! Hold on, sir!"

We stopped and turned. They were thirty feet away and closing, silhouetted against the glow of a street lamp just off the corner. They had their hands in their coats too. As they closed in, the Handlebar said, "Mr. John Swain of Texas?" He started to take his hand out and John shot him square in the forehead. Freckles and I fired at the same time and I felt his bullet tug through the loose flap of my coat. He dropped his gun and fell forward and I knew he was dead by the way he hit the ground. It was over just that quick.

I expected the whole damn world to come running to see what the shots were about, and I was already putting a story together in my head about us being attacked by these two strangers, hoping like hell they weren't U.S. marshals. But there were no cries of alarm, no sound of running feet—only the sudden splashing of a school of mullet in the St. John's and the distant music from the saloons around the corner.

We went through their pockets and stripped them clean, then dragged the bodies into one of the warehouses and covered them up with a rotted canvas sail. We piled broken crates on top of that. It'd be days before the corpses worked up a stink strong enough to be smelled beyond the warehouse—and even then they might not draw much attention. Then again, some scavenging tramp might uncover them the very next day, you never knew.

We cut through the back streets to my boardinghouse room. As soon as we shut the door behind us, I poured us a drink. Then we went through their papers and found out they were Pinkertons. The Handlebar was James Kelleher and Freckles was Francis Connors. They had ticket stubs off that morning's train from Atlanta—and a Texas reward poster offering four thousand dollars for the capture of John Wesley Hardin.

The next morning he put Jane and the children on the westbound train. He'd bought their tickets for New Orleans in case somebody came nosing around the depot asking where the Hardin family had gone. But he'd told Jane to get off the train at Pensacola and hire a hack to Polland, a small settlement just across the border in Alabama where her kin were living.

John stayed in Jacksonville a few days longer to give them time to get away safely, and in that time nobody discovered the bodies. I told the police chief I was quitting the force to go gold hunting in the Dakota Territory with John Swain, and a bunch of the coppers made a lot of jokes about it—which was good, because it meant they believed me.

Two days later we were met at the Pensacola depot by Jane's Uncle Harris, just like John and Jane had arranged, and by nightfall we were in Polland.

And so we got into the logging business, me and John. We went partners with a lively buck-toothed fella named Shep Hardie and his nephew, an eighteen-year-old ass-kicker named Jim Mann. They owned some prime timberland about thirty-five miles up the Styx River but were short of the capital to log it. John and I put up the money for the necessary machinery and wagons and to hire four more loggers. The eight of us went upriver to the property and set up a work camp, and that's where we spent most of the following year, cutting timber and logging it. Some of it we floated down the Styx to the sawmills on the Perdido fork, and some of it we sold to companies that used mule teams to haul the logs to the railway west of us. It was damn hard work but it turned us a pretty fair profit.

Every now and then we took a day off and went to Mobile to put some of that profit to work on the card tables—and so those among us who had the notion could buy themselves a good time at one of the swell pleasure houses to be found in that lively, lowdown town. Mobile always smelled to me of low tide, pine tar, magnolias, and puke. It was full of hard trade—sailors and shipworkers and sawyers, card sharps and whores. I don't recall a time we went there that two or three of us didn't get a broken nose or cut hand or some other kind of barfight memento. Jim Mann always came back sporting fresh cuts and bruises. He was a fine wild-hearted boy who wore a black eye like a badge of honor. He would grin through his puffy lips and make some joke about how we ought to see what the other fella looked like.

One time in Mobile, John and I got into a saloon row with a couple of timber teamsters named Lewis and Kress, and a little later—and unfortunately for us—they somehow or other ended up shot dead in an alley. We were arrested and wrongly charged with murder, and we spent two long miserable days and nights in jail before we finally got things all cleared up—with a little help from our contribution of two thousand dollars to the Mobile Police Department. After that, we mostly stayed clear of Mobile and took our pleasures in Pensacola.

Pensacola was anyway where we always took on camp supplies. We'd send the goods by rail to Pensacola Junction—Whiting, as some of the locals called it—and a freight boat would take them up the Styx to our camp. After shipping the goods, we'd stay in Pensacola another couple of days for a bit of fun. Shep Hardie had grown up there and knew all the poker rooms in town. The best was run by Alston Shipley, the regional railroad manager who'd been a logging contractor before going to work for the railroad. He still cussed like a logger and was strong as a mule.

When we'd done with our good-timing in Pensacola, Jim Mann would take the rest of the crew back to camp while John and I stopped at Polland for a couple of days so he could visit Jane and the children. It was on one of these visits that Jane's Uncle Harris informed us that Wild Bill Hickok was dead. He'd read about it in a New Orleans newspaper a couple of months old. It happened in a saloon up in Dakota. Hickok was playing cards, sitting with his back to the door for some damn reason, and some tramp shot him in the back of the head. "It's a damn low shame," John said. "Bill deserved better than to get it like that." He was down in the mouth the rest of the evening.

Jane had use of a house belonging to her Uncle Harris, and I'd sleep in a small side room whenever John and I were visiting. I always did my best to mind my own business, but the house was small and the walls were thin. Jane had never cared much for John living way off in the timber camp so that she didn't get to see him more than once or twice a month. She'd get visits from her Polland kin, but most of the time she was alone with just the children for company. To keep the law from tracing them through the post office, they'd been careful not to write any letters back home, so she hadn't been in touch with her family since leaving Texas. Still, she'd been a good soldier during the first few months of our logging operation, and their reunions were always full of affection. Late at night I'd hear their bed creaking and thumping with all the affection they'd stored up since they'd last seen each other.

But as time went by she found it harder to bear their separations. She complained she was lonely and that it was hard to raise the children properly when they hardly ever got to see their daddy. Why couldn't he run a saloon again, or go back to cattle shipping or butchering like in Jacksonville? John would say that for now the logging business was the only safe way he had of making money. He reminded her that he was a seriously wanted man and nobody but her and me and a couple of her Polland kin knew who he really was. If he opened a saloon or went back to the cattle business, he'd be sure to be recognized by somebody, and next thing you know the law or the bounty men would be down on him. She might not see much of him now, but he reckoned she'd see a lot less of him if he was dead and buried. John was right about the whole thing, of course, and I'm sure Jane knew it, but that was still a hard way to put it to her, and it made her cry. We'd been logging for close to a year by then, and Jane was about to give birth to their third child, so I could see why she felt like she did.

One morning near the end of June, as we were finishing up a visit to Polland and about to head back to the timber camp, John's brother-in-law Brown Bowen showed up. John had told me about him. He'd described him as one of those sorry creatures other men can't stand to have around. He was always trying too hard to be one of the boys, to be included in the doings of men, but all his

efforts to be liked had exactly the opposite effect. Nobody
ever asked his opinion or laughed at his jokes or listened
to his stories. The only claim to notice he'd had in his life
was being brother-in-law to John Wesley Hardin. Then
one day he shot a drunkard sleeping in an alleyway, an
old rumpot most everybody had liked. He killed him for
no reason except he was pretty drunk himself and feeling
low because nobody liked him. John said the boys would
have hung him on the spot if the sheriff hadn't been right
there to arrest him and hustle him off to the Gonzales jail.
Even then, a mob would've got him that night for sure if
Jane hadn't pleaded with John to do something to save her
brother from the noose. So John went to the sheriff and
money changed hands and that evening Brown Bowen escaped. John put him on a midnight train to Florida with
the warning that if he ever came back to Texas he'd let
the boys hang him next time. And now here the fella was.

It didn't take but five minutes to see how right John was
about him. Brown's smile was phonier than a medicine
barker's, and he never looked you square in the eye. He'd
been drifting all over Florida since leaving Texas, following one trade after another—hunting for plumes and gator
hides in the southern glades, wrangling for a cattle outfit
on the Gulf coast, cutting logging trails in the cypress
swamps, farming on the lower St. John's, a few other
things in a few other places. He tried to sound like he was
an expert at all of it, but it was my guess he'd done so
many different things because he couldn't do any of them
worth a damn.

When he heard we were logging up on the Styx, he
wanted to throw in with us. John told him sorry, but we
had a full crew. Brown Bowen said John just didn't like
him was why he wouldn't take him on. John said, "You're
right, Brown. I shouldn't of lied. The truth is I *don't* like
you and don't want you near me, you're right." And that
was that. Jane looked like she might want to scold him
for being so hard on her brother, but she didn't. She just
folded her arms over her swollen belly and kept quiet.

Brown stood there with his mouth open and watched us go.

We'd been back in camp a couple of weeks when word came up the river that Jane had given birth to their second daughter. John had told me that if the baby was a girl they were going to name her Callie, and he broke the news to me by sticking his head in the bunkhouse and yelling, "Callie's home, Gus! She got there three days ago!" We all lit cigars and passed around a bottle to celebrate.

A few days later I came down sick and was either shitting or throwing up every ten minutes. All I was good for was laying real still in my bunk. I couldn't even fart without soiling my pants. I tried to last it out, but after another few days I was full of fever and too weak to stand, so John had me loaded in a wagon and told Sweeny the Swede to take me to the doctor in Mobile.

As they loaded me in the wagon, John joked with me not to take too long about getting my sorry ass back to work. He and the boys were about to make another run to Pensacola and he joshed about all the fun I was going to miss out on. Then he slapped me on the shoulder in farewell and Sweeny giddapped the team and we set out down the logging trail.

I was tended by a gap-toothed doctor named Amons. He gave me some god-awful medicine to drink five times a day and told me to stay in bed and eat nothing but mashed greens and in a few days I'd be fine. Sweeny checked me into a hotel that faced out on the bay and made arrangements with a restaurant down the street to bring me my greens every day. Then he wished me luck and headed off for Pensacola to catch up with John and the boys.

Doc Amons's medicine might of been the worst stuff I ever tasted, but it surely did the cure. In fact, it stopped my runs so good I didn't have a decent shit for the next six months. My fever broke after two days, and in two more I was back on my feet and able to walk down the street for my first real food since I'd took sick—a beefsteak the size of a saddlebag, best thing I ever tasted.

The next day I felt strong enough to get moving, so I paid up my hotel bill and went down to the depot to catch the early train to Polland. I figured John was either already there, after his run to Pensacola, or soon would be.

When the hack got me to the depot, there were hundreds of people mobbing the place. I asked the driver what was going on. "You ain't heard?" he said. "John Wesley Hardin. They caught him yesterday in Pensacola. Texas Rangers. They brung him here and put every policeman in town around the jail house. Word is, they're aiming to take him back to Texas today. Everybody's waiting to have a look at him."

I waited at the station with everybody else, waited to see for myself if he'd really been arrested. I didn't believe it. He said he'd never be taken at gunpoint, he'd go down shooting first. If they nabbed someone, it wasn't him.

An hour later we got word the Rangers had believed his friends were waiting at the station to free him, so before sunup they'd taken him by wagon to the rail station in Montgomery. I knew then it was all bullshit. Nobody'd captured John. It was just one more of the stories people were always making up about him all the way from Texas to Florida.

I took the late train to Polland. On the way I wondered if John would laugh at the story of his "arrest" in Mobile—or worry that such stories were being told too damn close to his hideaway. Then I got to Polland and found Jane in tears and I knew the truth of it.

PART FIVE

THE
CONVICT

———— FROM ————

The El Paso Daily Herald,

20 AUGUST 1895

Henry Brown testified as follows:

"My name is H. S. Brown. I am in the grocery business in El Paso with Mr. Lambert. I dropped into the Acme Saloon last night a little before 11 o'clock and met Mr. Hardin and several other parties in there, and Mr. Hardin offered to shake with me. I agreed and shook first; he shook back, and said he'd bet me a quarter on the side he could beat me. We had our quarters up and he and I were shaking dice. I heard a shot fired, and Mr. Hardin fell at my feet at my left side. I heard three or four shots fired. I then left, went out the back door, and don't know what occurred afterward. When the shot was fired Mr. Hardin was against the bar, facing it, as near as I can say, and his back was toward the direction the shot came from. I did not see him make any effort to get his six-shooter. The last words he spoke before the first shot was fired were 'Four sixes to beat,' and they were addressed to me. For a moment or two before this he had not spoken to anyone but me, to the best of my recollection. I had not the slightest idea that anyone was quarreling there from anything I heard."

(Signed) H. S. Brown

—————————— F R O M ——————————
The Life of John Wesley Hardin as Written by Himself

"I was at a terrible disadvantage in my trial. I went before the court on a charge of murder without a witness. The cowardly mob had either killed them or run them out of the county. I went to trial in a town in which three years before my own brother and cousins had met an awful death at the hands of a mob. Who of my readers would like to be tried under these circumstances?"

———

"When we got to Fort Worth, the people turned out like a Fourth of July picnic, and I had to get out of the wagon and shake hands for an hour before my guard could get me through the crowd."

———

"I knew there were a heap of Judases and Benedict Arnolds in the world and had had a lifelong experience with the meaning of the word treachery. I believed, however, that in jail even a coward was a brave man."

———

"In 1885 I conceived the idea of studying law. . . ."

—————————— F R O M ——————————
The Daily Democratic Statesman
(AUSTIN, TEXAS)
AUGUST 25, 1877

MORE GLORY FOR THE ADJUTANT GENERAL AND THE STATE TROOPS

WESLEY HARDIN ARRESTED AT PENSACOLA, FLORIDA

———

General Steele and the efficient State Troops under him have for some time been quietly working for the arrest of the notorious and desperate John Wesley Hardin, the terror of the Southwest, and the glorious news of his arrest at Pensacola, Florida, is announced by dispatch to the Adjutant General from Lt. J. B. Armstrong, who left this city on this mission, accompanied by Private Duncan, on the eighteenth instant. The arrest of this notorious character with two of his men and the killing of another adds new laurels to the achieved honors of the State Troops. . . . The following is a copy of the dispatch received by Gen. Steele yesterday morning:

WHITING, Alabama, August 23.

Gn. Wm. Steele, Austin:

Arrested John Wesley Hardin at Pensacola, Florida, this afternoon. He had three men with him, and we had some lively shooting. One of their number was killed, and the others were captured. Hardin fought desperately, but we closed in and took him by main strength, and then hurried aboard this train, which was just starting for this place. We are now waiting for a train to get away on. This is Hardin's home, and his friends are trying to rally men to release him. I have some good citizens with me, and I will make it interesting.

J. B. Armstrong
Lieut. State Troops

Jack Duncan

John wired me in Dallas saying he'd been put in charge of running down John Wesley Hardin and wanted my help. General Steele had authorized him to appoint me a "special Ranger" for the job. I sent a telegram right back saying I'd do it and he could expect me in Austin on the morning train. After making a reservation, I went to my boardinghouse and packed a bag, then went to Sally McGuire's to celebrate with a Duncan Special. A Duncan Special was one girl to mount up on and another to lay on her back behind me with her face between my legs, doing whatever interesting things she could think of with her mouth and fingers while I rode her partner. Then they'd switch off and we'd do it some more. That particular night cost me a pretty penny, since we went at it till almost dawn. I just did make the train, looking like something the cat dragged aboard, and mighty aware of my reek of stale jissum and whorehouse perfume.

John met me at the station and gave a grinning snort at the smell of me. We went straight to the Red Rock saloon so he could fill me in. He was heavyset and going bald in front. The more hair he lost off his head, the thicker he grew his walrus mustache. He was a damn fine peace officer, quick and fearless. We'd worked together several times before, and he knew I was the best detective in Texas. I'd say I was the best in the country but it might

sound like bragging. He also knew I'd jump at the chance
to help him hunt Hardin. It wasn't every day a man got
the chance to get on the state payroll just to try and collect
half of a four-thousand-dollar arrest reward.

He said he had a tip that Hardin was in Florida. I said
I'd heard that rumor like everybody else, but Florida was
a long way off and a damn big place to go searching just
on account of hearsay. But John thought it was more than
a rumor. He said that a year ago the Pinkertons had got a
tip he was in Jacksonville and sent two men down to check
it out. Three months later their rotted remains were found
in a riverside warehouse. They'd both been shot. "Anybody might of killed them," John said, "but I got a feeling
it was our man." He had a hunch Hardin was still in Florida, though he likely wouldn't have stayed in Jacksonville.
I put good store in John's hunches, and even more in my
own—and my hunch was he was right.

Family, I told him—family was the way to find him. A
man on the dodge might never get in touch with his friends
or his partners, but if he had family or other close kin,
that's who he'd contact if he contacted anybody at all. And
Hardin had plenty of kin.

John had naturally thought of that. Hardin's wife and
child were said to be with him, wherever he was, but for
weeks now John had had a man watching Hardin's mother's house up in North Texas, near Paris, where the family
had moved after leaving Comanche. Preacher Hardin had
died just a few months before, but there'd been no sign
of Wes Hardin at the funeral. John's man in Paris was
bribing the postmaster to keep close track of the Hardins'
mail, but nothing had come from or been sent to Florida,
and all the senders and recipients could be accounted for.
None of them was Wes or Jane Hardin using a false name.
John had other men spying on Hardin's East Texas kinfolk, but they hadn't turned up anything either. I said I
didn't think they ever would, not through Hardin's people.
But what, I asked him, about *hers*?

*   *   *

We went down to the Sandies and snooped around on the sly. We learned that Neal Bowen, Jane's father, had a country store for sale in Coon Hollow, and we came up with a plan. I'll be the first to admit we were damn lucky in the way it worked out—but like the man said, I'd rather be lucky than good. While John laid low in Cuero, I went to Neal Bowen and introduced myself as Hal Croves from Austin and said I was looking to buy a store. We hit it off pretty well, and he naturally invited me to live in his house for as long as it took me to inventory the store and study his ledgers and make up my mind to buy the place or not.

It didn't take long to learn his mail routine. He'd stop in at the post office in the mornings, read his letters at home before dinner, then store them in a trunk in the parlor. I checked in that trunk every day whenever I had the chance. There were bundles of correspondence in there, and it took me a week of peeking through them before I'd had a look at them all. There was nothing in there from Wes or Jane Hardin, nothing that even hinted at their whereabouts.

And then, just when I'd stretched the sham of taking inventory and examining books about as far as I could, Bowen received a letter from his son Brown, who'd written it from an Alabama backwater called Polland. Brown was still wanted in Texas for a murder he'd committed years earlier, but he didn't interest me at all except as a possible lead to his brother-in-law. His letter was mostly about some property he owned in the Sandies that he wanted his daddy to sell for him. He hadn't been faring well and was in need of money. It was a self-pitying letter, and I read it with a growing irritation until I reached its last lines. "My sister has just born a baby girl," he wrote, "and they have called her Callie. She joins me in sending our love."

Except for some things I'd done with naked women, I'd never felt such a nice rush up my backbone. I saw the future in a flash: we'd slip into the burg nice and quiet, and if we didn't spot him right off we'd stake out their house and wait our chance and it would damn sure come and by God we'd have our man!

But first I had to take my leave of Neal Bowen without arousing his suspicions. John and I had arranged a ploy. I sent a telegram to "Bill Alworth" at the Duchess Hotel in Cuero, saying, "Bill, I like the store." The next morning here comes John into Bowen's store with his Ranger badge pinned on his coat and throws down on me with a shotgun and says I'm under arrest. You could've knocked Bowen over with a feather when John tells him my name ain't Croves, it's Harris Cobb and I'm wanted for horse theft in Travis County. He put the cuffs on me and got me mounted up and we trotted out of Coon Hollow with him cussing me good and loud and saying he'd blow me out of the saddle if I tried anything smart. Bowen and a bunch of other citizens watched us go with their eyes bugging in their heads.

We galloped straight to Cuero and took the next train to Austin. John took me with him when he reported to General Steele and told him what we'd found out. The general was impressed and congratulated me on my detective work, then went off to Governor Hubbard's office and came back in an hour with the arrest warrant. That night we were on a train for Alabama. We played cards and sipped at a flask of rye as the dark countryside flashed past the coach window. Every once in a while we'd look each other in the eye and just grin and grin.

Rather than get off the train in Polland and risk tipping him off that we were there, we went on to the last Alabama stop, eight miles farther east at Whiting. The place wasn't anything more than a tiny station house, a water tank, and a few small houses set at the edge of the piny woods. The midday air was hot and heavy and smelled of wood pulp. We went in the depot to ask the stationmaster where we might rent ourselves some mounts and found a handful of men gathered around a short, hard-looking fellow with a fresh blue goose egg on his cheek. He was telling the story of the fight where he got the bruise.

He'd got into it with a bigmouthed peckerwood and had
beat the rascal like a rug. We were a circle of grins around
him as he acted out the whole fracas for us, punching and
kicking the air and enjoying hell out of it all over again.
"About the time I've got him looking like stomped-on
sin," he said, "the sonbitch turns tail and runs off till he
sees I ain't about to chase him for the pleasure of whup-
ping him some more. So he stands over there across the
tracks and hollers, 'Just you wait till my brother-in-law
gets back, Shipley! He's John Wesley Hardin is who he
is and he'll shoot you dead as soon as spit!' " Everybody
roared at that. Me and John just looked at each other, and
I guess my eyebrows were up as high as his. You see what
I mean about how our luck ran on this thing. "Sorry son
of a bitch," Shipley said. "Can you beat that? I hollered
back, 'Yeah!—and *my* brother-in-law's Jesse James!' I tell
you, that fucking Bowen's crazier'n my Aunt Reba, and
that woman talks to the *trees*."

"Pardon me, sir," John says to him, and shows him his
Ranger badge. "I wonder if we might have a private
word?"

When Shipley found out Swain really *was* Hardin, he got
all excited and said he'd be glad to help us any way he
could. "Hell, I like the fella fine as Swain," he said, "except he's the luckiest man with a hand of cards I ever saw.
Takes me a week to win back from the sailors what he
wins off me in one night. But hey, if that bastard Bowen
really could sic him on me, well, I don't need *that*. Besides, ain't I heard something about a *reward*?"

I nearly laughed out loud at the look on John's face. He
and I had agreed that I was in for half the reward—two
thousand dollars—and that if he cut in anybody else, the
cut would come out of his half. He took Shipley aside and
they dickered for a while. I never did find out how much
he gave him. For all I know, John shared out his whole
half of the reward to everybody who helped us. But he
never was after the money; he wanted the glory of bring-

ing in Wes Hardin. For me, two thousand dollars was glory enough.

Whatever John paid Shipley, he was worth it. He was a mother lode of information. He knew for a fact that Hardin was in Pensacola just then. He'd gone to buy supplies for a timber camp he was operating upriver in Alabama. "He just sent the goods through today," Shipley said, "and he's bought a ticket for tomorrow's train to Polland."

He ordered a special engine and car for us and we rolled into Pensacola late that afternoon. A cool salt breeze was coming off the bay from under a high purple line of thunderheads. Our arrest warrant was for Alabama, but if we could take him in Florida we would, and damn the legalities. We'd leave that worry to General Steele.

We determined to take him when he boarded for Alabama. As much as he hated to do it, John decided we'd best get the local law to back us up, just in case the thing got mean. He went to the Escambia County sheriff, Will Hutchinson, and brought him in on the play, him and his deputy, Ace Purdue—and of course cut them in for some portion of the reward.

We stayed in the sheriff's office all morning and afternoon, planning our moves. Hutchinson insisted on putting riflemen on the rooftop of the hotel adjacent to the depot. "We're talking about a desperate killer," the sheriff said. "I've read all about him, you bet. A few rifles on the roof will make a damn big difference if it comes to a shootout." John argued against the riflemen but finally had to give in if he wanted the sheriff's help. But he told Hutchinson that if any of his men opened fire for any reason except Hardin running out of the car with a gun in his hand, he'd hold him personally responsible. "Remember," he told him, "this reward's for his *capture*. If he's killed, there'll be no reward for anybody—and that would make Detective Duncan very angry." I did my best to look menacing. "Don't you boys worry none," Hutchinson said. "It's my cousin Nolan who'll be in command of the shooters. I've used them boys before and they always done just fine. They can follow orders, you bet.''

If any of them had taken a look up at the hotel roof, they would have spotted the shooters for sure. Those stupid peckerwoods kept peeking over the top of the wall to see what was going on, instead of keeping their heads down like they'd been told to do. But Hardin and his friends were joking and laughing and not paying much attention around them. Hardin had been living in that region for over a year by then without a bit of trouble from the law. He'd gotten to feeling safe there. That was our big advantage.

There were maybe eight or nine other passengers boarding for Alabama. Hardin was accompanied by three fellas who worked with him at the timber mill. Shipley said the youngster named Mann was tough as he looked and would be quick to fight if he had the chance. The other two—Shep Hardie and Neal Campbell—had never been known to even carry a gun.

John and Hutchinson stood over by the baggage car, smoking cigars and chatting like a pair of old pals. I was standing with Shipley and Purdue near the ticket agent's window. As Hardin and his party headed for the smoking car, he looked our way and Shipley and Purdue smiled and raised a hand to him. ''What say, John,'' Purdue said. He'd sat in on plenty of poker games with him at Shipley's. Hardin smiled at him and Shipley and said, ''Hey, gents,'' and gave me a quick look-over and a nod, and I nodded back. They went aboard and we watched them through the big coach windows as they made their way to the rear of the car. Jim Mann took a seat on the window, facing front, and Hardin sat beside him, on the aisle. The other two sat in the facing seat. I looked over at John. He tossed his cigar under the baggage car and tugged down his hat. It was the signal to make our move.

John and the sheriff went up on the platform at the rear of the smoking car and stood ready while Shipley and Purdue and I entered the car from the front. Shipley and

Purdue were a few feet ahead of me. I kept looking out the windows and waving as we moved down the car, like I was bidding good-bye to somebody out on the station platform. "Say, Swain," Shipley said, "you going to give me and Ace a chance to win some of our money back tonight?" Hardin laughed and said, "Sorry, boys. Got to tend to business for a while. I'll be back next month with another fat poke you can try and take off me."

John and Hutchinson came in through the rear door with their pistols in their hands. The two sitting with their backs to me, Campbell and Hardie, looked up at them. "Hey, Will—" one of them started to say, just as Hardin turned to look.

"Texas, by God!" Hardin yelled. He made a grab under his coat for his gun but John lunged forward and cracked him hard on the head with his pistol as Shipley and Purdue dove on him and grabbed his hand away from his coat and they all went tumbling to the floor in a struggling, cussing heap.

As Jim Mann jumped up and pulled his pistol, I shot him twice in the chest. He fired a wild shot into the back of the car and fell against the open window—and the riflemen on the roof opened up on him like a firing squad. Blood flew off his head and neck and he fell through the window and onto the platform as the rifles kept firing and firing. I dove for cover beside Campbell and Hardie, who'd already hit the floor. A storm of bullets whacked into the side of the car, thunked into the coach seats, twanged off the steel wheels. "Cease fire! Cease fire!" Hutchinson was screaming. "*Cease fire* goddamnit!"

The rifle fire eased off and finally quit altogether, but Hardin was still making a fight of it. He was on his back and Shipley and Purdue had pinned his arms out at his sides, but John and Hutchinson were having a hell of a time trying to get hold of his kicking legs. A kick caught Hutchinson flush on the mouth and knocked him back on his ass. I dove in and grabbed one of Hardin's legs and managed to pin it down as John sat on the other one. He jabbed the muzzle of his pistol under Hardin's jaw and

said, "Surrender, you son of a bitch, or I'll blow your
damn head off!"

"Shoot, God damn you! Shoot!" Hardin said. He was
breathing like a bellows and blood was running out of his
hair where John had hit him. "You bastard!" Hutchinson
shouted, wiping at his bloody mouth. He pushed between
me and John and managed to whack Hardin in the face
with his pistol before John shoved him away. "This man's
my prisoner!" John shouted. "Anybody mistreats him, it'll
be me!"

The whack in the face set the blood pouring from Hardin's nose and took a good bit of the starch out of him.
We hauled him up and sat him down and John cuffed his
hands behind him and around the seat's armrest. "Get this
thing moving!" John yelled. "*Now!*"

Shipley ran out on the platform and signaled for the
engineer to start the train rolling. As the car jolted and
began to move, I yanked Campbell and Hardie off the
floor and shoved them into a seat. They had their hands
as high as their arms could stretch and looked scared shitless. "I don't know what Swain's done," Hardie said,
"but me and Neal ain't done nothing, we swear!" I told
them to shut up and patted them down to be sure they
were unarmed.

Purdue sat on a seat arrest and held his pistol inches
from Hardin's head. I looked out the window as the depot
fell behind us and saw the shooters on the hotel roof staring down at the bloody corpse of young Jim Mann as a
crowd began closing around it like a pack of scavengers.

As soon as we were clear of Pensacola we all busted out
laughing and yeehawing and clapping each other on the
back. "We done it!" Hutchinson hollered, grinning like a
keyboard through his swollen purple lips. "We damn sure
done it!" Even John couldn't keep the smile off his face.

Hardin had regained his senses, though his nose was
still leaking blood and swollen like a fat strawberry. He
kept insisting he was innocent. "Listen," he said, "you
boys got the wrong man. My name is John Swain and I

run a timber camp on the Styx River. You can ask any-body." John and I laughed. I sat down beside him with a grin I could feel all the way to each ear and said, "You're John Wesley Goddamn Hardin is who you are, and you're under arrest for the murder of Deputy Sheriff Charles Webb of Brown County, Texas. We're taking you home, Wes."

We stopped at Whiting so all the frightened passengers could get off the train. We released Hardie and Campbell, since we had no charges on them, and John got off a telegram to General Steele in Texas, telling him we'd made the arrest but weren't in the clear yet. Hardin had plenty of friends between us and Mobile, and we figured they'd probably form up fast and try and rescue him. So what we did was highball right through Polland, his Ala-bama stomping ground—speeding right past all the sur-prised people on the depot platform who'd been waiting for the train—and straight on to Mobile.

We took him off the train in Mobile and clapped him in a cell while John sent a telegram to Texas requesting the proper extradition papers. The Mobile sheriff posted six deputies with shotguns all around the jail. A train to Flor-ida came through an hour later, and Shipley and Hutch-inson and Purdue got on it after receiving many reassurances from John that he'd be in touch with them about their shares of the reward.

When we got back to the jail we found out he'd talked the sheriff into bringing him the best lawyer in town, some fella named Watts, who'd listened to his story and gone straight to a judge with a writ of habeas corpus. Another ten minutes and he would've been long gone—and legally. John had to talk fast and furious to get the Mobile judge to give us till that evening to get the proper papers. "Boys," the judge said, "you know good and well that what you done ain't exactly legal. But if this man *is* John Wesley Hardin, I'll be damned if I'm going to be known as the stupid son of a bitch who turned him loose on a technicality. I'm giving you till midnight to get the Texas requisition papers in front of me.'' Twenty minutes before Hardin would've been released on the habeas writ, the papers came from Governor Hubbard's office, and the way was clear for us to take him back to Texas all legal and aboveboard.

By then the whole town knew who we'd locked up in their jail, and the street out front was mobbed with people wanting to see him. What's more, they'd all heard we meant to take him out on the early-morning train to New Orleans, and the depot was jammed with even more people waiting to catch a glimpse of the notorious Texas man-killer. ''I ain't about to take him out through that crowd,'' John told the Mobile sheriff. ''He's got too damn many friends around here who could be hiding among all those people, just waiting for the chance to throw down on us.''

So we snuck him out the back door of the jail in the middle of the night, escorted by two deputies, and took him by wagon up to Montgomery and boarded a train for Decatur.

Once we had him on the train out of Montgomery, he finally admitted who he really was. But he never whined nor pleaded nor blamed anybody else for his troubles. He said he'd shot Webb in self-defense and would be able to prove it in a fair trial. The way he told the story, I thought he might come clear, but John said you never could tell what might happen in a courtroom. ''I seen men I damn well knew were guilty walk out free as birds,'' he said, ''and I seen men I knew were innocent end up in the rock quarries or swinging from a rope.''

At least a man stood a better chance in a courtroom than with a mob, Wes said, and there was no arguing with that. He told us he was impressed with how smooth we'd pulled off his capture, and wanted to know how we'd tracked him down. When I told him, he said, ''That stupid no-count sonbitch''—referring to Brown Bowen. ''It's God's own wonder how him and Jane could of come from the same seed source.''

*   *   *

We had to spend the night in Decatur before catching the morning train to Memphis. In exchange for his promise not to try to escape, we allowed him to write a letter to his wife and send her some money. We would have let him write her anyway, even without his promise, which neither John nor I took to heart. Any man will naturally promise not to try to escape if he thinks it might get you to let your guard down. *I'd* make that promise. What man with any sense wouldn't? And if the guard got careless and let me get the jump on him, I damn sure would. And if it was a rope he might be taking me back to, and there was no way to escape but to kill him, well then . . . you do what you have to do to keep alive. There's no plainer truth on earth.

Anyhow, we cuffed his hands in front of him to let him write the letter and, later, to eat his supper, which we ordered brought up to the hotel room. But I never took my eyes off him for a second while he was cuffed in front—which proved to be wise, because when John handed him his supper plate and turned to say something to me, I saw Wes's eyes cut to the revolver in John's hip holster, not six inches in front of his face. I grabbed John and yanked him away from Wes so hard he fell over a chair and banged his head on the bedstead and cussed me out good. I stood there with my gun drawn on Wes and said to John, "You best take a bit more care with this young rascal." Wes just looked at me all innocent and said, "Good Lord, Jack, you don't think . . . ? Hey, I gave my *word*!" But his eyes couldn't hide how ready he'd been to snatch John's gun. Another half a second and John and I would've ended up in our own blood on the floor, I don't doubt that one bit.

After that, John was a good deal more cautious with him, and Wes never got such a chance again the rest of the trip. From then on, whenever we brought his cuffs around in front to let him eat, I'd sit across from him with my pistol cocked and pointed at his head. "God *damn*, Jack," he once said with a grin, "you sure know how to take the taste out of a meal. You *still* don't trust me not to try to get away?'' And I said, ''Sure I do, Wes—as much as you trust me not to blow your head off if you try.'' He smiled and said, ''Me and you, Jack, we understand all about trust, don't we?''

The news of his arrest preceded us to Memphis, Little Rock, Texarkana—all the stops on our way to Austin—and every station on our route was chock-full of people wanting to have a look at him. We had a private car and naturally kept the doors locked and the windows open only at the tops. We had our shotguns ready at every stop. Most of the spectators cheered and waved at him and held up signs saying, ''Free Wes Hardin!'' and ''We Love You Wes!'' and ''Hardin is Innocent!''

But not everybody felt that way. At the Little Rock depot, a rough fight broke out between a group of young men with a banner saying ''Hardin Is a Hero'' and a group with a big placard saying ''Hang the Mankiller.''

People gave goods to the conductor to pass on to him—baskets of food (we ate like kings on that trip), bottles of whiskey, good luck pieces ranging from rabbit's feet to old coins to arrowheads, and envelopes of money, most with just a few dollars in them, but one with fifty dollars and a note saying, ''Sorry it aint more, your a good man and god bless.''

I tell you, it was an amazing thing to behold, all those people rooting for him—all those pretty girls calling his name! ''Damn, boy,'' I said to him as we stared out the window at the mess of pretty things blowing him kisses at the Dallas depot. ''I believe a man might smother to death under all that affection.'' He grinned and said, ''Maybe so—but what a damn fine way to go, don't you think, Jack?'' His face lit up every time he saw such crowds cheering for him. ''Lookit them all,'' he said. ''You really think all them people can be wrong about me?''

There was a telegram for us in Waco, warning that the crowd waiting at the Austin station was too large to control. When Wes heard that he went a little pale and said,

"You boys swore you wouldn't let no mob get me." John said it might be a mob wanting to hang him or one wanting to set him free, but either way he wasn't going to take any chances.

He stopped the train a few miles outside of Austin and we rented a hack from a livery for the rest of the ride in. All of us were nervous now for different reasons. "Wes," John said, "if you try to break, I swear I'll kill you." I didn't say anything, but I had a picture of my two thousand dollars flying off in the wind if Wes got away. Wes just shook his head and said, "I ain't gonna try a thing, John—you just keep the mob off me."

We'd made the mistake of not holding the train back till we got into town, and it got there ahead of us—and so the crowd naturally found out real quick from the crew that we were coming in by hack. Just as we turned the corner toward the jail, we saw the horde rushing at us from the other end of the street.

John and I each grabbed Wes under an arm and ran him in through the jail-house door just barely ahead of the clamoring crowd. A deputy bolted the door behind us and the sheriff was quick about posting armed guards at every window. He'd already asked the governor for help to guard Hardin against mob action or a jailbreak attempt, and the governor had promised to reinforce the Austin police with State Rangers.

For the whole time Wes was in Austin, the crowds milled outside the jail day and night—some people wanting to lend support, some wanting to see him hang, most wanting just to have a look at him so they could tell their grandchildren they'd seen John Wesley Hardin with their own two eyes.

Austin had the strongest jail in Texas—solid rock outer walls, floors and interior walls of sheet iron, and a double set of steel bars as thick as my wrist around each cell. He didn't lack for visitors. When he wasn't giving an interview to one reporter or another, he was conferring with one or more of his lawyers. He'd retained two of the best criminal attorneys in Texas to defend him. I met an uncle of his named Bob Hardin, and a cousin named Barnett Jones. Together with Wes's mother, they'd pooled their money to pay the lawyers.

For our part, John did all the talking to the newspaper boys who wanted the story of how we'd come to capture the most famous desperado in Texas. We'd become heroes of a sort ourselves, but nothing on the scale that Wes was. Lord, the good-looking girls in the crowd outside that jail! They sent him cakes and cookies and flowers and locks of their hair. They sent him love notes. Some sent him bits of their underclothes in boxes wrapped in fancy ribbon. When I went to see him to say so long, he was wearing a fresh red rose in his lapel and held up a lacy strip of white cotton for me to see. "The gal that sent this said in a note that it was from the shimmy she wears every night to dream about me." He tossed it to me through the bars. It was scented with perfume to make you faint. "You best take it. I wouldn't want my wife to ever find it among my laundry." The guard let him out into the runaround so he could reach through the second set of bars and shake my hand. "You're a damn good detective, Jack," he told me. Best praise I ever got.

Ten months later I got into a drunk argument with Sally McGuire about who-knows-what and that high-strung bitch shot me. In the *balls*. Took one of them clean *off*. I nearly bled to death on the floor of that damn whorehouse before the sawbones got to me and saved my life. But I was left a one-walnut man. A few weeks later I got a note from Austin saying, "Jack, I hear your children will only be three feet high. Coulda been worse—you could be squatting to piss. Take care. JWH."

—————— F R O M ——————
The Daily Democratic Statesman
(AUSTIN), 29 AUGUST 1877

JOHN WESLEY HARDIN

———

THE PRISONER INTERVIEWED IN JAIL

———

A reporter of the STATESMAN called on . . . Hardin in the Travis County jail, where he is confined in one of the lower cages near the entrance. He was found in a quiet but pleasant humor, and showed but little objection to being interviewed and making himself agreeable . . . in his own words:

. . . I am a prisoner and must stand trial. All I want is to be allowed to appeal to the law of the land, and I hope the officers of the law will protect me for this end. My relatives and friends have met death at the hands of mobs and I want protection, while helpless, against anything of a similar nature. I am satisfied that there are those who would, if opportunity permits, not allow the law to take its course with me. I want to stand trial. I am sick and tired of fleeing from it and would go away if I could. I must see the end of it, and all I ask is that a mob not be permitted to

MURDER ME,

for I believe I can show that I did not have anything to do with the killing of Webb. Had my friends not killed him I might have done so, but it would have been in self-defense.

HIS PERSONAL APPEARANCE

Hardin is only 25 years old, and has quite a youthful appearance. He is of light complexion, wears a modest mustache and imperial, is 5 feet 10 inches high and weighs

155 pounds. He is mild-featured and mild-mannered, with a mild blue eye, and talks pleasantly enough. He says he has no fear of the law, and that he is ready for execution if condemned, but he claims to be innocent, and he is charged with much that he never thought of. He wants the authorities to protect him against mobs, for it is mob violence alone that he fears.

———————————— F R O M ————————————
The Daily Democratic Statesman
(AUSTIN), 29 AUGUST 1877

CASTING OUT OF DEVILS—HOW TEXAS DOES IT

Murderers and thieves have suffered fearfully of late in Texas. Two notorious scoundrels, Ringgold and Gladden, are imprisoned or dead. King Fisher is incarcerated or has been released on bail remaining under the surveillance of the state troops. Scott Cooley was arrested and died in a spasm of rage and chagrin. Bill Longley sweats and sweats in the Giddings jail. Ham White, the famous stage coach robber, makes cigars for life in the West Virginia penitentiary. Jim Taylor, of the Taylor gang of desperadoes, was killed when resisting arrest at San Sabas last Thursday. His pal Hoy was killed under like circumstances the day before. Both fell before the guns of the state troops. Bill Taylor, brother of Jim, breathes hard and is nervous to the last degree, with three of the Sutton gang here in the Travis County jail . . . Wesley Hardin, the most reckless murderer ever known in Texas, is committed to our jail. He has killed, so the story goes, twenty-five or thirty white men, besides Mexicans and Negroes.

. . . Between Bell and Coryell counties there is a tree of death. Beneath one great, sturdy, bended branch there have been suspended, a prey to eagles and carrion birds, like the sons of Rizpeh, seven admirable devils thus "cast out" of Texas. In Lee County, within a few months, twelve or fourteen scoundrels have been remorselessly hanged by the people and danced on nothing into eternity.

. . . But the facts we state show that the end of desperadoism and lawlessness has come, and all the terrible facts recited tell the bloody-handed, cowardly villains who still wear pistols and knives girt about their bodies that this of Texas is no longer a healthful atmosphere. They should migrate. The people are surfeited with devilish deeds, juries are now doing their duty, and sure and swift justice is meted out. The frontier of Texas is no longer a proper place of refuge for continental knavery. Mexico must be its receptacle, and fortunate for Texas will be the day when the use of the pistol and the knife is more rigorously punished here than in Massachusetts.

Cletus Starr

In all my days as a Ranger we never put a prisoner under heavier guard than we did Hardin when we transferred him to Comanche for trial that hot September. The two biggest rumors were that his gang would try to free him on the road to Comanche—and that a huge vigilante mob had sworn to string him up before he ever set foot in court. Our whole outfit—Ranger Company 35, under Lieutenant N. O. Reynolds, as good a lawman as I ever knew—was assigned to escort Hardin to trial and repel rescuers and lynchers both, whoever came at us. We put him in irons from neck to ankles and propped him on the seat of a barred prison wagon. Half the company rode in front of it and half brought up the rear. We had a chuck wagon too, and an arms and ammunition wagon, and a remuda as big as you'd see in most cattle outfits. In addition to regulation sidearms and carbines, each of us was carrying extra saddle revolvers and a shotgun with buckshot loads. I mean we were ready for *war*.

At every town along the way, people came out in droves to have a look at him. No matter how far from the nearest town we might make our camp, they'd show up by the hundreds. Most of them would stand well away from the wagon and talk about him like he was some sort of wild animal exhibit, but the gawking didn't seem to bother him much. I guess he'd gotten used to it by then. Some would tell him good luck, and he'd say thank you very much, always real polite. Plenty wanted to shake his hand, and he never refused. One old fella pressed right up to the bars of the prison wagon and said, "Why, son, there ain't a bit of bad in your face. Your life has been misrepresented to me." At another place, a real pretty red-haired gal said to him, "I wouldn't have missed seeing you for anything—not even for one hundred dollars." Hardin winked at her and said, "I hope you think it's worth it, pretty thing." She said, "Oh, my, yes! Now I can tell everybody I have seen the notorious John Wesley Hardin and he is so handsome!" Hardin laughed and said, "Yes, well, my wife thinks so."

We didn't have any real trouble on that trip. Things didn't get truly tense until we arrived in Comanche. We had so much chain on Hardin he couldn't even stand up, never mind walk. It took six strong men to lift him out of the wagon and carry him bodily into the jail. There was a huge crowd of spectators, of course—some calling out encouragement and some calling him a lowdown killer who deserved nothing but a rope. There were plenty of cussing matches and now and then a fistfight broke out. Our scout brought word that a mob of two hundred vigilantes, most of them from Brown County, was camped just on the other side of town, ready to ride in and take Hardin out and lynch him.

Sheriff Wilson was plenty worried about a mob action against his jail, and he'd deputized thirty-five local citizens to help repel any attack. His idea was for his men to be inside the jail and the Rangers to guard the outside, but Hardin told Captain Reynolds he didn't trust the local deputies. "If a mob does attack," he said, "who's to say these local boys won't side with them and let them in? They sure enough let my brother hang. It'd be a whole lot smarter if *your* men were inside and the sheriff's men outside, don't you think?" Reynolds did think so, and that's how he set up the guard details. It chafed the sheriff that Reynolds put more faith in Hardin than in the Comanche lawmen.

The next day the town was buzzing with a rumor that

the vigilantes were about to storm the jail and take Hardin
by main force. So Captain Reynolds put out a word of his
own: if the jail was attacked, he would not only order his
men to shoot to kill but would turn Wes Hardin out of his
cell with a loaded pistol in each hand. He truly meant it—
and he told Hardin so. Hardin thanked him and said justice
in Texas would be a lot better served if it had more lawmen like him working for it. Some citizens were outraged
that a Ranger officer would threaten to do such a thing,
but I reckon the mob believed him, because they never did
attack.

I drew assignment as a courtroom guard, so I got to witness the whole proceeding. I've since seen a lot of legal
trials, but not many as hostile to the defendant as that one
in Comanche. The night before it began, me and some
other Rangers took a few drinks in the company of a newspaper editor named Quill, and he told us five men on the
jury had taken part in lynching Hardin's brother Joe three
years before. The barkeep, a fella named Wright, said he
knew for a fact that the presiding judge had once been
hoodwinked by Joe Hardin in a land deal.

The law of the time wouldn't permit a murder defendant
to take the stand on his own behalf, and most of the witnesses who could have testified for Hardin were either
dead or on the dodge from the law themselves—or had
been run out of Comanche County by the vigilantes. There
really wasn't much Hardin's lawyers could do to defend
him. The only thing he had going for him was the state's
own poor skill at prosecuting him. Because Hardin wasn't
the only one to shoot Charles Webb, the prosecution set
out to prove a conspiracy to murder. They claimed that
Hardin and Jim Taylor and others decided to murder Webb
because he intended to serve state warrants on them. But
the prosecution's own witnesses had to admit that Webb
had been the first to shoot—and even though the state
claimed he'd done so only when it became obvious that
Hardin and his friends were about to gun him down, their
argument sounded thin to me.

He was convicted of second-degree murder and sentenced to twenty-five years with hard labor in the state penitentiary at Huntsville. The judge denied his lawyers' motion for a new trial, and they immediately filed an appeal with the state Court of Criminal Appeals. He was ordered back to jail in Austin until the appeals court ruled on his case.

We took him back the same way we'd brought him— chained down in the wagon and guarded by all of Company 35. A gang of hard cases trailed us out of Comanche at a distance. The first time we set up camp for the night, some of those jackasses hid out in the trees and kept hollering stuff like "We got you a new necktie right here, Wes!" and "You're gonna get what your brother got, Hardin you son of a bitch!" Hardin had forty pounds of iron hanging all over him and looked as spooked as you'd expect any man to under such circumstances. Every time Reynolds sent men out to try and catch the night-callers, they'd shut up and move to another part of the woods. Then as soon as our boys got back to camp they'd start up again. Reynolds finally ordered us to fire a few carbine rounds into the trees in the direction the voices came from, but even that didn't quiet them down for long. It wasn't only Hardin whose nerves got put on edge that night. The next day they followed us till about noon before finally turning back.

During his first few weeks in the Austin jail he somehow managed to shape a couple of pieces of tin into keys— one for his cell and one to the lock on the runaround, the big barred cage around the cells. Somebody—we always suspected Manning Clements—had slipped him a six-inch piece of hacksaw blade, and every night, after letting himself out of the runaround, he'd go to work cutting on the bars of the jail's back window. The other prisoners knew what he was doing, of course, since you can't keep such a thing a secret in a jail, and one of them sold him out to the jailers for an extra ration of supper. When we examined the bars of the back window, we saw that two of

them were nearly cut through. Another night of hard sawing with the little bitty blade—we found it hid in his mattress lining—and he'd of been out. After that, we kept a
guard posted at the runaround door day and night, and
another posted directly under the back window. "I don't
hardly blame you for trying to escape, Wes," Reynolds
told him, "but if you'd got out that window, the jail-yard
guards would of shot you down like a dog in the street."
Hardin answered, "That'd be better than dying like a rat
in a cage." He had a point, you ask me.

I was on guard in the visiting room one time when his
wife and children came to visit. His face was bright as a
harvest moon, he was so happy to see them. But she
looked tired. There were lines in her cheeks and dark circles under her eyes, like she hadn't slept good in a long
time. The children were respectful but standoffish. Hardin
tried hard to sound encouraging. He told her to be brave
and strong and so forth. She mostly whispered, and it was
hard to tell from her face what she might of been saying.
I did hear her say, "Of course not—there's nothing to give
up *to*!" Said it sharp, and for a second he looked at her
like she'd cussed him. When they left, he stared at the
door like he was looking at something long ago and far
away. I know for a fact he wrote her just about every day
he was waiting to hear from the appeals court. I guess she
probably had a lot of good reasons for not writing him
back near as often.

I never did understand the workings of the appeals
court—why it could be so fast to rule in some cases and
took so damn long in others. Like the difference between
the time it took them to decide Hardin's case and how fast
they decided Brown Bowen's.

Hardin had been in jail for months already when his
brother-in-law was finally extradited from Alabama on a
warrant for murder in Texas. He was put in a cell not too
far from Hardin's, and it was real clear there was no love
lost between them. Whenever they saw each other in the

runaround, Wes would damn near snarl at him, and Bowen was always bad-mouthing Hardin to the other prisoners. The way I heard it, they held each other to blame for getting caught by the law.

Bowen was a cocky sonbitch who figured there wasn't a way in the world he would be convicted. "Ain't no witnesses," he said. "It's my word against a dead man's." A few weeks later he got taken to Gonzales for trial, and as it turned out, there *had* been a witness. A young fella named Mac Billings had seen Bowen commit the murder—he'd shot a passed-out drunk for some reason nobody knew. The jury stepped out of the room for a few minutes and came back with a hanging verdict.

When Bowen was returned to Austin while his case was appealed, he wasn't near so brash as before. He licked his lips a lot and looked to be in a constant sweat. He spent a whole day talking to his lawyer—and then the two of them announced to reporters that the man who'd really committed the murder Bowen was convicted of was John Wesley Hardin. Bowen claimed he hadn't said so before because he wanted to protect his sister's husband—and he hadn't expected to be found guilty. He said Mac Billings had lied to cover for Hardin.

Neal Bowen, Brown's father, came to Austin to beg Hardin to confess to the killing and save his son's neck. Hardin told him he wouldn't make a false statement—and that a true one wouldn't help Brown in the least. Bowen stomped out of the jail with a face like a storm cloud. I heard they never talked to each other again.

In early May Brown Bowen's appeal was denied, and we took him to Gonzales to be hanged. Over three thousand spectators turned out on the appointed day. He once again declared that Hardin was the guilty party, not himself. Then he was hooded and his legs bound together and the trap was triggered. The hangman wasn't too good at his work, though, because I counted to thirteen-Mississippi before Bowen finally stopped twitching.

I never felt a bit sorry for Brown Bowen, but I couldn't help thinking how hard things must have been for Jane.

Her whole family had come to hate her husband, and they cut all ties with her when she refused to turn her back on him. She went to live with Hardin's mother.

Four months after Bowen's hanging, the court denied Hardin's appeal. In its written opinion, it made reference to "the enormity of the crimes of John Wesley Hardin," which sounded to me like they'd denied the appeal as much because of *who* he was as for what he'd done. Reynolds thought the same thing. "The court ain't sure if he killed Charlie Webb in self-defense or not," the lieutenant said, "but they know damn well he's Wes Hardin and has killed plenty others, and that's enough for them to shut the iron doors on him."

We took him back to Comanche for formal sentencing, then set out with him and three other prisoners in a wagon once again flanked front and rear with a heavy guard detail. At Fort Worth we put them aboard a train—a prison car with barred windows and double-thick, double-locked doors—and headed for Huntsville. Every station on our route was jammed with gawkers, with people praying for him and people cursing his damned soul. The depot at Palestine was so crowded, people were jostling and shoving each other off the platform. We later heard a young boy lost his foot when he fell on the tracks as we went rumbling by.

Red Presley

He got to Huntsville early one morning in October. There were a lot of eyeballs on him when the prison wagon came into the main yard and the guards took out him and three others, including a bank robber and a boy who'd killed a fella in a fight over a girl at a church picnic. Wes was shackled to a blacksmith who'd got two years for trying to kill a storekeeper who kicked his dog, and the smitty looked about to piss his pants, he was so scared to be in prison with the likes of us. Two years!—hell, that's nothing. A man ought be able to do two years on his goddamn *toes*. I'd already been inside for seven years and had thirteen to go. A lot of the cons were doing thirty, forty, *fifty* years. An old boy named Weeks was pulling ninety-nine years *and a day*. He'd got the sentence from a smart-ass judge in Houston. "Could of been worse," Weeks liked to say. "Shitfire, it could of been *life*." That smitty, though, he couldn't bear up: before he'd been in the walls two months he dove off the second tier and smashed his head like a melon on the stone floor.

Wes was the big attraction, of course, and he damn well knew it. Even with the shackles on him he walked like a man used to getting attention. Most new fish would turn away real quick when you looked them in the eye as they crossed the main yard on the way over to Processing, but not him. He wasn't about to be rattled by a bunch of yardbirds. Some of the hardrocks hollered to him that they aimed to find out just how tough he was. He just looked at them and spit between his teeth.

A con who clerked in Processing said they had to use nearly two full pages to record all the scars he had on him. After he was washed down, he was given his skunk suit and his mustache was shaved off and his hair was cut down to the scalp like the rest of us. He was brought into the row just before lockdown that evening and put in a cell with Snake Miller. Snake was the only con on the row who usually celled alone. The rest of us kept our distance from him. He was crazy as a moonstruck dog and liked to kill things with his hands.

Right after lights out, we heard the scuffle in their cell. Didn't neither one let a holler through the whole thing, but we could hear them thumping and cussing and grunting hard. The row guards heard it as clear as we did, but they weren't about to put a stop to it. Hell, that's *why* they'd put Wes in there in the first place. Snake Miller was their favorite way to soften up any new fish who came on the row thinking too much of hisself. The loudest sound of the fight was the last one—there was a kind of wet crunch and everything got quiet. Next morning when they took the padlocks off the doors and opened the cells, they found Snake on the floor with his busted head still leaking blood on the stones. Pieces of hairy scalp were stuck to the door bars. Wes had some lumps and scratches but looked spruce compared to Snake. Smiley and Groot were the row guards—real sons of bitches—but they laughed when Wes said Miller must of been trying to break out by using his head. They had Snake carried over to the hospital. A couple of days later the morning orderly found him with his throat cut.

Wes got assigned to the wheelwright shop, which is where I worked, and where we got to know each other. I was from Liberty County, and it turned out we had some common acquaintances in East Texas.

He hadn't been there two months before he had a plan

for breaking out. It was a good plan except for one thing—
he had to bring ten other cons in on it. That was a mistake
and I tried to tell him so. "The place is crawling with rats
who'll sell you out for a tiny piece of cheese," I told him.
But he wouldn't believe cons wouldn't stick together in
trying to escape. "In or out, Red?" he said. I knew better,
I truly did, but of course I was in.

What we did was dig a tunnel from under the wheelwright shop to the prison armory, about seventy yards
away. Every evening, the guards—including the saddle
bosses, the horseback guards who took convict work gangs
to the fields every day—stored their weapons in the armory before going to supper. We figured to cut our way
through the armory floor, arm ourselves, get the drop on all
the guards, shoot anybody who resisted, and set loose
every con in the place—all except for the rape fiends, of
course.

The shop had all the tools we needed. Working in three
shifts of four men each, we broke through the floor in the
rear room of the shop, dug down about seven feet, and
tunneled straight at the armory. The tunnel was just big
enough for one man at a time, and each man in a shift
would work for an hour before being spelled by somebody
else. The man in the tunnel always took a handful of
empty flour sacks and payed out a strong cord behind him.
Whenever he'd fill a sack, he'd tug on the cord and the
men keeping watch up in the shop would pull the sack out
and dump the dirt in one of the privies behind the building.

It was pitch-dark down there, so we had to work by
feel. Some of the boys were scared shitless of working so
confined under the ground—but they forced theirselfs to
do their share. They'd come out breathless and white-eyed,
hands shaking, and make jokes about learning the mole's
trade. I admit I was one of them. Every time a clod of dirt
fell on me I'd think the tunnel was giving way and I'd
have to lock my jaws to keep from screaming with the
fear of being buried alive. There ain't been much in my
life to spook me like being in that damn tunnel. But hell,
it ain't nothing a man won't do to try to set hisself free.

The wheelwright was in on the plot. He was a Swede named Johansen and he'd admired Wes since long before meeting him. He took Wes at his word that five hundred dollars would be coming to him once we'd made our escape. "All you got to do or say or know," Wes told him, "is nothing."

We were all of us strong as oxen and the work went fairly fast. It was fall and the weather had turned cool, so the digging was easier than it would have been in summer. Every night I went to sleep with the smell of dirt in every one of my pores. It smelled like freedom. And our reckoning turned out to be perfect. In three weeks we reached a point directly under the armory. Then we dug up to its pine floor and by God we were there.

On the evening of the break I could feel my heart punching in my throat while we watched the armory from the wheelwright shop, waiting for the guards and saddle bosses to put up their guns and go eat. Wes had wanted to be the one to do the cutting through the armory floor and the first to arm hisself, but so did I and a couple of the others, so we drew straws to decide it. Weeks got the shorty and gave us a shit-eating grin.

As soon as the guards and bosses put up their guns, Weeks dropped into the tunnel and started crawling for the armory. I was right behind him, then Wes, then the others. When the tunnel turned upright again, Weeks stood up and slipped a sawblade between a couple of the floor planks over his head and started cutting. The chinks in the pine boards let just enough light into the well of the tunnel for me to make out the dark shapes of Weeks's boots right in front of me. I could smell the sawdust drifting down and feel it on my hands.

"What's taking that sawyer so damn long?" Wes said behind me. "Hold your horses, boy," I said. "I reckon you'll be free soon enough." I heard him chuckle, and I had a powerful urge to laugh out loud. "You about there?" I whispered up to Weeks. "Just about," he said.

He stopped sawing and gave a grunt, and I heard wood cracking and then break free. "Got it!" he said. One of his feet raised up to get a foothold on the side of the tunnel. I heard him grunt again and his other foot disappeared as he pulled hisself up.

I squirmed forward into the well on my belly and sat up. But before I could get my feet under me and stand up, there was a hell of a blast up above and Weeks came tumbling down on top of me. I knew he was dead by the weight of him. I felt his strong-smelling blood running hot and thick over my face. I kept wondering how he could be hollering so loud if he was dead, and then finally figured out that it was me doing the hollering.

Of the ten cons we'd brought into the plan, seven had ratted it away to the guards. One got hisself a full pardon, two were made trusties in another building, and the others got reassigned to farms outside the walls.

When they found out what we were up to, the guard captain—a hardass named Brockman—and some of his men had stashed extra shotguns in the shed behind the armory. On the day of the break, they'd gone through their usual routine of putting up their guns, then they went around to the shed and got the shotguns and sneaked back in the armory through the side door and waited real quiet for us to come up through the floor. When Weeks poked his head up, Brockman blew it off with both barrels.

They give me and Wes both fifteen days in the hole on bread and water, him in one building, me in another. I heard they give him a whipping too that damn near killed him. I never did see him again. When they took me out, they put me to work in the tannery, the most miserable, most stinking work there ever was. And I had to do it with a ball and chain they clamped on my leg, which they said I'd keep until I'd proved I could be trusted without it. It didn't come off for another eight years. To this day I walk kinda funny because of having it on for all that time.

—— Ed Klostermann ——

The hole was a lightless cell about five feet high and four feet square. Its door was solid steel except for a small hinged slot at the bottom for pushing through the prisoner's ration of bread and water once a day. The usual stay was three to seven days, depending, but if an inmate had been particularly troublesome—and Hardin surely was during his first six or seven years behind the walls—he could get up to fifteen days. What's more, we were under full authority to add to a con's discomfort in a variety of ways during his stay in the hole. His bread would certainly be moldy, and on occasion might even be soaked with "yellow gravy" dispensed from a guard's bladder. His drinking water would likely be dipped from the privy.

But nothing we did to their food and water was as punishing to most inmates in the hole as the cramped darkness itself. Some men adjusted to it, but many could not. Isolation in total and prolonged darkness will unleash the demons in a man's mind like nothing else can. Prisoners of weak will would start to scream within hours of the door closing on them. Others lasted a day or two before they began to howl. And once a man started screaming in the hole, he'd still be screaming when we came to take him out, even if his vocal cords had quit on him. They'd come out with eyes like loco horses and blood in their mouths and wouldn't be able to talk for days. The whole time they were in there, they were obliged to relieve themselves on the floor and wallow in their own waste. They'd come out smelling worse than you could believe possible of a human being. They'd be purblind in the sudden light. After fifteen days in the hole, some never recovered their proper vision. Some couldn't stand up straight or walk steadily for days afterward. A prisoner once described the hole as being as dark and foul as the devil's asshole. It was a crude but apt description.

Hardin always got through his stays in the hole a whole lot better than most. When we opened the door at the end of his first time in there, he was on his back and had his legs straight up against the wall—a position the smart ones figured out as a way to keep their knees and back muscles from knotting up on them and losing their stretch. He seemed indifferent to the cockroaches crawling over his filthy nakedness. He squinted hard against the light and said, "*Already?*" He was a genuine hard case, all right, and I was certain he would never leave Huntsville alive.

After his first escape attempt, we riveted a ball-and-chain to his ankle—a punishment usually reserved for the worst of the repeat offenders—and put him in a cell with a lifer named John Williams, a big mule-faced con who was the row turnkey. He was also the best snitch we had on the row. He could convince the hardest cons of his loyalty to them. And because they believed he had the trust of the authorities—his position as turnkey was proof of that—they considered him a valuable confidant. We would have been at a grave disadvantage against the cons if it weren't for snitches like Williams—but most of us saw them the same way the cons did: as worthless, dishonorable trash who would betray anybody for cheap gain. It is satisfying to know that a snitch's luck will sooner or later run out. Williams's ran out two years later when somebody overpowered him in his cell, sliced his tongue off at the root, and held his head back until he drowned in his own blood. Rumor had it that a row guard had tipped the cons about Williams. Perhaps so.

It took Williams more than a month to gain Hardin's trust, but eventually he did. He informed us that Hardin had somehow managed to cut through the rivets that held the ball-and-chain shackles around his ankle and had replaced them with a clever tap-and-bolt assembly. "He can take that ball off as quick as slipping off a sock," Williams said. He also said Hardin was planning another escape attempt. The worst punishment we could give him for cutting off his ball-and-chain was a trip to the hole, but if we caught him trying to escape again, we could whip him. So we let him think he had us fooled about the ball-and-chain, and we bided our time.

A few weeks later Williams knew most of the details of the plan. He was in on it himself. Hardin had formed wax impressions of all the padlock keys on Williams's ring—which Williams had to turn over to the guard sergeant every evening after locking down the row. It was Hardin's intention to fashion keys from pieces of tin to fit the locks on every cell on the row. Some night after lockdown, he would release the other cons on the row; they would overpower and disarm the night guards, and then shoot their way out or die trying.

A few days later Williams said Hardin had finished his keys. He'd had Williams test them on the locks and they all worked perfectly. "That boy's a right wonder with his hands," Williams said. "I believe he could make him a pocket watch from a tin can if he wanted." The break was set for Christmas Eve.

Just after Williams locked down the row that evening, I posted guard details with shotguns at both ends of the row, and then Ballinger and Meese and I rushed into Hardin's cell. He'd just taken off his ball-and-chain and was retrieving his keys from under a floor stone. He fought like a wildcat, breaking Meese's nose and nearly biting off one of Ballinger's fingers. I kept clubbing at him with my hickory stick, but it was hard to get a clear swing at him in all the rolling and tumbling. I finally landed some hard ones square on his head and took enough fight out of him for Ballinger and Meese to get him pinned and cuff his hands behind him. The rest of the row had been roused by the sounds of the fight and was roaring like a zoo at feeding time.

The lanterns in the drafty whipping room threw trembling shadows on the stained stones. It was so cold our breath showed in pale puffs. Wales was waiting for us, his sleeves rolled up on his muscular arms and the whip coiled in his fist. Ballinger and Meese each held Hardin by an arm and Lawrence had him in a choke hold from behind. It was all he could do to breathe. The warden had ordered us to give him a full whipping, then throw what was left of him in the hole for a week.

We stripped him naked and tied the end of one rope around his wrists and the end of another around his ankles, then stretched him facedown on the stone floor, Ballinger tugging on one rope and Lawrence on the other. He wriggled like a fish on a line and cursed us in a fury. Wales stepped up and uncoiled the whip with an easy twitch of his wrist. "You already got you some good scars, boy," he said, "but you ain't seemed to learn much by way of getting them."

The whip consisted of four leather harness straps, each about three feet long and two inches wide, attached to a foot-long hickory handle. Wales was a master with it and made every lick crack like a pistol shot. He'd snap his wrist one way to cut into the flesh, and another to pull the wounds open wider. The limit on lashes was thirty-nine, which was enough to kill a man. I knew because I'd seen it happen. But if a man couldn't take it, that was his bad fortune. He should not have done whatever he did to bring the whipping on himself. The convicts had a saying: "Don't make a slip if you can't take the whip." It was an admonition worth heeding.

With the first twenty-five licks, Wales opened him up from shoulder blades to tailbone. His ribs showed through in several places, and we'd all been spotted with his blood. I told Wales he would kill him if he persisted in hitting him in the same places. He glared at me and said he didn't need anybody to tell him how to do his job. His face was dripping sweat and his shirt was soaked through. He was in a temper because he'd been unable to make Hardin cry out until the seventeenth lick. No con had ever before lasted past the twelfth stripe before screaming, and none had ever taken all thirty-nine without losing consciousness. Only Meese had thought Hardin would go past twelve without yipping, and he won big in the betting among the guards. Nobody had been foolish enough to bet he'd be conscious at the end.

After one more to his ribs to remind me who the whipping boss was, Wales gave him the rest across the buttocks and the backs of his legs. When it was over, Hardin had fainted and looked like he'd been attacked by wolves. We took the ropes off him and poured water over his head, then pulled him to his feet and half dragged and half carried him down the hall to the hole. He left a smeared trail of blood behind him. On our way back to the block, Lawrence said, "He don't look all that good. No salve on them bad wounds, nothing to eat the next seven days hardly, nothing to *drink*? I don't reckon he'll make it." Ballinger said he didn't think so, either, and they both looked at Meese, who smiled and said, "Five dollars says he does."

Meese won again, though not by much. When we took Hardin out of solitary he couldn't walk on his own. His back was a massive ugly wound, oozing pus and blood and festering with maggots. He was on fire with fever and half out of his head. The warden thought he was exaggerating his pain and refused to admit him to the prison hospital, but he did permit the doctor to treat him. It was a month before he was up on his feet again—with a fresh new set of scars to carry to the grave.

For years he wouldn't quit trying. He took more beatings than any con I can recall. And then one day we got a new deputy warden, a former Ranger named Ben McCulloch. It so happened he and Hardin knew each other from some ten years or so before when they drove cattle together. He told Hardin he was sorry to see how poorly fortune had treated him. Hardin laughed and said it hadn't treated him as poorly as it had McCulloch. "Ain't much lower a man can get than a damn prison hack," he said. "You must of displeased the Lord a good bit more'n I have." Some guards took offense at such talk about our profession, but not McCulloch. He laughed along with Hardin and said, "Maybe so, Wes, maybe so."

I'm convinced McCulloch saved Wes Hardin from dying in prison. He had a good many long conversations with him and advised him many a time to quit trying to escape and to instead apply himself toward being a good convict and cutting time off his sentence. His argument to him was real simple: "If you keep doing like you been doing," he told him, "you'll die in here for sure. You'll die of a beating or a bullet or just plain choke to death on your own mean rage. And even if you somehow manage to stay alive all the twenty-five years, what then? You'll be old and broken and not worth shit. Your wife will be older than her years, Wes, for all her worrying over you. You'll never know your kids. They'll be grown and long gone before you leave this place."

It must have sounded to Hardin like he was being advised to surrender, which just wasn't in his nature to do. But he was no ordinary con—he wasn't stupid—and I think it goes to show how damn tough he really was that after his talks with McCulloch he never tried another break, not once in the next ten years.

He nearly died anyway—of an old wound, a chronically infected patch of raw flesh on his side, the result of a shotgunning he'd received more than ten years before. It suddenly abscessed so severely he could not stand up. It was an awful-looking thing—high-smelling and full of rank yellow pus and thick, constantly oozing, half-clotted blood. The doctor treated the wound the best he could. The rest, he said, was in the hands of God. With the warden's approval, he assigned an inmate nurse to tend to Hardin in his cell till he recovered or he died.

At first his condition worsened by the day. Every morning, I arrived at the row expecting to be told he had died in the night. He was sopping with fever and out of his head. His hair was plastered to his head like riverweed. His bloodshot eyes receded into deep black wells. His nurse was an effeminate little convict named Maylon Donaldson—whom the convicts had called Sister May until he was made a nurse, and then they called him Florence. He tended the wound as the prison doctor had instructed him—he mopped Hardin's brow, he spooned broth to his mouth, he sang softly to him. Sometimes Hardin would loudly address his wife, declaring his love for her, praising her eyes and breasts and the feel of her skin. Florence told me he sometimes laughed like a crazy man and babbled about the way he got his wound. "Goddamn tinhorn"— Florence said he once shouted—"shoots me *then* and kills me *now*." I heard him speak many other names in his delirium besides his wife's and children's. He often mentioned Joe, and somebody named Simp.

After four weeks he was skeletal as death. Nothing the doctor did for the wound seemed to improve it. And then his fever suddenly lowered and he slowly began to recover. But still the wound refused to close up properly, and the fever lingered like a low fire. Occasionally it flamed up again for one or two weeks at a time, and he'd sink back into a half-delirious sweat. Then the fever would drop once more and he'd regain his senses and manage to sit up and eat a few mouthfuls of whatever Florence spoon-fed him. For week after week he continued in this tenuous up-and-down pattern of recovery and relapse. All in all, eight months went by before he finally mended.

It was then he began his serious study. His father had been a Methodist minister—which explained much about his own thorough knowledge of the Bible and his easy familiarity with books. He devoutly attended the prison Sunday School. Every day, just as soon as he was done with his assigned work in the boot shop, he would retire to his books. McCulloch was pleased by his turn in character and would visit him in his cell to press encouragement.

He read history and philosophy and politics. He recognized me as a somewhat educated man and delighted in engaging me in discussion on a variety of abstract topics—the nature of evil, the power of personal will, the origins of society, and so on. These conversations were enjoyable although I sometimes lost track of my own points as well as his. He studied everything—even arithmetic and science. I recall the time he demonstrated Archimedes' principle of displacement to me and Florence in his cell, using a bucket of water and his foot. "I get it," Florence said. "The point is, if you put your foot in a full bucket, you'll spill water on the floor and get your foot wet. Makes sense to me." His dictionary got so worn its pages began to shed like old leaves, and McCulloch presented him with a new one.

When he made up his mind to study the law, he asked McCulloch to recommend books in both criminal and civil proceedings. The captain said he wasn't familiar with any law book besides Blackstone's, but he forwarded Hardin's letter to a friend who was a member of the Texas bar, and Hardin soon received a comprehensive list of readings in jurisprudence. Shortly afterward, he had law books piled all over his cell and was hip-deep in legal study. He joined the debating club and argued circles around everybody in it. McCulloch and I heard him declare against women's suffrage one evening and both of us were swayed by his arguments. He had the lawyer's stamp, no doubt about it.

I've mentioned that Florence had an effeminate manner. To be blunt, he was as queer as a purple egg—the sort of fellow called "sweetmeat" by the other cons, especially the "chickenhawks," the hard cases who preyed on them at every opportunity. But his assignment to the hospital included hospital living quarters, which put some protective distance between him and the chickenhawks on the main rows. He rarely went into the yard or even to another building unless there was no way to avoid it, and whenever he was outside he always kept in sight of the guards.

The safest he'd ever been in prison was during the eight months he was assigned as Hardin's nurse and lived in the two-man cell with him, away from the main population. Once Hardin was back on his feet, however, Florence had to return to his own quarters in the hospital. A few weeks later a couple of chickenhawks cornered him all alone in the hospital storeroom. In addition to sodomizing him, they beat him so badly he was hospitalized with both arms broken and his jaws wired. He was a little fellow and looked even smaller under all the bandages. It was three weeks before he could move his bowels without a heavy loss of blood. I'm sure the hawks had threatened him with even worse if he talked: he looked terrified and told the investigator he hadn't gotten a look at the men who did it.

Then Hardin went to visit Florence and they had a private chat. The next afternoon a chickenhawk named Beady staggered into the yard from behind the wood shop with blood streaming down his face. He'd been jumped from behind and never saw the man who'd cut his eyes out. The day after that a hawk named Kimble was found behind the laundry building beaten so badly with a lead pipe that he spent the rest of his days in an idiot's fog. The word spread that Hardin had done the jobs and would do worse to the next man to lay an unwanted hand on Florence. The warden questioned him about the rumors, but he denied having had anything to do with the assaults. He had iron-solid alibis in both cases. "I will admit I'm not real sorrowful about what happened to them," he told the warden. "They were terrible bullies and I believe they deserve what they got." I don't know if he knew it, but the warden believed so too.

Yes, there were rumors that Florence was Hardin's personal chicken. I don't know if they were true and I don't care. What would it matter? It was a prison, and a man might do things in prison he wouldn't dream of doing outside of it. I *do* know that nobody ever harmed Florence again in the two years before he was released. And I *know*

he was Hardin's friend. And I *know* Hardin wasn't one to
let a friend be bullied. Those things I know.

Officially, Hardin wasn't supposed to write more than
two letters a month, but I knew he was bribing some of
the guards to slip out letters to his wife several times a
week. It wasn't an uncommon practice, and since it helped
to keep the prisoner's spirits up and permitted the guards
to make a few extra coins, we generally turned a blind
eye. As for *her* letters, well, sometimes several weeks
would go by without one, and he'd be long-faced until one
finally arrived.

I knew more about his family than he ever told me
because I was good friends with Harvey Umbenhower, the
prison censor. It was Harvey's job to read every piece of
mail the prisoners sent out and that came in for them. I
ate dinner in the officers' mess with Harvey nearly every
day, and through him I learned that Jane had never got
along very well with Hardin's mother, with whom she and
the children had gone to live when he got put in the walls.

"I don't believe I ever seen a letter from her that didn't
have some complaint about the old woman," Harvey told
me. "Or one from the mother that didn't have something
bad to say about the wife. It's got to be rough on a fella
who loves both his wife and his momma to be getting
letters from them with one always bitching about the other.
Hardin tries to smooth their feathers the best he can, and
sometimes he even writes to the two of them on the same
letter so one can see what he's writ to the other, how he's
begging them both to try to get along."

When Jane at last had enough of Hardin's momma—or
Hardin's momma had enough of Jane—or both had had
enough of each other, most likely—she and the kids went
to live with Manning Clements and his family on his ranch
in the hill country. Harvey said her letters from San Saba
were just as full of complaint as ever, only now it was
mostly a lack of money she groused about. "You got to
wonder what a woman thinks a man can do about that
when he's locked up in the goddamn penitentiary. What'd

she expect him to do, print some up in the shop here? Go
out and rob a bank?'' Harvey's own marriage had come
to a bad end a few years earlier—his wife had run away
to Dakota Territory with a piano player—so he wasn't real
sympathetic to a woman's side of things.

He told me she finally took the children and went back
to her home county of Gonzales to live with Fred Duderstadt and his family. Duderstadt and Hardin were old
friends from their days on the Chisholm Trail. According
to Harvey, Duderstadt had helped to set her up on a little
farm of her own. ''*Now* she complains about how goddamn hard it is for a woman to work a farm by herself
and how she works from sunup to sunset and thank the
Lord little Johnny's old enough to help her in the fields
with the crops and with the hogs and with this and that
and the goddamn other. I tell you, Ed, it tires my mind to
read that woman's constant carping. It makes me wonder
why he ever tied hisself to her in the first goddamn place.''
I said I supposed he loved her. He sighed and gazed off
to someplace where he probably saw his sweet and pretty
and long-gone wife. ''Yeah,'' he said, ''I guess so. He for
damn sure *still* loves her too. His letters are just full of
love for her. You know, he ain't never told her of the pain
he's knowed in this place?—other than the pain of being
apart from her and the children, I mean.''

The prison letters of John Wesley Hardin

To Jane:

My knowledge of wayward, forward men and women is that they lead wicked, miserable lives and die wretched deaths. The gambler dies a blackleg, the prostitute dies a whore. The thief falls into a thief's grave, and the sepulcher of the murderer is the assassin's sepulcher. This is the general rule. Their ways are hard, their days are sombrous and sad, their nights starless and sleepless; their hope for time and eternity has faded away and they await their terrible doom with trembling and fear because their end is dreadful and certain and terrific. . . .

To John W. Hardin, Jr:

Son, should any lecherous treacherous scoundrel, no matter what garb he wears or what insignia he boasts, assault the character and try to debauch the mind and heart of either your sisters or mother, I say son dont make any threats, just quietly get your gun, a double-barrel. Let it be a good gun: have no other kind. And go gunning for the enemy of mankind, and when you find him just deliberately shoot him to Death as you would a mad dog or wild beast. Then go and surrender to the first sheriff you find. . . .

To his family:

Dear Jane, I have selected several pocket verses from my thesaurus; their sentiments are mine. I hope that each of my dear children will adopt them as theirs and learn each verse by heart—and as am earnest of this, I ask each to inform me of this fact at their earliest opportunity. Assuring you of my unalloyed, unwavering love, and wishing for your prosperity in the fullest sense, I close by sending each of our loving children a kiss and ask you to accept as proxy in my behalf. JWH

MOLLY: "Keep thy passions down however dear; thy swaying pendulum betwixt a smile and a tear."

JOHN W. HARDIN JR: "The trust that's given, guard; to yourself be just; for live how we may, yet die we must."

SWEET LITTLE JANE: "Soar not too high to fall, but Stoop to rise; we wasted grow of all we despise."

Judge W. S. Fly

His transformation, according to officials at Huntsville, had been truly miraculous. Despite having been a most intractable convict during his first few years in the penitentiary, he had, after thirteen years, become a model prisoner. He was held up to the other inmates as supreme proof and example of what a man might make of himself behind bars if he truly tried. The prison superintendent had informed Wesley that if he persisted in his remarkable reform, he would likely be set free within the next two years.

Wesley was elated by the prospect; but his elation was shadowed by another ominous legal cloud. Namely: he was still under indictment in DeWitt County for having killed a man there twenty years before, a deputy sheriff named Morgan. It was quite possible that he would be granted an early termination of his present sentence only to be put right back in prison upon conviction for the Morgan killing.

His plight was brought to my attention by Billy Teagarden, whose father had been my dear friend for many years. Billy and Wesley had been friends since boyhood and had been corresponding with each other of late, and Billy advised me that Wesley wished to retain me as legal counsel in the matter of the Morgan killing. I had to confess admiration for Wesley Hardin's astonishing feat of character reformation, and I said I would be pleased to represent him. Shortly thereafter I received a most impressive letter from Wesley himself. That he was no ordinary convict was immediately evident in his intelligent composition and ready grasp of legal principle. Clearly his study of law had taken effect.

I visited him in Huntsville, and we put our heads together and devised a strategy. He agreed that *if* the DeWitt charge would be reduced to manslaughter, and *if* the judge would permit his sentence (normally two to five years for manslaughter) to run concurrently with the one he was already serving, *then* he would plead guilty as charged—even though, as he repeatedly assured me, he was not in the least guilty. "That man Morgan forced my hand, Judge Fly," Wesley told me. "He gave me no choice but to defend myself, which is something I always could do real well."

I assured him I was certain the incident transpired exactly as he claimed, but it was possible a jury in Cuero would not share my certainty. It was because of a jury's unpredictable nature that he was willing to plead guilty to a crime he did not commit—*if* the conviction would not add to his time in prison. The scales of Lady Justice sometimes take ironic tilts.

I discussed the matter with Bubba Anderson, the state attorney in Cuero, with whom I happened to be friends. Because Bubba had no ax to grind with Wesley—and because he wanted to rid his old caseload of the Morgan killing—and because even a manslaughter conviction of Hardin would look good on his prosecutorial record and improve his chances of achieving the political future he was after—he was willing to accept the plea bargain. Bubba then went to see the judge who would hear the case—and because Bubba and the judge were drinking companions and long-time associates at a poker club, they had no difficulty reaching an accord.

Once everything was in proper legal alignment to assure a favorable dispensation of justice in the matter of the Morgan killing, I delivered the news to Wesley. He was quite gratified, of course, so much so that he arranged for a cousin in Gonzales County to meet in a certain Cuero saloon with a representative of the DeWitt County Council for Law and Order and deliver to him a cash contribution toward the Council's good works. The Council for Law and Order was an unofficial organization whose small but influential membership was comprised of some of the most important judges in the region, including the judge who was to hear Wesley's case in Cuero. Another undeniable truth about the scales of Justice is that nothing so emphatically affects their tilt as the impressive heft of gold.

The trial was held in Cuero on New Year's Day of 1892, and proceeded exactly as arranged. The whole thing took less than twenty minutes. We entered a plea of guilty and the judge handed down a sentence of two years' imprisonment to run concurrent with sentence being served.

That trip to Cuero was the first time Wesley had been outside the walls of Huntsville in more than thirteen years. Immediately prior to the trial, his family was permitted to visit him for a few minutes in a courtroom side chamber. I was in the chamber with him, discussing some last-minute points pertaining to the proceedings, when a deputy came in and announced they had arrived.

Suddenly Wes seemed nervous and unsure of himself. It had been a long time since they'd last seen each other. He had shown me photographs of his children which his wife had sent to him over the years—but it is one thing to see children grow up in a sequence of pictures, and quite another to come face-to-face with them after long separation. The only photograph he had of Jane was one which showed the two of them standing arm-in-arm in Jackson Square in New Orleans. She was smiling widely, her hat in her hands, her eyes happy, her light hair lifting in a breeze and shining in the sun. Wesley looked lean and grinned confidently under his cocked hat, his thumbs hooked in his vest.

"I've been in prison more than twice as long as we lived together," he'd said softly, staring at the picture in his hand. It was remarkable how young he yet looked. He was heavier now than in the photograph—not with fat but with the muscle of hard labor and the settled flesh of confined living. For all the punishment he'd taken during his early years in Huntsville, his face remained fairly free of scars, and his eyes were still quick and keen. His vitality of spirit was rare among long-time convicts.

I patted his arm encouragingly and excused myself, then followed the deputy into the outer room, where the family was waiting to be ushered into the chamber. With them was Fred Duderstadt, Wesley's long-time friend who had been of such great help to Jane and the children during Wesley's incarceration. He introduced himself to me, then presented the family. Molly, the eldest at eighteen, was a striking lass with lively eyes and a determined countenance, and little Jane, a slight fair thing of thirteen, was as pretty as a porcelain doll. John Junior was a strapping buck of seventeen or so and looked every bit the rugged ranch hand he had become under Fred Duderstadt's tutelage. They were all extremely well mannered but somewhat subdued, which I supposed was natural, given the circumstances.

Jane was a shock. Her hair was completely gray and her face deeply lined. Her shoulders sagged. Her eyes were dark wells of suffering. When I gently shook her offered hand, the bones under her pallid skin felt fragile as matchsticks. Her weak smile roused my heart's pity. She had become an old woman at the age of thirty-five.

The deputy led them into the chamber. In a few minutes Fred returned and we went outside to smoke on the portico. He commented on how well Wesley appeared—and a moment later confirmed my suspicion that he was thinking the same thing I was when he said, "It's hard on a woman, I reckon. They can't help but stand by and suffer. It wears on them." I had to agree. During the brief trial a few minutes later, she sat directly behind Wesley, and I believe most of the spectators in the courtroom took her for his mother.

*   *   *

My efforts on behalf of Wesley did not end with the Cuero trial. No sooner was he returned to Huntsville than he engaged me in his quest for a full pardon from the state of Texas. Although he was assured of gaining his release from prison in another year or so, his full civil rights could be restored only by a pardon from the governor, and he now devoted himself zealously toward acquiring that legal absolution.

It was certainly an auspicious time to petition for it. His heroic achievement of self-reform had been hailed by Huntsville officials and widely publicized by newspapers throughout the state. Dave Hamilton, newly elected to the legislature, had joined Billy Teagarden's unflagging efforts on Wesley's behalf. But the most favorable factor in his quest for pardon was the governor himself. James Stephen Hogg, "the people's governor," the first Texas native to govern the state, a wellborn man who'd grown up poor and was a fervent champion of the downtrodden, had just won a strenuous reelection campaign. If there was ever a governor whose sympathies might be moved by a plea from a convict of demonstrably reformed character, that governor was Big Jim Hogg.

Wesley labored hard and diligently on the careful composition of his petition. It included a detailed account of his crime and all the mitigating factors relating to it, and cited legal reference as it applied to his trial and the testimony rendered thereat. He had not proceeded very far, however, when he was distracted by the news that Jane had been taken seriously ill. In a frantic exchange of letters with his children he was assured that their mother was recovering well.

Perhaps so, but not for long. She soon fell ill again, this time even more seriously than before. I heard the bad news from Billy and immediately wrote to Wesley to inquire if I might be of any service to his family. I received no reply. I learned from Billy that Wesley was writing daily letters to his children, admonishing them to do everything possible for their mother and constantly plying them with questions about her condition. He sent me a brief note near the end of October. "I spend my days and nights beseeching the Lord to make my darling well," he wrote. "I am confident He will not abandon her, she who has suffered so much on my behalf." To his children he wrote: "Any serious mishap to your lovable mama would be . . . a calamity irretrievable and irreparable."

On the sixth of November, 1892, Jane Hardin died. I was told that her final words were, "Oh, sweet Jesus, *yes*!"

He grieved in the dark solitude of his cell. A guard reported that he'd chewed his tongue bloody. The officials feared he'd gone mad. They said he sometimes howled in the night. Billy suspected that had it not been for his love of the children, Wesley might have ended his own life. "His whole excitement about getting freed soon," Billy said to me, "was because he and Jane would finally be back together. But now . . ." He turned his palms up and shrugged.

Jane was buried near her childhood home of Coon Hollow, and Wesley's children were taken in by Fred Duderstadt and his family. Except for quite brief letters to the children, Wesley shunned contact with the outside world. He answered no letters—perhaps did not even read them. He would receive no visitors. The guards reported that he simply lay in his bunk and stared at the stone ceiling.

But one cannot grieve forever, after all. One either recovers or goes mad and that's the end of it. Over the next few months he slowly came back to life. He wrote letters of gratitude to Billy and to me and, I'm sure, to many others who had expressed their condolences and offered to help in his time of deep sorrow. And then he resumed work on his petition for pardon.

He submitted an early draft of the petition to me for critique, and I was most impressed by its clarity and cohesion, as well as by its astute legal references. With but minimum guidance from me, he had crafted a legal instrument of no less quality than those composed by attorneys of long practice. Indeed, it was in some ways superior. Unlike most legal documents, his was informed by a general semantic clarity and ease of style. In November of 1893 he forwarded the completed petition to me and asked that I deliver it personally to the governor, with whom I had by then become warmly acquainted through several audiences on various matters of law and politics.

John Wesley Hardin was released from the Huntsville Penitentiary on February 17, 1894. He was forty years old and had been in prison for fifteen years, four months, and twelve days. One month later, his petition for pardon was granted by Governor Hogg. I forwarded it to Wesley with the following letter:

> *Dear Sir—Enclosed I send you a full pardon from the governor of Texas. I congratulate you on its reception and trust that it is the dawn of a bright and peaceful future. There is time to retrieve a lost past. Turn your back upon it with all its suffering and sorrow and fix your eyes upon the future with the determination to make yourself an honorable and useful member of society. The hand of every true man will be extended to assist you in your upward course and I trust that the name of Hardin will in the future be associated with the performance of deeds that will ennoble his family and be a blessing to humanity. Did you ever read Victor Hugo's masterpiece, "Les Miserables"? If not, you ought to read it. It paints in graphic words the life of one who had tasted the bitterest dregs of life's cup, but in his Christian manhood rose above it almost like a god and left behind him a path luminous with good deeds. With the best wishes for your welfare and happiness, I am, yours very truly,*
>
> W. S. FLY

PART SIX

THE PISTOLEER IN EL PASO

PROCLAMATION
By the Governor of the State of Texas

To All to Whom These Presents Shall Come:

Whereas, at the spring term, A.D. 1878 in the district court of Comanche County, State of Texas, John Wesley Hardin was convicted of murder in the second degree and sentenced to the penitentiary for twenty-five years; concurrent with which sentence is a sentence for two years in the district court of DeWitt County, Texas, January 1, 1892, for manslaughter, and

Whereas, For the reason that he has served out his term of sentence and was discharged from the penitentiary on the 17th day of February, 1894, that good citizens ask it;

Now therefore, I, J. S. Hogg, Governor of Texas, do by virtue of the authority vested in me by the constitution and laws of this State, hereby, for the reasons specified, now on file in the office of the Secretary of State, do grant to said convict, John Wesley Hardin, full pardon in both cases and restore him to full citizenship and the right of suffrage.

In testimony whereof I have hereto signed my name and caused the seal of the State to be affixed at the city of Austin, this 16th day of March, A.D. 1894.

J. S. HOGG, *Governor*

GEO. W. SMITH, *Secretary of State.*

F R O M

The Life of John Wesley Hardin as Written by Himself

''Readers, you see what drink and passion will do. If you wish to be successful in life, be temperate and control your passions; if you don't, ruin and death is the inevitable result.''

— Cicero Allenwood —

He stayed at Fred Duderstadt's place for a while when he first got back. His children had been living there ever since their momma died. Even before they'd moved in with Fred and his family, they'd been neighbors for years and years. For most of their life Fred had been the main man in it, the one to always help them out when they needed helping. Considering that Wes had been in the penitentiary for the last fifteen years, it's only natural that they saw Fred as more their daddy than they did him. It had to be some awkwardness among them when Wes finally came back to them and said something like, "Hello, children—Daddy's home!"

By the time he got out of Huntsville, Molly was a full-grown woman of twenty-one and was engaged to marry young Charlie Billings. The talk was that Wes didn't much approve of the match but couldn't make Molly back down from it, nor Charlie either. His boy Johnny I knew real well. He was one of Fred's cowboys, and a danged good one. He rode like he was born to the saddle. I heard that Wes tried to talk both him and Molly into going to study at college in Austin, but they neither one wanted anything to do with college. Little Jane didn't hardly know him at all, having only been but about a year old when he went to prison. But he was set on them all living together like the family they were. He rented a nice little house in Gonzales—he'd always liked the town and it had always liked him, and he'd decided it was where he wanted to try and make his living as a lawyer. None of his children were happy about the move to town, but he *was* their daddy, and they did love him and want to please him, and so they went to live in Gonzales with him.

It wasn't long before he passed his State Law Examination and had his license to practice. He opened an office, in the Peck & Fly Building across from the courthouse. I met him after church one Sunday. Him and his children attended services regularly, most often with Charlie Billings in their company, since he'd come to town to visit with Molly nearly every week. On this particular Sabbath, Wes was asked by Preacher Kinson if he'd lead the congregation in a prayer, and he'd done it as good as any preacher could. I went up to him after the service and told him so. He invited me to dinner and I gladly accepted, and from then on I had dinner at his house almost every Sunday. We'd sit out on the gallery afterward and have good talks over cigars and some of Molly's fine coffee. I tell you, if you didn't already know who he was, you'd never guess that once upon a time he'd been the most feared mankiller in Texas. He was knowledgeable and well mannered, and most always dressed in a clean black suit and tie. It was obvious he enjoyed being the daddy of the family, even though it was sometimes just as clear that, grown as they were, Molly and Johnny and Jane didn't much care for being treated like children.

One day I asked him to join me for a drink in the Glass Slipper Saloon, but he said, "No, thank you, Cicero, you go on ahead. I don't associate with John Barleycorn any longer myself." It might of been true: nobody saw him take a drink the whole nine months he lived in Gonzales. Nor do any gambling either. And far as I know, he didn't make so much as a single visit to either of the pleasure houses at the edge of town. He said he intended to be an upright citizen and, by God, he was surely a better one than most.

I don't recall him having but about a dozen cases the whole time he lived in Gonzales, and they were just small

matters having to do with contracts and such as that. He
had plenty of free time to stop by the jail-house gallery
every afternoon to jaw with us—me and Sheriff R. M.
Glover and Deputy Bob Coleman and a bunch of regulars
who liked to get together to argue politics and tell stories
and pass along the latest jokes. Wes fit right in. He told
dandy stories and everybody liked him. Naturally, there
were lots of things we all would of liked to hear him tell
about—like the killings he'd done, and the time he backed
down Hickok in Abilene, and what Bill Longley was really
like, and what it'd been like in Huntsville all them years,
and . . . oh, hell, a hundred things. But you don't just up
and ask a man about such personal things as that. You
might hint around the subject a little, but that's all. If a
fella wants to tell a personal thing he will, and if he don't,
well, it's his right to keep it to himself.

One afternoon, though, he did show us something we'd
all been damn curious about. The talk had somehow got
around to the old cap-and-ball revolvers which had long
since given way to the cartridge loaders. R.M. and Bob
and me all carried Peacemakers, and asked Wes what he
thought of them. He said they were fine pistols, all right,
and owned one himself, but he still believed the old army
Colt .44 was the best gun he'd ever used. Then he says,
"Ain't I seen one of those cappers on your gun wall,
R.M.?"

R.M. went in his office and got it. Wes checked to see
it was unloaded and then twirled that piece as pretty as a
pocket watch on a chain. He spun it up in the air and
caught it in his left hand and kept it right on twirling. He
tossed it over his shoulder and turned around quick and
caught it in his right and held down the trigger and fanned
the hammer with his left hand so fast all you saw was a
blur. He handed the piece back to R.M. with a grin. "They
say Bill Longley could fan six rounds that way faster'n
you can sneeze."

I tell you he had some mouths hanging open. Who
would of thought a man could handle a gun that way after
fifteen years in prison? No question he'd been practicing

at home—but *still*. After Wes left for supper with his children, Bob Coleman said, "I believe that man is *every*thing with a gun I heard tell he was." I don't recall anybody disagreeing.

Wes never showed it, but he had to've been unhappy about not getting many cases. I don't think the wolf was at his door, but he might of been hearing it getting close by. Things weren't going all that well in the family, either. Molly couldn't stand being separated from Charlie as much as she was and her moping was getting worse by the day. Finally she just up and went back to the Duderstadt ranch. Wes didn't like that one bit and went out there to retrieve her. But when he got there and they all talked it over, he decided to let her stay at Fred's. What else could he do? If he'd made her come back to Gonzales, she would of been constantly miserable. More than anything, he wanted the family to be together, but not if it meant making his children unhappy.

With Molly gone, things at home got worse. Little Jane missed her sister and pleaded with Wes to let her go back to Fred's too. She wanted to be with Molly, she said, she wanted to be with her friends. So Wes let her go too. His boy Johnny didn't like living in town any more than the girls did, but he was a good and loyal son, and if his daddy wanted him at his side, then that's where he'd be. The truth is, he was blazing at the bit to go back to cowboying with Fred. Fred would come to town fairly often to visit with him and Wes, and Johnny couldn't ever get enough of hearing all about how things were going at the ranch. The fact is, Fred missed Johnny as much as Johnny missed him. I know this because Fred used to tell us so when he'd stop by the jailhouse and have a drink with me and R.M. before heading back home. It was a sad situation all around. I couldn't help thinking how bad Wes must of felt to know his son really preferred to live with Fred than with his daddy. But he did know it, and because Wes Hardin was never a bully nor a selfish man, and because he loved his boy enough to want him to be happy, he finally gave him permission to go back to Fred's. Johnny never asked to go, mind you. Wes gave the permission on his own. I can still see them riding out of town, Johnny and Fred, with Wes standing in front of the livery and watching him go.

I don't believe Wes had ever been so alone in his life as he was after Johnny left. Even while he was inside those prison walls, he knew he had somebody waiting for him to get out and come home to, and so he wasn't alone, not really, not in the way I'm talking about. But now, with Jane dead and buried and his children grown and gone from him, well, I reckon his heart had to been feeling hollow in a way that just can't be filled by anybody's consolations. I know what I'm talking about. I lost my wife Martha to the smallpox when I wasn't but twenty, and not all the friends and kinfolk in the world could fill the hole she left in my heart like an open grave. I guess I tried to drink myself to death. After a while I didn't feel much of anything; and once you reach that point, you either stop breathing or you start making your way back to the living. All I'm saying is loneliness can be worse than any sickness, and there ain't a thing that can be done about it except to last it out if you can. That means trying to find something to do with yourself—besides drinking and picking fights, I mean—till you get over it or till you don't.

What Wes found to do with himself was to get involved in the next election for sheriff. R.M. wasn't running again, and it looked to be a close race between the two candidates wanting to take his place—Bob Coleman, the Populist Party nominee, and Old W. E. (Bill) Jones, the Democratic candidate, who'd been sheriff once before, back in the '70s. When Wes found out Old Bill was running, he wrote an article in *The Drag Net* (one of the town's two newspapers, whose motto was "We Admire No One in Particular"). In it, he said that Old Bill Jones had helped him to escape from the Gonzales jail back in '72. He said Old

Bill was a crooked lawman back then and would surely be as crooked again if he got elected. If Gonzales wanted an honest sheriff, he said, they'd cast their votes for Bob Coleman.

Lord, what a ruckus he stirred up! Practically overnight the election became a contest between Old Bill and Wes Hardin, who wasn't even a candidate. Old Bill responded with some articles of his own in *The Gonzales Inquirer*. Who in his right mind, he asked the readers, would take the word of a damn convict who'd murdered dozens of people? He called Wes and Bob Coleman a pair of liars, and he accused Bob of recruiting Wes on his side of the campaign by promising to make him his chief deputy if he won the election. Old Bill asked the good citizens of Gonzales to consider if they were ready to hand Wes Hardin a badge and give him armed legal authority over themselves.

Tempers boiled all over town, and most political arguments ended in a fistfight. Some men thought that even if Wes's accusations against Old Bill were true, it was low of him to make them after all these years. If Bill *had* helped him to break jail, it was a mean way of thanking him for it to tell the tale now. Others argued that if Old Bill *had* been a crooked lawman, nobody, not even Wes, was obliged to keep it a secret. By telling the truth about Jones, Wes was showing just how completely he himself had reformed.

Then Wes announced that he wouldn't stay in Gonzales County if W. E. Jones won the election. If Old Bill got voted sheriff, he said, the enforcers of the law in Gonzales would be more dishonest than those who openly violated the law, and he himself would not live in a county that would accept such corruption.

It was the closest election we ever had. Over four thousand votes were cast and carefully counted. And when the dust all settled, the winner—by eight votes—was Old Bill Jones.

A couple of weeks later, Wes went out to the Duderstadt

ranch and said his good-byes to his children and to Fred and his family. The next morning he loaded his trunk on a wagon, hitched his saddle horse to the back of it, and giddapped the team on out of Gonzales County, heading west.

— Annie Lee Lewis —

They met at a Christmas party and were married two weeks later—and they saw each other for the last time just a few hours after that. Merciful Jesus! I have heard of whirlwind romance, but that of my little sister Callie and Mr. John Wesley Hardin was a fools' tornado! It was an astonishing episode from first to last, and I'm sorry to say they deserve the ridicule they received for it.

He was *forty-one* years old, for goodness' sake. Callie was seventeen. He had a *daughter* her age. I was twenty-four and felt like a child beside him. They said he killed forty men before being sent to prison. The wickedest boy Callie knew at the time was Marcus Framm, who once shot a farmer's prize hen with a squirrel rifle. You see my point: the differences between them were far greater than their years.

The Christmas party was given by the Dennisons, neighbors of ours in London, and was partly in honor of Mr. Hardin, who had very recently moved to Kimble County from Gonzales and opened a law office. He had not yet been out of prison a year. The Dennisons were related to the Hardins and quite close to Jefferson Davis Hardin, Mr. Hardin's younger brother, who lived in Junction, about fifteen miles south of London. But, until the party, they had never met Mr. Hardin himself.

It is important to know that Callie had always been a

willful and rebellious girl with a taste for stories of adventurous outlaws. She was an avid reader of dime novelettes. I used to chide her for her silly interest in such lurid literature, but my disapproval—as well as Mother's—only seemed to increase her enjoyment of it. Willful—she was simply willful. Father, who is said to have been a bit of a rapscallion in his youth, did not seriously object to Callie's reading such trash—but then Father never objected in any way to Callie. She was his favorite. Mother always said they were cut from the same rebellious cloth.

Not that Callie lacked for feminine wiles—she was an incorrigible coquette. The truth will out and I must be honest. But although I admit to a grudging covetousness of her perfect face and figure, I most adamantly deny, as some have suggested, that I was envious of her to the point of rejoicing in her humiliation with Mr. Hardin. Nonsense! She is my sister and I love her dearly. There *were*, however, occasions when she played the coquette to such extreme that I secretly wished to grab her and shake some sense into her. The occasion of our initial meeting with Mr. Hardin was just such a time.

On being introduced to him at the party, Callie fairly gushed. "Why, Mr. Hardin," she said, trilling like an addled songbird, "I am ever so delighted to make your acquaintance. I feel as though I'm meeting a legend in the flesh. Father has often praised your great courage in opposing the hateful State Police." Lord.

And him, forty-one years old and dressed impeccably in a handsome black suit and silk tie—and you'd have thought he had never been flattered by a pretty young thing before to see the silly grin he gave her. We all knew he'd been married for only a short time before going to prison and that he was a widower by the time he got out. And though one might suppose that fifteen years in the penitentiary would blunt a man's social grace, it obviously did not completely dull his. "Miss Callie," he said, "I would fight the entire State Police force all over again—*and* the Texas Rangers to the last man—if that's what it took to have the honor of the next dance with you.''

He *was* handsome—in a weathered sort of way. He was tall and ruggedly distinguished and his dark hair was only lightly seasoned with gray. His brows were thick, his jaw strong, and he wore a heavy mustache. But his chief feature was his eyes, which were at once alluring and yet fearsome—if that makes sense. They were as darkly gray as storm clouds and exuded a confusing mixture of independence, cruelty, and loneliness. Little wonder that Callie, with her penchant for renegade spirits, would be entranced by eyes as those—the eyes of the lonesome outlaw and all that.

She did not leave his side the entire evening. When they were not dancing to the fiddles, they sat together in a corner, sipping punch and conversing with goodly animation, so utterly indifferent to everyone else it was rude.

As Father's hired man Johnston drove us home at the end of the evening, she told me their chief topic of conversation had been the book he had begun to write, the story of his life. She was thrilled that he'd deigned to discuss such a personal undertaking with her, and of course she thought that his autobiography was the most wonderful idea. *She* would certainly rush to purchase a copy of the book, she assured him, and she was absolutely certain many other readers would too. As they'd bid each other good night, she invited him to come visit her at home. ''He has always loved the name Callie,'' she informed me. ''His younger daughter was named Callie at birth. The only reason he later changed it to Jane was to honor his wife. Isn't that wonderful?'' I wasn't at all sure *what* she thought was wonderful, but she did not really expect an answer.

Father was rich. He'd gone to the War a penniless young man and risen to the rank of captain by the time he came home after Appomattox. He became a cowboy and quickly learned the cattle business. Before long he was a drover, and eventually became one of the most successful stockmen in our part of the state. Furthermore, he had bought more and more land over the years and was now the largest property owner in Kimble County. But his fondest memories, he always said, were of his days as a young cowboy driving the herds to Kansas. Mr. Hardin, it so happened, had also been a cowboy in his youth, and within five minutes of making each other's acquaintance when he came to visit—a mere week after the Christmas party—they were deep in loud reminiscence about those *glorious* old days on the Chisholm Trail.

"Excuse us," Father said to the rest of us—including Callie, who had put on her best dress in honor of Mr. Hardin's visit—"while I get to know this old rascal a little better." They retired to Father's study to continue their talk about the old days on the trail. The moment the door closed, Callie stamped her foot and said, "He came to see *me*, not to talk to Father about stupid old cows!" I believe she would have stormed into the study after them and created a scene if Mother hadn't prevailed upon her to mind her manners—as well as conspired to retrieve the men from the study by having supper served earlier than usual.

They'd had a few drinks of whiskey in the study—Mr. Hardin claimed they were the first he'd tasted since "my period of employment with the state," as he amusingly phrased it—and their effects were quite obvious on him. His eyes were mischievously bright, his voice louder, his gestures broader. He smiled at Callie constantly and even winked at her across the table a time or two. Callie was delighted by his indiscreet attentions and beamed upon him as radiantly as the full moon framed in the window. Mother was somewhat nonplussed, but Father was a bit fired with whiskey too, and unmindful of all the flagrant flirting. When we'd done with dessert and coffee, Mr. Hardin asked Father ("Captain Len," he called him, quite aware of the way he was addressed by everyone in the county) for permission to take Callie for a short ride in the buggy. Father said of course, wholly ignoring Mother's deep frown.

When they returned, less than an hour later, Callie was smiling as mysteriously as a cat. Mr. Hardin took another drink with Father, then shook his hand and bid us all good evening. That night, as we lay in our beds in the darkened bedroom, Callie told me Mr. Hardin had asked her to be his wife. "Good Lord, Callie!" I said.

"I haven't said yes or no," she said. "I really didn't expect that. I told him I'd have to think it over." She pushed up on an elbow and stared at me in the dark, looking like a pale shadow in her cotton shimmy. "Are you shocked, Annie Lee? Just think—you'd be sister-in-law to John Wesley Hardin, the most famous desperado in all Texas." She giggled like a devilish child.

"But he's old enough to be your *father!*" I said. "And he hasn't a handful of dirt to his name."

"Oh, *you!*" she said. "Nobody else would say a mean thing like that. You're just jealous!"

Mother was shocked when Callie broke the news. I know she thought Mr. Hardin too old for Callie—and far too familiar with the world's harsher truths. But she simply said that marriage was a serious decision and perhaps Callie and Mr. Hardin ought give themselves a little more time to discuss it. Father, of course, thought the marriage was a splendid idea and would brook no talk against it. Callie had to remind him that she had not yet accepted the proposal. "But I know you will," Father said with a sly grin. Callie just smiled at him and kept mute.

The following day she received a letter from Mr. Hardin, asking for her answer to his "proposition." He also told her that on his way home the previous evening, he'd been thrown hard from the buggy when a coyote spooked the horse. His face had been bruised and his ribs cracked, he wrote, but he was sure he'd be fine in a few days.

When Callie showed the letter to Father that evening, he smiled widely. "And what is your answer to his proposition to be, daughter?" he asked. Callie's face was difficult to read just then. She studied Mother's sad look for a moment, then met my own stare directly. I suppose my disapproval must have been visible, because Callie twisted her mouth at me in disdain, and then said to Father, "My answer will be yes." Father beamed and told her he wished to meet with Mr. Hardin about the matter as soon as possible. "I'll write to him today," Callie said.

There is another story about the way he acquired the broken ribs and the bruises on his face. Rita Maria, wife of one of Father's ranch foremen, was my prized confidante, my informant about life in the rougher reaches. *Her* source was her husband Francisco. He told her that on his way home to Junction after his visit Mr. Hardin had stopped at an isolated roadside inn to have a drink or two. It was said he was already a little drunk when he arrived, and in a short time he was drunker yet. He began to brag to the bartender that he would soon be a force to reckon with in Kimble County. But his loud bragging soon wore thin on some of the other patrons, most of whom were rough cedar choppers. Hard words ensued and Mr. Hardin challenged one of the choppers to a fistfight. They went outside and fought under the moon in a wide gully behind the building. And that, Francisco told Rita Maria, was how Mr. Hardin had received his injuries—or so he had heard.

I overheard Mother and Father late that night in their room. "He has killed men, Leonard," Mother said. "He has been in the penitentiary for most of Callie's life! He is taking advantage of the poor child—yes, *child*—who doesn't know her own mind. What he really wants is the property he'll gain from the marriage. Surely you can see that. Why else would such a man want to marry one so young?"

And Father said: "Callie is a child no longer. She's a grown woman and it's time she married. One spinster daughter in the family is enough." (The remark cut me, but not to the quick—I'd long since grown accustomed to such sidelong slashes of his displeasure with my maidenhood.) "Yes, the man committed crimes," Father said, "and he has paid a dear price for them. Prison cost him the family he once had, and he is lonely for another. He needs a young woman to give it to him. He is a man of courage and fortitude, and we are honored—*honored*, do you hear?—to have such a man attach to our family. Now that's the end of it.''

Within the week Mr. Hardin was at our house once again, this time to confer with Father about the details of the wedding. Callie was shocked by the sight of his face, which was still livid with purple and yellow bruises, and she was unusually subdued at the supper table that evening. When Mr. Hardin told Father that he'd been quite busy writing his memoirs, Callie gave him a stricken look, as though he'd revealed a secret that was theirs alone.

After supper, she and Mr. Hardin went for a long walk in the south meadow. When they returned she was in better spirits, and the smile she gave me was pure wickedness. Her eyes were dancing and her cheeks were flushed. A leaf of grass clung to her hair. Mother saw it too, and her lips went thin—but of course she said nothing. Mr. Hardin grinned stiffly and had a drink of whiskey with Father, whose celebratory mood had him drinking a good deal more than usual of late.

They were married on January 8, a chilly but brightly sunny day, in the county courthouse in Junction. Callie looked beautiful in her white dress, and Mr. Hardin, despite the lingering traces of bruise on his face, looked quite distinguished in his black suit and stiff collar. It was a small ceremony, attended only by our family and a few close friends—and of course by Mr. Hardin's brother, Jefferson Davis, and his wife. A grand ball was scheduled for later that afternoon, and all the important families in the county would be there. While Father conveyed the bride and groom to the home of family friends to refresh themselves and await the hour of the ball, Mother and I and a number of helpful neighbors and kin began preparing the courthouse room where the ball would be held. The room had been cleared of furniture except for several long food tables along the wall and a stand at the front of the room where the string band would play.

A short time later the tables were laden with steaming platters and covered dishes, with pies and cakes, bowls of punch, and jugs of other potables. The band was tuned and ready, and the room resounded with the laughter and conversations of more than a hundred people. Father checked his pocket watch and said, ''They'll be here any minute now.''

The time of their scheduled arrival came and went. Father repeatedly consulted his watch and his face grew grim. The conversational din had assumed a quizzical tone, and the guests stirred restlessly. ''Perhaps there's been an accident of some sort,'' Mother said in a strained voice. Father decided to go check on the matter, and Mother insisted on going with him. They instructed me to stay in place and placate the guests as best I could.

People do not believe me when I say I don't know what happened. I can see their disbelief in their faces. They think I'm withholding the truth from them out of deference to Callie or simply for the perverse pleasure of keeping the knowledge to myself. But it is the truth: even today I do not know. Neither does Mother. And Father remains the most confused of us all—except perhaps for Mr. Hardin, who, if he were to be believed, had no explanation whatsoever for Callie's perplexing conduct. I asked her about it again and again during the first few weeks, but she absolutely refused to discuss the matter with me. She finally told me that if I did not stop questioning her, she would cease speaking to me altogether. She put an end to Mother and Father's interrogations in much the same way: she threatened to leave home and live with a cousin in Dallas.

I only know what everybody else knows. I know that the friends at whose home they awaited the start of the ball left for the courthouse an hour prior to the appointed time. They thought Callie and Mr. Hardin might appreciate a period of privacy together before the party. And so, for that hour, they were alone in the house. I also know that just as Mr. Hardin and Callie were walking from the house

to the buggy to come to the ball, Jefferson Davis Hardin
and his wife drove up in their own buggy to accompany
them to the courthouse. According to Mr. Hardin, Jefferson Davis greeted them by saying, "Howdy there, Brother
Wesley—and howdy to that sweet little child you robbed
right out of the cradle." His brother said it jokingly, Mr.
Hardin told Mother and Father—but in an instant Callie
was in tears and dashing back into the house.

Mr. Hardin said he was so stunned that for a moment
he stood there and watched her go. Jefferson Davis
laughed loudly and hollered after her, "Good golly, little
girl, you ain't got to *prove* it to nobody!" Mr. Hardin said
he chided his brother for his remarks and then hurried into
the house. But Callie had locked herself in a room and
refused to let him in or even to answer his pleas to tell
him what was wrong. Mr. Hardin said he tried vainly to
explain that his brother had merely been joking about her
being a child, but still she would not come out of the room.
He was finally forced to break the door open with his
shoulder, he said, which unfortunately only added to her
distress. She raced from the room and out to the gallery,
where she sat in a chair and hugged herself and cried re-
lentlessly and refused to look up into his face. He could
not even touch her without prompting her to greater hys-
terics.

That is the way Father and Mother found them—Callie
hunkered in a chair on the gallery, weeping uncontrollably
and seemingly deaf to Mr. Hardin, who knelt beside her,
speaking earnestly. When Mr. Hardin saw Father and
Mother approaching, he said, "Look, Callie, here are your
parents," and touched her arm. "She shrieked like the
devil himself had put a hand to her," Mother told me. She
shrieked and ran to Father and clutched tightly to him,
sobbing and begging him to please, please take her home
immediately.

Mr. Hardin followed along in his buggy and, on arrival
at the house, continued to try to speak with her. But she
shut herself in our room upstairs and absolutely would not
see him or even answer his entreaties at the door. Father

tried to serve as emissary to her from him, but to no avail. Mother then tried her best to secure some explanation from her, but Callie adamantly refused to discuss it, even with her. Finally, she screamed, "Tell him to go away! Go away and never never *never* come back! *Never!* I never want to see him again! I never want to hear from him! I never want to hear his name! *Never!*" They might have heard her all the way out on the main road.

And so Mr. Hardin took his leave of us, looking haggard and confused. Father promised him that he would continue to try to persuade Callie to "come around." Even Mother, no champion of Mr. Hardin, was mortified by Callie's horrendous behavior and assured him that Callie would soon calm down sufficiently to explain what was troubling her. "I'm sure everything will be fine," she said. He thanked them both for their efforts on his behalf and said he too was certain that everything would soon be straightened out. But, quite frankly, he did not look as though he believed that in the least.

He did not return to London again. He moved to the home of friends in Kerrville, about thirty-five miles southeast of Junction. At first, he corresponded with Father almost daily, inquiring after Callie and reporting that he was working busily on his book. He invariably included a separately enclosed letter addressed to her. But she just as invariably refused to accept it, and Father was obliged to keep sending them back to Mr. Hardin with his regrets.

His correspondence slowly dwindled, and he ceased to enclose separate letters to Callie. His missives now came but once a week. They were notes more than letters, and they reflected an exhausted hope of ever being reconciled with his bride.

The whole pathetic episode has provided grist for the local gossips ever since, but I have steadfastly refused to blush before the fact of my sister's embarrassment. Why should I? The gossips are absolutely right: those two had no business whatsoever getting married to each other. Their ridicule serves them right.

In early spring we heard from him for the last time. He wrote that he was going to Pecos to try a legal case. He did not mention Callie, which was just as well. By then Father had succumbed to her entreaties and retained a lawyer to initiate divorce proceedings. Mr. Hardin left for West Texas in April, and he never returned.

Among the many leading citizens of Pecos City now in El Paso is John Wesley Hardin, Esq., a leading member of the Pecos City bar.

In his young days, Mr. Hardin was as wild as the broad western plains upon which he was raised. But he was a generous, brave-hearted youth and got into no small amount of trouble for the sake of his friends, and soon gained a reputation for being quick-tempered and a dead shot. In those days when one man insulted another, one of the two died then and there. Young Hardin, having a reputation for being a man who never took water, was picked out by every bad man who wanted to make a reputation, and that is where the ''bad men'' made a mistake, for the young westerner still survives many warm and tragic encounters.

Forty-one years has steadied the impetuous cowboy down to a quiet, dignified peaceable man of business. Mr. Hardin is a modest gentleman of pleasant address, but underneath the modest dignity is a firmness that never yields except to reason and the law. He is a man who makes friends of all who come in close contact with him. He is here as associate attorney for the prosecution in the case of the State vs. Bud Frazer, charged with assault with intent to kill.

Mr. Hardin is known all over Texas. He was born and raised in this state.

—— Hudson Duvall ——

El Paso was the last wild town in Texas. With Mexico just across the Rio Grande, and the New Mexico Territory a stone throw north, the town was placed real well for anybody on the dodge from the law. It's no wonder it attracted all the desperadoes it did. The only way to keep a rein on so many bad actors was with some of the toughest lawmen in the country. Jeff Milton, who'd been a Ranger and a U.S. marshal and was absolutely nobody to fool with, was the chief of police. "Any man I kill had it coming"—that was Jeff Milton's motto and everybody knew it. Deputy U.S. Marshal George Scarborough was another quick ass-kicker you didn't want to cross. Old John Selman, who some said had been more of a bandit and mankiller than any of the men he ever arrested, was constable of the first precinct. His son, John Junior, was a city policeman. Like I said—the law in El Paso was every bit as hardcase as the outlaws. And some said it was every bit as crooked.

I'd come to El Paso that winter, and by spring I'd had enough of the place. It was too damn dangerous for a man of my profession. I was a dealer—poker mostly, sometimes blackjack, now and then faro. I worked at the Gem Saloon and did fairly well for myself. But it was a rare night that somebody at the table didn't accuse me of pulling stunts with the deal, and things sometimes got fairly tense before cooler heads persuaded the hothead to

accept his loss with a little more grace. But cooler heads
didn't always prevail: one night a dealer was shot dead
just two tables away from me. The killer was arrested and
eventually convicted and hanged, but that didn't bring the
dealer back to life even a little bit. Sore losers are a constant hazard of the trade, of course—it's one of the first
things a gambler learns. But El Paso sure seemed to have
way more than its share of men who took personal offense
at losing.

It was Hardin who finally convinced me it was time to
shake El Paso's dust and head for California. He came to
town in April—but even before he arrived, the word was
out that he was coming. Somebody telephoned the news
from Pecos, where Hardin had been pressing a suit for a
cousin-in-law named Killing Jim Miller, and the saloon
district buzzed about it for days. I recall a newspaper story
saying Hardin should be welcomed in town because he
was an inspirational example of how a man could reha-
bilitate himself in prison and triumph over his sordid past.
But the saloon rats weren't interested in any model of
reform—they wanted to get a good look at John Wesley
Hardin, the famous pistoleer. Some of them had been children when he was packed off to Huntsville Penitentiary,
but even among most of the older roughs he was
something of a living legend—the quickest, deadliest pistoleer in Texas, the man who made war against the State
Police, the man who'd had to replace the grips on his
pistols more than once because he'd cut so many notches
in them.

The local lawmen weren't nearly so glad as the saloon
rats to have him in town. I heard that Jeff Milton and
George Scarborough met him at the station with shotguns.
They warned him against carrying a gun inside the city
limits and told him to watch his step. It must've been an
interesting conversation. Hardin supposedly told them he
had no intention of making trouble and hoped nobody
would give him any. He said he wanted only to be a good
lawyer, and it's a fact he opened a law office on the second

floor of the professional building across the street from the Gem.

The first night he was in town he came into the Gem and was greeted like some kind of hero. At one point he had a dozen fresh drinks on the bar in front of him, each one bought by a different man. Everybody wanted to be able to say he'd bought a drink for the one and only John Wesley Hardin. Everybody wanted to be his friend. Everybody wanted to hear him tell about facing down Bill Hickok and about the way he gunned down Charlie Webb in Comanche. They gathered round him like some kind of one-man freak show, which I guess in a way he was. The first few times he came in, he accepted the drinks but only threw back a couple of them, and he politely declined to tell stories about his past. He said those days were long gone and he didn't really care to relive them, thank you. But it just wasn't in him to ignore all that admiring attention, I guess. It was pretty obvious he liked it, and I don't guess he got too many free drinks all the time he was in prison. By the time he'd been in town two weeks he was knocking back most of the drinks the boys bought him and grinning bright-eyed at the crowd gathered round as he demonstrated the ''road agent's spin'' he'd used on Hickok. No question he could twirl those pistols. I heard he was putting on the same show in saloons all over El Paso.

He started sitting in on some of the card games in the Gem, and I know a few of the boys sometimes lost hands to him on purpose, just to make him happy and to stay on his good side. But the fact is, he was a reckless card player, and sometimes the boys couldn't lose a hand to him even when they tried. I'd always heard he was a hell of a gambler, but you never would've known it from the way he played in the Gem. To make things worse, he was one of those bad losers I mentioned before, especially when he'd been drinking.

One night he got into a stud game at my table and by midnight was just about cleaned out. He was red-eyed and surly and in no mood for the general joshing and chuckling at the table. When Buck Elliot laid down four nines to take the biggest pot of the night—which Hardin had been sure he was going to take with his full house of aces over fives—well, it was too much for him. He said, "Shit!" and sent Buck's cards flying off the table with a quick backhand sweep of his arm.

Everybody said, "Hey now!" and "No need for that!" and so on. They'd all got pretty familiar with him in the couple of weeks he'd been in town, and the familiarity had eased them off their tiptoes around him. Maybe that was part of what was bothering him, I don't know. All I know for sure is what happened. He jumps up and says, "I've had enough of your card tricks, boy!" He was talking to me. I was stunned. "*I* don't play card tricks!" I said, and the others quickly backed me up. "Hud's no cheat, Hardin," Bill Lepperman said, and Jerome Bradstreet chimes in with, "It ain't his dealing costing you, Hardin, it's your playing."

"Save the bullshit for your gardens, you sonbitches," Hardin says, and pushes back his coat flaps so we can get a good look at the one pistol on his hip and the other hung in a vest holster. He never did pull them—Buck and the others lied about that. He just let us see them, and that was enough. "The whole bunch of you been playing me for the fish all night long," he says, "but that damn game's over. This pot's mine and I'm taking it. Anybody's got objections, all he's got to do is stand up and make them."

None of us stood up or said anything more, and he raked up the pot and stuffed it in his pockets. I had a derringer in the waist pocket of my vest, but it might as well have been a frog for all the use I was about to make of it. That was the moment I made up my mind to move on to California.

As soon as Hardin left, Buck went out in search of a lawman, and a few minutes later was back with Old John at his side. John listened to everybody's story, then him and Buck set out for the Herndon House, where Hardin lived. But as they were walking past the Wigwam Saloon they spotted him at the bar.

The way Buck told the story, he was right at Old John's side as John stepped up to Hardin and told him he was under arrest. But Mack Tracey, who was working the bar that night, told me Buck hung back by the doors, ready as a rabbit to run for it. Buck claimed Old John backed Hardin down, but Mack told it different. He said when Old John told Hardin he was under arrest for robbing a card game, Hardin said he didn't do any such thing, he'd only taken what was rightfully his. Old John said he could tell it to the judge, and Hardin said, "I'm telling it to *you*, uncle." There weren't but about six people in the saloon at that late hour and they all hustled out of the line of fire. No telling what would've happened next, Mack said, if Jeff Milton hadn't come in just then.

Chief Milton heard one side of the story from Hardin, then the other from Buck, then said to Hardin, "If you can prove they were cheating you, I'll do something about it—but if you can't, then you're in the wrong, and you know you are. Now you told me yourself when you first got to town you didn't want any trouble. I'm holding you to your word."

Hardin said he knew he'd been cheated but couldn't prove it. "Then I'll have to arrest you for robbery, Wes," Chief Milton told him.

"I'll have that pistol," Old John said, and started to reach for the pistol on Hardin's hip. But Hardin stepped back from him and squared off. "No you won't," he said. "Jeff can arrest me, but *you* can't arrest one side of me, you murdering old buzzard. I know all about you."

Mack said Old John's eyes flamed up and for a moment it looked like he might pull—but he didn't. "If Old John was ever going to pull on Wes Hardin in a stand-up gun-fight, that was the time he'd of done it," Mack said. "The man had just called him a murderer, for Christ's sake. But Old John didn't get old by taking chances in a stand-up fight, if you know what I mean—and if you ever tell him I said that, I'll call you a bald-ass liar."

Anyhow, that's what I saw of John Wesley Hardin with my own eyes in El Paso and what I heard about him with my own ears. Jeff Milton took him before Judge Howe and the judge made him repay the money to Buck, then fined him twenty-five dollars.

They say Hardin and Jeff got to be friends after that and often took a drink or two in the saloons together— and George Scarborough with them. Some say the three of them got to be thick as thieves and even conspired in the killing of Martin McRose. I wouldn't know. By then I was on my way to California. But I do know that Hardin and Old John weren't friends for even a minute. Between them, it was bad blood from the start.

Hector Gomez
———— O'Keefe ————

There's nothing worse can happen to a man than to fall in love with a hot-ass bitch. That's what happened to Marty. Hell, she used to give *me* some looks, and I ain't *nothing* to look at. If it had a dick, she was interested.

Me and Vic and Tom were at the cantina table in Juárez with them when Scarborough told Marty that Hardin was keeping company with his wife. He said it real casual, while he was rolling himself a smoke. He said everybody in El Paso knew it too and was having a good laugh about it. Marty's grin looked like wood. He said what the hell did he care, she wasn't his wife no more. He said he'd divorced the no-good tramp in Ojinaga a coupla months ago, so she could fuck all El Paso for all he cared. Bullshit. He was lying to try and save face. Whenever Marty was really steamed, a big vein on his forehead would swell up, and just then it looked about to pop.

"Well," Scarborough says, "you mighta divorced her and all, like you say, but I bet those fellas laughing at you in the saloons across the river don't know it. I bet *Hardin* don't know it."

He was smart, Scarborough, egging Marty like that. A couple of days earlier, when he figured Marty was holding out on him, he said he'd arrest him next time he crossed the river. Old Selman had throwed a fit about being cheated and said he'd shoot Marty if he set foot back in

Texas. But now Scarborough wanted to deal. "Cut me half the take from the cows," he said, "and I'll set Hardin up for you." He'd trick him into showing up at the railroad bridge in the middle of the night and Marty could be laying for him and let him have it.

"What about your bigmouthed pal Selman?" Marty says. "He want the *other* half of the take?" Scarborough says, "Fuck Selman. Old bastard don't know how to get along. This is between you and me." Marty wanted to know how he would get Hardin to go to the bridge in the middle of the goddamn night, and Scarborough says, "Hell, me and him are big buddies now, ain't you heard? I'll tell him a dealer I know is selling some guns to some Mexes at the bridge tonight and wants to hire protection for himself in case the greasers try a cross. Hardin'll go for it. He's trying to prove he's still the man he was before he went to the pen. Been pushing his luck lately."

"I'll push his fucking luck," Marty says. All right, he says, it's a deal—only he ain't giving Scarborough a nickel until after Hardin's taken care of. "Sure," Scarborough says with a big phony smile, "I trust you. Just don't forget to bring the money." Marty gives him a go-to-hell smile back and says, "Don't worry about that, George. I always keep my money on me—all of it. It's the safest place." Scarborough says, "All right, then—the rail bridge at midnight," and heads back to El Paso to set the thing up.

That night, Marty posted me at our end of the bridge with my Remington repeater to cover their retreat if they had to make a run for it back to our side. Then him and Vic and Tom went out to the middle of the bridge to meet Scarborough. There was a mist on the river, but the other side was lit up by a streetlight good enough for me to see everything. At the far end of the bridge, a pair of ice wagons stood on one side of the tracks. George Scarborough came out from behind one of them.

They met out on the bridge and talked for a minute. Scarborough pointed to the wagons like he was saying that was where Marty could lay for Hardin. Marty nodded and they all headed that way.

As soon as they got to the end of the bridge, Scarborough pulled his gun and shot Marty twice in the head and jumped off to the side just as rifles opened fire from one of the ice wagons and a shotgun blasted from the other. Vic and Tom went down before they could clear their holsters. I ducked behind one of the bridge posts and watched from the shadow. Hell no, I didn't shoot. It wouldn't of helped Marty and Vic and Tom one bit, but it likely woulda brought the shooters running over to kill me too.

All that shooting didn't take five seconds. Then Scarborough scoots out and takes out Marty's gun, fires it in the air and drops it on the ground, then quick cleans out Marty's pockets. The police captain, Milton, and a man the next day's newspapers said was a Texas Ranger came out from behind one of the wagons, both of them with carbines—and from behind the other wagon comes Wes Hardin with a shotgun. I'd always figured Milton was in on the deal for those cows we rustled in Little Texas. The Ranger too, I guess. Lawmen—Christ! A dog's hind leg ain't as crooked as a lawman.

Hardin gave the scattergun to Milton and hurried off down the street, but Scarborough, Milton, and the Ranger stayed and smoked cigars while a crowd of excited sports came out of the nearby saloons and gathered to gawk at the bodies.

The newspapers said they were shot for resisting arrest on warrants of cattle rustling, but the talk in the saloons was that Hardin had paid Scarborough and Milton to kill Marty so he could have Beulah McRose for himself. Well, he wanted the bitch, all right, and he got her—but he did his own shooting, like I said. The others were just paying Marty back for crossing them. While they were at it, they crossed Old Man Selman too, for some damn reason. Hardin musta been behind it, though—because just look how Selman got even with *him*.

── Beulah McRose ──

Early that summer, my husband made a deal with some people in El Paso to move a herd of cattle down from New Mexico. Two of those people, he said, were George Scarborough and John Selman. He didn't mention Jeff Milton—maybe because Jeff wasn't in it, maybe because Martin didn't know he was. Anyhow, they told Martin they had a buyer out at Van Horn all ready to take the cows off their hands at a real nice profit. They were stealing the herd, of course—that's why they contracted Martin to move it for them. He had a reputation for expertise in that regard. I once heard him describe his profession as the low-overhead approach to the beef business.

I married Martin because I was young and bored and didn't know much except that I wanted some excitement in my life. My brothers taught me to ride and shoot when I was still in pigtails, and I always envied them their freedom to roam and take their pleasure where they found it. I won't be stupidly coy and deny that I'd known men before Martin, but they were mostly dullards of the sort to be found by the bushels in small towns—clerks and druggists and drummers. Men with stiff collars and soft hands and eyes as oily as their hair. Now and then I'd fool with a farmboy. Their muscles were hard, but I wanted no part of their sweat-and-dirt futures. I'd never known a

truly exciting man until I met Martin. He took me away
to the bright lights and loud music and fast smoky pleasures of Galveston and San Antone. He taught me the
mean comforts of whiskey, and many of men's secret sex-
ual delights. Before long, however, I found out he was not
the man I thought he was. I began to suspect that he was
afraid of losing me, and one dark night, when he whispered that I was the only one he'd ever trusted, I knew I
was right. I realized how much stronger than him I was,
and I couldn't help but hate him a little for disappointing
me so bad.

Scarborough gave Martin half his fee before he left for
New Mexico and promised to pay the rest on delivery of
the herd to a small ranch just east of El Paso. Martin took
Vic Queen, Hector O'Keefe, and Tom Finnessy with him
and went up to Little Texas to get the cows. Two weeks
later he got back to our rented house in town and woke
me in the middle of the night, still smelling of dust and
horse sweat. He said they'd run into some hard luck on
the way back with the herd. They were attacked by rustlers
just a few miles north of the Texas border and had the
cows stolen from them. "We were lucky to get out of it
alive," he said, and I heard the lie in his voice. That's the
trouble with a liar: he even lies to the people he doesn't
have to. He undressed in the dark, saying he was worried
because he didn't think Scarborough and the others would
believe the herd had been rustled. "Guys like them," he
said as he got in bed and ran his hand over my breasts
and down my belly, "think the whole world's as crooked
as they are." Both of us laughed, only he didn't know we
were laughing at different things.

The next day he telephoned Scarborough and set up a
meeting with him and Selman in Juarez across the river.
Before leaving he gave me an envelope full of money for
safekeeping. I saw him put another thick envelope in the
inside pocket of his coat. Then he kissed me and left. As
soon as he was gone I counted the money. It was more

than four thousand dollars. I knew he was in over his head trying to cheat men like them.

That evening Hector O'Keefe came to me from Juarez with a message from Martin. He was one of Martin's best friends. He'd had most of his nose bitten off in a fight when he was a boy, and I could never look on him without a little shudder of repugnance. The damn fool would actually make eyes at me. He told me Scarborough and Selman hadn't bought the story about cattle rustlers. They accused Martin of selling the herd himself and pocketing the money, and they had demanded their share of the take. Martin swore to them he was telling the truth and said the best he could do was return what was left of the advance payment they had given him, though he'd had to use most of it to pay his hands and buy supplies. The meeting broke up in a flare of bad tempers. Scarborough said he'd arrest Martin on any one of several rustling warrants if he crossed back into El Paso before giving them their money. Selman said he'd shoot him on sight and charge him with resisting arrest afterward. Martin wanted me to see a lawyer first thing in the morning and find out what legal protection he could count on if he came back to town. If nothing could be done, I was to pack our bags and join him in Mexico.

I'd read all about him in the newspapers, of course—from all the early editorial hoorah about what a fine model of upstanding citizenship he'd made of himself during all those years in prison, to the recent story accusing him of holding up a card game in the Gem Saloon. And I'd heard the talk going around—that he hadn't done much business as a lawyer in the two months he'd been in town; that he was drinking like a drowning man every night; that he sometimes didn't stagger home till dawn, mumbling to himself. And that damn near every man in town was scared to death of him.

I told myself that if any lawyer could understand Martin's situation it had to be him. But that was only what I told myself. The truth was, I wanted to see him up-close. I wanted to know if he'd ever really been what they said he'd been. I was curious about him, what else can I say? Oh, hell—I guess I had the yens for him before I ever met him, it's simple as that.

He damn sure got some yens of his own when I showed up at his office next day and he took a good look at me. But he knew how to play the gentleman. He showed me to a chair facing his desk and prepared cups of coffee for us from a tray he'd had brought up from the cafe next door. He wore an impeccable black suit and smelled freshly barbered. It was fascinating to watch those large scarred hands stirring a teaspoon, jotting an occasional note with a fountain pen, or stroking his mustaches as I told him about Martin's predicament. All the while I was talking, his gray eyes drifted over me like smoke. I never wore a corset. I knew how interesting a man could find the contours of my shirtwaist and the way my skirt clung to my lap. I'd been getting yearning looks from men from the time I was twelve. But there was something more than that in his eyes, something beyond just wanting to touch me. At first I thought it might be loneliness, but I came to find out it wasn't that, not exactly, not in the way most people mean it, anyhow. I can't say what it was, only that it was always there, right from the start of—what shall I call it? our *liaison*—from the start of our liaison till the time I last saw him, less than two months later.

He listened to me tell about Martin's problem without once interrupting me. I hadn't meant to tell him *every*thing—not about the money Martin left with me, for instance, or the envelope he'd put in his coat—but I did. Every time I stopped talking, he'd stare at me like he could see right *into* me, and I'd start right up again, until finally I'd told him all of it.

He said he could likely get a judge to write up some kind of protective order, but added that such legal restraint would really be useless. "Legalities don't mean much to the men he's dealing with," he said. "They *are* the law. If they believe he has money which belongs to them, they'll get it from him or know the reason why.''

I asked him what should I do. That depends, he said. On what, I said. On how much you love your husband, he said. For a minute we just stared at each other. I swear I could smell the smoke in his eyes. ''Well,'' I finally said, ''sometimes I'm just not sure.'' He smiled and said, ''I admire your candor, Mrs. McRose.'' I smiled back and said, ''Yes, and that's not the only thing about me you've been admiring, Mr. Hardin.''

My heart jumped in my throat as he came around the desk, took me by the wrists, and pulled me to the couch. He pushed me on my back and yanked up my skirt. Up went my legs, off went my underclothes, down went his trousers. His hardness slipped into me so smooth and deep and fine I didn't even know I was howling with pleasure till his hand went over my mouth. ''*Damn*, woman,'' he said between grunts, ''they'll think it's murder going on up here!'' I laughed and came at the same time—which was a first for me.

A few minutes later—our breathing still ragged, our faces hot, our bodies cramped and sweaty and crushed together on that narrow couch—we grinned at each other and kissed for the first time.

The problem, Wesley said, was that Scarborough and Selman might find out I was holding some of the money.

''Would they harm *me*?'' I asked—as if I didn't know. He looked up at me and said, ''Only as much as they have to in order to get their money.''

It was the afternoon of the same day, and we were naked in his bed in the Herndon Lodging House. He was lying on his back, his head and shoulders propped up by a pillow, and I was astraddle him, slowly working my hips and feeling him deep inside me. An empty bourbon bottle glinted on the floor in the sunlight slanting through the window, and a half-full bottle stood beside the bed. On the little writing table by the window was the stacked manuscript of his book, his life story. He'd been writing on it every day, he told me, and was close to finishing.

We'd been at it all day—both the humping and the drinking—and neither of us had had nearly enough. "What should we do," I asked him, and rolled my hips wickedly. He growled with pleasure and plucked at my nipples. "That depends," he said, "on how much you love your husband." We both laughed out loud. And at the same thing.

The next morning Vic Queen showed up on my front porch and said Martin wanted me to go to Juárez right away. I thanked him for the message and started to close the door, but he blocked it with his boot. "He means *right now*," he said.

I had a hangover like a railroad spike in my skull and was in no mood for an argument. I excused myself for a moment and left him standing in the foyer while I went to the bedroom and got the loaded Remington revolver I kept under my pillow. I went back to the front room with the gun behind me, then brought it around and aimed it with both hands squarely in Vic Queen's face. "Get out of my house, you son of a bitch!" I said. "And *I* mean right now!"

He raised his hands to his shoulders and backed out onto the porch. He said, "Marty's gonna be damn mad, Beulah." I slammed the door shut and watched him through the window as he stomped off down the street toward the river.

When I saw Wes in his room later in the day and told him what had happened, he said not to worry, that he'd had a talk with George Scarborough that morning and Martin wouldn't be a problem much longer. He poured two drinks and handed me one. "Hair of the mangy mutt," he said, and we touched glasses and drank.

I had a pretty good idea what he meant about Martin, but I figured it was best not to ask too many questions. What you don't know can't implicate you as an accomplice. The whiskey sparked in my brain and bloomed in my belly like a little fire flower. Wes pulled me to him, ran his hands over me from neck to hipbone, and bit my lower lip. Then our clothes were sailing through the room and we were laughing and grabbing at each other and falling into bed in a naked tangle of arms and legs and tongues.

They shot Martin dead on our side of the Mexican Central railroad bridge. Milton and Scarborough and a Ranger named Frank McMahon. Milton told the newspapers Martin was wanted for cattle rustling and had been hiding out in Mexico. He said he'd gotten a tip that Martin and some of his "gang" would be crossing into El Paso on the night of June 19 to commit a robbery, and he had set a trap for him.

"The fugitive resisted our attempts to arrest him peaceably," Milton said. "We were forced to defend ourselves when he drew his weapon and opened fire."

Yeah sure. Wes looked at the newspaper over my shoulder and said, "Damn shame. Like the man says, crime does not pay." I looked up and said, "Not if you're dead, it doesn't."

We were the only two at Martin's funeral. A few days later I received a package with Martin's effects. It contained his clothes, his gunbelt and empty holster, his boots, and an envelope with thirteen dollars. By then I'd moved in with Wes in the Herndon House, and everybody knew I was his woman.

One night we fucked on a sandbar in the river under a bright half-moon. We were well away from town and both banks were covered with heavy brush. "You think somebody's peeking at us?" I whispered. The idea of it was exciting. He chuckled and said, "Sure do." I sat up and looked all around. The moonlight blazed on my tits and belly. "Who? Where?" I said. "God," he said, "everywhere." Now *I* had to laugh. I hugged him tight and rolled on top of him. "I *heard* you were a preacher's son!" I said. "Tell me, what's Lord Jesus think about us carrying on like this?" He nuzzled his face between my tits and said, "He thinks it's real nice we follow the

Golden Rule with each other, you and me.''

A couple of times a week we'd check into a fancy Juárez hotel room with a bathtub large enough to hold the both of us. We'd soap each other to a thick creamy lather and just run our hands over our slippery flesh till we couldn't stand it anymore. We found all sorts of ways to do it in tubs, on tables, in hacks, on chairs—standing with him behind me at our wide-open window with all our clothes on and the back of my dress hiked up to accommodate our humping while the lights of the city blazed down below.

We did everything we took a mind to. I'd tickle his balls with my tongue. I'd wrap his cock in my hair and caress him through it like a glove. I'd roll ice chips in my mouth and then lick him like a stick of candy. He'd pour wine on my cunny and press his face to it and slurp it up. He'd look up at me from between my thighs and grin and tell me the little man in the boat was standing practically on tiptoe. ''I *know*,'' I'd say through my teeth, furious for him to get back at it. He'd tease my nipples to stones with a flamingo feather off my hat, then turn me over and play the feather along the crease of my ass and twirl it lightly in the tiny hairs down there. For every trick I taught him, he taught me two.

And we drank. Sweet Christ, did we drink! Through all of July we were naked and half drunk more often than not. About a year later I would discover the wonders of an opium pipe, and the hazy, floating, unreal sense it gave me was very much like the feeling I had when I was naked and drunk with Wes.

Whenever we did put on our clothes and venture into the streets to get something to eat or just take a walk through the park, we drew stares. I could hear the whispers in those eyes: *John Wesley Hardin and his woman. The killer and his whore.* Those eyes glared at me—but they cut away damn fast when Wes turned toward them. I'd pull Wes's arm tighter against my breast and give all those sons of bitches my best go-to-hell smile. We were like a tiny independent country of two surrounded by the alien nation of El Paso. And it felt perfectly natural.

One night when we were in bed, the light from the window facing the street made my private hair glow like a coal fire. Wes pretended to warm his hands at it, then laughed and buried his face in it.

"I can't get enough of this," he said, "I just can't." After all those years in prison without his share of hair pie, he was doing his damnedest to try and catch up.

Sometimes when he went out for cigars and the newspapers I'd leaf through his manuscript. He usually worked on it an hour or so in the morning and sometimes a little more in the evening while I took my bath.

Christ, what a story. I suppose a good deal of it was true, but I couldn't imagine anybody's life being *that* full of blood. What I remember most about it, however, was the total lack of self-pity—and I loved him for that.

Every day, drunk or sober, he practiced with his pistols, and I never got bored with watching. He'd stand in front of the mirror, one gun on his hip, one in a vest holster, and he'd practice for a solid half hour. He'd never say a word the whole time. He'd draw and *click*, draw and *click*, changing positions, drawing and clicking from every which way, shooting himself in the glass over and over, looking himself dead in the eyes. I have posed in my skin for painters, and the look on his face was the look I saw on theirs. I know it sounds silly, but I always got the feeling he was disappointed when he was done—like the only thing that would have satisfied him would have been to beat the fellow in the mirror to the draw.

But God *damn* men anyway! They all talk like they can never get enough of sex, but that's only because they don't get enough chance *at* it. But you let them have all they want of it and they get their fill damn quick.

After a month of going at it with me day and night, he started pining for an evening in the saloons with the boys. The card tables, the dicing at the bar, the beer and the happy bullshit. I'd made him fat on sex and now he was feeling skinny for the saloons. He didn't say it, but I could tell. One night he said he was going for a newspaper and then didn't come home till nearly three in the morning, smelling like a bar rag. I was so mad I didn't say a word to him all the next day. That afternoon he said he was going to the office and I said something smart-ass about his office having swinging doors. He said I'd best not talk like I was his mother or his wife because I sure as hell wasn't either one. He slammed the door so hard behind him some of the plaster flaked off the wall. That remark about not being his wife hurt a lot more than I care to admit even now.

He came reeling in at four A.M. and flopped into bed with all his clothes on and started snoring up a storm the second his head hit the pillow. I'd been hefting the bottle pretty good myself and was ready for a fight, but I passed out right after he did.

The next morning I was still sore about that "wife" remark, but that's not the main reason I was so mad at him. Mainly, it was because I was afraid. I'd been having such bad dreams. I was afraid somebody was going to shoot him dead while he was running around out there drunk. And I *hated* being afraid, I'd always hated it more than anything. I was furious that he'd made me be so frightened for him. And then *he* gets all closemouthed and sulky with me, like *he* was the one who'd been wronged and *I* was the one who should apologize. So there I was, scared for him and angry that I was. Naturally anger got the upper hand.

"The great John Wesley Hardin," I said, "staggering around drunk in the streets like some rumpot. Real impressive. I always heard you were such a fearsome fellow, and now I know why. People are afraid you might breathe on them."

"You'd know a lot about the smell of rumpots," he said. "I guess that's a fact."

"Those saloon tramps aren't your friends. You're nothing but a sideshow to them, don't you know that."

"You don't know a goddamned thing."

"I know when I'm making a fool of myself, which is more than I can say for you."

"Nobody calls *me* a fool."

"Fool, fool, fool!"

He backhanded me into the wall and I felt the blood run hot out of my nose. I went at him with both fists swinging. He caught my wrists, so I tried to knee him in the balls, but I lost my balance and fell down. He gave my hair such a yank he nearly broke my neck. I bit his wrist and he yelped and smacked me on the side of the head hard enough to make me see stars. Next thing I knew, we were wrestling around on the floor and one of my tits came free of my dress and he caught hold of it. I felt my nipples turn hard as bullets. I grabbed him by the hair and pulled his face down to me and bit his lips so hard the blood popped into my mouth. He growled deep in his throat and pinched my nipple hard and his stiff cock jabbed against my belly. As he shoved my skirt up and yanked off my drawers, I undid his belt and caught hold of him—and then we were humping hard and loud on the floor until we both came like we'd been dropped from the ceiling.

It was exciting, all right—but I wouldn't want to do it that way every night of the week.

Anyhow, that knockdown session on the floor didn't really settle anything. At supper the next night he said he had a case to try in Van Horn and would be gone a couple of days. I wanted to go with him but he said no, he'd be too busy with the case and didn't want any distractions. I didn't believe he had a damn case, but I kept it to myself. The truth was, he hadn't opened a law book more than a couple of times since the day I first walked into his office. Later on, when it sure as hell didn't matter anymore, I found out my suspicions had been right—the case he'd had in Van Horn was a redhead named Lil.

I was miserable about him being gone—and mad at him, and afraid of every bad possibility prowling through my imagination. A few hours after his train pulled out that afternoon, I was whirly-eyed drunk. I'd lately been drinking like a catfish anyway, and the minute he was gone I started pouring myself the drinks even faster than usual.

I don't know why I did what I did next. Hell, I was so drunk I couldn't remember much about it the next day. I recall sitting at the window, drinking and looking down at the people in the street, talking and smiling at each other like they didn't have a care in the world. I remember feeling like I was going to bust wide open if I didn't do *something*. According to the arrest report—and to a lot of witnesses—what I did was go traipsing down Overland Street with my Remington in my hand, pointing it left and right at people, and laughing like hell when they scattered like scared chickens. They say I hollered, "I'm John Wesley Hardin, you sorry sons of bitches, and I can outshoot any swinging dick in town!" That's not as hard to believe as the claim that I shot out a streetlight at eighty paces. I was a good shot, but I couldn't have done it sober, I don't think.

I have a fuzzy recollection of John Selman—the policeman son, not the murdering constable father—sweet-talking me on the street and asking me to hand over the pistola. I remember the gun slipping out of my hand and discharging when it hit the sidewalk and the bullet ricocheting off a wall. He said in the report that I dropped it when I tried to twirl it. He quick grabbed it up and put the arm on me.

That was it for the sweet-talk. He was real sarcastic about calling me "the grieving widow." He said—and plenty of witnesses backed him on this too—I cursed him like a muleskinner all the way to the jail. He said I told him Wes would give him a new asshole right between the eyes for treating me so low.

He wanted to jail me till I sobered up, but Jeff Milton wouldn't have me put in a cell. Jeff took me direct to Judge Howe, drunk as I was. I know the judge gave me a lecture—I have a vague picture of his face looking all serious and his big thick finger shaking at me. I had a terrible feeling the next day that I'd laughed and said something nasty about what his finger looked like, wagging up and down at me that way. Anyhow, to make a long drunk story short, I was fined fifty dollars and Jeff Milton took me home.

Wes must have heard about it the minute he got off the train. He came charging into the room and threw his valise against the wall. It knocked his manuscript off the table in a flutter of pages. He looked like he was ready to rip me to pieces. I could see how hard he was fighting to keep himself under control. He sat on the bed with his fists tight and white on his knees and made me sit in a chair across the room and tell him my side of what happened. I did the best I could, considering how little I could remember about the whole thing. I wasn't lying when I finished up by telling him I was sorry, and I didn't talk back when he said, "You sure are. You're about the sorriest bitch in this whole sorry town." I figured I had that coming.

He poured himself a glass of whiskey and sat there sipping from it and staring at me without saying anything for a long time. I kept my mouth shut and waited for him to make up his mind about what to do. I was sorry for what I'd done, but I wasn't going to let myself get beat like a dog for it. I'd decided that if he tried it, I'd holler out the window like I was on fire.

But the whiskey seemed to soothe him. He put the empty glass aside and rubbed his face with both hands and made the most tired sound I've ever heard in my life. Then he got down on his hands and knees and carefully gathered up his manuscript and stacked it on the table. Then he took me by the hand and we got in bed with our clothes on and just lay there holding each other gently. I could feel his heart beating hard against my breast.

He *had* to do something about it, though, something loud and public. He couldn't see it any other way. He was John Wesley Hardin and nobody, by God, could arrest his woman and speak to her like she was some common tramp. It was a point of pride with him. That's why I still refuse to accept the blame for what happened afterward, no matter what people say. I knew my stunt in the streets was wrong, and I was sorry I did it, and I told Wes as much. But I could have apologized till Doomsday and it wouldn't have done a thing to ease his injured pride—his "honor," as he called it. He had to do something about the way Young Selman had treated me or it would look like he was admitting his woman wasn't worth defending—and only a man without honor would ever attach to a worthless woman.

"For God's sake, Wes," I said, "it's almost the twentieth century. Nobody gives a damn about such silliness. Why don't we just leave this awful place? Let's go to Santa Fe. Let's go to Denver." The look he gave me was more pitiful than angry.

The next morning he went out and found Young Selman walking his beat and gave him loud hell for arresting me. I heard all about it from Patsy Webster, one of the dozen witnesses. She said Wes called Young Selman a bully and a coward for arresting a woman. "You wouldn't have dared done it if I'd been in town," Wes told him. They say Young Selman looked scared but held his ground and took the bullyragging with his mouth shut. Wes almost always wore a gun or two in defiance of the town ordinance against doing so, but he usually kept them out of sight under his coat or vest. This time, however, he opened his coat wide so Young Selman could clearly see the pistols. "I'm giving you fair warning," Wes told him. "You come near her again and you'll answer to me."

He was quiet and moody during the next two days. He cleaned his pistols and practiced his quick draws. He dealt himself hands of cards. Now and then he sat at the little writing table and wrote more of his book. In the evening he'd put on his guns and go down to one or another of the saloons, have a couple of drinks and play a few hands. My heart would lodge in my throat from the minute he walked out the door until the moment he came back. I couldn't help feeling he was trying to prove something—though I can't say what it was or who he thought he was proving it to. He drank steadily but only got drunk enough to stay loose. I believe his head was just full of snakes.

Sometimes, when he didn't know I was watching, I'd see him staring at himself in the mirror with such intense concentration he looked like he was trying hard to place a face he hadn't seen in a long time. He made love like he was dreaming about it instead of really doing it. His touch, his kiss, even his cock—they all felt like a stranger's.

That Saturday he said he'd been thinking over what I'd said about moving to Santa Fe, and he now thought it wasn't a bad idea. "The territory needs lawyers," he said. "We can get a new start, breathe some mountain air that's not full of desert dust."

It was wonderful news—but when he said he wanted me to leave ahead of him while he took care of closing his office and paying off a few bills and such, I felt a shiver run through me. He wanted me to go up there right away and check into a hotel and start looking around town for a nice office for him. I said I wanted to wait so we could leave together, but he said no, we'd do it the way he said. We nearly got into an argument about it, but I caught myself in time to avoid it. All right, I said, we'd do it his way.

On Sunday morning I left El Paso on the train for Santa Fe. I'd had a sleepless night and was red-eyed and jumpy. The passing landscape glared so whitely it hurt to look out at it. The air lunging through the open windows was as hot as desperate breath and didn't do a thing but swirl dust through the coach. Still, I was so tired the rocking car lulled me into a sweaty, fitful sleep.

Just before we reached Las Cruces I dreamt about Wesley. I saw him standing at a long brightly lighted bar in a dim saloon, tossing dice and laughing. Then a shadowy figure came up behind him and pointed a long accusing finger at the back of his head. . . .

The loud bang of a coach window woke me with a start, my throat tight and pulsing wildly—and the train whistle shrieked like the devil in grief.

... This morning early a *Herald* reporter started after the facts and found John Selman, the man who fired the fatal shots, and his statement was as follows:

"I met Wes Hardin last evening close to the Acme Saloon. When we met, Hardin said, 'You've got a son that is a bastardly, cowardly, s___ of a b___.'

"I said: 'Which one?'

"Hardin said: 'John, the one that is on the police force. He pulled my woman when I was absent and robbed her of $50, which they would not have done if I had been there.'

"I said: 'Hardin, no man can talk about my children like that without fighting, you cowardly, s___ of a b___.' "

"Hardin said: 'I am unarmed.'

"I said: 'Go and get your gun. I am armed.'

"Then he said: 'I'll go and get a gun and when I meet you I'll meet you smoking and make you pull like a wolf around the block.'

"Hardin then went into the saloon and began shaking dice with Henry Brown. . . . I sat down on a beer keg in front of the Acme Saloon and waited for Hardin to come out. I insisted on the police force keeping out of the trouble because it was a personal matter between Hardin and myself. Hardin had insulted me personally.

"About 11 o'clock Mr. E. L. Shackleford came along and said: 'Come on and take a drink but don't get drunk.' Shackleford led me into the saloon by the arm. Hardin and Brown were shaking dice at the end of the bar next to the door. While we were drinking I noticed that Hardin watched me very closely as we went in. When he thought my eye was off him he made a break for his gun in his hip pocket and I immediately pulled my gun and began shooting. I shot him in the head first as I had been informed that he wore a steel breast plate. As I was about to shoot a second time someone ran against me and I think I missed him, but the other two shots were at his body and I think I hit him both times. My son then ran in and caught me by the arm and said: 'He is dead. Don't shoot anymore.'

"I was not drunk at the time, but was crazy mad at the way he had insulted me.

"My son and myself came out of the saloon together and when Justice Howe came I gave my statement to him. My wife was very weak and was prostrated when I got home. I was accompanied home by Deputy Sheriff J. C. Jones. I was not placed in jail, but considered myself under arrest. I am willing to stand any investigation over the matter. I am sorry I had to kill Hardin, but he had threatened mine and my son's life several times and I felt it had come to that point where either I or he had to die."

(Signed) John Selman

— Samuel Peckinpah —

I arrived in El Paso on the nineteenth of August, a hot Monday evening I shall never forget.

After asking the depot agent for directions to the Herndon Lodging House, I plunged into the tumult of the streets. The city was raucous with rumbling and clanging streetcars, clattering wagons, clopping hooves, barking dogs, the bray and snort of livestock, with shouting and whistling and laughter, with the cries of newshawks, with music blaring from every saloon—piano and hurdy-gurdy, banjo and guitar, and lustily, badly sung songs.

The sun was almost touching the mountain looming over the town, but the air was still thick with heat and dust. It was pungent with horse droppings and the peppery aromas of Mexican cooking, with the smells of creosote and whiskey and human waste. Old women in black *rebozos*, their faces as dry and cracked as desert earth, hunkered on the sidewalks with their bony hands extended for alms. Through the open door of a shadowy saloon came a great crash of glass, followed by several resounding smacks, a heavy thump, and an explosive chorus of loud laughter. Four boys on a corner were laughing as well, and poking jackknives into the malodorously bloated carcass of a large black dog, raising a horde of fat green flies with every whooping stab.

It was, as Fox had told me it would be, one tough town. I refer to Richard Kyle Fox, publisher of *The Police*

Gazette, the most popular periodical of our day. Its specialty was sports, but its larger appeal was rooted in its zealous reportage of sex and violence. Every week the shocking-pink pages of the *Gazette* presented a plethora of crime, scandal, bizarre spectacle, madness, and death. *Gazette* readers feasted on each new issue like scavengers alighting on fresh carrion. "I give the American working man what he wants in a newspaper," Fox often boasted, "the real stuff of life!" And I, who in my youth had been a serious poet with dreams of capturing the light of the stars in my verse, had now been in his employ for over six years. Indeed, I was one of his star reporters. So veers life.

I was in El Paso to try to gain an interview with John Wesley Hardin, the infamous mankiller. Fox had only recently heard about him and had become instantly enthusiastic about the subject. He was a man of sequential obsessions, and his obsession of the moment was the Wild West. He thought an interview with Hardin would be perfect for the *Gazette*. "It's a splendid tough tale, this Hardin fella's, full of life's hard truths," Fox said to me in the New York office. "Old West killer does a big stretch in the pen and then, on being set free after many cruel years, takes up the mantle of the man of law. He follows the straight and narrow, he does, but then stumbles and falls to the evil wayside once again, for the leopard can't change his spots after all, can he now? I hear he robs saloons at his whim, that he shot a man dead in a fight over a woman. I hear he's a fearsome drunk and most of his fellow citizens want to see him dead, they are so frightened of him. Well, I want to know the details, Sammy lad—as will our readers. Go and get those details, my boy, and write them up for us in your particularly enthralling style, hey?"

That was how I came to be on the loud streets of El Paso on that sultry evening of August 19, 1895.

At the Herndon I was told by the landlady—one Mrs. Williams—that Mr. Hardin was not in and she did not know where he was. "Go poking through the saloons and I guess you'll sure find him," she said. Her sneer couched on her face like a bad-tempered cat.

The nearest saloon, The Show, was across the street and just around the corner. As I quaffed my first stein, I made known that I was a *Police Gazette* reporter interested in Hardin, and the barkeep began talking my ear off, as I'd expected he would. The *Gazette* was venerated in every tavern in America, even in such remote outposts as El Paso. The Show wasn't yet busy at that early evening hour, and a handful of other gents soon gathered around me at the bar, taking exception to some of the boniface's assertions and delivering their own opinions about the city's most famous resident. Among the things I found out was that Hardin's chief antagonist in town was a constable named John Selman, who carried a formidable reputation of his own as a man to be reckoned with.

The boys at the bar knew as much about John Henry Selman as they did about Wes Hardin, and they regarded him with nearly equal awe—and equal fear. Selman, I learned, had fought for the Confederacy before moving to Texas. The way they'd heard the tale, he got married, fathered a daughter and three sons, and made his daily bread as a dirt farmer for a few years before settling near Fort Griffin and getting into the cattle business with a partner named John Larn. His first turn as a lawman came when Larn was elected sheriff of Shackelford County and appointed Selman as his chief deputy.

One day a band of Comancheros stole a ten-year-old white girl and her six-year-old brother from a farm a few miles west of Fort Griffin, intending to trade them to the Comanches. Selman and two army scouts tracked them for weeks, all the way across West Texas, before finally catching up with them in the Davis Mountains. They returned with the two children alive and seven Comanchero scalps dangling from their saddle horns.

Not a man at the bar doubted the truth of that story, not even those who were no admirers of Selman. "Old John's done lots of things over the years, I expect," said a man in a white skimmer, glancing about cautiously to see who might be overhearing, "some of them not altogether legal, if you know what I mean." Another man chuckled and added, "Hell, some of them not altogether *Christian*!"

Not long afterward, Selman killed a bad actor called Shorty Collins who was trying to gun down Sheriff Larn. There was a good deal of dispute—then and now—about the cause of the shooting. Some said Collins was in a heat because Larn and Selman had double-crossed him in a cattle rustling scheme. Whatever the case, the story holds that after killing Collins, Selman went hard outlaw for the next few years, that he went to New Mexico and formed a band of rustlers and robbers called the Seven Rivers Gang.

When he next returned to Texas, he was arrested and charged with rustling, but the case never went to court and eventually the charges were dropped. Then his wife became ill and died. He was broke and feeling aimless, so he parceled out his young children among various families and wandered off in search of better fortune. A few months later he showed up in Fort Stockton, debilitated with the smallpox. The fearful citizens wouldn't have him among them. He was taken to a spot about two miles from town, laid under a canvas cover to protect him from the sun, supplied with a cask of water, and left to his fate. "Old John's told this story himself more than once, in more than one saloon," one of my informants told me. "I guess it's true. He sure enough has the pox scars on his face to prove it."

According to the story, Selman was saved by a Mexican cattle dealer who was passing by in a wagon on his way back to his ranch. The Mexican's young daughter was with him, and they put Selman in the wagon and took him along. The daughter tended to Selman every mile of the way. Each evening, when they made camp for the night, she bathed him with lye soap and then fed him a steaming bowl of *menudo*, a fiery dish of tripe cooked in chile peppers. By the time they crossed the river into Mexico, Selman was fairly well recovered. "John always has said it was the *menudo* saved his life,'' a man at the bar remarked. ''He still eats a bowl of it a day.'' Several heads nodded sagely. ''That stuff'll cure you or kill you, one,'' someone else said.

When they reached her father's ranch in Chihuahua, Selman and the girl got married. John went to Texas to retrieve his children but was able to find only his two youngest sons, Bud and Young John. He lived in Mexico for years, and his boys were practically raised as Mexicans. It was said he became best friends with a murderous local captain of *rurales*—the national police force created by the Mexican dictator Díaz—and that he sometimes helped track down fugitives for a portion of the reward. When his second wife died, he and his sons, now grown, moved back north of the river. To El Paso.

That was six years ago, and all my informants agreed the town was even wilder then than it was now. But even though he was starting to get along in years, Old John still had a lot of pepper in his blood. He quickly earned a reputation for drinking and gambling with the hardiest of them—*and* for being able to handle himself in a row. El Paso was always in need of tough lawmen, and in '92 he was elected city constable.

The following year, at age fifty-seven, he married a sixteen-year-old Mexican girl. She was far younger than his sons, both of whom were so angrily embarrassed by the marriage they refused to speak to their father for months. Old John supposedly said, ''I don't know what they're acting so put out about. Ought to be *proud* their pappy can still cut such a spicy mustard. I reckon they're just jealous.'' He eventually reconciled with his boys, and one of them, Young John, himself became a city policeman.

Of the eight or nine men at the bar of The Show saloon, four claimed to have witnessed John Selman's killing of Bass Outlaw in a local whorehouse just the year before. The other men at the bar all snorted derisively and said they'd bet none of the four had been anywhere near the place. ''You'd have to build another six floors on that cathouse just to hold everybody who's sworn he saw the shooting with his own eyes," one man said, and everybody but the four avowed witnesses had a good guffaw.

Bass Outlaw was a notorious bad actor who had been a Texas Ranger until he was fired for drunkenness. He then became a deputy U.S. marshal. On the night in question, he was drunk and in a fury because the girl he wanted to sport with was engaged with another customer. He loudly proclaimed his intention to go upstairs and kick open the door of every room until he found his favorite whore. Old John was sitting near him and said, "Hey now, Bass, you don't want to be busting up everybody's pleasure up there. Just wait your turn." At that moment, Texas Ranger Joe McKidrict turned to Outlaw and said, "Bass, you're too drunk to fuck anyhow."

The words were barely out of his mouth before Outlaw drew his pistol and blasted a hole through his heart. As Selman went for his gun, Outlaw shot him twice in the leg—then Old John put a round through Outlaw's eye and blew out the side of his head and the fight was done.

"Old John's had a hobble ever since," someone said. "The man can't walk ten feet without his cane."

"That's true," said another, "but his damn gunhand don't need no cane. That's what Hardin best keep in mind."

The noisy streets were deep in twilight when I came out of The Show and made my way up Utah Street, heading for the Acme Saloon. The sky along the mountain rim was the color of fresh blood. As I reached the corner, I glanced to my left—and there on the sidewalk, not ten paces from me, stood John Henry Selman and John Wesley Hardin, looking quite ready to kill one another.

They were standing face-to-face with three feet between them. I'd heard them described so thoroughly that I recognized them both instantly. A few other pedestrians had also taken notice of them and were hastening across the street or retreating down the sidewalk. Most people in the vicinity, however, remained wholly unaware of the confrontation from first to last.

Selman gripped his cane in his left hand and his right was ready to go for the gun on his hip. Hardin stood with his hands on his coat lapels. I could not see if he was armed. I could see their faces distinctly, however. Both men were rigid with anger. They spoke sharply but not loudly, and the din of the street muffled much of what they said. If I'd been two feet farther from them, I'd have heard none of the conversation at all.

". . . know damn well . . . the goods off him. I know . . . cheated me!" Selman was saying through his teeth, his gray mustache twitching with anger. "I won't be cheated, you hear me? I won't . . . or anybody else."

"The hell . . . ," Hardin said. ". . . between you and George. *He's* your partner, not . . ."

"What . . . George . . . damn business," Selman said. "I know . . . cheat me, you . . . I'm warning . . . square with me, and I mean soon!"

"Warning *me*?" Hardin said. "Nobody . . . a bucket of shit with a badge stuck on it . . . bastard son . . . nothing but picking on women."

Selman's face darkened with fury. He looked about to have a fit. A streetcar clattered down the street, its bell clanging loudly, and I couldn't make out any of what he next said to Hardin, nor what Hardin said in response. What Hardin *did* next, however, is still vivid in my mind. He held out his hands as though showing Selman he held nothing in them. Then he closed the lower fingers of both hands, keeping the thumbs upright and the index fingers pointing at Selman like pistol barrels. He flicked his thumbs down and mouthed the word, "Pow!" Selman stepped backward as though he'd been shoved. He looked astonished. Hardin grinned and slowly raised each index finger in turn to his mouth and softly blew on their tips, as though clearing them of gunsmoke. He then strolled across the street and went into the Acme Saloon.

Selman watched him every step of the way, his face inflamed with fury, then turned and saw me staring at him.

"Ah . . . Constable Selman," I said, "my name is Peckinpah. Of *The Police Gazette*. I wonder if—''

''*Kiss my ass!*'' he said, and stalked away.

When I told Hardin I was with the *Gazette* and offered
to buy the next round, the first thing he wanted to know
was whether I'd covered the Sullivan-Kilrain bare knuckle
championship fight six years earlier. ''We heard about it
in the pen,'' he said, ''but I've never met anybody who
saw it with his own eyes.''

I hadn't been at the fight either, but I knew several of
the reporters who had, which made me the nearest thing
to an eyewitness he'd yet met. So I was obliged to reca-
pitulate for him everything I could recall about the progress of that epic battle as it had been told to me. I admitted
I'd been astonished by the outcome, that I'd never expected Sullivan, sodden drunkard that he was, to withstand
the assault of the younger and quicker Kilrain under the
roasting Mississippi sun. When Kilrain drew first blood
and Sullivan paused to vomit in the early going, I told him
that the reporters all figured Sully was done for. Hardin
seemed enrapt. ''But he wasn't done, was he,'' he said,
''that old warhorse?'' He certainly was not, I agreed. After
seventy-five rounds spanning two hours and sixteen
minutes, Kilrain's seconds threw in the sponge. Hardin
smiled widely. ''Never bet against the warhorse,'' he said.

We were standing at the end of the bar nearest the front
door, and I signaled Frank the bartender for another round
for us. Hardin's interest took another turn when I told him
the *Gazette*'s chief correspondent for the Sullivan-Kilrain
fight had been none other than Steve Brodie, the famous
bridge-jumper, who was a good friend of mine. I then had
to expound at length about the various jumps I'd seen
Steve Brodie make. I told of more than once having seen
him pulled unconscious from a river, blood running from
his nose and mouth and ears, sometimes his ribs broken
and his shoes knocked from his feet. Dozens of men and
boys were killed every year in their attempts to emulate
Steve Brodie.

''Damn, but that man's got daring!'' Hardin said. ''And

he can surely take a beating, can't he?'' John Wesley Hardin is the only man I ever spoke to about Steve Brodie who never said he wondered why a man would risk his life and take such beatings jumping off high bridges.

He said he'd be pleased to grant me an interview for the *Gazette* on one condition—that I didn't call him a "pistolero." I had suggested that my lead-in would refer to him as the most famous pistolero in the West. "I never did much care for that word," he said. "Sounds too damn Mexican." Well then, I asked, what term would he prefer? Gunfighter? Shootist? Pistolman? Mankiller? "They called Wild Bill the Prince of the Pistoleers," he said. " 'Pistoleer' always did sound properly American to me." All right, I said, "pistoleer" it was. I'd call him the *King* of the Pistoleers. He smiled and said, "Sounds about right."

We never did get to the interview. He was far too persistent in interrogating *me*—particularly about the writing craft. He told me he'd been writing the story of his life for the past several months and was very near to completing the book. He asked me question after question about techniques of narration, exposition, and description—though he did not know the proper terminology for many of these things. I said I'd be happy to read his work and offer whatever helpful criticism I might. He smiled almost shyly and said he'd be grateful.

I kept trying to shift the conversation to the subject of himself, but he much preferred to hear about the stories I'd covered for the *Gazette*—about the execution of William Kemmler, the first condemned man to die in the electric chair, a process that took more than eight minutes and left the carcass half cooked; about the white slavery rings I'd investigated in New York's lower depths; about the sex scandals and the opium dens and the labor riots; about crimes of passion. When I at last managed to ask him about his beginnings as a desperado, he was perfunctory. "Just say I was drove to it by murdering Yankee occupation troops and carpetbaggers. Anybody who wants to

can read about it in my book. But tell me, what's the
strangest thing you've ever seen?"

A few minutes later a friend of his named Henry Brown
came in and informed him that Old John Selman was sitting on a keg on the sidewalk in front of the saloon.

"His son Young John and Captain Carr came along just
now and I heard him tell them to stay close by and be
ready for trouble with you," Henry Brown said.

"Just like the old coward to ask for help," Hardin said.
"How's he look?"

"Hard to say," Henry Brown said. "But he ain't smiling."

"Bastard's scared," Hardin said. "No bushwhacker
likes the idea of going up against a man face-to-face.
Reckon I'll let him stew in his own sweat a while longer.
Let him think some more on the way things stand."

"And then what?" I asked. "Will you go out and face
him down?" I tried to mask my excitement with a tone
of nonchalance—but, in truth, I was heady with the prospect of witnessing a dime-novel shootout between two famous gunmen.

"Well now," he said with a smile, "let's just wait and
see what happens." I think he knew how I was feeling
and was amused by it.

He shook the bar dice with Henry Brown to decide who
would buy the next round. I told him I'd witnessed the
exchange he'd had with Selman across the street, but that
I hadn't overheard enough of it to know exactly what was
going on. "I know you rattled him with those two-gun
fingers," I said, and we both chuckled. "You see how he
flinched when I shot him with these .44 caliber fingers?"
Hardin said. "Old jasper damn near had a heart attack."

Hardin had been leaning on one elbow on the bar as we
conversed, frequently glancing into the back-bar mirror to
check the front doors. Quite abruptly he tensed and slipped
his right hand up inside his coat. I looked toward the doors
and saw Old Selman standing there, his eyes locked on
Hardin's in the mirror, his left hand braced on his cane,

his right hanging loosely by his holstered .45 Colt.

He wasn't alone. But the man with him—who I later found out was one E. L. Shackleford—was no fighter. Indeed, he looked extremely nervous to be standing so near to Old John Selman at the moment. To be truthful, I was not entirely at ease standing so close to Hardin as I was.

Shackleford bolted toward the rear of the barroom, saying loudly, "Back here, John. We'll have a drink with R.B. and Shorty." R. B. Stevens, the proprietor of the Acme, and a fellow called Shorty Anderson were taking a drink together just inside the open door of the private room at the rear of the saloon. There were only a handful of patrons in the Acme at the moment.

Selman stood rooted for a few seconds, holding Hardin's stare in the glass. I looked at Hardin just as he slowly and silently mouthed the words "*Do . . . it,*" at Selman.

Selman's face seemed to turn to wet clay. Hardin smiled and withdrew his hand from his coat. He aimed his index finger at Selman's image in the mirror and softly said, "Bang." Then laughed aloud.

Selman broke his gaze, flushing furiously, and hobbled after Shackleford into the back room.

Hardin grinned at me and said, "Only took *one* finger to shake him up this time." He smiled broadly all about the room. "Sammy," he said, clapping me on the shoulder, "I'll roll you for the round."

He suddenly seemed twenty years younger—barely more than a boy—a happy, confident, carefree boy. His eyes danced brightly and his smile was a fierce contagious thing. He snatched up the dice cup and said, "I can't lose, boys, not me. But I don't want to make street beggars of you, so let's play for quarters." And he didn't lose, not once in the next ten rolls against me and then six in a row against Henry Brown.

When Selman and Shackleford came out of the back room, Selman's face looked as rigid as his cane, but his eyes were red-hot and whiskey-bright. I could feel the heat of his anger as he went past us. He didn't even glance our way as he headed for the front door. In the back-bar mirror, Hardin watched him go out, and I heard the low chuckle in his throat. He picked up the dice cup, shook it, and rolled the dice. He laughed once more and said to Henry Brown, "You got four sixes to beat."

As Henry reached for the dice cup, I put a match to my pipe and turned to Hardin. He was smiling happily at himself in the mirror, his hands laced together on the bar. He was utterly and completely a picture of self-satisfaction.

Then his eyes shifted and his smile vanished and I followed his gaze in the mirror and saw Selman standing inside the doors, aiming his Peacemaker at the back of Hardin's head. Selman shouted, "*I will!*" And fired.

Even in the roar of the gunshot, I heard the bullet crunch wetly through his skull and clank against the frame of the back-bar mirror. A second gunshot thundered and the bullet smacked against the wall as Hardin slumped to the floor on his back. Selman rushed up and shot him twice more at point-blank range. Then another copper—Young Selman—was clutching Old John by the arm and shouting, "Stop! Stop now! You've killed him!"

Old Selman looked crazed. Young Selman took his gun and ushered him away from the body, talking to him rapidly and earnestly. A bright puddle of blood was spreading from under Hardin's head and a red rivulet ran down his face from a hole over his half-closed and shattered left eye. The other eye was open wide and dead as glass.

My ears rang with the pistol shots and my eyes smarted from the gunsmoke. I saw Shackleford and Henry Brown hurrying out the rear door. I wanted to leave too, but was afraid that if I released my grip on the bar my legs would fail me.

In an instant the saloon was in full tumult, jammed with babbling gawkers shoving against one another for a better look at the corpse of John Wesley Hardin. Each new arrival had to be told by the man who had arrived just before him what had happened. There was argument and angry gesticulation.

I heard a man explaining loudly to another that Selman

had beaten Hardin to the draw and shot him squarely through the eye.

A gaggle of whores from the house around the corner entered in a perfumed rush of swirling skirts and a jabbering frenzy. There was gasping and cursing and an outbreak of weeping. Some of them stooped and dipped handkerchiefs or the hems of their underskirts into the blood on the floor. I saw one gently touch Hardin's face. I saw one stare at her bloody fingertip a moment, and then lick it.

Stevens, the proprietor, and a lawman named Carr tried futilely to drive everyone back and stood arguing over the body. Stevens wanted the dead man removed from the premises at once, but Carr said adamantly that he would not do any such thing until the police chief showed up and took charge. He sat on his heels beside the body and searched it—and withdrew a pair of pistols.

A man later identified to me as Jeff Milton pushed his way through the crowd, the Selmans close behind him. He said, "All you, get the hell back, goddamnit!"—and back they fell.

He and the Selmans stared down at the dead man on the floor. Old John was grinning like a lunatic. He poked at Hardin's shoulder with the tip of his cane. "See, Jeff?" he said. "You see? Like I said! He went for his gun and I killed him. I did it!" He put his hand out to Milton. "Shake the hand of the man who killed John Wesley Hardin."

Milton glanced at Selman's hand as though he might spit into it. "This man," he said, pointing at the body, "was shot *in the back!*" He stared at Selman with hugely profound contempt, then stomped away.

I saw Stevens crouch beside the bar and pick something up between thumb and finger. Smiling like a prizewinner, he showed me the bullet that had passed through Hardin's head. He dropped it in a whiskey glass and set it on a shelf behind the bar for display.

The undertaker's assistants arrived and took the body away to the parlor, where it was examined by a team of

physicians for their official report. Within hours, photographs of Hardin's naked corpse, his several wounds
starkly evident, were being hawked on the streets.

This report appeared in *The El Paso Daily Herald* of 20
August 1895:

> *The following evidence was given Justice Howe this*
> *afternoon by the three physicians whose names are*
> *signed thereto:*
> *"We, the undersigned, practicing physicians,*
> *hereby certify that we have examined the gunshot*
> *wounds on the person of the deceased, John Wesley*
> *Hardin, and it is our opinion that the wound causing*
> *death was caused by a bullet; that the bullet entered*
> *near the base of the skull posteriorly and came out*
> *at the upper corner of the left eye."*
> *(Signed)*
> *S. G. Sherard,*
> *W. N. Vilas,*
> *Alward White.*
>
> *The wounds on Hardin's body were on the back of*
> *the head, coming out just over the left eye. Another*
> *shot in the right breast, just missing the nipple, and*
> *another through the right arm. The body was em-*
> *balmed by Undertaker Powell and will be interred at*
> *Concordia at 4 P.M.*

John Wesley Hardin was buried in the Concordia Cemetery in El Paso. Inscribed on a small plate fixed to his
coffin was the phrase, "At Peace." None of his kin were
in attendance at the funeral, only myself and a handful of
curious onlookers—and a veiled woman dressed in black.
She left immediately upon the casket's lowering in the
ground.

John Henry Selman was indicted for murder and stood
trial in El Paso. His attorney was Albert Bacon Falls, who

later became Secretary of the Interior and went to prison for his part in the Teapot Dome scandal. Falls argued that Selman acted in self-defense. The jury could not reach a verdict, so the judge ordered a new trial and released Selman on bond. The night before I departed El Paso I saw him ensconced in a dark corner of the Wigwam Saloon, half drunk but looking sharply at every man who entered the premises, his mind likely occupied with visions of young pistoleers seeking their portion of fame by way of the man who killed John Wesley Hardin.

John Selman, the victor of not less than twenty shooting affrays in Texas, the exterminator of "bad men," and the slayer of John Wesley Hardin, is dying tonight with a bullet hole through his body. About three months ago Selman and United States Deputy Marshal Geo. Scarborough had a quarrel over a game of cards, since which occurrence the relations between them have not been cordial. This morning at 4 o'clock they met in the Wigwam Saloon and both were drinking. Scarborough says that Selman said, "Come, I want to see you," and that the two men walked into an alley beside the saloon, and Selman, whose son is in Juárez, Mexico, in jail on a charge of abducting a young lady from there to this side, said to Scarborough: "I want you to come over the river with me this morning. We must get that boy out of jail."

Scarborough expressed his willingness to go with Selman, but stated that no bad breaks must be made in Juárez. Scarborough says that Selman then reached for his pistol, with the remark, "I believe I will kill you." Scarborough pulled his gun and began shooting. At the second shot Selman fell, and Scarborough fired two more shots as Selman attempted to rise. When Selman was searched no pistol could be found on him or anywhere around him. He says he had a pistol, but that it was taken from him after he fell and before the police reached him. Scarborough's first shot hit Selman in the neck. The next two shots also took effect, one through the left leg just above the knee and the other entering the right side just under the lower rib. A fourth wound in the right hip is supposed to have been caused by Selman's pistol going off prematurely, as the ball ranged downward. Scarborough is about 38 years old. He was born in Louisiana and was raised in Texas, and for several years was sheriff of Jones County. Selman was raised on the Colorado River in Texas. He was about 58 years old and has lived a stormy life. When not drinking he was as gentle as a child, but he did not know what fear was, and has killed not less than twenty outlaws. He was a dead shot and quick with his gun. He was an old officer in the service. Some years ago he fought a band of cattle thieves in Donna Anna County, New Mexico, killing two and capturing the others, four in all. He killed Bass Outlaw, a deputy United States marshal, in El Paso a few years ago.

EPILOGUE

"True, it is almost as bad to kill as to be killed. It drove my father to an early grave; it almost distracted my mother; it killed my brother Joe and my cousins Tom and William; it left my brother's widow with two helpless babes . . . to say nothing of the grief of countless others. I do say, however, that the man who does not exercise the first law of nature—that of self-preservation—is not worthy of living and breathing the breath of life."

From *The Life of John Wesley Hardin as Written by Himself*

ABOUT THE AUTHOR

James Carlos Blake was born in Mexico and raised in Texas. He has won the *Quarterly West* Novella Prize and the national Authors in the Park Story Award. *The Pistoleer* is his first novel. He lives in Florida.

TOP WESTERN TITLES FROM JOVE BOOKS!

__HIGH MOUNTAIN WINTER
  by Frances Hurst   0-515-11825-7/$5.99
It was 1850, and a young nation looked westward to the promise of new land and a new life. But Maryla Stoner's destiny takes a different turn when her family dies on the journey west and Maryla must survive the high mountain winter...alone. Based on a true story.

__ME AND THE BOYS
  by Ellen Recknor   0-515-11698-x/$5.99
Sixteen-year-old Gini Kincaid had hair of flame and a spirit to match. Running with outlaws, her name was on the tongues of righteous and criminal folk across the Southwest. And she had a mouth that got her into all kinds of trouble...

__THUNDER IN THE VALLEY
  by Jim R. Woolard   0-515-11630-0/$4.99
Falsely accused of trading with Indians, Matthan Hannar barely escaped the hangman's noose. He ran for his life through the treacherous valley, eluding scalpers and surviving the wilderness. Now, for the sake of a woman, he was going back...where the noose was waiting for him.